the book of lies

the book of lies

Felice Picano

alyson books
los angeles | new york

MANUFACTURED IN THE UNITED STATES OF AMERICA.
PRINTED ON ACID-FREE PAPER.
COVER DESIGN BY CHRISTOPHER HARRITY AND RON GOINS.

THIS TRADE PAPERBACK IS PUBLISHED BY ALYSON PUBLICATIONS,
P.O. BOX 4371, LOS ANGELES, CALIFORNIA 90078-4371.

FIRST PUBLISHED BY LITTLE, BROWN AND COMPANY (UK): 1998
FIRST ALYSON BOOKS EDITION: NOVEMBER 1999
FIRST ALYSON PAPERBACK EDITION: SEPTEMBER 2000

00 01 02 03 04 a 10 9 8 7 6 5 4 3 2 1

ISBN 1-55583-592-9
(ALSO PUBLISHED WITH ISBN 1-55583-541-4 IN HARDCOVER BY ALYSON BOOKS.
ORIGINALLY PUBLISHED WITH ISBN 0-316-64315-7 BY LITTLE, BROWN [UK].)

LIBRARY OF CONGRESS CATALOGING-IN-PUBLICATION DATA
    PICANO, FELICE, 1944–
        THE BOOK OF LIES / FELICE PICANO.—1ST ED.
        HARDCOVER: ISBN 1-55583-541-1; PAPER: ISBN 1-55583-592-9
        I. TITLE.
    PS3566.I25B66 2000
    813'.54—DC21   99-38406 CIP

CREDITS
•COVER PHOTOGRAPHY OF SUNSET BY PHOTODISC INC.
•AUTHOR PHOTOGRAPH BY GERALD INCANDELA.

To Andrew Holleran

CONTENTS

The Baron told her only Art meant anything.

Edward Gorey, *The Gilded Bat*

PROLOGUE

'Every man of substance and imagination has his Dark Lady of the Sonnets,' Mr Crassius used to tell us in English class. 'She doesn't have to be a lady. She doesn't even have to be a she. Some time or other in the life of the fully lived man, someone will come along and seize the senses and the emotions so fully, you are left gasping, pleading for relief. It's a roller-coaster ride. To heaven – and to hell! And if you haven't been driven completely insane, in the end all you ask is to escape without too much humiliation.'

Mr Crassius would hyperventilate a bit as though words alone couldn't adequately explain what he meant, his eyes would goggle out of his head, beads of perspiration would appear upon his usually blank face with its line-patterned forehead and along the side of his large, and very unRoman nose, which he'd quickly wipe off, and we students would sit there totally embarrassed yet secretly pleased, doing all we could not to giggle, until, as would invariably happen, Crassius would suddenly pop out of his self-induced trance, straighten out his tortoiseshell glasses, pat down the front of one or another of the several tweed vests he always wore over a starched white shirt to class, and once again he'd become our boring, middle-aged English teacher.

The result of these infrequent bouts would leave us boys in no doubt whatsoever that Mr Crassius himself had once had such a 'Dark Lady' in his life, and that he'd barely escaped her eldritch clutches with what he now (to us who knew its humdrum details as only students in such a closed world could) laughingly called his life.

On those rare mornings following such an outburst, we'd explode out of his overheated classroom at Lovecraft Hall, spill in a group across the icy steps and onto the poorly snow-swept paths of Tipton, asking each other in that half-mocking, half-sincere manner of all adolescents in all countries of the world and all times in history whether or not any of us hoped for such an all-encompassing love, such a thorough overhaul of our emotions, and we six closest – the little group that had come to hang out together the most often, known to ourselves and others on campus by the silly if not entirely inaccurate name of 'The Thought Club' (sometimes to our detractors as 'The Taut-Trousers Club') – would debate this issue with complete thoroughness until we'd reached our next class across the quad or had otherwise broken up, headed variously on our own ways.

I was always the skeptic. I'd call Crassius an 'old lameoid' and repeat what my father always told me, 'Men are ruled by money and power. Women are ruled by love.' And Nicky Ballette would grab his crotch and say 'I'm ruled by this!' (So true, and one reason why we were known as the Taut-Trousers Club). And we'd laugh and punch his arm and tumble with each other into the white, pure snow banks that seemed to fill the northern New England quad almost half of the school year, horsing around until one of us shouted, 'Hey! This faggot grabbed my dick!' or something equally offensive, and we would pile on top of the alleged offender for a free-for-all in which we managed to vent our aggression by punching someone while at the same time having the satisfaction of having our genitals handled, before one of us – Wayne or Herb – pulled himself out of the squirming mess, acting suddenly dignified, and said in his most manly fourteen-year-old tone of voice, 'I don't know about you queers, but I've got swim practice (or chemistry class or School paper) to go to.' At which point we'd slowly unscramble from the heap, giving our closest neighbor a sneaky, final jab or knuckle-rub before straightening out our rumpled, snow-covered, hard-on-tautened Levi's and corduroys, and split up into twos and threes to go off and do what was required by our prep-school careers for the next hour.

It's true that I never believed in Crassius's Dark Lady theory. Not through prep school, not later on in my undergraduate years at Harvard, not while I was getting my MA at Columbia, and in truth I never in my life ever expected to believe the theory. But that seems ages ago, before I arrived at UCLA to study for my doctorate under Irian St George, before I fell under the spell of his well-known personal charms, academic brilliance and suave persuasiveness . . . But wait! I don't want you to get the idea that the elderly Franco-Armenian-American scholar – personally delightful as he might have been – was my Dark Lady. Ridiculous as that sounds, I sometimes wish it were true, because it would be so uncomplicated. Well, relatively uncomplicated, compared to the more Byzantine and unpalatable truth.

No, while St George is undoubtedly responsible for leading me onto the path I eventually took, it wasn't at all him. And no, it wasn't (though people have speculated, gossiped) even the great author Damon Von Slyke, at whose home in the Hollywood Hills I ended up living that fateful summer, ostensibly to catalogue the enormous mass of thirty-eight years of his manuscripts and papers preparatory to their being packaged and sent off (sold off really, and for a pretty penny) to a prestigious university library back East. After all, Von Slyke was in Europe all that summer: from London to Hamburg to Majorca. Once the job was set up and the keys to the house handed to me, and Conchita, the maid's, days arranged, I was left alone. I think we only slept one night in the place, he in the master suite, I in a guest bedroom across the courtyard with its ceramic colored Cuernavaca tiles and fountain.

It's really so difficult to begin to explain how it all happened, to explain *what* happened; it all became so snarled up and confused, so fraught with non-essential matters, encumbrances having to do with gaining tenure and securing academic standing, with publicity and publishing, with the personal lives of, well, of myself, among others. So, let me just say straight out that none of it was planned, there was never any malice aforethought, certainly no hint that I'd find anything quite so explosive.

And yes, if you must have it spelled out, it all happened by accident (though Von Slyke and St George would tell you there's no such thing as 'accident'): the accident being that among Von Slyke's scores of cardboard boxes of manuscripts and papers I discovered . . . a manuscript . . . and through that single, at first utterly baffling and later on revelatory discovery, I made other discoveries – not only of works, but of the existence of a certain person until then totally unknown to any scholar or historian of the 1970s and 1980s. And how as a result of discovering this person, I unearthed his various relationships to and effects upon not only Von Slyke, but also Dominic De Petrie and Jeff Weber and Aaron Axenfeld, on Cameron Powers and Rowland Etheridge, on Mitchell Leo and Frankie

McKewen and Mark Dodge, all the members of the legendary Purple Circle (as well as his effect upon some of their hangers-on), and thus his centrality of influence upon what we know to be that bursting bright nova of American literature in the last decades of the twentieth century.

So, yes, that was the key moment, when everything changed, although I didn't know it at the time, thought something else was going on, certainly not anything that would forever alter my understanding, my sense of values, my life itself. And yes, it's only natural, after all that, that a little thing like a belief would also easily fall victim.

I'm still not certain this is how I should do it. Or even if I *should* do it. Except there are so many people who hate me now for what happened, who blame me and who are convinced it was deliberate, that I wanted to undermine and expose, sought to destroy, carried secret prejudices, harbored low motives from the very beginning. From before the beginning.

None of which is true: I swear it!

I'm getting nowhere, circling, and circling, like a half-blinded bird over some fallen morsel. Bird of prey, others would say, over some not yet fully dead creature. Carnivorous insect, even others would say, attracted to the putrid, rotting flesh of long-dead carcasses.

Maybe I'd better try at what was the actual beginning – I don't know how else to do it – the late morning that I drove my newly leased Celica convertible to Von Slyke's house . . .

Book One

THE VON SLYKE PAPERS

From the pubescently trembling onset itself, we'd dared
aspire to that lofty elevation, into the nearly godly
presence our incomplete knowledge hinted at, and
which our as yet untried instincts assured us existed;
not at some vast remove, but instead here at hand,
fluttering almost peripheral, within our grasp; if only
we dared...extend ourselves

Damon Von Slyke, *Systems for Approaching Emmeline*

IT WAS A LATE MAY MORNING as I drove my newly leased, late-model Celica convertible to Damon Von Slyke's house. Being a relative stranger to the so-called 'Southland', I was closely following his directions, from Westwood along Sunset Boulevard through the famous Sunset Strip, turning at Laurel Canyon first onto Hollywood Boulevard, then, a few blocks later, turning again onto Franklin Avenue, where I cruised several blocks high above the old and imperfectly revitalized Hollywood of our day: a residential neighborhood redolent of the Cinema town of two-thirds of a century ago; lengthy blocks where 1920s high-rises with French names and Gallo-Gothic architectural ornaments were interspersed with vaguely Spanish-style garden apartments. The north side of the street was suddenly different, covered in foliage – spindly poinsettia trees with blackish bark and hot red flowers larger than your head, grotesquely twisted pine trees, lush candleflower bushes, fragrant eucalyptus, mixed with cerise bougainvillaea's papery flowers and clumps of Birds of Paradise, growing hard and straight like primeval cycads, all of it luxuriant and tropical, Eocene and slapdash, designed to hide yards and yards of twenty-foot-high wrought-iron fencing and gates, behind which lay Runyon Canyon, several semi-public gardens and a score of big silent-movie-star mansions put up when the town below was a handful of Victorian wooden houses along a newly macadamized main street.

After driving past twice, I at last found my turn onto the liana-overhung gloom of a dead-end road and, slowly inching along its narrow length, located the frond-hidden sign. Following Von Slyke's earlier instructions, I used my car phone to call.

'Hi!' Von Slyke answered, as always sounding about twelve years old. 'You made it! Now when we hang up, point the phone at the sign, hit the pound key and dial these numbers, 7-5-8-8. It spells S-L-U-T,' he giggled, 'and shall, sluttishly, let you in.'

I did as instructed and a large, until then invisible, gate clanged and drew inward. I drove the Celica into what might have been a scene out of a Disney animated movie: a curved gravel driveway defined by huge trees susurrating in the breeze so that every one of their millions of purple flowers stirred, their brown-black limbs and trunks dark against a background of bushes white with what smelled to be jasmine and honeysuckle, all of it – trees, jasmine, honeysuckle – perfuming the air as though it weren't outdoors, but within the labyrinth of a sultan's most secret harem.

I slowly circuited a softball-diamond-sized island of grass and flowers, dominated by a Spanish-style bird-bath set in a mass of pink and orange azalea, out of which, at the Celica's approach, a fistful of large blue birds exploded into the air. They wheeled as I slowly passed what looked like the hedge-darkened front of a single-story house, and arrived at my next turn, the *porte-cochère* built into an extension of the house's stucco front wall, where, as previously instructed, I parked next to Von Slyke's expensive-looking silver sport utility vehicle.

Looking deeper into the driveway, I could make out through the tangle of wild oleander what old architecture books called a 'motor court' and, beyond it, the three closed doors of the garage, festooned with lilacs. The unexpectedly long stuccoed wall seemed shut, the deep-set windows at varying heights of a tower-like structure – wreathed in more bougainvillaea – appeared closed up. The heavily carved, deep-stained wooden door, barely visible through trailing yellow hibiscus, was sealed off.

I walked around to what I supposed to be the front of the house, seeking ingress. I'd just spotted a path along which I determined my steps would lead past a two-story window, barely visible behind yet more, this time orange, hibiscus blooms, and from there into a partly covered entryway when I heard Slyke shouting from a direction ninety degrees away, 'Here! Over here!'

He was on the opposite side of the circular driveway, beneath two more of the unearthly-looking purple trees, sprawled upon the floral cushions of what seemed to be a once white-painted, now weather-mottled wickerwork lounge chair. A battered tan Maine fishing hat with curled brim lay high on his ginger and white hair. He wore soiled white painter's pants and an oversized T-shirt that barely hid his bulk, but, like his voice, his face was much younger than the sixty-five years I knew he'd amassed.

He'd been writing something on a pad of yellow foolscap and seemed to hastily finish off a sentence before closing the pad and covering it up with a cellular phone as I approached, threading my way through the azalea, so the birds which had just resettled on the lip of their bath once more rose, large and bright blue and surprisingly soft-voiced. I was still half turned to watch them when I reached the chaise.

'May the bluebird of happiness shit on your head!' Von Slyke laughed. 'They're genuine California bluebirds. During the fall and winter, they feast on the olives from those trees –' he pointed to the dark foliage of what I'd taken to be the front of the house – 'which fall by the bushel and stain the pathways black and drive my gardener to distraction. God knows what they eat in spring.'

While putting out a white hand to be shaken, he added, 'You're even handsomer than I remembered from our brief meeting. And such a butch name: Ross Ohrenstedt! Not that you don't look butch enough to carry it. You unquestionably do.' He finally let go of my hand. 'Have a seat –' pointing to a wrought-iron chair drawn up next to the chaise. 'Want some coffee? It's cold, I'm afraid. It's always cold. In fact one of the best-kept secrets about southern California is how, despite the constant year-round heat, everything is always getting cold. Cole Porter wasn't kidding when he wrote in that song, "She hates California. It's cold and it's damp." You don't believe me?'

'No, I believe,' I said. 'It's just all so . . . you know, so pretty and clean and so, well, so fabulously verdant. Back East everyone gives this place a bad rap. I'm embarrassed I'm not finding it so.'

Everything – table, hat, lawn – was covered with, patterned by, scores of fallen purple blossoms. I bent to pick one up. Odorless. So where did that musky smell come from? The bark?

'Whatever are all these purple trees? They're unreal.'

'Jac-a-ran-da!' Von Slyke said. 'Or yak-a-rahn-da, if you prefer Spanish. Although I'm not certain they're Spanish to begin with, or even native. They look like they should be from Bali or someplace like that, don't they? I do know the entire city was planted with them for the 1932 Olympic Games. And I do mean everywhere. Even South Central.'

'I hope,' I quickly said, 'I've not come at a bad time. I didn't mean to interrupt any writing.'

'No, not at all. I do all my writing in the morning. This was just a letter.' He smiled boyishly, despite the hair-color job that needed immediate and serious touching up and the pasty-colored sagging skin of his cheeks and jowls and the overcartilaged (by age and good food and drink) nose and ears. Von Slyke smiled boyishly, just as it's been reflected in the hundreds of photos of him and on TV interviews and in those two documentary films made about his life; boyishly, as though that was Von Slyke's natural role in life, not at all a put-on, as others have darkly hinted; and I thought with a thrill, here I am, at his house, and despite Dr St George's warning that Von Slyke could be simultaneously charming and devious, he was being instead comfortable with me, polite.

'My mother,' Von Slyke said, clearly amusing himself with what was about to come, 'a woman of decided views, now deceased, totally despised California, although I don't believe she ever in her life stepped foot here. She was personally offended by anything having to do with the state. She would hear some news report about it on the radio or read some item about it in a newspaper and she'd snort and harumph. I'm not kidding, she would actually snort and harumph. Only time I ever heard anyone do that. Her worst put-down of a person was that they'd moved to Los Angeles, or worse that they'd "gone Hollywood", which she always said as though it were between inverted commas, and had come from the title of some slashing exposé, an article by Clare Boothe Luce she'd read in her youth perhaps. So naturally . . . this would be where I ended up. What do you think it means when a person has "gone Hollywood"?'

He'd stopped me by the suddenness of the question, coming in the middle of all that flattery and candor, and I had to remind myself that he still wasn't certain of me, didn't trust Irian St George's estimation but had to know for himself, and might – like some character out of some old *Märchen* – be determined to test me. I decided to be completely open.

'I used to think it meant a person had become stuck up, snobby, all façade. But recently someone who's lived here a few years told me what he thought it meant and I've thought about it and I've come to adopt his definition. So, here it is: going Hollywood means being able to stand up old friends, stiff former acquaintances, not return phone calls and letters of former lovers and . . . this is the key element . . . being able to rationalize it all by telling yourself you're too busy making money and getting famous.'

'Bra-vo!' Von Slyke applauded. 'Said with the cynicism, slashing wit and honesty of a true follower of the Purple Circle! Rowland Etheridge must be squirming with delight in his dark little grave, deep in Ole Virginny! But you know –' he was suddenly thoughtful – 'if you come here, stay here in this house while I'm away all summer, sorting out that utter bedlam of papers inside, you'll be right in the very heartless heart of Hollywood: zip code, town line . . . Why, even the phone number spells out Beachwood, like in the '60s song: Beachwood Five-Six-Seven-Eight-Nine. Doesn't that intrigue you? Scare you?

'No, of course it doesn't,' he answered himself. 'After all, despite your stellar face and spectacular body, you're not just some Santa Monica Boulevard clone looking to break into TV commercials, are you? You're a Serious Scholar. And all such ideas are totally beyond you. What was it exactly that St George told me about you? That you're his most promising colleague in a decade. That you'd read all of the Purple Circle's works while still in grade school –'

'That's not exactly true,' I interrupted. 'I discovered your novel *Instigations* in my prep-school library. I don't know how it had gotten in there, frankly, because all the other books were pretty old and conventional. And to tell the truth, I'm not even sure now I had a glimmer of what your book was about at the time. I did know it excited me far more than *For Whom the Bell Tolls* or *Catch-22*, which is what we were reading in class that term. And, of course, your book opened a door . . .' I let that hang, not wanting to say too much. 'It was only later, when I was in Cambridge, Mass., that I got around to reading all of your work. All of *all* of your work,' I added, meaning the entire group he'd belonged to briefly, famously, a quarter-century before, and lest he think I was flattering him.

Clearly I'd said what he wanted to hear, because Von Slyke's eyes, which had up until now been focused on me in a general sort of way, with darting, openly evaluational glances at my well-muscled arms, legs and crotch – I'd been clever enough to follow St George's guidance in accentuating it with a one-size-too-small pure-cotton white T-shirt, tartan flannel gym shorts, custard ankle socks and 'natural' leather work boots – now looked at me fully face to face. I could at last gauge whether or not the writer's eyes were 'a junkety, watery blue like the flotsam-filled Great South Bay two days after some remarkably disappointing storm', as he'd written of the protagonist of the novel I'd first read, which after all – and not all that early in his life – had made his name. Or if, instead, Von Slyke's eyes were 'iced and sharp, like the trined iron sides of one of those over-polished slide rules mathematics nerds suddenly sweep out of their chem notebooks and apply to a numerical riddle', as he'd written of another protagonist, Jamie Dollinger, in the more recent *DOS: Manuscript in Distress.*

'You're an assistant professor at UCLA?' he added, rather than asked. And when I nodded. 'You don't have summer classes?'

'I didn't . . . but Dr St George asked me to take over a class another professor couldn't handle because of family problems. It's undergrad Twentieth-century American Lit. But I did manage to subversively get stories by Capote, plays by Tennessee Williams and Elizabeth Bishop's poetry onto the classes' dozen required books, which isn't bad: one out of four. And I added tons of Purple Circle books to the additional reading list . . . I can easily handle an undergrad class and do the cataloguing, if that worries you.'

'I don't for a second doubt you. It's no wonder St George adores you,' Von Slyke said. 'Do you do other favors for him? Personal ones?'

Before I could register what he'd asked, Von Slyke answered himself, 'Of course you don't. You're probably terribly insulted I brought up the subject. What you must think of me! I'm such a ditz sometimes. I blame it on all that cocaine I sniffed at Studio 54. I'm certain now it forever stripped my brain cells of common sense. Not that I ever was a member of the place, like Dom and Mark of course.' He meant other Purple Circlers, Dominic De Petrie and Mark Dodge. 'I was far too unattractive to be a regular of that, or indeed any of the really select clubs in the '70s. Whereas they, especially Mark, virtually lived at Flamingo! But, you know, one of the things that no one seems to get anymore about we Purples was that we were buddies. And the others were always were so sweet, the

way they'd go out of their way to make certain I wasn't left out of
their reindeer games. Every year like clockwork I was invited to the
White Party and the Black Party, the opening party and the closing-
for-the-season party. The Leo-McKewens would call me a week before New Year's and say, "Don't breathe a word, but we've got tickets to Studio One for the big night, two suites at the Château
Marmont and at least one high-priced hooker slash porn star apiece
for the weekend." And when I'd ask, "But how, darlings? I can't afford to pay my Balducci's account, never mind fly to LA and buy
hustlers!" Mitch would reply, "It's taken care of. Don't ask how."
And Frankie, listening in on the other phone line, would add, "Assume it's an anonymous admirer. That's always my policy." Rowland thought our jaunts were paid for by "burning" credit cards
stolen by some of the Leo-McKewens' more louche African-American boyfriends! Whereas Cameron—' Cameron Powers, another
member of the Circle— 'we were still going together at the time—was
certain it was all thanks to some Mafia connection they'd made
staying every fall at Mitch's family place on the Jersey coast. But
Cameron was from the hill country of Mississippi and from the
minute he hit Manhattan he claimed to see mafiosi everywhere. He
used to tell me that when he first moved to New York as a hustler
himself, his biggest-tipping customers were what he liked to call
"Massapequa Tonys and Staten Island Vitos". While we lay in bed,
Cam would recall each encounter and describe his Johns' bodies in
extensive detail. Although he may have merely done that from boredom...or even to titillate himself. Whatever am I thinking? You
don't want to hear any hundred-year-old gossip, do you?'

Before I could protest that it was exactly such gossip I wanted to
hear, that everyone who was in any way interested in the Purple Circle wanted to hear, Von Slyke stood up, pushed down to either side
the shirt that had ridden up his middle and swept off his hat to ruf-
flingly hand-comb his hair. 'Serious as you surely must be, doubtless
you're bored to distraction by an old queen nattering on, and far too
polite to ask me to gather my wits and show you into the library,
where your real interest in being here lies. You have to forgive me!
Puddles' —Peter? Patrick? What was the name of his current
lover?— 'says I've grown so used to those idiots we call fans, and so
accustomed to the attentive vacuity of the media always nosing

around, I've come to assume everyone's equally grasping and shallow.' Before I could say a word, Von Slyke had taken off, headed back to the house.

I followed. At one point followed so closely I almost tripped on the surprisingly tightly rooted ground cover of gray-green stems and tiny blue flowers I only at that moment recognized from their overpowering odor must be fresh rosemary. Until now, I'd hadn't a clue where the herb came from, how it grew, what it looked like, never mind that it had such strong roots and pretty flowers.

We were at the other side of the house, hidden until now in hedges, and Von Slyke stopped and scratched his head. 'I'm wondering if I locked the library door. Yes, I think I did,' he replied as I caught up to him, and he lurched off again, this time onto the concrete path that led—as I'd earlier guessed—to the entryway. The whole front of the house was a sweep of adobe laid on so thick it looked like solidified peach ice cream sculpted to scoop up and slide down, to be hollowed out by a doorway here, a window there, a chain of columned nooks and niches. We went under an overhang into a partly covered-over terrace, overgrown with ferns that flourished tempestuously in the abundant coolness. A half-dozen tiny windows gated in wrought-iron abutted on either side a double door; the dark wood carved in arabesques accented by oversized wrought-iron knockers and handles.

Von Slyke flung open the doors and gestured me over a worn alabaster lintel. 'Welcome to Casa Asunción Maria Estrella Herrera y Lopez,' he said grandly, adding in a lower voice, 'That was the name of the Tijuana whore it was originally built for.'

A single long, cool, low-ceilinged corridor floored in blood-red tiles led in either direction to brightly sunlit, high-ceilinged rooms: a venous artery connecting two huge organs. Like the exterior, the interior walls also sported irregular little cave-like openings: one could peer through them into the upper level of a two-story, thick-raftered dining room, approachable only via wrought-iron railed stairways at either end of the corridor.

We headed right, and Von Slyke stopped, turned and stood while I caught up. Still playing tour-guide, he pointed toward the huge dining room with its open-brick fireplace, enormous refectory table, score of chairs along either wall, Viking-ship sideboards dappled in sunlight from multipaned windows with French doors leading to a central terrace.

'Although this house has seen in its day, I was assured, many, many orgies,' Von Slyke began, 'it is said that at one particular party given by the actor George Peppard, now deceased, in the year 1964, when he had leased this house and was possibly the handsomest man in the land, some twenty-two underaged girls from the San Fernando Valley were simultaneously deflowered on that very table, at least five of them personally by their host, wielding, besides his allegedly formidable member, his hands, feet and a variety of garden vegetables, several of which were never recovered.'

He smirked and we ended up laughing together. 'The house doesn't look half this big from the outside,' I said.

'Like the Peppard petard! But in truth it's hu-uge! You'll probably never end up using the wing opposite.' He pointed beyond the fireplace, where, through an open doorway, I could just make out the pale furnishings of a sitting room. 'Although naturally you're welcome to. The West Wing, as we call it here at Casa Herrera y Lopez, contains the formal living room, my sitting room and bedroom – in a tower I languish like Mélisande! The East Wing –' we'd stopped again and were now looking down another lengthy, dark-tiled corridor which ended, apparently, in mid-air – 'contains the library, maid's quarters, closets galore, two lavs and, down those steps, a kitchen, breakfast room, laundry, pantry, and at the end a suite of two guest bedrooms and bath. You'll probably live there. It opens onto the courtyard, close to the food and the garage. You won't have to traipse through all this.'

'I know it's rude to ask,' I began, 'but you bought this house from your royalties, right?'

'Aren't you a doll to say that. But the truth is, I couldn't earn royalties enough to buy this heap if I'd written day and night, lived in a garret and never spent a dime – none of which is even remotely true. No, the very sizable downpayment that allowed me to move in was thanks to the film rights some utterly crazed producer paid for *Heliotrope Convertible*. What?' He looked shocked. 'You didn't see the movie based on my fourth novel?' He smiled. 'Well, sweetie, neither you nor the rest of the universe. But do I care?

'And this,' he continued in his tour-guide voice, stopping at the doorway, 'will be your domain. Or is it demesne? One's never certain of the usage. Fortunately, here's a dictionary handy. Several, in fact, in several languages, all of which I profess to know and none of which I really do know, including, unfortunately for my readers, English.'

There are photos of Von Slyke's library on the back of his last three books, all of them purposely, somewhat campily, in allusion to author shots of earlier times. On *DOS: Manuscript in Distress* he's dressed in tweeds and cravat, standing on one book-wall ladder, halfway up, holding open a volume, facing the camera. On the back of *Epistle to Albinoni* he's on the corner of his huge Craftsman's desk, some old album across his lap, his open-necked white shirt and still-blond hair all but glowing in the backlight of the huge window behind. On the cover of *Canticle to the Sun* he's upon the Mission-era fainting sofa, his costume satiny black to contrast with the strong patterns of the Lloyd Wright upholstery, one arm languid behind his head, his eyes hooded, his lips puckered in a pout.

So even though I thought I knew the room – and of course Dr St George had spoken of it as 'possibly the ur-library, the ideal author's work room', even so, I wasn't prepared for how high the bookcases rose to the ceiling on three sides, how rich and fine and how beautifully stained the dark-grained wood was, how many volumes were on those shelves, how their sheer mass managed to dwarf the huge desk, the sofa, almost dwarfed the huge pane of glass flooding it all with sunlight.

While I stood in awe, Von Slyke was already at one wall, going through what I assumed were reference books, muttering, until he looked up. 'Perch anywhere.

'Aha! Under "demesne" with an "ee" and an "es", it says "in law, possession, as of one's own. But formerly" – a second definition – it meant "the land or estate belonging to a lord, and not rented or let, but kept in his hands". While domain with an "o" and no "s" means a land under a single ruler or government.'

'So technically,' I summed it up, 'neither word is correct. Since the house belongs to you, not me. What dictionary is that?'

'This,' he patted the worn carmine cover, 'is my all-time favorite and, it turns out, the oldest dictionary here, and the one I use most. The College Edition of *Webster's New World*, copyrighted 1962. A college graduation gift. Not that all of them aren't good. Oh, except the Random House defines love – the word I use checking out any new dictionary – as quote "a strong passion between those of the opposite sex" unquote.'

'A little homophobic?' I suggested. 'This place is . . . well, as described, truly something. Your papers are . . .?'

Von Slyke stood up, put down the *Webster's*, went to the wall of books opposite the window. Reaching behind a few volumes, he must have pressed a button because the entire thing suddenly swung open.

'Can you believe it!' he exulted. 'The moment the real-estate agent showed this to me, I creamed in my jeans! A secret panel behind the bookcase. Every moment of my recent life was as though nil, and my true existence as Nancy Drew could pick up again where I'd dropped it, aged nine and a half, in that humid Midwestern suburb where it is perpetually three o'clock on an August afternoon!'

A little hallway behind the hinged book-wall showed two doors: one led to another – by comparison to this chamber – more modestly sized, inexpensively paneled inner library, maybe eight feet by six, its shelves up to the dropped ceiling filled with ancient long-playing records, peeling paperbacks and, on one wall – I noticed instantly and instantly wanted to get my hands on – dozens of manuscripts inside of and partly peeking out of their rubber-band-shut cardboard boxes, all strewn haphazardly on the shelves amid plastic bags spilling open with letters and envelopes. They didn't appear to be in order, nor did the scores of hard- and soft-covered notebooks among them, not to mention the stacks of old newspapers, magazines and quarterlies in which I assumed Von Slyke's work had first appeared excerpted. Equally unarranged seemed the boxes on the floor in front of and blocking the shelves, cartons originally used for Chablis and Volnay and Margaux, now filled to their cracked cardboard brims with what even the most cursory glance told me were typesetting manuscripts and unbound galleys released from the printers.

The other door led to a dainty powder room, with old-fashioned standing porcelain sink and toilet. One odd note: a poster for Ivory Soap, *circa* 1919, featuring sailors taking a bath onboard some destroyer.

'Perfect for a sudden whiz,' Von Slyke said, adding, 'There's a full bath with tub and stall shower directly behind this. It opens onto the maid's room. I seldom use it.'

'The maid is here all day?'

'When I'm staying in the house Conchita is in from noon to eight as a rule. She cooks and does light cleaning. For any heavier cleaning she calls in her sister or her daughter to help. I'll leave checks on the desktop for her to pick up weekly. That's the way she prefers to be paid.'

'Then she goes home at night?'

'To Bell Gardens. It's only forty-five minutes to an hour, depending on freeway traffic. Occasionally, however, she'll sleep over. She usually asks if it's okay beforehand. But there are times she's asked and I've forgotten, and she's so quiet I don't remember she's even in the house until the next morning I wake up and she already has coffee made for me. She's an absolute doll, and speaks a lot more English than she lets on. I once caught her reading a Barbara Taylor Bradford novel, and when I suggested she might like to read one of mine she said, "I appreciate that, but, Mr Von Slyke, your books are all on the Pope's list of No." Isn't that heaven? I dined out on it for a month!

'Do you want to meet her?' he suddenly asked. 'You will sooner or later anyway.' He went to the desk and hit the buttons of an angled unit that I'd earlier supposed was merely a telephone-answering machine, and now had to assume was also an intercom. '*Conchita. Soy yo, El Jefe.*'

Before I could tell him not to bother, Von Slyke said, 'I could use some coffee. You?' Then, in response to my nod and a squawk from the intercom, 'Coffee for two. Coffeemate and sugar substitute. We're in the library.' Turning to me, 'Now that you've seen the mess in there, shall we discuss what you're to do? Maureen – that's the woman who's taking the papers – says her people at the Henry Timrod Collection have a particular method of accounting for every item. She said they could make a list when they get the papers there, but St George and what little bit remains of my own good sense say I should have a list made before it all leaves.'

'A master list, it's called,' I explained. 'You definitely ought to have one made, if possible listing each item, it's length, its genre and form, where it's been published, if it's unpublished, what draft number it is. A copy of that list should go to your agent and your executor.'

'I feel better already about your coming here today,' Von Slyke said. 'I seem to live – to thrive, if you must know – in an amount of chaos others find unacceptable. It does me good to know there are sweet, smart lovelies like yourself able and willing to take charge and elicit order out of this –' His hand traced curlicues in the air. 'At any rate, Maureen sent a copy of the collection's guidelines.'

He'd placed himself on the edge of the desk as in one of his photos and I'd sat, as he'd gestured for me to do, in a slatted wooden chair opposite. I looked at what he handed me. 'This is pretty standard,' I said. 'I took a course in Primary Sources and Bibliography in grad school. We used something similar. If I can I'll input it into my laptop, augmenting the program I've already set up.'

'You have your own computer? I don't have to rent one?'

'I've got a new Toshiba. Nine ninety-six MB. Six ports for two faxes, two modems, a Net line and a satellite TV hook-up. It's on the seat of the car. If you want, I'll show you the program I intend to use – I'm sure I can interface it with these parameters in a few minutes.'

Von Slyke's eyes had grown alarmingly large. 'Not altogether necessary, dear. In fact, I'm completely computer illiterate.'

'I thought you did several on-line appearances every year. I'm certain I downloaded one LesBiGay lit chat room off the Net last year.'

'I sat there and talked. Someone else typed in the words,' Von Slyke said. 'I'm not proud, but the truth is it scares the willies out me. I'm even a lousy typist.'

Keyboardist, I mentally corrected.

'In fact none of we Purples ever . . . what am I thinking? Dom –' De Petrie, he must mean – 'had a word processor as far back as the early '80s. I remember him showing it to me, and us laughing and laughing over "word processing". What else do writers do but process words?'

'Without a computer –' I was unable to hide my mystification – 'how do you write?'

'With a pen! On paper. You must think I'm some stone-age

throwback! But it's worked for years. I write in a big notebook. When I'm done with a section, or chapter, or a complete piece, Puddles inputs in his computer and prints it. I correct it, he does a copy and I send that. Now,' he added with a sort of wink, 'the really fabulous part about this extremely antiquated method of composition is that it produces a great deal of what librarians of rare-book collections refer to as "autographs". Which is nothing but handwritten stuff but is worth a great deal more cash than typewritten manuscripts, never mind computer-printed ones.' Von Slyke smiled. 'And when one spends money as I tend to . . . My mother, a woman who said whatever was on her mind, told me when I was boy – among many stupid and useless things – two that were utterly practical, for which I daily thank her. She said, "Damon, you're a sloppy boy. When you grow up you'd best find an occupation that allows you to afford one servant to clean up after you."' Von Slyke paused, and pouted. 'The other thing she told me was that I was lazy, and I'd better find a line of work that didn't require much effort. Well, that took a while.' He laughed. 'She couldn't have been more correct. Tell me –' a sudden change in direction, tone of voice, a sudden leaning forward – 'about your own family, Ross.'

Another little test. Calm me down, let me think I have the job, then ask me something personal and possibly crucial. Okay, I'd play the game. 'Nothing much to say, Mr Von Slyke –'

'Damon, dear,' he corrected me.

'Damon . . . I'm the youngest. My sisters are eight and seven years older. Dad worked for Big Blue, so there were computers in the house from the beginning. He left IBM during one of their '90s upper-management "downsizings" and opened his own software firm. He's done well. Mom was a housewife until I was in junior high, then she went back to school for an MA in education. Went to work for the local Board of Education, and ended up heading the County Board, and now she's angling for the top position at the Connecticut State Board. My older sister has a baby-clothing part-nership, Melissa Jane. She's Melissa. It's quite successful. My other sister, Judy, married Bart Vanuzzi, the Forty-Niners quarterback. She's his professional and financial manager, and his publicity agent.' Before he could say anything, I now interrupted myself to add, 'I know what you're thinking, they're all overachievers. While I –'

'While you, according to Irian St George, you are the great white hope of American literature scholarship. Does that sound racist? I never seem to know what's correct anymore. And here, always at exactly the right time, is Conchita with our coffee.'

Given her name and what I'd gotten from Von Slyke, I guess I expected the maid to be someone small, dumpy, wide as she was tall, swarthy, middle-aged and uxorious, wearing a bandanna and floral housecoat. Conchita turned out to be at most thirty-five years old, with an absolutely striking head as though off an Amerindian carving: shapely oval face highlighted by almost triangular cheekbones, small nose, Siberian hazel eyes, large lower lip, thick black hair cut short. She wore no make-up on her clear, dusty-olive complexion, and I know this was Hollywood but Conchita was dressed less like a housemaid than like an unemployed actress: an oversized charcoal-colored knit sweater that barely reached her hips over a skin-tight black leotard that did everything to accent her slim figure and Rockette legs before ending in what looked to me like expensive silver-black Capezio slip-ons.

She'd brought in a delicate wooden Japanese tray onto which she'd placed a silver and Pacific-blue hand-thrown ceramic coffee pot, mugs, and plates, with a half-dozen almond-studded Italian anisette cookies.

Von Slyke introduced us. Conchita's hand was small, soft-skinned, firm and quickly withdrawn. I remembered what my ever-horny Tipton pal Wayne used to say about Latin women: how, with a few modest glances, they could size you up and let you know they were available. Maybe Wayne would have been able to tell if Conchita was flirting. I couldn't.

'See what I mean,' Von Slyke was saying, 'ask for a simple cup of coffee and this . . . marvelous, really . . . is what you get.' He'd begun pouring the steaming coffee and sniffed its fumes. 'This is the Dominican I brought back from Grand Caicos, isn't it? Perfect for mid-afternoon.' He was handing me a cup and one of the loaf-like cookies when the phone rang.

It rang twice and the machine answered, Von Slyke's taped voice sounding higher-pitched and even more archly inflected than in life. Then the beep. A live voice: male, bass, in a bad mood. 'Damon!

Ron Preston here. What in the hell do you mean by that message
you left on my phone?'

Von Slyke almost fell off his perch reaching for the receiver. 'Ron?
Damon! Can you hold a sec?' To me, 'My publisher. I'd better take
it. Why don't you let Conchita show you to the guest wing?'

As I hightailed it out of the room behind Conchita, I heard Von
Slyke's voice take on an totally new iron edge. 'Ron, I don't see
what you're steamed at. I'm the one who's just been stilettoed in the
back.'

I admit it, I was so fascinated by Von Slyke, had I been alone I
might have lurked in the corridor and listened. Instead, all I could do
was follow the swaying hips of Conchita past the dining-room balcony and down the stairs, to where the corridor achieved ground
level, its left side full-length windows and glass doors opening to the
large interior courtyard with its happily splashing Mexican fountain
even more ornate than its matching frontyard bird bath. To the
right was the kitchen, also in Spanish style and dark wood, opening
to a lawn. I could make out a patio under a rectangular umbrella
protected by a bougainvillaea-enlaced fence, the breakfast room and
finally, at the end, perpendicular to this wing, two dark, cool-look-
ing bed-sitting rooms.

Conchita left and I wandered, sipping coffee, into and around the
two rooms, noting that they were separated by a bathroom with a
stall shower big enough to hold a basketball squad and a closet the
size of my bedroom back in Westwood. One bedroom had floor-to-
ceiling doors that opened to the breakfast patio, while the other led
to the interior courtyard and fountain, the superior view.

I stepped through the French doors to the central terrace, admir-
ing whomever had laid out and planted it. Later that summer, when
he visited, someone into architecture told me Fewling designed,
landscaped and built the place in 1932; he'd seen photos of it in a
book on West Coast residences. The six-foot overhanging roofs of
the two long wings provided loggias bordering areas shaded by
large trees, including two forty-foot-high Washingtonia palms that
must have been planted when the house was first built. Several
chaises and a low table had been placed where the sun was most
constant during the year, yet so anyone sunning would be cooled by
fountain spray. In the far corner, near the high dining-room

window-walls, a table and two chairs had been set up, half hidden behind succulents: a good lunch or outdoor work spot. I ambled toward another little courtyard set deep between the bedrooms and the garage, where another sitting area was arranged beneath a vine-covered pergola dripping a mini-jungle of vines that would in mid-August be heavy with grapes. There, in the nook formed by the West Wing – Von Slyke's bedroom – and the eight-foot fence hiding the motor court, set amidst succulents and bamboo, was an outdoor whirlpool bath.

I could picture myself with the laptop under the pergola, could picture myself outside the dining room stretched on the chaise by day listening to my headphones and reading, could picture myself warmed and soothed in the Jacuzzi by night as constellations glittered in the dark skies overhead, and I couldn't help but compare it all to the two tiny, airless, thin-walled, overpriced rooms I'd taken off campus to be near UCLA. 'Don't flub this!' I warned myself. 'You've got to be here this summer. You simply have to. And not just because St George expects it of you, or because Von Slyke needs the cataloguing done, but because you need it. Desperately. If only to prove you don't need Chris!'

I didn't let myself think more about the personal disaster that had seemed to accompany my slow, steady ascent in the academic world; although I knew that I also somehow hoped that all this might become the magical setting of some new love to come my way. Come and remain, this time. Talking to Von Slyke of my family, I'd not been able to forget how I'd managed to alienate each of them, one by one, even those who'd loved me the most: either by my big mouth or by my lifestyle. That fellowship to UCLA had appeared just in time for me to achieve my long-overdue independence, with Irian St George taking on the role of fairy godfather and engorging the amount further by dipping into some until then unknown to me departmental fund, so I was able to make the coast to coast move and take the position, study under him, write that book on the Purple Circle, whatever it would turn out to be (I had ideas but nothing specific) which would solidify my status and launch me in academia for life. What better place to start than in Damon Von Slyke's garden, near his manuscripts and letters and . . .

'More?' Conchita at the glass door leading into the kitchen, holding a Chemex pot. When I said no, she said, 'He's done,' with less of an accent than I'd expected, before she vanished back in the kitchen.

When I'd reached the corridor outside the library I wondered how to announce myself and hesitated. Good thing, because it turned out while he wasn't shouting, Von Slyke was still on the phone. '. . . never have two dimes to rub together,' he was saying plaintively, 'and you can't i-mag-ine the squa-lor!'

I backed off and stood indecisively. I was wondering if he were talking about himself – did he honestly consider himself to be living in poverty and squalor? Did he honestly think that a publisher who paid out what I'd heard were six-figure advances would believe it? – and if not himself, then whom was Von Slyke talking about?

I counted to five hundred and knocked on the adjoining wall. A second later, Von Slyke's face appeared, enlaced in phone and wires, still listening. He smiled seeing me, quickly mouthed the words 'One more minute', vanished again, talking loudly so I could hear he was trying to sign off.

Finally he was done. 'What did the old lady call them in that Henry James novella? Publishing scoundrels? She couldn't have been more precise. You're fortunate: whomever you find at whatever university clever enough to print your work probably will not be motivated by, on the one hand, vanity about your literary stature, and, contrarily, dependent on some accountant's bottom line. Come in, sit down, have more coffee, another anisette. I will. After all the pain I've endured with that dragon of egocentricity, I'm entitled to some smidgen of pleasure!'

During the phone conversation, Von Slyke must have moved the mahogany captain's chair from behind his desk, because he now turned it to face me, sat down and began to loudly and happily munch, dropping crumbs all over himself yet not seeming to care. He periodically washed it down with a swipe at his coffee mug.

I got up the nerve to say, 'Is all this about a new book?'

'Yes,' he replied tonelessly. 'I'm not sure whether it's a memoir, a novel, a meditation or simply an affront! It's called – are you ready, dear? – *The Gulls*! Everyone hates the title. My publisher. My agent. My editor. Everyone hates the book. Everyone hates me for writing it.'

'I like it,' I said, truthfully. 'It's different. Although I will admit it's not very Von Slykean.'

'Bless you for good sense. That was exactly my point. Although try to tell that to these idiots . . .' He took another swig of coffee and suddenly asked, 'Before you embarrass me by asking me what it's about . . . how it is that you met St George? And are you aware of what an utter tramp he used to be?' Another sip, then, 'Obviously you're not. But in the bad old days of the Club 8709 – one of the great bathhouses of our time – your very own mentor, Dr St George – at that time still a stunner – would actually take up residence weekends at a time in one of the upper-floor cubicles, where he would entertain gentleman callers by the baker's dozen, lying supine and naked on his little cot with the door left ajar. How such an unregenerate bottom could survive *la peste* is completely beyond me. But there are those who insist he's actually a fifteenth-century sorcerer, able to command time and space, who decided to take up residence in Holmby Hills as a diversion, and woe to whomsoever questions him on any of the Elizabethans, all of whom he personally knew and by whom he was most assuredly buggered.'

'Those rumors periodically sweep through Rolfe and Royce Halls,' I admitted. 'But I thought they only went back to Queen Anne's time.'

'No, no, it's the little things that give St George away. Saying "tup" when he means to say screw and his constant surprise at the efficaciousness of indoor plumbing.'

'How did you meet him?' I dared ask.

'We all met him together. Wait, no, it must have been Mark Dodge who first met him. St George was infatuated with Mark – as who wasn't in those days? Yes, that's right, I believe Mark met St George on Mark's book tour for *Keep Frozen*. That book, you surely already know, was the Purple Circle's first success, and, I must say, it didn't at all hurt that Mark possessed godlike beauty and male-model poise. Everyone wanted to meet him, to know him, to be fucked by him. For years, I'd go out on my own tiny tours, to dreary gay clubs on third-string campuses in the sticks, and the first half-hour of any encounter was always spent fielding questions about Mark Dodge. "What's he really like?" Meaning, what and whom did he really like in the sack? I faked it of course, because I didn't know a thing, never having had the pleasure myself. Dom did, though, but then Mark and De Petrie both were in the innest of in crowds in the Pines–Flamingo set and I believe for one year they were more than lovers, they were that most intimate of all gay relationships: dance buddies!' Von Slyke giggled at his witticism. 'There was someone else who slept with Mark in our group. Who could it have . . .?' He thought, seemed to remember, didn't like the memory and moved on. 'At any rate, St George met Mark at a reading at the old Walt Whitman bookstore in San Francisco when it was located on Sutter Street and that wonderfully lemon-mouthed Charles was running it. Way before your time, I'm afraid. I suppose St George was teaching at Berkeley then. And when Mark came back to New York sporting hickeys, carrying a case of the clap the size of a steamer trunk, he said we should meet St George, we'd love him. And we did!'

The phone rang again. Von Slyke cast it a dirty look but went on eating his cookie, saying, 'We're not talking to that beastly man again. Now tell me. You read my novel in prep school. And then what?'

I was about to reply when the machine picked up and it was not Ron Preston but instead a woman's voice, saying, 'Damon, are you there? It's Midge. I just spoke to Preston and I know you're there. Sulking. Attempting suicide. Doing something irretrievably messy. Please pick up, we've got to –'

'My agent!' Von Slyke held his head with both hands. 'I'd better take it. Why not get a refill?' handing me the empty cookie plate.

He took the receiver, moaning 'Mid-ddge' into it as I once more left the room. This time, I did stay close enough to the open doorway to hear him say, 'I'm not committing suicide because I'm not changing one fucking word, not one fucking comma, not one fucking semicolon of that manuscript. Who does that editor think she is? Demanding changes? When we all know she got the position by giving Preston blowjobs under his desk and she couldn't spell if her life depended on it, for Chrissakes!' Followed by silence. Then, 'I know, I know, I know.' Followed by, 'Mi-id-dge, you surely know the advance money is spent already . . . How do you think I took the summer place?' I noticed the dark head of Conchita just coming up the corridor stairs and decided I'd heard enough.

When I handed her the plate, she said, 'I just washed the floors.
It's all wet. We'll have to go the long way.' She led me past the open
doorway, where Von Slyke was moaning into the receiver,
'Never! . . . Never! . . . Never!' Back through the front corridor and
outside, around the house, toward where I'd met him before, detour-
ing at the bougainvillaea-filled fence I remembered lay outside the
breakfast patio.

'You wait here.' It felt to me as though Conchita dismissed me,
but maybe I was just being oversensitive. In the bright sunlight,
among the proliferation of plant life, as she walked away, Conchita's
jet hair had a red sheen and she looked more vulnerable than
indoors.

The meeting was going well, despite my forebodings and anxi-
eties. Von Slyke seemed far too distracted by his own life to test me
with as much rigor as he'd probably planned. So, thanks to the
interference of unrelated external events, I'd probably manage to slip
by. Once again slip by in my life. If I could just keep my side of it
going a little while longer, these interruptions might end up being
helpful to me. But I had to admit they were anxiety-producing.
When I went inside again and Von Slyke asked what of the Purple
Circle I'd read, what should I do? Tell him I'd read all their books,
as well as the two volumes of the group *Reader* and Thaddeus
Fleming's study of their works. Yes, sure, of course. What else? The
Erling Cummings biography of the Purples? Hadn't that been dished
to filth by Jasper Goodstern in some book review, the *Washington
Post Book World*? And hadn't Jasper been one of Von Slyke's pro-
tégés when he'd taught at Stanford in the late 1990s? Someone had
said that. So surely that meant Von Slyke also hated the group biography. Too bad those two planned bios of him hadn't been published
yet. And Irian's own full-length study of Dominic De Petrie, but
that only touched on Von Slyke's work. I'd felt so sure coming here
today, so on top of all the material, so certain. And now . . .

I became slowly aware that I was hearing a regular noise. I turned
around where I stood and there was Von Slyke banging on the inside
of the big library window to get my attention.

'You're probably already ruing that unhappy day you chanced
upon my novel in prep school,' was how he greeted me when I got
back into the library. 'But then what can I say, except that you

possibly now understand better than most what a dreadfully waste-
ful and ridiculous life we poor authors are forced to endure and why
it is a far, far better thing to forgo completely and remain in the
comfy groves of academe.'

'Here,' he thrust them into my hands all a-jingle, 'are the keys to
the house. They're vaguely marked. If you can at all make it, try to
be here and sleep over tomorrow night. I'll need a little help getting
all of my bags into the Trooper fairly early the following morning.
You wouldn't want to waste your precious time driving me to the
airport? You would? You are an angel. Make a list of what you like
to eat not already in the fridge and Conchita will buy it. She shops
at Mayfair Mart every Friday. She changes the beds every Monday.
You know where the laundry is. Just dump stuff there. Or do it
yourself. Anselmo comes twice a month and the electric leaf-blower
makes a frightful noise, but he appears to be physically attached to
it, and whines awfully if he can't use it, so what is one to do but bear
it? I'll call or fax once a week to check up and I've left numbers
where I can be reached.'

By now, in addition to talking fast, Von Slyke was quickly walking me out the library to the front door. 'I hope you won't be too utterly bored here. Don't have wild parties. Or at least don't have loud
ones so the neighbors complain. And whatever you do, don't let in
some tall skinny number named Hector when he rings the bell at
three in the morning. Unless, that is,' he added as we now reached
the driveway and he rushed me to the Celica, 'you don't mind paying a C-note for the privilege of being called a sick perverted *mari-
con* while you suck a short, unwashed dick.'

Von Slyke shook my hand, simultaneously bussed my cheek and
shoved me into the car, before scurrying off into the house.

I'd driven halfway back to UCLA when I looked at the set of keys
in my hand and realized what had happened: these were the keys to
Damon Von Slyke's house. I was in.

'...so, you see, in "The Yellow Room", Charlotte Perkins Gilman
was doing more than writing a psychological tale of a nervous housewife's breakdown, she was prying open a dialogue about the place of
women in American life that was already an issue in her own day.'

The seating in the classroom was arranged so it faced west. I could see over the twenty-two heads to where, from this second-story window in Royce Hall I had an unobstructed view across campus split by a half-dozen verticals from sixty-five-foot cypress trees planted years before, flanking the terrace and partly hiding Drake Stadium. It was a breezy, lazy summer morning, the air flavored by salt from beaches only a few miles away, where I was certain more than one of my listeners would be headed after class.

I went on: 'Let's remember that this story was written in the years before the so-called Great War, during the height of the Suffragette Movement, and that the central focus of these early groups was obtaining the right of women to vote. The deeper problems of a woman's place and worth and future in our society would require another half-century to come to the forefront again. When we read Jewett, or Edith Wharton or Willa Cather, even Dorothy Parker and Pearl Buck, always keep this underlying feminist emphasis in mind as contextual background.'

During the last speech there was a noticeable if almost subterranean shifting of sneakers and sandal soles against the wooden floor. Only a half-hour in the faculty lounge the day before classes had begun confirmed what I'd heard from several grad students: in previous summer sessions the course I'd taken over had been considered a 'cinch'. Professor Fusumi was known as a sweet man who loved American literature and didn't believe in failing grades. He usually held the class in the nearby Rolfe Hall auditorium, where some sixty to seventy-five students would spread out in the dimly lighted fan-shaped room to nap, work crossword puzzles and do other homework. Word had gotten out late that Fusumi had been forced to return to Okinawa to care for a dying father, and that an upstart named Ohrenstedt had taken over. Despite that lateness, the class was one-third its normal size and I'd moved it upstairs, where I could see the students and where they'd have to remain awake. It wasn't lost on me that at least a quarter of the faces belonged to upper-class jocks so out of the loop they were now stuck with a course where they'd have to actually read. Half of the rest looked like English or language majors who'd already read much of what we would discuss, and the remainder were out-of-department with a passing interest in books. Naturally, it was the jocks scattered around the room that I went out of my way to provoke.

'Next class we'll be discussing F. Scott Fitzgerald's novel *The Great Gatsby*. Please have it read by Friday. Any questions? Yes . . . bear with me, I'll learn all of your names soon, I promise,' I said, checking the seating chart. 'Mr Rice, is it?' Here I was play-acting. I'd noticed him from the minute he'd walked into the class a week before – a rugby player's lean body, alternating knots of muscles and planes of long bones, an undeniable physical presence in his '80s polo shirts and overwashed jams, topped by a square head, brooding unshaven face, fine facial features focussed on his dark eyes, abundant ebony eyelashes and bushy eyebrows, the whole framed by the current trend: an overgrown helmet of jet-black hair. 'Raymond Rice?'

'It's this reading list you gave out.'

'What about it?'

'You said that we've got to choose one of the authors to do a term paper on.'

That in itself must have been a horrible surprise to him and the other jocks.

'You'll also need to have read at least one author from each page of that list to discuss on the written-essay portion of your final exam . . .' I added, introducing yet more future horrors.

'Right!' he said, and while big basketball-playing David Ben-Torres in the back row let some books fall to the floor in undisguised surprise and disgust at this new turn of events, Rice gamely went on, 'Well, what I wanted to ask was, and I don't know if I was the only one who noticed it, but how come all of the last page of the list, the last two decades of the twentieth century, it's all . . . well, lesbian or gay writers?'

'Will anyone address that?' I asked. And seeing a hand raised in the same lateral row as Rice, 'Ms Agosian?'

'The lion's share of the books on the last page of the list were written by members of a group called the Purple Circle, which more or less created and perfected gay literature between 1975 and the second millennium,' she said in a most professorial manner.

Her polished delivery clashed with her appearance, which was pure Neo-Valley Girl. Given her tanned-to-perfection olive skin and undyed-looking cornsilk blond hair worn in a single off-the-shoulder pigtail, she seemed to be third-generation Armenian and something else, Danish or Dutch perhaps, with voluptuous hips and small breasts barely restrained within a trendy faux-foil parachute outfit: not pretty, but sexy.

'In English One,' she added, 'our professor said the Purple Circle is considered to be a major crystallization of *fin-de-siècle* American lit, with far-reaching implications for our time.'

'Thank you, Ms. Agosian. If you'll recall, Mr Rice, the subtitle of this course is "The Outsider as Insider". Each author we'll be reading and discussing represents a gender, ethnic, racial or geographic minority that produced a substantial body of its own literature, which in turn illuminated all American life and mores. Women, African and Asian-Americans, Southerners –'

'What about Fitzgerald?' Rice refused to stay put. 'We're reading him next and he wasn't a minority writer.'

Pamela was raising her hand, so I simply pointed to her and she took over. 'From our day and distance, we think of Fitzgerald as part of the ruling hegemony, a white male Midwesterner. But in his own day he was an outsider, barely assimilated out of Irish immigrant status, and only by his father's self-made wealth and his education at Princeton.'

I watched if that stuck in Rice's Irish-American craw.

'Maybe so,' Rice argued back at her, pleasing me by his tenacity, 'but Fitzgerald didn't write about Irish immigrants living in slums. He wrote about people who lived in big houses, worked as stockbrokers and had lots of money.'

'Ms Agosian?' I asked.

'It's true that Fitzgerald mostly wrote about what he considered to be his audience but what many critics believe is his greatest literary creation, the character of Jay Gatsby, breaks the mold. Gatsby is an immigrant, Jay Gatz, born in Eastern Europe.'

'He's still not an Irish immigrant,' Rice insisted.

'No,' she countered, 'but Fitzgerald suggests he might be Jewish: the ultimate American outsider of the time.'

'Yeah, but –'

I interrupted. 'In every case, Mr Rice, class, it was the outsider's perspective that cut most deeply into the national psyche. And by the end of the last century, while much assimilation had taken place for women, Native Americans and African-Americans, lesbians and gays remained the most evidently disenfranchised group. So it is that they – and especially their leading edge, the Purple Circle – produced the books many of us turn to today. Aaron Axenfeld's *Second Star from the Right* and Dominic De Petrie's *Adventures of Marty* are perennial sellers, especially among teens, not only because they're entertaining but for the depth of the questions they ask about what constitutes self-identity and the honesty of their answers. How many of you have already read them?'

More than a dozen hands were raised. 'You see, Mr Rice . . .' I let my case stand. 'That's why we'll be discussing this group in some detail. I suggest you read their work . . .' He'd raised his hand again, on his face I read a look of intransigence. 'You're not going to tell me you have some reason not to read them, some religious beliefs, say, against this material, Mr Rice?'

'No,' he quickly replied, 'but when my male parent saw it, he went Q-bomb on me for an LA minute, you know what I mean, asking if I was planning a transgen op and all.'

'I condole with you, Mr Rice. But isn't one function of a university to broaden education? If he has a problem with your reading list, your parent may address it directly to the Languages Department head and the Dean of the college. Both approved this syllabus.'

Rice, now the unwelcome center of other students' attention, was more brooding, embarrassed.

'Or perhaps, unlike most young men, you're personally squeamish reading about sex?' I mischievously suggested. And before he could answer I gave him a hand-up. 'You realize that even the most socially heterosexualized among us can pick up tips from these books.'

The class laughed.

'No, no.' He retreated into his dark, closed-face handsomeness. 'I'll read them.'

You'd damned well better read them if you want a passing grade and a spot on next year's team, you little bigot, I thought, but smiled serenely instead.

'If that's all the questions, till Friday, same time, same web-site,' I added, which got an appreciative titter.

One of the lit major students, Danielle Tsieh, stopped at my desk to ask if I'd consider looking over something she'd written. In a previous term's course on twentieth-century journalism, she'd done a paper on the relationship of the Purple Circle to the rise of the lesbian/gay media of its day, and her professor had sent it off and it had been accepted by an academic quarterly. All she had to do was expand it. Could I vet the piece before she sent it off? I said I'd be happy to.

The basketball guard, Ben-Torres, was outside waiting for me when Danielle and I exited last out of the classroom. 'I'm holding down a job this summer,' he said, mentioning a famous old CD shop a few blocks away on Gayley Avenue. 'It's the only way I can afford to take summer classes. An' I don't know if I'll be able to do all the required reading.'

'Gatsby's only 120 pages,' I replied. From this close up, the skin on his hollowed cheeks and below his lower lip was quite pitted. The same hormones that had raged throughout his body a few years back, causing sudden growth to his height and girth, had plagued him with acne. His eyes were surprisingly pale, gray-green, his lashes as naturally lavish as a made-up girl's.

'I know, but I read slow. I'm not dyslexic or anything. It's just that it doesn't always sink in . . . Last year, I read some books that could have been on your list,' he offered, 'I remember them, and I could go back and refresh my memory. Can I use them instead?'

'Which books?' I asked.

'Capote's *In Cold Blood* and the one you mentioned in class, De Petrie's *Adventures of Marty.*'

'Did you like them?' I asked. I was guiding Ben-Torres along the corridor toward the metal-railed stairway, feeling a bit like that energetic, ambitious little tugboat in some kid's book from my childhood trying to steer the big ocean liner into dock.

'Well . . . I couldn't say I enjoyed the book about the murders,' Ben-Torres replied.

We so-called verbal types make fun of the seriousness of those who are less Ariel-witted and I'm usually no exception, but I felt his words were thought out, measured, not so much portentous but as though each word counted, meant something to him.

'It was shocking. Except it explained the two guys a lot better than the movie. I read the book after I'd seen a video,' Ben-Torres

explained. 'I'm kind of slow sometimes and I didn't really understand what made those guys tick. I figured if I read the book . . . I
guess that's why you have to read . . .'

'Exactly!' I encouraged him, 'And the other book?' I asked, even
more curious how he'd explain De Petrie's romp through sexually
liberated 1980 gay Manhattan.

'Parts of it were funny – and weird! I thought someone should
make a video of it too. But I guess it'd be too pornographic . . .'

'Well . . . erotic. I hear it's under film option. How did you come
to select that book?'

'My roommie here at school made me read it. He's gay, a really
neat guy, and he said it would help me understand him.'

Well, maybe, I thought. Ben-Torres's roommate wouldn't have
been the first to use *Adventures of Marty* for sheer titillation, or as
an aid to seduction. But I didn't want to say so and spoil their relationship.

Just then three male students tore past us, barely touching the
steps as they flew down the flight of stairs, onto the landing and out
the building door. Two were screaming, 'Motherfucker!' at the first,
who kept puffing out, 'Shit! Shit! Shit!' as he fled.

'I'd say you're a neat guy going out of your way like that for your
roommate,' I said, and touched Ben-Torres's huge bicep.

He blushed, lowered his Maybelline eyes and all but said, 'Aw,
shucks.' I could see how all of this might have driven the roommate
into masturbatory fantasies, seduction plans, ecstasies of anticipation. I wondered how far an acne-pitted jock would go to keep
dormitory peace.

We'd reached the bottom of the stairs and, like the superb young
gentleman I now knew he was, Ben-Torres held the door open for
me. As soon as we got outside, I heard familiar voices, around the
corner, on the other side of the building, where another little porch
was placed off another entry: Ray Rice and Pamela Agosian were
there, and they were still arguing. It looked as though, inadvertently,
I'd thrown them together.

'Read what you can this term,' I said to Ben-Torres. 'Keep me
informed on your progress. You can use either of those books on
your term paper and final. I'll keep your work situation in mind
when I'm making up final grades.'

Big grin. 'Thanks Mr Ohrenstedt,' and he loped off down the
steps and into the quad, shouting out, 'Hey, Ray! I'm going to eat.
You coming?' to Rice, who replied, 'Yeah, sure,' and loped off
alongside him.

Von Slyke had referred to the state of his papers as 'an utter bedlam',
and while his favorite dictionary gave the definition of the word
'bedlam' as the slang contraction of Bethlehem Mercy Hospital – the
early mental institution famous in eighteenth-century London – and
its second definition as any very noisy and confusing place, neither
of which seemed relevant, his usage of the word turned out to be,
after all, not that wildly inappropriate. 'Chaotic', 'baffling', 'bewildering' and 'utterly befuddling' are a few other terms Von Slyke
might also have applied, as I found out for myself and nearly to my
grief.

I'd assumed that some general order prevailed among the morass
of paper upon those secret chamber shelves on which Von Slyke's
manuscripts and letters and notes had been lain. Possibly because I
thought that once I'd gotten past the obvious messiness of their
bestrewal, I would happen upon a more basic level of internal con-
sistency, one reflecting first the steady growth and later the
efflorescence of Von Slyke's career and reputation. All I need do, I
thought (foolishly, erroneously), was dust off each box, each rubber-
banded group of papers, thumb through the pages to ensure they
were all the same piece of writing, align the edges, note down what
was within according to those aspects detailed in the bibliographic
program I was using on my PC, then rebox or reseal the papers a bit
more securely.

For perhaps the first five or six batches of papers I came upon,
this was exactly what happened. These works represented the early
years of Von Slyke's career, the late 1960s and early 1970s, when he
was first living in Manhattan, fresh from college in the Midwest.
He'd been young, attractive, if photos are to be believed, at times
slender, at others tanned and somewhat muscular. After flailing
about a few years in part-time occupations and freelance work of
low pay and no future, he'd secured a full-time job: 'trainee' as an
insurance company statistician. But Von Slyke was already writing
at least an hour every morning before work – a habit he would

never entirely grow out of – as well as on weekends and vacations, penning his first plays and stories.

Talented, hopeful and ambitious, young Damon was still completely closeted in his writing, but by no means in his personal life. During the first decade or so in New York he had three live-in lovers, various boyfriends and several of what he himself described as 'physically active if emotionally hopeless' love affairs with heterosexual yet experimentally inclined young men. (A sign of more naïvely freewheeling times, difficult to conceive of in this post-AIDS era.)

Naturally enough, since the Purple Circle hadn't yet 'created' gay literature, none of Von Slyke's personal life was reflected in the content of that first period of writing, except perhaps with the lightest of allusions, the most ambivalent of touches. As a result, Von Slyke's first work, when it did appear in print, was welcomed with if not the proverbial open arms, then at least with semi-extended fingertips by what passed in those days for the New York literary world. (Although if one were to believe the unsparing journals of Dominic De Petrie and the gossipy correspondence of Mitchell Leo, Von Slyke's personal charm and 'sucking up' to some of those literary lights might also account for the early notice his works received.)

Those more or less orderly packets of manuscripts and papers within my purview that first week of the summer I lived in the Hollywood Hills hacienda contained what there was of what we have since come to know as Damon Von Slyke's juvenilia: nine early stories of various lengths in at least three versions apiece, two published in small, long-discontinued literary magazines of such short life, such minuscule subscription and newsstand distribution rates that even I, who'd studied the period's 'little mags' and done a paper on them for a graduate class, had only heard of one – admittedly the one in which had been published Von Slyke's best-known early tale, 'Fantasietta on a Sad Pierrot'. All of these early stories had then been subsequently rewritten and eventually published during the Von Slyke 'boom' under the not altogether inappropriate collective title, *Spun Sugar*.

Besides the fiction, I also happened upon a few reviews of long-forgotten books Von Slyke had done and two essays. The first, titled 'Meeting Mr Maugham at the Russell Square Hotel', I took as a *jeu d'esprit*, possibly a Nabokovian joke, as I've found no corroborative evidence that Von Slyke ever met the British writer, let alone visited London before he was himself aged forty, by which time Maugham was long dead. The second piece, 'On the Neglect of Balzac', takes as a jumping-off point two incidents – Lucien de Rubempre's arrival at the Paris Opéra and, later on in the novel, the poisoning of Esther's greyhound – in *The Splendors and Miseries of Courtesans*. This essay appears to have arisen from some deeper well of Von Slyke's being. Balzac's late novel – with its veiled yet central homosexual relationship – is a disturbingly prescient, possibly seminal book in Purple Circle studies (De Petrie and Axenfeld note it) and the essay posited several themes – self-identity versus accepting other's version of identity and the question of being 'elective' or 'choiceless', motifs which would become central in Von Slyke's and other Purple Circlers' works.

Expected among the early manuscripts I went through were the two one-act plays, *Representations in Indigo*, which according to accompanying papers opened to a very few, decidedly mixed, reviews in an Upper East Side Manhattan theatre (now closed but in the 1980s transformed into the popular 'Bridge and Tunnel' discotheque Mistinguet) when Von Slyke was twenty-one. Capping it all were the manuscripts containing the early masterwork *Systems for Approaching Emmeline*, his first critical success, a novel revelling in Von Slyke's oddly slanted perspective and unique prose style – at this time at its most richly descriptive.

Besides being 'densely written' and 'sexually indecisive', the early work of Von Slyke – whether fiction or drama – was problematic in other ways, as critics were harsh in pointing out. Plotlines, when they existed at all, were, as one reviewer unkindly put it, 'indecipherable', and when decipherable were deemed 'smarmily suggestive and indeed morbidly unhealthy'. This about work which to our time is almost chaste in its closetedness. 'Byzantine in the worst, most dark-corridored, back-alleyed, shilly-shallying sense of the word,' the *New York Times* dismissed the plays. 'Approaching new levels of tortuous, torturing, discomprehension' whined *Atlantic Monthly* of the novel.

Despite these nay-sayers, the work was, after all, noticed. The novel especially. The aged, still vitriolic novelist and film critic

Parker Tyler predictively announced 'a major new voice fresh out of the despicable American wasteland – a transformative and healing book'. The nearly senile Anglo-Indian author Aubrey Menen, reviewing the book in the *Sunday Times*, advised readers that Von Slyke was a 'young eagle unfurling powerful prose pinions'.

It now seems almost natural that *Emmeline* would be taken up and adored; what must amaze us was that it was done on so limited a front, primarily a few cognoscenti, mostly by the vast number of then still-closeted gay reviewers, authors, critics, academics and hangers-on.

This was also the period in which Von Slyke possessed as friend, confidant, amanuensis and, most importantly, copy-editor that extremely ambiguous character in all of the histories and studies to date of the Purple Circle, Jonathan Flitch. He hadn't yet become the 'bitter and cynical harridan' Dominic De Petrie later described in his autobiographical novel, or 'the great foul rotting spiderlike cloaca of gay literature' that Frankie McKewen had mixed metaphors to not quite name in a thinly disguised portrait in his posthumously published novel. It was thanks to Flitch, however, that I got as far as I did in cataloguing the early work. Whatever faults of character or personality he later revealed as a magazine editor (and they were evidently many and extreme), Flitch possessed two positive qualities that should leave followers of the Purple Circle forever in his debt. First was that intrinsic orderliness of mind and habit historians and scholars are forced to depend upon – and applaud when they find it – and second an absolutely unshakeable belief in Von Slyke as an important writer.

That I was able to deal relatively rapidly with the slew of earliest Von Slyke manuscripts is due to the fact that they'd all first been typed up by Flitch from Damon's handwritten autographs. Typed up twice (on an electric Smith Corona Super-Coronet *circa* 1964–6, with a defective 'g' key that lifted every second time it was struck), so each manuscript exists in what might be called a 'pure' version, as well as in the 'working' version, the latter distinguished by 'outside' editorial comments and emendations. On a few pages of the autographs so altered, one can make out in faded ink and smudged pencil comments in Flitch's hand, suggesting an intimate literary relationship, one where Flitch gave the writing a first read-through and responded in an unforced manner.

The manuscript of *Instigations*, for example – the first of Von Slyke's work I'd read, the original of which I'd been searching for from the minute I'd returned to the hacienda from driving the great man himself to LAX and having seen him fly off East in a Delta jet, leaving me free rein in the little hidden office. In the four (!) typed versions one sees not merely Flitch's editing, but also several others' emendations, despite the fact that all versions were typed on the same electric typewriter, indicative of Flitch's effort. These several groups of emendations are often at loggerheads with each other, suggesting that by this time Von Slyke was no longer solely relying upon Flitch for literary advice.

For example, on page ninety-two of the manuscript (page seventy-six of the published book) I'd marked MS#2, Flitch had written in the margin in comment of a Von Slyke page-and-a-half-long simile 'marvelous!' whereas the same simile on page ninety-two of MS#4 has commented in the margin in what I take to be Dodge's hand, 'Dame – was it really "like" all that?' with a suggestion that most of the simile be deleted, cut to two lines. This is what appears in MS#4 and in the finished book.

Now, it's a well-known fact, according to both McKewen's and De Petrie's journals of these early years, when the Purple Circlers first began meeting each other, as well as throughout the letters of Axenfeld to Leo and McKewen during those annual spring months they lived in Florence, that *Instigations* evolved quite slowly, and was probably written over nearly three years (this Von Slyke himself confirmed in an interview with *The Advocate*).

It was begun as a short story, then added to and published in another form in *Christopher Street*. What would be the second chapter of the novel was emended again, obviously by Mark Dodge, and published later that same year in his path-breaking anthology, *Young and Gay*. Both the first and the fourth chapters of the book were first orally presented at readings of the Purple Circle, in the Leo–McKewen's Upper West Side apartment and at Mark Dodge's Chelsea penthouse.

In each case, handwritten comments and alterations on the typed manuscripts in Von Slyke's own hand are obviously in response to critiques by the others. Most of these seem to have found their way into the final form of the book.

The fourth and fifth – i.e. the final chapters – also show this kind of emendation. They were presented by Von Slyke in the only two public readings we know the Purples to have done together: one in Manhattan and brought about by, of all things, a nascent film group; the second in Boston, co-sponsored by members of a local university's English department who seemed to personally (perhaps sexually) know Cameron Powers or Jeff Weber, in conjunction with a local independent bookstore.

Confusing as these several versions of Von Slyke's first financially successful novel are, they approach the limpidity of a Montana mountain stream compared to what happens once Jonathan Flitch falls out of the scene and other helpmates move in.

The works of what might safely be considered Von Slyke's second or middle period, the novels *Heliotrope Convertible* and *Pastiche Upon Some Themes Alluded to by Gustave Flaubert*, and the non-fiction *Rejection: A Masquerade* exist in a dozen versions apiece. Even the original handwritten ones are a mélange of paper colors (puce, mauve, pale canary) and sizes (though standard letter size 8½ × 11 inches, prevails), as well as in different colors and thicknesses of ink and pencil (some teal, most in blue-black).

Partly this was aesthetic posturing, partly it was because Von Slyke was then 'editor' of – i.e. only on-staff writer of – and thus constantly traveling for – a short-lived Condé-Nast magazine geared toward the so-called 'Airline Sophisticate'. This may also explain why one draft of chapter six of the *Pastiche* can be found entirely penned with a sculptural Italic point upon richly textured paper, watermarked by the stationer of the Ritz-Carlton Hotel in Atlanta, Georgia. Of course, other factors still unknown to us at this date may have come into play.

We have hints and suggestions from other Purple Circlers, in addition to Von Slyke's early typist's rebarbative personality, of reasons behind the waning influence of Jonathan Flitch upon Von Slyke's life, never mind what would come to be known pre-emptively as his style.

Damon had begun dating, then living with, the younger and somewhat more louche Cameron Powers, the least prolific and certainly the biographically murkiest figure among the group. We do know that the earlier years of Powers's tragically short life included a stint as an actor and yet another as a director and 'dramaturge' with a Lower East Side theatrical company of peripheral importance. More than one of Von Slyke's letters refer to the various elderly gentlemen – some wealthy, a few famous – who'd befriended the young Southerner when he was still in (their common friend and correspondent) James Merrill's elastic locution, a 'male Thais' – i.e. before Powers settled into Von Slykean domesticity and literary circles.

We know of Powers's personality that he was 'a good time girl (*sic*) whose Mississippi charm' – according to Frankie McKewen (in his heavily autobiographical, posthumously published novel *A Boy from Quad Cities*) – was 'Vivien Leigh crossed with Messalina: so long as she (*sic*) cares for you it's lilies and Jasmine tea and Whitman samplers, but get in her (*sic*) way or cross her (*sic*) and the lilies don't fester, they fuckin' explode in your face'.

Flitch himself never openly referred to Cameron Powers's new influence on Damon's life or to the growing estrangement between himself and Von Slyke, neither at the time nor even very much in later years. In fact, when he was interviewed for an obscure journal whose editor rightly recognized how crucial Flitch had been in discovering and aiding not merely Von Slyke but two decades further of younger gay writers, Flitch merely said of Powers that he and Damon had first been introduced 'in a club named, I believe, Scuzz, a block or two off the West Side Highway'.

Reading De Petrie's trenchant second volume of memoirs, *Chrome Earrings*, we find a significant gloss on this meeting place: he describes Scuzz as 'a suck and fuck palace supreme', colorfully adding that it was 'a true dive with shirtless studs endlessly fondling their baskets in front, chains separating the front room from the dimly lighted back room, where said studs and other young hotties spend many hours nightly in "receptive" positions, i.e. either on their knees blowin' or on their backs against the torn baize of the pool table, gettin' porked'.

Flitch did often say that in later years he and Damon remained in contact and friendly. In the same vein, once he'd achieved success, Von Slyke was known to go out of his way – in often misguided and failed attempts – to obtain positions, occupations and various offices for his former secretary, when Flitch had fallen on difficult times.

Possibly the changing circumstances and the naturally evolving inequity of their relationship were adultly accepted by the two of them. More likely – and according to Cummings and other biographers – Von Slyke fell 'hard' under the influence of Cameron Powers, and when that relationship was over, of several other young men, all of whom also exerted considerable sexual power over the by-then late-thirties to mid-forties author.

Oddly, we find almost no textural indication in Von Slyke's work of the far greater personal influence of Cameron Powers, despite the three years they lived together (years of great Purple Circle activity) and despite the fact that Powers later became a noted book editor for a subsidiary trade paperback line of Simon and Schuster.

Whatever the reason, not the work but the manuscripts, the proofs and the care and upkeep of the Von Slyke papers ended up suffering most. While the 'Powers Years' may be characterized by what might be termed literary multichromaticism, the years in which Von Slyke was 'in thrall' to the athletic Herve Fraser seemed to encourage utter disorganization among his papers, while those (thankfully not too many) months during which he was in love with honey-blond Achilles Ashe were bereft of any literary output.

Thus, as I soon found out, the orderliness of the papers and manuscripts continued to worsen the further along the shelves I reached. Fully handwritten and typed-out early, middle or final (even near-final versions) of *Verbatim*, Von Slyke's follow-up to *Instigations*, as well as the next novel, *Leaving Riverside Drive*, were scarcely to be located in the secret chamber. True enough, printer's proofs existed, several copies each of three-foot-long, unpaged galleys, as well as bound 'uncorrected' galleys, but it was only when I was going through another half-dozen unmarked cardboard boxes that I located what turned out to be parts of earlier manuscripts of the two books, in no particular order.

Another bag marked Von's (an LA area supermarket), which I merely thought contained letters, turned to hold much of the first autograph of *Leaving Riverside Drive*, as well as some of the stories later collected in *The Japonica Tree* (a title and title story that – with its Southern setting and dialogue – a decade later, represents whatever influence Powers exerted over his more distinguished partner).

From there on it truly becomes chaotic. Another box marked 'Tax Records??' which I briefly looked at ended up containing several sections of *Verbatim*'s first draft. A third cardboard MS box, pencil-scrawled to read 'Publisher's Royalties Statements', did indeed contain some of those financial reports, but also, it turned out, the rest of what might have been a second draft of *Leaving Riverside Drive*, which, when I later compared it to the finished book, was more complete than what I'd found in the supermarket shopping bag. By this time I'd reached boxes on which what I now recognized as Von Slyke's hand had written 'Insurance Policies/Will' and 'Electronics Manuals and Guarantees' and I didn't at all hesitate.

Inside I did find manuals and guarantees, but also two autographs of the short stories 'When in Despair with Fortune' and 'Hair Gallery', and, in addition, penned on the inside leaf of the manual for someone's – Fraser's? Ashe's? – Panasonic Business Partner 150 Laptop Computer, the opening paragraphs of Von Slyke's seventh novel exactly as they would appear in finished form, I mean *DOS: Manuscript in Distress*. The title had been taken from a chapter heading of the computer manual, circled by Von Slyke, reading 'Word Processing Problems: When Your MS is in Distress'.

Evidently – I was forced to conclude – any paper or plastic bag, shopping bag, boxlike container, business, manila or expanding envelope, sheaf of curling paper wrapped in twine or gathered by yellowed Scotch tape, any papers clipped or stapled together, any laundry or grocery list, the back of a PEN Club rejoin reminder, the whiter areas of the Metropolitan Opera Annual Performance Schedule, the margins of correspondence from his health-care provider, the backs of fan letters, the edges and reverse side of a natal horoscope he'd received as a fiftieth birthday present, the obverse of a bank statement, in fact anything and everything made of paper or able to contain paper might contain a draft or manuscript of Von Slyke's work.

He'd not thrown out much, although seeing what actually remained it was obvious that through sheer sloppiness, inaction, lack of attention and general attrition, losses, possibly even great losses, had unquestionably occurred. If I were to catalogue it right, I had to scour every single inch of the inner room for paper, no matter how it might be marked or unmarked, no matter how unprepossessing a possibility it might appear at first to offer, if only to locate what Von Slyke's totally unorganized yet pack-rat-like mentality had left behind.

Scour it and then lay it out in some systematic fashion. For that the library itself proved to be far too small, and I was forced to begin moving material into the huge dining room. Beginning on the table and then, as each new draft, version or proof of one of the thirteen books or any of the more than two dozen magazine pieces appeared, laying it down row-like so that eventually, when there were a dozen drafts or torsos of, say, his title essay of the most recent uncollected essays, 'G. B. Shaw and Samuel Goldwyn: The Author as Moralist', the row extended along the tabletop and far onto the dark-tiled floor.

I'm going into detail here, because I want to be very, very clear about the facts: I was not looking for anything in particular. I was looking for everything Von Slyke had written, aware that I might find anything, anywhere.

I'd become convinced that I would know what I'd found once it was in front of me. Damon Von Slyke might have been sloppy and disorganized, yet, as he'd reminded me himself, he also lived quite well and, as was common knowledge, he was unstintingly generous with friends, and thus always short of funds. After he'd made his name with *Instigations*, not a single article, story or essay, not any paragraph with his name on it longer than a book-cover blurb, was ever again written 'on spec' – or free. It was all deemed 'salable' and I can attest that it was sometimes sold to several buyers on various continents simultaneously, both in periodical and book form, as well as later on appearing in a variety of anthologies, often several times over.

Also, after Von Slyke's first fame, nothing he wrote remained 'in progress' or in development for very long. Pieces might be revised, but less so as time went on (despite the prevalence of 'differing' MSS), and seldom were they as much rewritten as earlier works. They might be retitled, but again that too soon ceased. As a result, knowing what constituted Von Slyke's finished and published work after about the year 1982, essentially you knew Von Slyke's work, period.

All of which goes to explicate my great, my utter surprise when I was pulling apart the various typewritten pages of one particular typed draft of *Heliotrope Convertible*, reading a sentence here, a line there to confirm it was that book and no other, and also to confirm for myself this particular version's placement among all the other drafts (or sections of pages that never made it into the finished book but eventually found their way into, say, both the *Pastiche* and *Leaving Riverside Drive*) and there, in front of me, in several neatly printed pages, in a typeface I'd never come across in the perhaps 3,000 pages so far that I'd placed around myself in the large dining room, written in a style that only a glance was needed to confirm was neither early, middle nor late Von Slyke, indeed not to be confused with even 'experimental' or the freewheeling 'diversions' of Von Slyke, but unlike anything that I'd been checking through and reading, was the following: a single, seemingly complete manuscript, without title, without author identification, without pagination, without apparent provenance, indeed without any reason for existing at all.

I've gone back in my memory again and again to that moment of discovery. As though within it I can find some clue, some hint, some inkling of what was to come.

I recall the exact time of finding the manuscript not only because of my surprise but because just a few seconds before the total and utter strangeness of what I held in my hands had made an impression on my consciousness, I'd been momentarily startled out of my concentration by a sudden noise, a little thud, something hitting one of the many panes of the great dining-room window wall above my head. I don't know what I thought caused the noise. One of the small, hard-skinned lemons dropping off a bough and somehow blown by the wind, perhaps. I don't know if I even thought that far. All I know is that I had been concentrating on the papers in front of me, had already espied and laid one tentative finger upon the first page of what would constitute the manuscript, and suddenly I was distracted.

I can visualize the scene, and often have: I was sprawled out on the tiled floor, amidst the dozen or so lines of manuscripts snaking more or less evenly along the floor, and I was riffling through the MS version of *Heliotrope Convertible* when I suddenly found these alien papers and I stopped, put the thing down and began to separate them, looking to see how many sheets were out of place, inspecting them carefully in the hope that this would produce instant identification, noting the lack of upper-right-hand pagination, common to all of the MSS so far.

In my mind, in that ongoing internal monologue we all possess, it went sort of like 'What *is* this? *This* doesn't belong here!' with a soupçon of something else, something like, 'Where *does* this belong? Hell, I'm going to have to search through all of it until . . .' Then I heard Conchita coming, the by now familiar soft splat splat of her dance slippers against the tiles approaching along the corridor suddenly also strange: strange because the normally so dignified, even staid Conchita was clearly running, running along the corridor, up the stairs and onto the balcony along one side of the upper part of dining room, running, breathless, then she was standing there saying in a voice in which she didn't at all attempt to hide panic, 'What do you know about birds? A little bird flew into the window. I don't think it's dead.' And when it took me a second to respond. 'Please!'

Her fear and her urgency impelled me into motion. Even so, some instinct told me this was a time to be especially careful. I grabbed the pages of that strange little manuscript I'd just happened on and I carefully placed them far away from all the other papers, on the seat of a dining-room chair against the opposite wall, where I was sure to find them again. Then and only then did I run up the stairs and follow Conchita along the corridor and outside into the hacienda's central courtyard.

At first I didn't see anything, even though Conchita kept pointing and saying, 'There! There!' Then I did see: about three feet away from the dining-room windows, on a section of tile outlined by overgrown grass. The minute she'd said 'bird', I'd assumed it would be a bluebird, since they were so prevalent around the front of the house, and sitting in the wickerwork chaise the previous afternoon I'd noticed bluebird parents teaching fledgelings to fly. What I saw now, however, was a much smaller bird, not three inches tall, a sort of finch, with dark green, almost military green, feathers, a contrasting golden-gray vest front and yellowy-green feet.

It was tipped on its side, like a toy that had fallen over, and though it seemed to be stiff as a board, it also appeared to be shivering. At first I thought its wing was broken, which would have spelled doom, but as I bent down – trying not to scare the tiny thing too much by my huge looming presence and as I edged all around for a better look, it appeared as though no wings were bent. Sensing my presence so close, the bird seemed to go totally still.

Conchita gasped, 'Es muerte!'

'I don't think it's dead. I think that's a protective reflex. Should I pick it up? It seems to be cold.'

'It's a baby,' she said. 'I heard that sometimes if people touch them, the parents reject them.'

The little bird began shivering again. I, meanwhile, felt conflicted. If I picked it up, would that help? I intuited that just holding it warm in one hand would convey caring and health somehow. If the bird were merely in shock, that would even help. On the other hand, I didn't want it rejected once it was well enough to return to its nest because of what I'd done and perhaps starve to death.

'I'm going to pick it up,' I announced and turned to Conchita for encouragement.

She looked pained and maternal. Suddenly I found that I could understand what I never had before: the attractiveness of all those suffering Madonna paintings and statues. 'Yes, help it. It's so small, just a baby,' she whimpered.

Calming it with my voice, I picked up the bird and held it loosely but securely in my cupped, partly open hands. It stopped shivering, and I thought it was playing dead. I held it for what seemed ten minutes, until the long muscles along the sides of my calves began to feel stiff and I slowly began to rise. Just then I felt motion in my hands, and I hunkered back down again and slowly partly opened up fingers to look.

'What?' she asked.

The little bird was trying to stand up. It was still shaky on its legs and fell back again. I cooed and calmed it with my voice. 'I don't think anything is broken. It may be in shock. It's so amazingly smooth and soft,' I added.

The little finch was still trying to stand up and falling against the giant geography of my hands and fingers. Its feathers were minute, amazingly iridescent. Its little beak was bright yellow and quite hard-looking. Its eyes were dirt brown, ringed with a vague pale blue, the way a full moon is held within a milky corona the night before rain. They were perfectly round eyes, open, staring ahead: unfocussed. At last it found its balance. I could feel sharpness and pressure from its claws as it grasped onto the loose skin of the palm of my hand as though it were a branch.

'It's alive. It's getting better,' I said.

The little bird's head half swiveled for the first time. Then its little beak bent down and rapidly preened its chest feathers, making quick little dives under its wings to groom there too. The wings opened a bit, closed again, which must have thrown it off balance, as the little bird fell over onto my fingers. But it got up again right away, and did its grooming and checking once more, in the same order as before. Then it looked at me, first with one eye, then turning its head around, with its second eye. It was intensely active, intensely alive. I found myself thinking how in olden times people referred to those living as 'the quick'. As in the 'the quick and the dead'. This tiny bird was undeniably 'quick'. Another shuffle of the wings, then so fast I didn't see how, it darted out of my hands.

'Wow!' I fell backward onto the courtyard tiles.

'There!' Conchita pointed.

The bird had flown only a few feet away to a sill of the stone fountain, where it sat continuing to preen itself, then turned to take tiny sips of water.

'I think it's all right.' I hoped to convey relief.

'Look!' Conchita pointed to the lip of the fountain.

Two larger birds of similar if slightly lighter colored shades of plumage had arrived. The parents? They hopped nearer, seemingly chatting with inquiring chirps, then, as identification was confirmed, nearer, and at last began nuzzling the little bird, alternately grooming it and themselves. Yes, the parents. With the sudden, darting movement I'd recognized as finch-like, all three suddenly flew off together. It seemed as though they'd gone in the direction of some nest hidden within the grape-arbored pergola at the back of the courtyard.

I'd regained my balance and stood up, dusting fallen leaves and garden pollen off my shorts.

'Mission accomplished!' Now I really did feel relief. The bird was fit again and it had not been rejected.

We stood in the hot courtyard sunlight a few seconds more, not looking at each other, listening to birds.

'You're a good man,' Conchita said, startling and a little embarrassing me.

We went back to the house. I'd just resettled into the dining room among the papers when I recalled the manuscript I'd found before. I got up and looked at it and once more thought, 'It doesn't belong here.' So I left it where it was on the chair seat, and returned to the work I'd been doing, the hard sorting, the pulling apart of irrelevant dross to arrive at Von Slyke gold. I was there another five minutes or so when Conchita appeared again on the dining-room balcony. This time she was holding a large cup.

'I made *chocolate*,' she said, pronouncing it in Spanish and making it seem much more exotic. 'You need a break.'

As I took the cup and sipped the rich and deliciously semi-sweet liquid, I thought I saw admiration in her eyes.

It was only much later that evening, after I was sure I'd gone through all of Von Slyke's library papers and had pretty much located and fairly much to my satisfaction laid out various versions of his novels and stories, that I went back to that manuscript. I'd put it off, the way a child puts off what he knows will be the most delicious piece of candy in a large selection.

As I picked it up again, something inside me rolled and spun with excitement, telling me that what I held, what I was about to read, was something special, incredibly special, perhaps unprecedented. I don't know what I expected to come upon. Certainly not that old cliché of scholars and bibliographers: a manuscript of a masterpiece even the author himself had lost, forgotten. As I said before, I already strongly suspected it wasn't written by Von Slyke . . . but of course it could have been written by someone else famous, another one of the Purple Circle, for instance, or even . . . Well, Von Slyke knew so many writers.

Now, of course, I know with far more certainty what that tight, hot little knot of excitement roiling my stomach was: it was a more intelligent, better subconscious self warning me off.

Or is that also hindsight?

*

This is what I found and what that night I read for the first time:

'Now you boys better stop that, or your dad is going to stop the car and give you both a good spanking.'

'I'm not doing anything,' Francis pouted.

'Yes, you are!' Paul declared. He was younger by two years and the constant butt of his brother's unwanted attentions.

'Well, you started it!' Francis now defended himself, unaware that he'd just admitted guilt.

'You started it first,' Paul insisted. 'You started it this morning, back at the house.'

'You started it before then. You started it last week!'

'I don't care which one of you started it or when,' their irritated mother said. 'I want both of you to stop it. Right now. Do you hear me, Francis?'

'Yes, Ma'am.'

'Paul?'

'Yes, Mamma.'

She turned around and they were once again face to face, with the boredom of looking at the back of the front seat, by now endlessly stared at, yellow threading through darker brown material, or with looking outside at the highway, where the sides of the road on either side appeared identical to what they'd been looking at a half-hour before, and an hour before that, and an hour before that. At least hitting each other had been something different.

'I don't know why you boys can't play nice games!' their mother now said. 'What happened to that Parcheesi set?'

'We've played that already,' Francis spoke up.

'Play it again!'

'Don't want to,' he mumbled.

'What did you say?'

'How about counting cars?' their father suggested. 'You did that a lot the last trip we took.'

'That was different,' Francis said. 'There were more cars.'

'Yeah!' Paul added. 'And better ones!'

'More foreign models. Not all Fords and Oldsmobiles!'

'Well, I don't care what you boys play, just so long as you

keep quiet!' their mother asserted. 'And don't fight!' she added. 'How much longer do we have, Bill?'

'Can we stop?' Paul asked.

'We just stopped a short while ago!' their mother said.

'He's gotta go again,' Francis sneered.

'No, I don't!'

'Didn't you do number one and number two back there?'

'Yes, Mamma.'

'He did not. I was watching. He only did number one!'

'I'm hungry!' Paul whined. Being youngest he could get away with occasional whining.

'Here's two Pecan Sandies for each of you.' Their mother handed the big luscious cookies over the backseat wrapped in fluffy pink napkins already oily from the dessert.

'I'm going to eat one and save the other,' Francis said smugly.

Paul tried to do the same, but after he'd finished the first one, his resistance broke down and although he only nibbled at the second cookie, soon it too was gone.

They tried playing the car game, but the most exotic model either of them saw was a Studebaker.

In the front seat, their mother was napping, her head flung against the car seat, snoring quietly. Their dad took advantage of her being asleep to open his window vent and to light up one Salem Menthol after another, free of her nagging that he was going to end up in an iron lung like her cousin Warren. Dad even hummed a tune that Paul recognized, as an occasional plume of smoke flew back into the car for Paul to thread his fingers through, still amazed smoke had no density.

Paul saw what looked like a foreign car and quickly said, 'Left window! Volvo.'

Francis craned his neck to see. 'Where?'

'There. Just went past. Dark green.'

'That was no Volvo. It was some old American car. Wasn't it, Dad?'

'Looked like a '39 Mercury coupé to me,' Dad said.

'Cheater!' Francis said.

Paul refused to play the game anymore. To make matters

worse, he was still hungry and Francis continually assailed him with the fact of his own uneaten cookie. He would open up the napkin and sniff at the Pecan Sandy, saved by his self-control, and even more so, Paul was sure, by Francis's love of needling his younger brother. *Mnn!* Francis would go, just like they did on TV commercials. Paul would think how much he hated Francis and wished he had another brother – any other brother!

After a long, irritating silence, Francis suddenly said, 'Bentley!' He sounded genuinely excited. 'See it, Dad?'

'Shh. Don't wake your mother!'

'Did you see it?' Francis whispered.

'Sure did, son.'

'I'll bet that's the most expensive car in the world!'

'Close to it.'

'That means I win,' Francis exulted to Paul, who was already sulking. 'I win the game and probably the next ten games we play.'

Francis stared up over the seat next to his mother's ear, obviously trying for a faster look for more Bentleys on the road ahead. Paul was furious.

Only Francis had made a mistake. He'd left his Pecan Sandy on the car's back seat, and Paul now saw a way to both satisfy his hunger and get revenge on his brother.

Quietly, sneakily, he opened the napkin, took out the cookie, fluffed up the napkin so it almost looked as though it was still full, then he leaned across the back seat as though he too were now searching full-time for rare autos out the back windows – meanwhile eating and savoring every crumb and morsel of the Pecan Sandy.

'Hey! Where is it?'

Francis pulled at Paul, who fell back onto the seat, laughing, the last crumbs from the cookie still clinging to his lips.

'Where is it?' Francis demanded.

'I said,' their Dad warned, 'don't wake your mother!'

'Where is it?' Francis whispered angrily.

'Where's what?' Paul stage-whispered back.

'My Pecan Sandy?'

'All gone . . . joke's on you!'

'I'll show you a joke!' Francis punched at him. Paul fended off the blow, though it fell on his wrist and hurt.

'Francis! Leave him alone. There are plenty of cookies up front,' their dad said.

'Yes, Dad,' Francis said.

But Francis didn't leave him alone. Instead he began to pull Paul down between the front and back seats. And Paul fought back. And while their father now didn't hear anything, because it had become a silent, earnest, deadly match, the boys were now aiming to really hurt each other, working silently away at twisting arms and ears, rabbit-punching each other, in almost totally silent fury.

Paul was smaller and naturally he was getting the worst of it, but he wasn't about to make a peep. Until Francis covered Paul's mouth with a hand and then punched him hard where he shouldn't have. Once, and before Paul could even react, once again.

'That'll show you to steal from me,' Francis whispered, his face contorted in anger.

Paul was trying to catch his breath, trying not to black out from the intense and now unceasing pain in his groin. Little cartoony stars danced in front of him, yellow and red and shiny blue. He was sure he'd have to be taken to the hospital, he hurt so bad.

Francis had moved back almost into a standing position, looking down at his brother, as though to look at his handi-work: the fallen, the conquered Paul. Half leaning against the back of the front seat, smug and sneering.

'You're not hurt,' he had the nerve to whisper. 'You're just faking it. Get up!' he repeated. 'Or I'll do it again!'

He dove for Paul. Paul turned his body to avoid having the punch land where it had been aimed. Francis tried again. By now, both of Paul's knees where drawn up against himself for protection. So, when Francis grabbed one of his legs and tried to get around it and punch Paul again, Paul simply used the other foot to push Francis off, as hard as he could.

It worked. Paul saw his brother slam back at an awkward

angle against the car door. He noted the astonished look on Francis's face as the door gave way behind him, and before either of them could say or do anything, Francis fell back and out. The very last of his brother Paul saw were the soles of his Keds.

Paul didn't believe it. Not even when the door fell shut again with a light thud and Francis was not in the car. For a few seconds more he was certain Francis was outside the car somewhere, hanging on somehow, just waiting for Paul to get up and feel better, before he made his appearance and came back punching even harder, getting even.

Somewhere behind Paul heard the screeching brakes of a car. He sat up, afraid to look back, looking instead at the rear-view mirror, in which his father's face was curiously peering, trying to see what had happened.

His mother's head rose too, sleepily. 'What is it?' she half yawned.

'Car behind us stopped suddenly,' Dad said. 'Guess some animal must have run out onto the highway in front of it.'

'Poor thing!' she half yawned. 'Did he run over it?'

'I guess so. He's completely stopped. Got out of the car.'

She turned and looked at Paul, then touched his face and peered past him, trying to see behind him out the car window. She lightly held Paul's head next to her own and she smelled so nice and warm from sleep he hoped she would never let go of him. But a second later, when she looked away and into Paul's eyes, she swiftly understood that something wasn't right. She searched the back of the car, and, not seeing what she was looking for, raised herself to look out the back window.

'Stop!' she shouted. 'Stop the car.'

Dad swerved, braking to the side of the road, shouting, 'Sit down. What's going on!'

'It's Francis! Francis isn't in the car! He's fallen out. My baby Francis. He's been hit. My baby! My baby!'

Then she was out of the car, and so was Dad, and Paul looked out back to where they were running, to the object huddled up and wearing Francis's jacket, now bunched up somewhat behind the left front wheel of what looked like a two-toned green Hudson Hornet.

Hudson Hornet: a great car to name, Paul thought. Too bad they weren't still playing the car game.

'I'm sorry, but Dr St George isn't in his office now,' the assistant said. Hopkins, I remembered her last name, but what was her first name? Something odd, Eleetra or was it Aleeta? No, that had been Prince Valiant's wife's name. 'I don't have you down as having an appointment,' she added defensively.

'I didn't have one,' I admitted. 'I was passing by and thought he might be free.'

'I am sorry,' she repeated. Now that it was clearly not her screw-up, she could afford to be compassionate. Also she knew how well Irian and I got along. 'I believe he's at home. If you'd like to call him?' She moved the phone over.

'Don't bother. It's not that important.'

'Or set up an appointment for tomorrow. He did say something about wanting to speak to you.'

'Don't bother . . . Maybe we should set up something.'

After some finagling with what looked from this angle to be a suspiciously blank schedule, it was worked out that I'd see St George the next day around noon – if, I glossed it – he bothered to come into the office at all.

In the hallway, I noticed a familiar back coming out of the little chamber that held faculty mailboxes. Although he was wearing yet another oversized, baggy rugby shirt, this time the shorts were light denim cutoffs, and so close-fitting I could easily see the squared-off concavity of his gluteus maximus. I resisted the impulse to grab one of those large shoulders to find out exactly how muscled and hard it was.

'We do terrible things to students who put anonymous letters into our boxes,' I said, in a mock-threatening tone of voice.

Ray Rice spun around. A clear look of guilt on his fine features: a creasing of his abundant dark eyebrows, a narrowing almost to slits of those jet eyes, nostrils flared.

'It's not anonymous,' he said. 'And it wasn't for you.'

'Oh? For Dr St George perhaps? A letter of complaint from your

male parent about my conspiracy to subvert Mom, apple pie and
Mother Church and pervert you through our reading list?'

'It's not my idea,' Rice said, surprising me by affirming what I'd
only that second come up with as an explanation for his presence
here. 'And I don't agree with it.'

'Don't you? I got the idea in class that you did?' When he didn't
answer, 'Or were you saying all that to establish your credentials for
the female students and the other athletes?'

'You've got me all wrong.' Rice's words came out hard, as though
compressed by how tight-lipped he was being.

'I trust a copy of that letter went to the Dean?' I asked.

Rice got even tighter-lipped. Meaning one had.

'It won't work,' I said.

'Gotta go!' Rice said, and took off.

'It won't work!' I repeated, following him. 'St George and the
Dean will both support me.'

We'd reached a turn in the hallway. This opened to a lobby of two
elevators and next to it a stairway. Ray Rice had already punched
the elevator button for 'down' when I arrived.

'St George and the Dean will both support me,' I repeated. 'Then
where will you be?'

Seeing that I wasn't about to leave him, he turned resolutely
toward the stairway's door. I got to it first.

'When they support me, where will you be? Have you thought of
that?'

Rice looked at me, then said, 'He did. My dad. He thinks if I do
this, you can't give me a failing grade in class.'

He pushed past me into the stairway, and in my surprise I let him
do so. But I followed him down the stairs, catching up with him on
the next landing and using my surprise to edge him into the wall.

Before he could react I said, 'Let me get this straight. If you set up
a complaint now, at the beginning of the course, because of the
course's content, and I give you a failing grade, then you can file a
formal complaint with the university board demanding a reversal
and claiming what? That I was prejudiced against you from the
beginning because of your so-called religious beliefs?'

Rice looked down.

'Answer me!'

'Something like that,' he slowly admitted, without looking up. 'My dad's a hot-shit attorney. He figured it all out.'

I let that sink in, then asked, 'Is that what you think?' When he kept his head down. I repeated, 'I asked you, Mr Rice, is that what you think? That I'm against you.' And when he didn't answer, I said, 'I'm not, you know.'

'It doesn't matter whether you are or not,' he said in that same tight, aggrieved tone of voice. 'He and the coach looked up your specialty. They found what you'd done your master's thesis on. They know what topic you've said you're planning to do a book on as a PhD candidate. They've worked it all out so that you're caught and you have to let me pass this course . . . so I'll make the team next fall.'

This plethora of information came fast and landed hard, as he'd intended it to. But I wasn't so easily intimidated.

'If I'm caught in this net . . . if I'm being manipulated by them . . . then, well, aren't you?' I tried to make him see reason. 'Even more manipulated and caught than I am?'

'You think I don't know that?' Rice amazed me by saying, and now he looked at me right in the eye, and I could see those jet eyes weren't all one shade of black but instead contained tiny specks of dark green, gray, olive green, hazel. 'You think I'm so stupid I don't know all that?'

'No, no, of course you're not stupid,' I said. 'I mean, if you do the class work, read some of the list, you'll pass. I never expected anything else, really. And I don't know what you've heard of me from other students, but I'm not a monster with grades. So I don't even begin to see why you would go through all this trouble . . . Why let them do this to you?'

Rice sighed and said, 'You don't understand. How could you? It's different for you.'

'How is it different? Explain. Try me.'

He gave me a theatrical sigh: stock in trade of the American adolescent. 'I let them do it to me because I have no choice. Because . . .' He sighed again, half shrugged and his eyes roved. There was no doubt about it: words were failing him.

Rice glanced up and down the stairs, then abruptly pushed me against the wall. At first I thought, he's unbalanced. He's going to punch me out, or shove me really hard out of his way and make good his escape. So you can imagine my astonishment when he did neither but instead grabbed my shoulders and then kissed me hard, and when, in my surprise, I gave way, he increased his grip on my shoulders and even held my head, pushed his tongue into my mouth and ranged around, kissing me with such force and completeness and need to invade me, I felt unable to respond at all.

'That's why!' He pulled away just enough to whisper furiously into my ear. 'I'm not the man they want me to be. Instead . . .'

Rice let go of me and bounded away, down the stairs, out into the splash of bright sunlight he created flinging open the door, which he uncreated as quickly into even greater obscurity as the door slammed closed, leaving me alone and stunned on that stairway landing, totally in the dark.

'. . . leave a message at the beep. I'll try to get back to you.'

Von Slyke's voice on the library answering machine. I'd not yet figured out whether or not to change it, although I'd done so on the machine in the bedroom I stayed in.

I was stretched out on the fainting sofa, a copy of Rowland Etheridge's *Desperately, Yours* open across my chest. I'd located it on the shelf in the library that held signed copies of most of the Purple Circlers' books. Spotting it, I'd noticed it was an original casebound publication, with the since then often reproduced photo of the two young men – the one in front's beautiful torso, the one in back enfolding him within his muscular arms and bent head. A glance at the copyright page told me this was a first – now rare – edition. The message on the flyleaf read, 'For Dame – from an avid worshipper. This excrescence of an offering. Be not too harsh!'

That so-Etheridge voice, and the astonishing first sentence – 'Semen does not, as has been often averred, taste like sea water, but instead like the stuff out of which is made the rings around Saturn!' – had pulled me into the book, but after a few pages the warmth of the early June day had conspired against me and I'd fallen asleep.

Only to be awakened by the answering machine, and by Von Slyke's voice itself saying, '. . . probably locate it in the . . .'

I leapt up and grabbed the receiver. 'Hello! Hello!'

Delight. 'You are there! How fortunate. I told Puddles you'd be out gallivanting in one of those Silver Lake bathhouses or perhaps simply extending your net of charm and beauty in one of those wonderfully trashy lounges on the Sunset Strip.'

'I was reading. I fell asleep a minute.'

'Reading?'

Did he want me to say one of his books or to be honest? Who could tell?

'*Desperately Yours*,' I said. I didn't know whether or not to apologize I never could recall the intricacies of how the surviving Purples had gotten along with those Purples now dead.

'That opening line!' Von Slyke turned out to be pleased; I'd made the right choice. 'When Rowland first read it at a Purple Circle meeting, Dom De Petrie kept murmuring something. I was next to him and I could just about make out what he was saying – it was "Rocks". Finally, Rowland, who'd been going on gamely, ignoring Dom's muttering, had enough. He stopped his reading with a great show of annoyance and asked what in the hell Dom was nattering on about. Dom looked embarrassed a second, then obstinately said out loud what he'd been saying under his breath and at me, "Rocks! The stuff around Saturn is composed of rocks. Ice and rocks." We were all flabbergasted, I mean totally nonplussed for what was a very long minute, then Rowland said in the sharpest and edgiest tone of voice he could muster – and believe me that voice of his could etch basalt – "Rocks! Schmocks! It's a metaphor, you nitwit!"'

When he was done laughing, I said, 'I was going to call you.'

'Is everything all right?'

'Oh, sure. The house is fine. Everything's great. I mean living here is . . . Well, I could really get used to it, as the saying goes. No emergency. But I did have a question . . .'

'Conchita's there?' Von Slyke interrupted. 'Everything's working out well with her? And Anselmo?'

'Conchita's fine. No problems I'm aware of. She's not here right now. Do you want to leave her a message?' Evidently not. So I went on, 'Anselmo was here the other day, but I was on campus all day and missed the noise of the leaf-blower. But everything green around the place looked neat and trimmed when I got back.'

'Lucky you. Listen, the reason I rang you up, besides of course to hear your creamy voice and to see if you were doing all right, is because when we got to Claridges and we went through our bags, Puddles couldn't find his international telephone book. He thinks he left it at home. He's desperate for the phone numbers and addresses of his sexy little friends all over Europe and he simply has to have it. Could you be a dear and go look for it? I'll give you my agent's Fed Ex number and you can send it by international overnight mail. He thinks he left it . . . Where, exactly, dear?'

A moment, while I sat poised over the pad of yellow foolscap I'd found on the wickerwork chaise-longue and taken indoors the day before, thinking it might rain overnight. Was this the one Von Slyke had finished a letter upon the afternoon we'd met?

'Puddles isn't all that clear. You'll have to go into the West Wing.' Then, speaking into the room where he was again, 'Do you have to shave now, dear? Can't you come to the phone and . . . Oh, bother the child! Ross, love, Puddles is paranoiac about international trunk calls. He thinks the CIA is listening in all the time or something. We'll have to do it ourselves.'

I was across the width of the hacienda and in the bedroom in a few minutes. It still smelled of cologne: I didn't recognize the scent, but neither did I associate it with the author, so I guessed it was the boyfriend's – Patrick? Peter? What was his name? I must ask Conchita some time.

I lifted the receiver and identified myself. I was trying to think how to bring up the MS I'd found when Von Slyke said, semi-exasperated, 'And to make matters worse, Puddles has only the vaguest idea where it is. Where are you, Ross, exactly?'

'Your bedroom. Sitting on the bed, left side, facing the curved wall and the window looking out to the motor court.'

'A writer's accuracy of description. There's hope! It's small and dark red. Check around the bed table where you picked up the phone.'

I did. A few automobile magazines.

'Nothing here. The drawer?' I suggested. He assented.

I found pornographic magazines with centerfold erections so large you could see every pore and count the pubic hair stubble. Plastic-covered coins of condoms. A box of over-the-counter sleeping pills. Another of antihistamines. Earplugs (which of them snored?). A tube of 'Lube'.

'Not here. Maybe the drawer on the other side of the bed?'

That table contained the TV and VCR remote. I flipped them on and instantly – muted – came on a pornographic videodisk of a bisexual scene. A big, long-muscled, square-butted blond with his single long braid over one shoulder, being fellated by a slender, cute, avid, naked, mahogany-haired younger man while he was also being anally licked by a lithe, attractive red-headed woman wearing black leather bra and V-shaped open-front panties. The man standing was swiveled toward the camera, so one arm and hand reached out to direct each of their heads, front and behind, to his pleasure. I freeze-framed it. And his figure, in fact all of their figures, seemed ancient somehow, mythic, or as though in imitation of some old artwork, a Cretan mural, a pre-Attic Greek vase painting. Were *kouros* ever blond or was it the bleached-out state of the found statues that made them appear so?

I continued to search in the bed-table drawer. This contained more foolscap pads, obviously Von Slyke's morning-in-bed writing material, pens, pencils. One pad looked as though it had been written in ballpoint and quite hard, I could make out some of the impression of lettering beneath. If I rubbed a pencil along it . . . Sure enough there was the word 'everything'. And the next sentence began 'Ross Ohrenstedt'. Wait a minute. Could this be the letter he'd been writing?

'Find it yet?' Von Slyke.

'Not yet. But I feel kind of weird going through all this,' I said. 'It's all so personal.'

'Oh, please,' Von Slyke demurred. 'I'm sure it's no different than what you'd find in the bedside-table drawer of any self-respecting homosexual in the universe.'

'I don't know about that.'

'It's not as if you haven't already been through all of my manuscripts. What is it Ruskin said, "Once rummaged, twice raped"? Did Ruskin say that? Did I just make it up?'

'Ruskin wished he said it. It's all yours, I think. And I really did rummage. I have to tell you, Mr Von Slyke, I pretty much ended up going through every piece of paper in your library and then some. And in fact, I came upon something I wanted to ask you about. It was with . . .'

I'd lost him. He was away from the receiver talking to the boyfriend. Then he was back: 'Puddles just had an inspiration. He was sure he placed it in his jet carry-on bag, but he thinks it could have slipped out while the bag was on the bed. It may have fallen to the floor.'

I got off the bed and began looking. Under the bed were another few porno videodisks, including the cover for the one still freeze-framed on the Sony, titled, I now saw with even more of a pang at bad puns than usual *Tom, Dick and Mary*.

What was that? Over there? I used the edge of one videodisk album to nudge the piece of cloth closer and managed to pull it out. Sat up and shook it off, although it seemed clean. A T-shirt reading 'Cocoa Beach Spa – Where the Dear and the Astronauts play!' and under the logo of an oddly flesh-colored space-shuttle zooming into the atmosphere, 'Really Get Your Rock(ets) Off!' Within the shirt's chest pocket was a small, worn, burgundy leather telephone book.

'Wait a sec?' I said. 'Does the first number read, "Andersson. Erik. Helsingborg, Sweden"?'

'You darling,' Von Slyke cooed into the receiver, then into the hotel suite, 'He found it! Naturally! Are you lucky!' Back into the phone, 'Was it wedged between the bodies of those two high-school softball stars I forgot under the bed, or just stuffed inside one of Puddle's "magnum"-sized scumbags?'

'Why don't I take down the Fed Ex number?'

After I had, and assured him I'd get it off to him next morning, I tried once more. 'Re the papers, Mr Von Slyke . . .'

'Damon, please! And is all of it as much of a horror show as I said it would be? I assure you, I'm wincing long-distance.'

'Not that bad,' I lied. 'It was disorganized, and I think I've located pretty much everything. I've got several MSS for each major work, and many, many more for nine-tenths of them. However, among them was one completely anomalous . . .'

'I just remembered!' he interrupted. '*Leaving Riverside Drive*, is in with my tax papers.'

'Actually, *Verbatim* is in with your tax papers,' I said. '*Leaving Riverside Drive*, or at least one version of it, was in among your royalty statements.'

'Oh dear! It really *was* a mess.'

'But I found everything.'

'I knew you would. I felt it in my coalescing old bones the second we met. I had the greatest faith in you.'

'Thank you. But, you see, among all of your papers, I found something else. Something that I don't believe is yours. I could be wrong, and if so I naturally don't want to include it.'

'Why not put it aside, and when I get back . . .'

He clearly didn't want to be bothered.

'Can't we see if we can straighten it out right now?' I tried. 'It's only a few pages. Typewritten, but not on Jonathan Flitch's typewriter.'

'It was *my* typewriter,' Von Slyke coldly interrupted.

'The Smith-Corona? A mid-'60s model?'

'My mother's college graduation gift to me. I was supposed to take a typing class too. But when I got to New York, I cashed the check and I used the money to buy a number from Red Hook named Spike and a bottle of B & B Brandy. They each lasted one night!' He laughed.

Despite the anecdote (by now I was certain Von Slyke had a million of them stored away in some vast, personal, wetware RAM), I'd felt the coolness begin to creep into his voice and I was trying to be delicate and courteous and not bring up anything questionable or annoying like the estrangement from Flitch, which might make him even cooler at the same time that I got the info I needed.

'I think I still have that typewriter somewhere. If not in storage with you somewhere, then in the place at Kauai. It must be years since anyone's used it.'

'Great!' I feigned an enthusiasm I hoped he'd hear as sincere. 'What you're telling me confirms what I was only guessing at. I thought the typewriter was used for every manuscript up to *DOS: Manuscript in Distress*. That naturally was printed up on computer laser jet. But then there are versions of your George Bernard Shaw essay and of the short story "Systematic Betrayal", both of which I knew to have been written later than the novel, that are typed on the Smith-Corona. Because they were written while you were on vacation?'

'Yes. I found this lovely boy to type for me. Dick long as your arm. Funny thing is, I located him through one of those retiree bulletin boards they put up in the local K-Marts. You are the cleverest thing on earth to have figured out so much from so very little. You're a regular Sherlock, aren't you? '

He'd warmed up a little, so I moved on, although gingerly. 'Well, it's what you took me on to do, and I am trying to do it right,' I added in further self-defense. 'For your benefit, naturally, and also of course for future readers and scholars. Which is why I'd like to clear up this business regarding the one little manuscript I found that seems so out of place.'

When he didn't moan or say no, please, don't, I took courage and went on. 'It's a short piece. Not even a story. An anecdote really. Perhaps part of a longer work. Two children riding in a car with their parents . . .' No response. 'Francis and Paul are the boys' names . . .' Still no response. 'It's not written in what I'd like to think of is any of your styles.'

No response. So I said, 'Mr Von Slyke? Damon?'

'I'm trying to think.'

'Well, that confirms what I believe: that it's not your writing and I won't have to include it. I had to ask, however, because I did find it between the pages of an early version of *Heliotrope Convertible*. I realize the Purple Circle was no longer meeting regularly at the time, but you were still seeing most of the members of the group socially. Could it be something one of the others wrote? Dodge? Leo? Weber?'

'I don't think so. Gosh, I really can't remember it at all.' He paused. 'You know . . . I taught briefly around that time. You couldn't possibly give me a year for this?'

'Eighty through eighty-two is as close as I can date it with any accuracy.'

'Well, maybe . . . I taught writing one year, both fall and spring. Two fiction-writing classes each term. It was at the West Side Y Writers' Voice Workshop. Too much work for too little pay. But I needed the money and the exposure. Is that still around?'

I said I didn't think so.

'My class met near the swimming pool. I would come in and have to fling open the windows no matter how cold it was outside. The room always reeked of chlorine. And this occasional hollow booming – I suppose whenever a swimmer turned under water during laps and hit the side of the pool wall to push off into the other direction. Oh, yes, and this one young man, halfway cute, who wrote about how strongly his girlfriend's vagina smelled. Not . . . good . . . writing! At the end of the term he wanted me to sign a statement he'd prepared saying I wouldn't steal his work. I told him, "I can guarantee you that a description of any vagina never has and never will appear in my work, save, and only in the rarest of cases, as an expletive." Imagine the effrontery!'

'Awful lot of nerve,' I commiserated. 'So you're thinking it might have been one of your students?'

'No,' Von Slyke said. 'I don't remember keeping any of their stuff. The thing is, I don't remember what you're describing at all. What was the theme of the piece?'

'Theme? I'm not sure . . . It was more of an anecdote. About . . . well, about fratricide. Unintentional fratricide.'

'I see,' he said, more soberly. 'So if it is by me . . .'

'Which it may not be!'

'Or one of the other Purples,' he amended, 'then it could be a crucial piece of what your brilliant mentor Irian St George calls "internal evidence".'

'Absolutely crucial.' I echoed the adjective he'd used.

'I, of course, had no brother,' Von Slyke said. 'Only two sisters, neither of whom I cared enough about to speak to after I'd reached the age of twelve, never mind deign to murder. But if, say, Mitchell Leo or Frankie McKewen or Dom De Petrie or Mark Dodge, they all had brothers, wrote it . . .' He let it hang.

'I know I must sound to you exactly like one of those "publishing scoundrels" you mentioned when we met, but it could be important. For the Purple Circle!' I added, trying to let him see it wasn't just my gain.

'I'd love to help you, Ross dear. But I simply . . .'

'Could I photocopy the MS on your office machine and put it in the overnight packet with the telephone book?'

'Fabulous! Do that! I'll look it over and . . .'

To change a subject I suspected was growing tiring to him, I said, 'I didn't know you'd taught.'

'Just that year. Oh, wait. No! One more term. In Bath of all places. Apple-cheeked British lads and lassies.'

To bring us closer, I asked, 'What if, and I'm not saying this ever happened, but what if one of your students sort of, you know, came onto you?'

'Has that happened to you, Ross? Well, of course it must have happened to gorgeous you quite regularly.'

'We're on-ly sup-pos-ing here,' I corrected lightly.

'Well, if it happened to me, and it did once, I'd drag the boy home and force him to sodomize me until we passed out.'

'I had that coming.'

'I'm telling the truth. Remember, Ross, dear, to whom you're speaking. I've had, and continue to have, nothing even resembling shame! . . . And I suggest you do what I did. Except, of course, you're probably not as utterly flattered by the boy's attentions as ugly old I was. Instead, you're probably trying to find a courteous way to get out of his hot little clutches.'

We went on in that manner until I was surprised by sudden motion in my peripheral vision and turned to see the 'freeze' had timed off the TV. Tom, Dick and Mary were going at it full-tilt.

'I'll send everything tomorrow,' I assured Von Slyke, when there was a suitable break in his conversation. We signed off.

I felt as though I'd accomplished a little: at the least, I'd confirmed for myself that the MS wasn't his, and managed to keep his interest and faith in me as strong as his mercurial temperament allowed.

After I'd hung up, I didn't leave the West Wing immediately. I remained on the double bed and watched the sixty-inch video screen as the bisexual scene got more active. Especially when I located the hand-held clicker that allowed me to zoom in for chosen close-ups. The images couldn't help but remind me that it had been some time since I'd had sex. Finally, I gave in to its unspoken message, shut off the bed lamp, lay back and, watching the three work toward climax, I masturbated. I used Puddles's Cape Kennedy T-shirt to wipe myself off and threw it into the hamper.

The letter on the foolscap pad turned out to be the one Von Slyke had been writing when I'd arrived at Casa Herrera y Lopez. He'd put it aside and only later picked it up to finish. It was addressed to Dominic De Petrie, which wasn't a surprise, as I knew the surviving Purples remained in contact; addressed to him in some town I'd never heard of but later, on a road atlas, did manage to locate, not

far from Provincetown, on Cap Cod. I don't usually read others'
mail, but since I'd been reading so much of Von Slyke's already, and
knew I was mentioned in the letter, I treated it as fair game:

Dear Dom

*You sounded better on the phone today. Both P. and I
think you ought to get away from that dreary shack and
come join us a while in Europe. You don't realize how much
you're adored in France. I'm rat-droppings in comparison.
We'll eat and shop all day, spending the university's ill-gotten
money, and go out everywhere and be atrociously blasé all
night.*

*Yes, Maureen and I agreed on a price for all my papers. So,
at last, I'll join with the rest of the Purples: letters, MSS,
everything. Ross Ohrenstedt will catalogue it all. He's one of
St George's boys at UCLA. A blessed-lad: smart, rich, built
and hung! When he first came across the lawn toward me, he
so resembled L. in the way he moved and how he held his
head and that tight body I thought I was having an 'eerie'
experience . . . v. disturbing for Her heart. Closer up, and
once he began to speak, the illusion revealed itself, but the
sense of 'deep resemblance' never quite went away. Despite
which, he'll be living here all summer while I'm gone.*

Come to Europe. Play with us. Love you.

Dame

So much for reading other people's mail. I was left with so many
questions after perusing this. Later on, during that summer, as facts
long hidden came to light, I would slowly begin to make sense of the
various references. All I knew at first was that I'd once more 'put
one over', this time on the brilliant Damon Von Slyke, who had concluded I was a 'blessed-lad'.

I also found out that his very mixed signals during that meeting had
not been because he was 'testing' me and was too distracted by other
matters, as I'd first foolishly supposed, but because I closely physically
resembled someone both he and De Petrie knew – initial L – though
how and in what context I couldn't tell; yet enough to make Von Slyke
nervous, circumspect. I guessed the L did not stand for Mitch Leo,

whom all photos show as being tall and slender, hardly what a word-smith like Von Slyke would call a 'tight' body. Also I also guessed that L was dead. Otherwise why would it have been an 'eerie' experience? Something about the way he wrote suggested Von Slyke had had a sensual relationship with L, although I couldn't be sure if De Petrie had too. And L had not been completely trustworthy.

The next day I naturally went through both the Fleming and Cummings books on the Purple Circle looking for a Larry, a Les, a Lawrence, a Lance, a Lionel, a Lonny, finding no one who seemed to fit the bill. More desultorily, for I was beginning to think it was something I'd never find out, or would do so only if Von Slyke him-self told me, I went back to the two volumes of Reuben Weatherbury's *Purple Circle Reader* to see if any L name indexed in McKewen or De Petrie's selected journals would leap out at me. None did, so I ended up spending a cheerful hour and a half instead enjoying two pieces printed there that I'd not read in a few years: Jeff Weber's moving story of love and loss, 'In the Tree Museum', and the excerpt about the three friends getting drunk and driving wildly in circles around each other by the light of the stars in the abandoned drive-in movie theater from Mark Dodge's third and final novel, *We All Drive Fords*.

'In-dub-i-ta-bly you're thinking, "Why are we meeting here, when surely St George can afford any place in town, including the new Chasens or the Ginger Garden?"'

This greeting as I arrived and settled into the Merlot-colored leather booth of the Hamburger Hamlet, a sixty-year-old standby in the campus neighborhood, so much a constant I'd hardly registered its existence until the invitation had arrived on my phone-answering machine. The Professor had evidently been sitting here a while – even though I was a minute and a half early – sipping what looked like a Dr Pepper Gingkola out of a tall, ice-filled, old-fashioned malted-type glass, his elbows placed on one of the big old brown leatherette menus splayed in front of him upon the Formica tabletop, staring at the substantial, post-adolescent foot traffic at the populous triple corner of Broxton and Kinross Avenues and Westwood Boulevard.

'My only question,' I said, 'is do they actually serve hamburgers here? I don't mean turkey burgers or tofu burgers or veggie burgers but with, you know, red beef and all?'

'Act-u-a-lly –' one of St George's picturesquely arched eyebrows raised an eighth of an inch, a feat he'd long perfected in front of seminars and departmental meetings – 'I believe they do serve them. Although –' an index finger flew up to specify point one – 'quite seldom.' A second finger joined it. 'Never to anyone under sixty. And only –' the ring finger joined the others – 'after they've sub-jected you to the most intense scrutiny.'

'Screening out potential health risks?'

'Screening out potential FDA inspectors!' Both arched eyebrows danced in amusement at his witticism.

'No, this place is fine, it's fun!' I said, pulling over a menu and looking over its many, many entries.

'Luck-i-ly,' St George began, 'you're young enough to still possess a digestion able to take on equal amounts of tofu and tufa. If you're not lactose-intolerant, as poor I am despite vats of masticating enzymes and oriental medications, I suggest you try the heav-en-ly . . . que-sa-dil-las!'

'Good idea!' A waitress appeared who was dressed like a Yogi and moved with the calm that suggested she'd just completed a ses-sion of t'ai chi in the kitchen. I ordered the appetizer, their version of a salade Niçoise and black coffee, which she assured me in a serene voice was not only decaffeinated but without a smidgen of free rad-icals.

'For-tun-nate-ly!' St George said. 'Wouldn't want any nasty free radicals hovering around the For-mi-ca.'

After she'd gone, I forced myself to say, 'You received the letter from that attorney? My student, Raymond Rice's, father?'

'Nat-ur-al-ly, yes, but that's all the most ridiculous twaddle. Not worth discussing. And not the reason I wanted to see you . . . It's going well with the Von Slyke papers?'

'Very. I found pretty much everything . . . and then some.'

'Some!' St George could make even a one-syllable word seem as though it had six syllables.

'Something not by Von Slyke,' I quickly said, to disabuse him of that idea. 'Something I found in the middle of a MS of *Heliotrope Convertible* that Von Slyke didn't recognize, that he's never heard of.

Not very likely with him. He remembers every comma he ever placed. Possibly by one of the other Purples.'

St George's lips pursed. 'Some-thing fas-cin-at-ing?'

'An anecdote. Probably autobiographical. Freudian. The unintentional killing of an older brother by a younger brother.'

St George's lips opened and closed as though he were sucking on a lemon, while behind them he quietly moaned.

'I sent Von Slyke a copy by Fed Ex,' I went on. 'I'm not expecting him to be able to identify it. I've checked all the obvious sources to see who might have done it.'

'Sty-lis-tic-al-ly,' he probed, 'it's what? Whom?'

'It's not Von Slyke or Aaron Axenfeld. And probably not Etheridge, either. It's too simply written. Possibly Jeff Weber, or Dodge, maybe even one of the Leo–McKewens. Could even be Cameron Powers, though Weatherbury claims he found everything Powers wrote, little as it amounted to. Whichever it is, it's early. Which, besides the subject matter, makes it valuable.'

'Aes-thet-ic-al-ly,' he felt me out, 'it's what? A trial run?'

'You mean for *Last Good Year for Cadillacs*? It's possible. De Petrie wrote so much experimentally and it could be preparation for the first volume of memoirs. Although,' I quickly added so he'd know I knew, 'I'm certain you must have gone through De Petrie's papers with the finest of fine tooth combs.'

'He . . . holds . . . things . . . back!' St George surprised me by saying. Four words, each one syllable each. I took the emphasis. 'I can't . . . say . . . what . . . he holds . . . back,' St George added, again monosyllabically, with great sadness. I could understand the emotion: St George was supposed to be De Petrie's literary executor.

Irian St George's face seemed to suddenly sag in despair in front of me and for the first time ever, and only really because of the strangely direct overhead illumination of the restaurant, I wondered if he used a make-up base on his face. I'd long ago concluded that his mustache was dyed, well, partly dyed to look lyart. It was black, with one stripe of white, while his cropped short and quite receding head of hair was steel gray. The mustache color had to be fake. But it fit so perfectly to St George's look, bringing out his soft, as though furred, ebony *Arabian Nights* eyes, his perfectly arched eyebrows, his long, bulbous yet sultanically aristocratic nose, that I never before cared if he painted it twice a week before a bathroom mirror.

'I'll show the MS to you,' I offered.

'E-ven-tu-al-ly. At the moment, you must find out who wrote it, and how you may u-til-ize it to best advan-tage. Before even your thesis. Say in a smaller paper, a few thousand words or so, placed in the *Modern Language Association Journal* . . . Or even in the ex-treme-ly fash-i-on-able Queer Studies rag, *Gender Flick*. It would do nei-ther of us any harm at all,' he appended pointedly, 'if you were able to place a tidbit there.'

I didn't have to read between the lines. St George was insinuating that he possessed solid contacts within both the *MLA Journal* and *Gender Flick*. I'd never been published in either periodical. And indeed, the two pieces I had sent in to the former on 'recommenda-tion' from professors at Columbia Master's Program – had been 'declined' with no suggestions for rewriting; meaning the editors were just plain not interested. Stung by the second of these rejec-tions, I'd been unable to stop myself from mentioning it to St George during one of our telephone conversations, months before I'd come out to California. He'd sighed dramatically, then began, 'Sure-ly you understand that American novelists are vir-tu-al-ly out of the picture academ-ically, unless of course they have at least one proven per-ver-sion to offer.' Doubtless meaning that my papers on Fitzgerald and Thomas Wolfe were useless because the subjects were unstylishly heterosexual: a turn of events which would have aston-ished both authors. Lacking publication, despite my superior class and paper grades, I had then lost out on the top two spots when departmental honors were handed out at graduation. And I would not soon forget the snub. Now, now . . . who knew but that this tiny unindentified manuscript I'd just happened upon in Von Slyke's papers might end up changing all that. Who knew but that the tiny thing might become a glittering ticket into the very heart of those same bastions that had consciencelessly barricaded themselves against me. I'd show those trendy fuckers I could play their game!

'Not to-tal-ly irrel-evant to this matter,' St George interrupted my cogitations, 'and you understand, this in-format-ion I'm about to relay is not in common circulation, nor for the ears of the hoi-polloi . . .'

I snapped to attention. 'My lips are sealed tighter . . .'

'Than your anus!' He finished the sentence for me. 'Yes, I hope so. This is my news. Professor Fusumi is not returning to us in the fall. Indeed, he's not returning to California at all in the near future. I've had a communiqué – tor-men-ted, na-tural-ly – but certain . . . You realize what this entails?'

My eyes were blinking at him. 'Fusumi's classes will open up. And eventually his tenure will go to someone else.'

'Add-it-ion-al-ly,' St George confirmed that and went on, 'and hardly to be sniffed at, is the Harold Robbins Chair Fusumi's been seated at these seven years . . . it's a sub-stan-ti-al en-dow-ment . . . the old hack was certainly generous . . . and as part of it, the mansion he once resided in, ten gor-geous-ly furnished rooms, campus adjacent on Club View Drive, backing the LA Country Club.'

'I see.' I tried not to let him see how much my breath had been taken away. I knew that house, not far from St George's. I'd been at it once, at a faculty tea. I knew that endowment, too. 'But taking over a summer course is one thing, taking over an entire chair –'

'In-ci-den-tal-ly,' St George butted in, 'the endowment is spe-ci-fic-al-ly for American literature of the twentieth-century and, unless I'm greatly in error, only one other candidate presents any com-pe-tit-i-on at all. We both know whom that is.'

'Waterford Machado. Does he know?'

'E-ven-tu-al-ly,' St George said, 'he must find out. But he –' index finger up in the air for point number one – 'teaches no summer course – as an emergency favor to the department. His proposed candidacy –' middle finger for number two – 'is mentored by a professor without great seniority, and –' ring finger up too – 'his thesis subject has not yet been approved.' The fingers folded gracefully into a loose fist. 'A single brilliant coup by, say, yourself . . .'

My quesadilla and drink arrived simultaneously.

I sipped, tasted, offered a taste to St George, who sniffed the cheese, jalapeno and tortilla but backed off and contented himself with watching me eat while staring fondly at me, like some giant cat, its furred elbows folded upon the Formica.

'Don't think I don't appreciate all this,' I said. 'But I won't even know where to begin. Do I contact De Petrie and Axenfeld and ask if they know who wrote it? And what if they say, as is most likely, they never saw, heard or read it? Then what do I do? Go through the

bibliography of what the Timrod Collection has of the Purples' manuscripts? What if, as is probable, it's not listed in the library? Do I
contact the heirs and executors and legatees of the dead members of
the Purple Circle? Phone and visit their aged mothers and married
siblings and by now grown nieces and nephews, their college roommates and old boyfriends? Is that what you expect? That I charm
them, win over their confidence? Rummage around their memories
and go through their basements and attics?'

'Ex-act-ly!' St George sighed out the word. 'You see, you *do* know
what to do.' His meal arrived and he settled into it. 'And you may
have to do more too. But by way of assistance and en-cour-age-
ment, I'll provide all phone numbers and addresses you may
require.'

I guess I stared at his response too long. He suddenly stopped
eating and once more lifted an eyebrow in my direction.

'Well . . . if you think so!' I concluded.

'O-ccas-ion-al-ly,' he said, and by his tone of voice he was clearly
changing the subject, 'I sat in when Fusumi was lecturing, and I
found the male students to be of an unusually healthy and salubrious sort. Tell me, Ross, about your students.'

'Jocks looking for a fast C.'

'Nat-ur-al-ly, troublesome Mr Rice is one such jock.'

'The jockiest. Co-captain of the school soccer team.'

The eyebrow raised again and St George attacked his food with,
I noticed, canines more than ordinarily pointed.

'Ex-as-per-at-ing-ly,' he finally said, wiping his lips daintily, and
seeming anything but exasperated, 'I believe I shall, after all, have to
see Mr Rice, the younger, in my office. Perhaps,' he added, 'directly
after soccer practice. Before he can, as the saying goes, hit the show-
ers.'

Which observation led to several others and thus ended any further conversation about the MS, which might explain how it all
moved into what I now see was Stage Two.

Book Two

THE WIDOW WEBER

She'd always gotten what she wanted, eventually. Even when she most complained that she had nothing. Especially when she complained that she had nothing

Jeff Weber, *Cheyenne August*

'. . . SEVEN FOUR,' THE PHONE MESSAGE said in what I recognized from some of his poetry recordings, as well as taped radio and video interviews, to be Dominic De Petrie's voice. 'If you're giving me a large sum of money and wish to discuss details of how to deposit it, leave a message. Otherwise don't bother. I *will not*, I repeat *will not* return your call, no matter who you are or what you want.'

As De Petrie had cunningly arranged, I was too surprised by the ferocious negativity of the greeting to gather my wits about me in time to leave a properly intriguing message before the phone machine shut itself off and the line went dead. I put down the receiver and sighed.

On the desk, next to the one-fourth-filled coffee mug I'd found in the kitchen and made 'mine' for the duration of the stay – a masked racoon holding out a revolver and a cup saying 'Hand Over the Java and No One Here Gets Hurt' – was a copy of the letter I'd written to De Petrie and to Aaron Axenfeld. A good letter, with exactly the right balance of respect and request, courtesy and requirement. I'd written it seven times, let it sit for two days, altering a word here, a line there. I felt like Oscar Wilde, who quipped he had spent all morning changing one word of a poem, and the entire afternoon changing the word back. It was a week since the letter had gone out and neither author had replied. Thus my phone call.

Placed on top of this photocopy were the letters I *had* received in response to the initial flurry of correspondence following my lunch meeting with Irian St George. One was from the library that was collecting the Purple Circle's papers, which I'd written to as Von Slyke's 'assistant' – well, wasn't I? The thirty-page pamphlet they'd sent was, according to the head of the American collection's secretary, 'as up to date and complete regarding what we have on hand here of the work of the other members of Mr Von Slyke's esteemed circle'.

I'd gone over the pages again and again and I'd red-lined three possibilities for the manuscript I'd found. Wild ones, even I had to admit. But also three that I hoped made some sense. For example, I'd decided that the fragment had taken place not in the eastern part of the US, but in the South or West. If asked to explain why, I would have to admit this was more instinctual, more of a feeling than anything that could be proven about the cadences of the language, the mother's diction, how more common car trips across longer spaces were in the 1950s and 1960s (the ostensible time frame). Little things like that. So, an untitled, unfinished short story written by Jeff Weber, who'd grown up in Wyoming, seemed a possible candidate. He'd been the Purple Circler driving earliest – at age thirteen he would daily use his family's ten-year-old Fairlane coupé to drive to school, twenty-four miles distant – or so he wrote in his final book, *Cheyenne August*. According to the person who'd done the Timrod Collection notation, Weber had written this unpublished piece at some unspecified time in Manhattan, definitely before his collection *Slights and Offenses* had been gathered for its 1979 publication, since all of the stories considered for inclusion there were already known. This piece had handwritten across its top but *not* a title 'What Occurred on Route 90' – i.e. the main road between Billings and Spokane, where Weber had taken pre-college summer school courses in 1965 before matriculating at Bennington. It was further noted as 'Six pages, double-spaced, typewritten. Ends in middle of a sentence. Three characters. Child narrator. A sketch. Not included in *Cheyenne August*.'

The next likely candidate was one of several unpublished sections of Mark Dodge's unfinished autobiography, excerpts of which had been published in Weatherbury's two volumes of the *Reader*, and which he – like Dodge – had sometimes referred to by the title *Framed by Life* and sometimes as *Man in a Jar*. Mark had also grown up in the West, and I knew from *Buffalo Nickel* that he'd written about taking car trips with his family. Perhaps the fragment had been a precursor to that book? An experiment? Mark Dodge's literary executor, his youngest brother, Thomas Dodge of Walnut Creek, California, had non-professionally (nonetheless quite usefully) notated one piece as 'some twenty typewritten pages with many handwritten ink changes, all about us kids together, three young brothers biking, fishing, fighting, plotting schemes to raise money, taking car trips to our Grandma and Grandpa in Stockton'.

Mark Dodge had himself begun driving at fourteen, his father's 'ancient, beat-up yellow-fendered, green-bodied Ford F-200 pickup that because of its coloration everyone called the Greenfinch' (cf. *We All Drive Fords*).

Finally, there was that mass of unfinished papers Reuben Weatherbury had filed at the Henry Timrod Collection as executor of Cameron Powers's estate. Powers was from the South, and like Dodge, and to a lesser extent Weber, had as running themes throughout his work driving, highways and automobiles. Of the six stories in the posthumous compilation *'Miss Thing' and the '41 Bugatti* (all collations of many drafts), three took place in and around highways and cars. I knew that Powers's father had at one point in his chequered career been a (not very successful) Pontiac–Oldsmobile dealer. During his single recorded interview with a short-lived literary quarterly out of Durham, North Carolina, in 1981, Powers had reminisced about how he and his girl cousins would play 'story' in the family station wagon while enduring long drives to their grandparents' home in the Blue Mountains of Virginia, and how especially good young Cameron had been at the game. Any of the unpublished, unfinished MSS in the collection, all with many titles each, might be what I had in hand.

No response had come as a result of my sending the little manuscript to Damon Von Slyke in a Fed Ex packet along with Puddles's address book, except a phone message on the machine saying, 'Thanks, Ross. Got it yesterday. It's getting rainy here and rain in London is too cliché, so we're off to Hamburg. Ciao.'

What I would have preferred was to visit the collection and go through it all myself, but it was 3,000 miles away and I was just getting to work on Von Slyke's cataloguing. It would be months before I had the time to go.

Second best, would be to have the library fax me some first pages, but this, I was advised when I phoned, was not possible. Mostly because while I was considered 'accredited' – i.e. due to the subject matter of the thesis I'd filed at UCLA's PhD program, my name was on file at the collection as an accepted Purple Circle scholar with most (if not total) access – even so, they only had one person on staff June and July, the secretary I was speaking to – a marbles-in-the-mouth Fairfield County native – Christopher Kovack, and as it was summer session with no bibliographic classes taught at the university the collection was attached to, Kovack had no undergrads to badger into doing grunt work. He'd fax stuff, if he 'got around to it', he assured me, making certain I knew this was totally dependent upon his free time, passing whim and possibly what I might offer him.

The two slightly more hopeful responses I'd received to my letters included a San Francisco Museum of Modern Art card of a 'hyper-real' Wayne Thiebaud painting of various pie wedges in a chrome circular cabinet from Thom Dodge saying that he and his brother's papers would be available to me, and listing his work hours and home and work phone numbers.

The other note was on Languages Department letterhead from Professor Tanya Cull, PhD, at Berkeley. I'd discovered Cull was the niece of Mitch Leo, as well as his executor, when flipping through Von Slyke's very up-to-date Rolodex file. Her correspondence to me read, 'What you described doesn't sound like anything Mitch wrote. I'm afraid I'm too busy getting my own new volume, *Revisions to the Hegemonic 'Norm'* (Univ. of Illinois Press) ready for the printer to be able to look for what you need until August first. But if you have to have it sooner than that and want to come look yourself – I've retained photocopies of the entire Leo oeuvre – let me know when.'

I began to plan a trip to the Bay Area to see Dodge and Cull. I'd phone my sister and stay with her and the quarterback in their skillion-dollar place in Presidio Gardens, which might also help mend fences a little in the personal relationships area. But it was only two in the afternoon and I decided I wasn't totally beaten down today: I could bear one more rejection. So I dialed the unlisted phone number I'd found in Von Slyke's desk directory for Aaron Axenfeld where he lived, on a small Florida Gulf island south of St Petersburg.

I'd prepared myself for an assault equal to that of De Petrie's phone message, even written down what I would say to Axenfeld whether he'd left a message or answered in person. Despite that, I was caught unawares when, after three rings, the phone lifted and a young laughing male voice said, 'You're wrong! Wrong! Wrong! Wrong! It was *not* Renata Tebaldi. It was Leyla Gencer, the Turkish coloratura, known to her claque as the "Marbled Halvah Soprano", who sang Adriana Lecouvrer at La Fenice in 1968 with Franco

Corelli. Don't say no. I have it on the very most reliable authority.'

'I won't say no,' I replied. 'Mr Axenfeld. Aaron Axenfeld?'

'Yes . . . but you're not –'

'Ross Ohrenstedt. Calling from Damon Von Slyke's office. I'm collating his papers. I sent you a letter a few days ago. I wondered if you'd received it, and if you hadn't, if I could ask you about something among the papers I'd found.' It all came out in a rush, since I didn't know how else to keep his attention.

'Well, you must think I'm out of my mind,' he said, his voice rising at the end to seem almost querulous, 'answering the phone as I did. And you're Ross . . .' He sounded as though he'd hang up unless I said the exact right thing.

'Ohrenstedt. I'm living at Damon Von Slyke's while he's in Europe this summer. I'm preparing his papers for the Purple Circle collection at . . .'

'Oh, right!' He still seemed completely fazed. 'I did get your letter. The problem was I didn't know how to respond.'

Could the little MS have been his? Axenfeld's? When I'd eliminated him almost immediately? 'You know the piece?' I asked, and my pulse was pounding so hard I could actually see it lifting the skin in that little hollow under my thumb in the hand holding the receiver.

'That's just it –' uncertainty even more evident in his voice. 'What I read did seem familiar. Yet when I racked my mind to think why, I came up with a blank.'

'Mr Von Slyke didn't recognize it either.'

'So, you're doing what there, exactly, with Dame's stuff?' Axenfeld now asked in such a forthright, almost accusing tone, so different from how he'd responded so far that I felt like an intruder.

I began to explain the process and had gone on for some time when I interrupted myself to say, 'Well, you must know what I mean. Someone must have done the same when you sent your papers off to the Timrod Collection.'

'My papers are still here. For the collection I gathered a few drafts of the published books and added some letters the Leo–McKewens sent from Italy.'

I thumbed through the catalogue: only two pages of the thirty were of Axenfeld's work. Every item listed was previously published.

'You mean there's more material not represented?'

He guffawed and was instantly contrite again. 'I'm sorry and you must think me terribly rude but, "Is there more material not represented?"' His voice dramatically rose in pitch, and he answered himself, 'Do gorillas have hair? Do hairburners have sex?'

'Then there's . . .' I tested the waters, 'a lot more?'

'You're probably too young to know the reference, but I've got an entire Fibber McGee room. McGee was a radio character in the '40s who had everything but the Pacific fleet in his closet. Whenever anyone would open it – lots of sound effects! Most of what I write, most of what I've written since 1972, goes directly into the room. Never to see the light of day. My literary Fibber McGee closet. Only a room.'

'An entire room filled with unpublished manuscripts?' In my mind, it glittered with treasures like some illustration out of Scheherazade's tales.

'Unpublished – and,' Axenfeld specified, 'unpublishable!'

'You would think so. Everyone knows how hard you are on your own work. How, when asked why you'd published only six books in twenty-three years, you replied, "That was five too many."'

'I *was* a bit hard. Even so, I know what's here. It is unpublishable.'

I wondered what decision his literary executors would make contrary to that opinion after he were no longer around to hold back the flood tide. It wasn't my duty to say anything, and more, if I did say anything, it might make him nervous and possibly destroy the work. Authors were doing that all the time.

'So, the manuscript I sent you, could it have possibly been by one of the others at your meetings?'

Fleming and Weatherbury had each, separately, gone over letters, journals, diaries and conversations to ensure that every page the nine members of the Purple Circle had read aloud to each other during their short-lived period together was not only listed but also published, then glossed and notated *ad nauseam*.

'It was so long ago . . . I keep thinking it was something Jeff Weber said,' Axenfeld admitted.

'A piece *he'd* written?' I tried. 'Was *then* writing?'

'No. I don't know . . . I'm losing it . . . It *was* Jeff. Maybe I can reconstruct it. Let's see. I'm pretty sure we were at Rowland Etheridge's place on West 21st Street, between Eighth and Ninth Avenues, and we were in that long front room of his with its bay window, and it was a break between the readings. Usually four of us would read each session. Two before and two after dessert. That way, we'd each get a chance to present work every other meeting. And although I usually dreaded it myself, the others fought for the opportunity, treating it as a privilege, which I suppose it was. At any rate, it was intermission, which I loved because that was the time for gossip and catching up, and fun and food. Rowland and Dame and yes, now I recall, Cameron too had gone into the kitchen to prepare coffee and food. I could hear Rowland and Cammy doing their high-pitched "Mammy and Scarlett O'Hara" camp routine, accents dripping with molasses on grits (I'm sure you know they were both Southerners) and Dame yelling, "Stop! Stop!" He was laughing so hard. The Leo–McKewens and Dominic had put on their coats and gloves and had just gone down the flight of stairs outside to where Mitch had parked the car to get something, a book Frankie had mentioned earlier, I think, Dame was interested in reading. And poor Mark Dodge had been pushed and shoved complaining out of the apartment into the hallway to smoke a cigarette, since Rowland had just stopped smoking and would no longer allow anyone to light up inside his apartment. Mark was smoking like a chimney but was also periodically banging on the apartment door and howling that he was going to freeze to death out there since Rowland's wasn't one of those chic Chelsea townhouses but instead a sort of O'Henry brownstone tenement and the hallway was unheated and it was a frigid mid-February. Jeff and I were sitting alone on either end of Rowland's ancient heirloom sofa from his parents' Rappahonack home, with its shiny green horsehair upholstery and jet-tipped black antimacassars. Our arms were across the sofa back, and we were looking backward out the bay window, at the frozen street below, ice riming the branches of the trees like lace, looking down at Mitch and Frankie and Dominic on the sidewalk. It was evening, lamplit by those yellow sulfur streetlights, and there had been a six-inch snowfall that day, and it had snowed once more after we'd arrived and the three of them were stripping snow off the roof of their Corvette and other cars and throwing big puffs of it at each other and laughing and pulling each other by their scarves and falling down in the middle of the still-unplowed, already frozen, snow-covered street. Jeff and I hadn't seen each other since the previous Purple Circle meeting several weeks before, or even spoken to each other on the phone. I don't recall if it was because we'd been too busy or what was the reason, but I felt guilty about it, and so we were talking about oh, who knows what, so much to catch up on, and I recall thinking how handsome he looked that night with his hair worn longer than usual, which I supposed was Dominic's doing, since they were palling around together at the time and it showed up in odd little ways, such as a "makeover" for Jeff from the more style-conscious Dominic. And so I guess the two of us finally got around to the story that Mark Dodge had read, yes, that's right, or rather the excerpt from that autobiographical novel that would later come out many years later, in the two *Readers* long after Mark died –what a shame that was, Mark was so gorgeous, and so nice! – and I think Jeff said how what we'd just heard had reminded him, Jeff, of another piece, something he'd just read, or . . . at any rate, a story about two kids fighting in the back-seat of a car. Then the food arrived, Rowland carrying a tray with coffee cups and plates, and Cammy holding the coffee pot and yelling, "Make way! Make way!" And Dame with this amazing cake . . . eight inches tall and round and frosted white, looking like some Gothic castle turret, and at that moment Mark and Dominic and the Leo–McKewens all came into the flat together, each carrying great handsful of powdery fresh snow, which they threw up in the air, so it was snowing indoors and Rowland had a hissy fit about how it would ruin the carpet and everyone began shouting and laughing and trying to calm him down and I'm afraid that swept away all talk or thoughts of stories so I simply don't remember anymore.'

Axenfeld's words had drawn me away from the desk in the library in Hollywood, away from the phone and completely into that world of wintry Manhattan and the nine of them, so young and so alive and active, with their foibles and their play and their mix-ups and desires, a long quarter of a century before.

It took me a second to come back. 'So Jeff Weber told you about the story. But did he say it was his, Jeff's own, story?'

Axenfeld sounded sad as he replied, 'The truth is, I just don't remember clearly what Jeff did say.'

I tried another angle. 'He didn't say it was Mark's story?'

'No . . . I don't . . . Sometimes the unconscious does marvelous things with memories if you just let it alone a while.'

'Well, thank you, Mr Axenfeld. I appreciate you're taking time out to talk to me like this.'

'I wish I could be more helpful.' He sounded genuinely sad.

'You were. Really you were,' I said to cheer him up, because now I'd concluded that he wasn't sad about not knowing what I wanted, but because he'd too well evoked that moment in February, and it had pained him so much to remember it. 'And maybe,' I added, hoping to draw him out a bit, 'someday, if you ever decide differently, you'll let me come organize your Sibber McGee room.'

'Fibber. With an "ef",' he corrected. 'And you are sweet. But you know what I just did suddenly remember?' Axenfeld asked in a different tone of voice and for a second I thought, he's got it, he's going to remember who wrote it.

But no. Instead, Axenfeld said, 'I remembered someone who would know better than I ever will. Bobbie Bonaventura!'

'Who?'

'She's there near you somewhere. Hold on, let me look in my address book.'

'Bobbie with an "i" and "ee"?' I asked. 'Bonaventura spelled as it sounds?' As I wrote it down, it sounded familiar.

'Actually it's Roberta. We knew her as Bobbie,' he said, seeming quite distracted, as I guess he searched. '"The Widow Weber", Dominic always called her. Which may be cruel but is not completely inapt. Bobbie went to college with Jeff Weber. Dominic said he thought Jeff and she might have been lovers for about two minutes. But they did continue to hang out together all throughout college and they moved to New York City together, and remained in contact all through later life. And, of course, she helped care for Jeff when he got sick. Here we go. Yes, California. Venice Beach. Is that far from you?'

'Not at all.' I took down the number and address.

No sooner had I done that than Axenfeld once again changed the playing field. 'You know, I wonder if she's still there. I'd heard, well, but you know how you could find her? Dominic told me she worked as a manager for one of the big bookstore chains there. What would that be? Waterstone's? Borders?'

'Not in one of the gay bookstores? West Hollywood or Silver Lake? Not in Mar Vista or Westwood? In a woman's bookstore?'

'No, not West Hollywood or Silver Lake. And the other places don't sound right either. Near where she lives, I think, he told me. She doesn't own a car. Is that possible in Los Angeles?'

'Yeah, sure, if she walks or rides a bus to work. She was Jeff Weber's closest friend, you say? And it's Roberta?'

'Yes, and Jeff's executor too, I believe. I remember someone, maybe Dominic, saying that Jeff's mother died only a year or two after he did, and because he'd lost his father and I don't think there were other siblings, Bobbie became his heir and executor. In fact, I'm sure that she arranged for his work to go to the collection. Because Maureen gave me her phone number and address. I spoke to her about the whole thing before I agreed to sign up with the collection. I also think Bobbie had something to do with getting Jeff's stories reprinted a few years ago.'

'*Slights and Offenses*, you mean. So she'd know if this piece was Jeff Weber's?' I said the obvious. 'Well, again, thank you. And I hope you won't think I'm sounding sycophantic, but I love your writing. Especially *From the Icelandic*. And I'm not alone in wishing you'd publish more of what you've got in that room.'

'You're very nice to say that.' He sounded genuinely modest. 'But you must now wipe your mind clear of everything I told you about my Fibber McGee room. Promise?'

When Axenfeld rang off, I put down the receiver and looked at what I'd written on the pad in front of me. 'Roberta i.e. "Bobbie" Bonaventura. The "Widow Weber"' and all of the real and possible info about her. Not a defeat at all. But a new lead.

I don't know how long it was before I began to notice that the library was silent. Not only the library but the house and outside too. No radio in the distance was playing Conchita's favorite 'oldies' station. No sawing razzed, no hammering machine-gunned from the workmen erecting garden structures in the abutting property. Not a hint of an ambulance beseeching or fire engine clamoring its

way down along Hollywood Boulevard. Oddest of all, there wasn't
a single chord of the omnipresent birdsong that had become a diurnal and nocturnal background hum. The light from out of doors,
though undoubtedly from a potent summer sun, appeared cold and
white. And though I knew that tropical orange hibiscus preened in
front of the window glass, for a minute it all seemed frozen out
there, frozen and quite still.

Could the past have such a powerful hold over a person its influence could be transferred to another, not even alive at the time? As
though memory weren't ephemeral and empirical as I'd always
thought, but permanent, a sort of decal?

I shivered.

Four phone calls later, I located Bobbie Bonaventura. As Axenfeld
thought, she was working for one of the 'Ultra-Super' bookstores
that had taken over the city, getting larger and more varied with
every year, less like a bookshop and more like a 1950s department
store with floors of books, CDs, CD-ROMs, magazines and newspapers, tons of tie-in theme merchandise: clothing, toys and
furnishings from the latest movies, videos and ROMs, multi-ethnic
restaurants, coffee shops – as well as LA's own riff on the new Pacific
Rim food craze, Bancha bars, where you could order anything – hot
soup to cold drinks to yogurt and ice cream – so long as it was made
out of green tea.

I'd guessed from the last address Axenfeld had given me for her,
and the fact that she didn't drive, that Bobbie would be somewhere
on the city's West Side, not far from where she lived in Venice.
Especially as the dozen Santa Monica and Venice streets parallel to
the Pacific ocean had been cleared of all auto traffic a few years
before, miles of road now pedestrian malls, with public transporta-
tion provided by electric trams running through what had been
narrow streets and back alleys.

It turned out that Bobbie managed the fantasy and science fiction
section of a brachiosaurus of a place at the Third Street Mall in
Santa Monica. This shop had not only absorbed its main competition, another chain up the street, it had also ingested two small
used-book shops (one formerly on the open mall, another a few
blocks away). In addition, it had eaten up the Penny Lane Used

CDs shop and the local Sam Goody's, the never that successful Warner Bros. emporium, the largest art bookshop in the city and a multi-theater cinema. All their stock and much of their interiors had been replaced intact within this new five-story building sited at the far end of Third Street's recent two-block northern extension at Montana Avenue. Actually, two existing structures, cleverly connected across what had once been road by a huge window-fronted indoor-outdoor food area, the three-story glass-paneled walls utilized for exhibiting videos day and night, inside and out, promoting items in one or another of the twenty separate departments.

From the huge central information desk, I was directed by a 'touch-screen' computer to the third floor, left, to where I'd been told Bobbie worked: at Blade Runner science fiction shop.

Growls, grunts and a sudden ear-piercing scream 'Dooooonnnn't!' assailed me as I stepped through the theft-deterrence device. A second was all it took for me to realize that it derived not from that sensor, or from any of the score of browsers indifferently squatting to read on the carpeted floors or leaning against the walls, but from a recent video, *Hellraiser Ten: The Magnetification of Pinhead*, reproduced from a grape cluster of eight monitors, hanging at differing angles from the middle of the shop.

Bonaventura was less easy to sight. I had to circle the purposely constructed maze of shelving twice before I at last came upon a short, thick-set, middle-aged woman with a steel-gray 'fright wig' of curly hair who looked as though she might actually be an employee. This had more to do with what she was doing than how she was dressed. Bonaventura wore the most washed-out blue shoulder-strapped farmer dungarees I'd ever seen over a pale pink T-shirt. The pastels and hairstyle – and even her rather blank face – made her look like an overgrown toddler. As she was awkwardly standing on, and trying not to fall off, a fold-out metal stool, alternately packing volumes of Arthur C. Clarke onto a top shelf and bending down to reach for more in a cardboard box that shared the narrow seat with her chunky 'Air-Dr Martens' mixed-media shoes, the physical resemblance to a three-year-old was if anything even more exaggerated.

'"Scott Fitzgerald says that when you're in real trouble, it's somehow always three o'clock in the morning,"' I said, quoting the opening of Jeff Weber's novel *Ode to a Porno Star*.

She stopped, books in hand, scowled and replied, '"But Fitzgerald was wrong. It was three o'clock in the afternoon, and there I was, on Christopher and Gay Streets, deep in dogshit!"'

'I just love it,' I enthused.

Without comment, she turned and put the books on the shelf. Without turning back and in a surprisingly gravelly voice, she said, 'So you a groupie? Or his long-lost son, looking to get your hands on the fab-u-lous Weber inheritance?'

'Neither. I'm an assistant professor at UCLA, doing a book on the Purple Circle. I'm currently working on getting Damon Von Slyke's papers ready to go to the Timrod Collection.'

She was not impressed. 'If you're going to stand there, make yourself useful. Hand me those books. My back is killing me.'

I did as she asked.

'I thought Von Slyke sold his papers years ago,' she said, and before I could reply, she added, 'I guess he was waiting to jack the price up as high as possible.'

I suppose I shouldn't have been surprised by her hostility, but I was. I tried another, less fraught angle of approach. 'When I spoke to him today, Aaron Axenfeld gave me your phone number and address. He thought you might be able to help me.'

She still wasn't looking at me; her chubby little hand would periodically shoot out and I'd place three or four books in it.

'I don't fuck guys a third my age. Sorry.'

I ignored that. 'I found something among Von Slyke's papers that didn't belong to him.'

'Thing?' she asked, reaching for more volumes. 'In the singular? Meaning only one? Not lots and lots of things that didn't belong to him?'

I ignored her imputation and charged on. 'A manuscript. A short manuscript. I thought . . . well, it might be Jeff Weber's. Actually –' her hand jutted out and I again filled it – 'it was Axenfeld who remembered Jeff talking about it. At a Purple Circle reading. It might be what you listed in the catalogue as an unpublished story.'

Her hand jutted out, fingers grasping for more books.

'The box is empty,' I reported.

'Take it down off the stool and get more books out of the other,' she ordered.

I did as she said.

'So?' she asked me.

'So, you're Weber's executor and allegedly know about his work. I wondered if you could confirm that it is or isn't his.'

'And if it is Jeff's?' she asked.

I hadn't thought that far, so I was forced to wing it. 'Well . . . then, after the proper consultation with Mr Von Slyke of course, the manuscript will be returned to where it belongs . . . You'll get it. Or the Collection.'

She didn't respond to that, and I continued mechanically handing her volumes until the box was empty.

'Next?' she said.

'That's all,' I replied.

She turned around and put out a chubby hand, which I took and held as she stepped down the shaky stairs of the stool. On the floor she was about five foot two, looking up at me. Frowning.

'You're not bad-looking. Maybe I'll revise my policy about screwing kids.'

'Do you want to see it?' Then I quickly revised that to, 'I meant the manuscript?'

'I know what you meant. No, I'm busy here. Bring it by my place.' She bent over and began punching apart the cardboard boxes until they were flat. She folded them under one arm. 'Say, seven. You have the address?' She was already walking away.

'Tonight? At seven?' I tried to confirm it.

She half turned around, scowling. 'You want to yell any louder? I don't think people up in Topanga Canyon heard you.'

'Don't you think it odd?' Pamela Agosian asked. She then specified, 'What H. L. Mencken wrote about the book? I'm directly quoting now: "No romantic novel ever written in America, by man or woman, is one half so beautiful as *My Antonia*."'

'What's so odd about that?' I asked, Socratically.

'Well, after I'd got the book and noticed the blurb on the back cover, I looked up Mencken in the encyclopedia. He was alive and active at the time Willa Cather was writing. So he must have known . . . you know, that she was a lesbian.'

'Not necessarily,' Michelle Tsieh countered. 'People didn't publicly reveal that they were gay until well into the 1970s and 1980s. Right?' she asked, turning to me.

'Maybe,' Pamela argued back. 'But they *were* writers. The avant-garde. And they were a small group. People in the same field. There had to have been talk, gossip. Surely Mencken knew.'

'I think he did know,' Bev Grigio put in her two cents' worth. 'I mean, the book is written from the point of view of this man in love with this woman Antonia. Yet the man is written by a woman. So I think what Mencken wrote about the novel not only reveals that he understood all the complexity, but that in writing what he did about it he was writing a sort of inside joke.'

All three young women looked at me for an answer. We'd left the classroom together, exited Royce Hall and advanced along Dickson Court in a group. Having reached the low, semicircular retaining wall that looked over a hill of grass down to Wooden Center, Drake Stadium and Pauley Pavilion, we'd stopped. The Santa Añas had been blowing through any arroyo and canyon they could find for the past two days. The air was flat-out hot, crackling dry, the sky such a perfectly enameled blue you actually felt it was a dome, as in those medieval illuminations. In class, the students were dressed as skimpily as possible in shorts and tops, sipping soft drinks. Even I'd had to resort to Evian every few minutes of the lecture. From where we four stood facing west, I could make out every leaf of every single tree beyond Circle and De Neve Drives, the air was that clear.

'Mencken died in the late '50s, Cather in the '40s. No one ever asked that question of the two of them while they were alive. And there's no one alive they both knew for us to ask.'

'What about "internal evidence"?' Michelle asked. 'What's right there in the text. Wouldn't that tell us?'

'Not really,' I replied. 'Of Mencken's statement, there's too little of text for it to be reliable. And anyway, wasn't that the great mistake of Lacan and the Semioticians forty years back or so, believing that a text must reveal what the author didn't or wouldn't want to reveal? Even at times despite the author's intentions? Isn't that why they're so discredited today?'

Below us, on the grassy slope leading down to the Powell Library's yellow plastic extension – put up as a temporary structure in the 1980s, and supposedly to be torn down, but so beloved by students and faculty alike for its sheer ugliness it had remained – a half-dozen jocks were stumbling and charging into each other, around a white-striped soccer ball. I made out Ben-Torres's figure among them, as well as another Basketball Bruin, Colby Granville, and wasn't that Ray Rice down there, trying to outknee that gargantuan Samoan linebacker? Looked like him.

'The Discoursists' failure,' Michelle began, 'as I understood it, was that they took a contrary view to the modernist credo that authors like Joyce and Mann consciously put far more into any work than we could ever take out of it. Whereas . . .' she wavered.

'What if,' Pamela asked, 'the author or authors are alive. And could be asked? Would Cather or Mencken ever tell us what they thought? What they meant?'

I wanted to tell them that was what I seemed to be coming up against with the living members of the Purple Circle. Not even the meaning, but merely whether something was their own work.

'You're saying,' Bev interrupted, 'that it is the function of a work of art to *be*, not *mean*?'

'Not only that. Maybe Cather would simply be too embarrassed. Think her lesbianism too personal a matter to discuss.'

'That's certainly possible,' I admitted. 'We are talking about people born and raised in the nineteenth century. They hadn't been exposed to the incredible publicity of electronic media that we've experienced. But the real question,' I suggested, 'is not whether Cather – or Proust or Wittgenstein either – were too embarrassed to air personal identity issues, but rather how *others* would deal with the issue. Reviewers, critics, readers. Publishers for that matter. For every Gertrude Stein who lived an "out" life, there were millions of lesbians who never dared. Even today, four decades after Stonewall, there are critics who go out of their way to deny the crucially inherent homosexual nature of these geniuses. They'll stand on their heads to persuade you that Wittgenstein's entire philosophic system *wasn't* constructed because he lived in such a homophobic world that he literally had to reinvent the universe. Or that Alan Turing's adolescent passion for another brilliant boy scientist and his complete alienation after the boy's death and because of his sexual nature *weren't* responsible for his breaking the German's Enigma Code in World War II, or for his discovering the cathode tube as the best data storage and retrieval path, thus enabling modern computers to exist. Our lives are so threaded through by our sexuality and how we perceive the world perceives our sexuality that anything we create *must* reflect it, even when we try most to suppress or hide it.'

I was at that moment – surrounded by three intelligent, questing students – feeling like a real teacher, as though this job I'd taken on without being at all certain about it was the right one. The exact right one. Thinking how Plato had felt with Aristotle in that stoa in Athens. Or Aristotle with the brilliant Prince Alexander as a student. So proud . . . When out of nowhere something swacked me on the side of the head.

'Hey!' all three women yelled at the same time.

Bev caught the soccer ball that had struck me, just as it caroomed off. 'Hey, you guys! Watch out! Someone could get hurt!'

I was momentarily stunned. It was more a glancing blow than a full punch but it grazed my ear. Which was still ringing.

'You all right, Mr Ohrenstedt?' Michelle asked. 'Why don't you sit down a sec?'

She took my arm as though to pull me down to the brickwork of the terrace wall. I resisted.

'You don't look right!' Michelle said. 'How many fingers?'

'None,' I replied, having caught my breath, balance and enough sight to see her fist held in the air. Then, 'I'm okay. Really.'

'You sure?' Pam asked. 'Want to go to the medical office?'

'No. I was just surprised.'

I could hear several guys now yelling, 'Throw the ball!'

Bev was about to throw it, when Pam grabbed the ball out of her grip and stepped over the wall, onto the grassy bank.

Ignoring their continued calls for the ball, now held close to her side, Pam shouted in a voice just looking for trouble, 'Which one of you assholes hit him? Which?' she demanded.

They ignored her and kept yelling at her to throw the ball.

'Screw you!' she shouted in answer and turned around, the ball still in her grasp. 'Let's go,' she announced. To me. 'I think you should see a medic. It might be a concussion and . . .'

Three players, Lorenzo Linden, Colby Granville and Tony Taponaupoa, hopped over the retaining wall and blocked our way.

'The ball!' Tony demanded in a big bass voice, one huge hand held out, fingers itching. 'Puh-leeze!'

'Are you the one responsible for his injury?' Pam asked.

'We're taking Professor Ohrenstedt to the infirmary.'

'I don't know about any injury. The ball.' Tony insisted.

Ben-Torres, Ray Rice and another guy were advancing from another angle, up the side of the hill, toward us.

'Give him the ball,' Bev said quietly. 'Don't cause . . .'

Pam headed us in another direction, and the three huge guys blocked us there too. 'Don't make me hafta take it,' the Samoan threatened, smiling to show a trendy red plastic front tooth. 'Think you can take it from me, fat boy?' Pam taunted.

For an answer he suddenly darted toward her. Pam pulled back and away and he slid past like a bull finessed around the cape of a matador. The two other guys each made a jump in her direction, and Pam wove back and forth, dribbling the ball, and as Lorenzo came too close, she threw the ball to Michelle. I heard Lorenzo grunt suddenly and saw Pam dance away. She'd just elbowed him in the ribs. Michelle dropped her bookbag and ran with the ball, putting distance between herself and the others. Bev also dropped her books and ran to join Michelle, blocking Colby. Michelle faked a hand-off to Bev that Colby fell for. So she popped the ball up to Pam, who'd gotten clear, and Lorenzo and Tony both charged her. She faked one, then the other, then handed off to Bev, who leapt up, hung onto Colby's shoulder and threw the ball over his head back to Michelle.

All this should have been good clean fun, if it weren't for the guys grunting and murmuring just loud enough for me to hear, 'I'll get you, bitch!' and the women mumbling back, 'Eat me, lard ass!' among other endearments.

Suddenly all six were headed my way. The ball was free, in the air, six sets of hands grabbing for it, but I'd jumped up first, highest, and I nabbed it, spun in the air, got my fingers tighter on the ball, turned a bit more still in the air and, having calculated right, came down just outside of the terrace on the grass, well away from the morass of limbs and bodies and grunts of 'Fuck! Shit! Bitch! Asshole!' Invigorated by what force I couldn't tell, I touched ground barely a second, leapt even further away from the crowd, held the ball close to my chest and turned again. This time directly into Ben-Torres,

Barry Thayer and Ray Rice. I put up a game fight, but where we were struggling the ground was hummocky, at a forty-degree angle, and all their arms poked different parts of my torso, so I simply let them take me down to the grass and, once there, I let gravity take its course and rolled down the hill, pulling the three of them along with me.

By the time I'd come to a stop, only Ray was still holding on. I was on my back, grasping the ball, but he fell on top of me, knocking out what was left of my breath. Using his superior strength, he held me down with legs athwart my thighs, held down my hands easily and popped the ball out of my grip into the air. Ben-Torres was motionless there and caught it with his sneaker tip, kicked it up once, tipped it higher, shouting, 'I've got it! I've got it,' and bounced it from his shoulder and then headed off into a new direction I couldn't see but could easily infer from where he charged next, away from us, joined by the others.

Ray meanwhile hadn't let go.

'Okay!' I said.

Instead, he continued to hold both of my hands back over my head, and leaned over to my right ear and said, 'I sort of like you in this position. I'd like to tie you down and have some fun.'

For a second or two I struggled. But of course I soon realized this was what he wanted. So I stopped struggling. He'd arranged his crotch near my sternum. I couldn't help but feel his erection.

I heard the voices of the three women approaching. 'C'mon, Ray. Fun's over. Let him up!' They still sounded psyched for action.

'We've really got to stop meeting like this, Professor,' Ray whispered as erotically as he could in my ear. He blew once hard, so I'd be in no doubt of what he meant. Then he was off me, gone. As I sat up and tried to catch my breath, I could see him running, shouting, up the hill, toward the other guys.

'I'm okay,' I said, but I let Pam and Bev help me up. 'You ladies are something, you know,' I added, dusting off my slacks and joining them in the ascent back up the grass.

'After today, none of them'll call us ladies,' Bev said, and all of us laughed.

One of the disadvantages of being dead, I believe Lord Chesterfield commented, is that it is rather difficult to tend to one's reputation. Of the nine members of the Purple Circle, five of them had had for the past few decades that very problem. And of those five, two had an even bigger problem. Cameron Powers had only published one book in his lifetime a travel book about Rome and its environs, unique and quirky, yet still a travel book – and as a result he'd never developed any reputation. Early pieces written about the group had mentioned him a bit embarrassedly as a book editor, or at times as Von Slyke's lover. As a result of Reuben Weatherbury's efforts on his behalf, Powers was better known posthumously than he'd ever been when breath still filled his body.

Jeff Weber's problem was different. Unlike the Leo–McKewens, he hadn't been social, hadn't constantly thrown dinner parties and afternoon teas, hadn't cultivated gay and straight authors or heiresses, or television anchorwomen, or well-connected men of a certain age entwined in Manhattan's 'uptown art scene'. He'd not spent two months every year in a European city, nor had he spent summers at a beachfront house entertaining. Also, unlike Rowland Etheridge, who had managed to beef up his faltering fiction-writing career by going on to write, direct and be extremely involved in plays, even if it was merely at various Off-Off-Broadway theaters and second-drawer university drama departments, Jeff Weber had stopped writing plays altogether after he left college and so had not managed to achieve a name in that field. And finally, unlike Mark Dodge, Jeff Weber had never had a beloved book which had sold a million copies, been translated into five languages and made him famous.

Instead, Jeff Weber had written and published a novel about coming out, in 1978, and a collection of short stories about the Manhattan and Fire Island gay scene, in 1979. *Ode to a Porno Star* had all the makings of a hit: it was told from the point of view of a young Midwestern naïf who arrived in New York the morning of the Stonewall Riot, and it dealt with just about every potentially amusing and poignant encounter such a hapless lad might have, right up to the absurd love affair with the spectacular man who happens to be everyone else's fantasy-figure. But for all its richness of detail and writerly strengths, there was something too restrained about the satire, something held-back in the romance, something not-quite-there re: the inner workings of the gay scene he was writing about. No surprise, as those who knew Weber admitted: that same restraint, that very sense of holding back, characterized him as a person. Damon Von Slyke, who of all the Purple Circlers claimed to have known Jeff best in the earlier years, was astonished to discover (and to reveal to Powers in a letter) that it had taken Weber ten years of what Damon had thought was a close friendship to reveal that he'd always hated his father and had gone out of his way to destroy by fire his father's most cherished possession – an old folio volume of Dante's *Inferno* with illustrations by Doré, which the seventeen-year-old boy had inherited.

Slights and Offenses, the book of Jeff's stories published in various magazines and anthologies, did have the satire, did have the gay-scene inner workings, did have the romance. De Petrie praised the book both in print and in private, writing in his journals that 'Jeff's delight in spinning a yarn for us over a littered dinner table, and the way Jeff transformed himself from a stylish West Side queen into some grubby old Pecos Bill or Gabby Hayes figure right in front of us as he narrated his tall tales and impossible sagas, have finally been caught, if momentarily, in two or three of the book's best stories.' But the book was, after all, a collection of short stories, difficult to market, and without that sustained reading experience a novel provides. It actually did better in sales and reviews than *Ode*, but still not very well. That depressed Jeff a great deal (according to De Petrie's journal entries, he even thought he'd stop writing), at the same time that it made him defiant (cf. a contemporary letter from Etheridge to Von Slyke in which Jeff declared he was as good a writer as any of them, and he would 'show them!'). As a result, Weber's editor wasn't able to offer him a contract for a third book he was working up: a never-finished novel about an eastern university town.

Almost seven more years would elapse before Weber published another book. *The Odds in Ocean Park* was based on a series of magazine articles he'd done about the effect of AIDS on various people: a week of a young internist's office visits by the freshly tested and newly infected, a nurse's month in an intensive-care hospital unit dealing with the disease, the opening of a hospice for those dying of AIDS in the eponymous area of Santa Monica, California.

Atlantic Monthly, the *New York Times Magazine* and *Los Angeles* had published the originals Weber had expanded into a book, and as a result the book was widely and quite well reviewed. The briefly public and open Weber of the days of the short stories was long past, however. He had withdrawn from socializing with the other Purples by then. He had moved to a small studio in Boerum Hill, Brooklyn, and he'd begun traveling a great deal for the magazine, work that was now paying the bulk of his living expenses. Axenfeld's letters to the Leo–McKewens, as well as McKewen's and De Petrie's journal entries of these years, mention the others seeing Jeff briefly, coming or going from errands on the streets of Manhattan, usually having just flown into town or on his way back out, headed to Bali or Ireland or the Comoros Islands. 'He was polite but distracted,' Axenfeld wrote. 'He remembered to ask after you two, but halfway through my brief recitation of how you were doing, he began asking after Dom and Damon.'

By November of 1985, when the book came out, the Purple Circle was long disbanded. Even so, Dominic De Petrie wrote in his journals that all of them except Mark Dodge (who was at the time himself hospitalized by a meningeal complication of the disease) were at Weber's publication party. De Petrie and Axenfeld had given the book-cover blurbs. Von Slyke reviewed it for the *Washington Post Book World*, and McKewen discussed it at length in his *Philadelphia Gay News* column. Despite this support from his colleagues, it was after all non-fiction, little better than reportage, not the work of his imagination, and Jeff Weber sharply felt the book would never be considered first-rate by the others. He wrote as much in a letter about the party to his new boyfriend: 'They all made me feel I was special. I am special. And a lot less than they are. Any of them.'

Possibly this attitude was exacerbated by Weber's internalization of his own infection by the HIV virus (he'd been diagnosed the week of the publication party), which would slowly come to take over his life, his relationships and his work. The relative success of *The Odds in Ocean Park*, did bring Weber more publication in magazines, more reportage, and for the first time in his life book royalties.

During 1986, Weber began writing the half-dozen interleaved stories that would form his final work, *Cheyenne August*. This last book, published October 1988, a month before his five-month hospitalization and death, combined the techniques of fiction, autobiography and reportage. As a portrait of small-town western characters, attitudes and mores, it is unique, useful and wonderful to read. As Thaddeus Fleming pointed out, Weber's voice was never stronger, more succinct, more flexible or more real. It's a summation of his work to that date. De Petrie got early galleys of the book and passed them onto Mitchell Leo in Europe with this note: 'This is the Jeff Weber we all used to know and enjoy so much in the '70s. The "ornery old bartender who'll bend your ear till you run screaming", the "blushing young maiden", the "half-drunk old Indian grandma", the "insane yet strangely prescient town castaway": they're all in the book, just the way he used to do them for us. Odd how the more Jeff distanced himself from us (and from his home back in the West), the more familiar, the more likable, he's become.'

But to get a sense of the strength and unity he'd achieved and for an idea of the direction Weber's work might have gone had he lived longer, one must turn to his ultimate work, what Reuben Weatherbury called Jeff Weber's 'masterly swan song', what Cummings called 'his most assured work': the story 'In the Tree Museum'. Published four years after his death in the first volume of the *Reader*, it is a Chekhovian tale of a doomed from the start, afternoon in a park encounter between two desperately love-starved young men from utterly different backgrounds, mental sets and cultures. 'On his deathbed,' Fleming had written in his study of the nine members of the Purple Circle, 'Weber achieved a single luminous vision of the human tragedy.'

Weatherbury had thanked Roberta Bonaventura of the Jeff Weber Estate for releasing that story for the publication of the anthology. And as the *Purple Circle Reader* had been my own first contact with Jeff Weber's writing, almost eight years ago, it had forever colored how I thought of him thereafter; that and the odd, sad photo of Jeff Weber, inside the book, caught just after a bookstore reading he'd done during the winter of 1980, snow on the window panes behind his backlighted head, his hair fallen over his forehead, his hand lifted as though in greeting or repulsion, his eyes staring off to one side of the photographer's lens.

And now I was driving through the fast – seventy miles per hour –

heavy – five lanes wide on either side, only five feet from bumper to bumper – six-forty p.m. rush-hour traffic on the Santa Monica Freeway, headed directly into the glare of a big red sun, just beginning to set over the Pacific Ocean, on my way to meet and speak with Roberta Bonaventura of the Jeff Weber Estate: Bobbie as she was known to most; the Widow Weber herself.

I left the Celica at the Venice Avenue public parking lot and took an open tram up aptly named Electric Court to where it became Hampton. A block east was Douglas Street. Finding the number was more difficult. This area was considered beachfront, densely built up: overarching trees closely abutted one- and two-story wooden-frame and adobe houses, seven-foot-high fences and gates, all on top of each other, with barely an alley between, and each one held numbers and sometimes half-numbers, behind which I supposed were flats.

Bonaventura's number was even more hidden and unreadable than most. When I had found it, hassled to unlatch the gate and got through a slot of a passageway made almost impassable by a pocket jungle of overgrown succulents, there was nothing but a screened door. I knocked and heard a TV. I shouted and heard what sounded like Bobbie's voice telling me to come in.

A narrow eat-in kitchen, leading to a shadowed office. The TV noise was coming from a third room. But as I tried to decide what to do, I heard a shout of 'Damn you!' and a fuzzy, soap-covered dog of no immediately discernible breed shot out from a door I'd not noticed, past me and through the screen door.

Bobbie Bonaventura dashed out of what I now saw was a bathroom, yelling, 'Get back here! Get back here!' She ran into the tiny yard, where the dog barked loudly but outmaneuvered her and wouldn't let itself be caught. She chased it, until I saw it cornered behind a thick-leafed plant with sharp tips, growling, nipping at her hand whenever she would get near. She finally said, 'Fuck yourself, stupid! Lick the goddamn soap off yourself!' The dog replied with a bloodcurdling howl.

Bobbie stomped back into the kitchen. She was wearing another pair of dungarees, cut above the knees, without a T-shirt beneath, and she was soaking wet. Outside the dog was still barking. She ignored it, went to the fridge, got out a mango-guava drink, swallowed its contents in a few gulps. Only then did she notice me, though both had had to maneuver around me before.

'Oh, you! Von Slyke's little amanuensis!' She made that last word sound utterly pornographic. 'Did you bring it?' And when I nodded, 'Well, I'm wet. Go into what my roommie calls our living room –' staring in the direction out of which the TV emanated. 'I'll dry off.' She offered a drink and I said no.

The living room was vacant, the TV set either tuned to or replaying a video of a local beach's volleyball tournament, a sport I'd never in my life seen televised before, but which I knew to be almost twelve-hour-a-day standard West Coast cable fare. I got comfortable on one of two big upholstered chairs, looking for the control panel or remote. I'd not yet located it when Bobbie entered. She was wearing a furry pink terry robe, her hair pulled back with a silver band. She held another drink in her hand, dropped into a chair and yelled 'Off!' at the TV, which shut itself off instantly. 'Now! Let's see what you've got!'

I handed her the manuscript. She read a few lines, furled through the pages, then got up. One door turned out to be a closet, probably a linen closet when this was still a bedroom, with a dozen horizontal wooden shelves. Each held a manuscript, or magazines, or envelopes. All very neat. All precisely labeled. She knelt to the lowest shelf, rummaged, found a manuscript, threw it in my lap.

It was a photocopy of what I'd brought her. Exact copy, page by page. Except on top of this version, on page one, written in fine green ink script was, 'Len Spurgeon's childhood story'.

I didn't understand.

'Len Spurgeon's childhood story?' I read it aloud. 'This is what you called an unpublished story in the collection catalogue?'

She dropped exhausted into the other chair and sipped at her mango-guava. 'That's Jeff's handwriting. The green ink. What did he write on top?'

It wasn't what she'd notated in the Purple Circle Collection catalogue as 'What Occurred on Route 90'.

'I don't get it.'

'It's Len Spurgeon's childhood story,' Bobbie said. 'At least what he claimed to be a story from his childhood.'

'But,' I tried, 'Jeff Weber wrote it!'

'I don't know who the fuck wrote it. It was typed on Jeff's old IBM Selectric, using the Elite Type Ball he used for *Ode to a Porno Star* and the stories in *Slights and Offenses*.'

I said what was obvious: 'Then it is Jeff's story?'

'If it's Jeff's story –' she tried to be patient – 'then why in screaming hell did he write it's Len Spurgeon's story?'

'Maybe Jeff used that name as a pseudonym. The way James Joyce used Stephen Dedalus to represent him,' I explained.

'Well, that would all be very literary and neat. Except that Len Spurgeon was a real person.' And when I looked astonished: 'A real person, who was Jeff Weber's . . . I daren't use the word lover, as that implies some smidgen of affection – so I'll simply say that he and Jeff fucked for a while. Several months.' And as I was taking that in, Bobbie went on, 'Around the time Jeff was writing some of the stories and the *Ode*. Which may explain to you why I did not include this with the other stuff that I definitely knew Jeff had written, when I sent his stuff to the collection.'

'And you didn't find this until?'

'After Jeff was dead. So I couldn't very well ask. I did go through his letters and things of the time, looking to see if he'd mentioned this story to anyone. I got nowhere.'

I had to get it right. 'Len Spurgeon was a real person.'

'Depends what you mean by "real." He lived, if by living you mean eating and fucking. And he fucked Jeff Weber but good. Actually and metaphorically. If that's real, then Len Spurgeon was real. I met him. Others met him. Satisfied?'

'Others? As in other Purple Circle members?'

'In fact, one of the Exalted Nine, Mr Wonderful himself, Mark Dodge, introduced Jeff to Scumbag Len.' She gulped more. 'Others knew Len. Prissy Etheridge. Mitch Leo.'

While she'd been speaking, the dog had sneaked back into the house, and was now lurking right behind the ajar door to the room. I could see it, but I wasn't sure if Bobbie could too, until she suddenly leapt out of her chair and charged. There was a great scrabbling of dog claws and human limbs on the floorboards as they went at each other. She must have gotten it by the tail or ear or paw, as I could hear her drag it howling and barking into the bathroom, where she swore loudly. I heard the dog let out two very loud barks, heard Bobbie yell and the dog take off through the house. It slid in front of the TV room doorway momentarily, hit the opposite wall, caroomed off, and scrambled in the other direction out the screen door into the yard. In those few seconds I could see that Bobbie had succeeded in rinsing off the soap, revealing an old gray Bedlington terrier.

By the time Bobbie had reappeared in her third outfit in fifteen minutes – big blouse and shorts – carrying more soft drinks, I was ready. I had brought an ultra-microcassette recorder with me. I'd hidden it in my top pocket and turned it on. I accepted the drink she offered and said in what I hoped was a properly naïve, sincere tone of voice, 'So, who exactly was Len Spurgeon and what did he do to Jeff Weber to make you hate him so much?'

'Really want to know?'

'Do Gorillas have hair?' I repeated Aaron Axenfeld's dictum to me of the previous day. 'Do hairburners have sex?'

'Okay,' she said, and I could tell she'd been waiting for years for this very moment, 'I'll tell you.'

'First, and there's a reason I'm asking this, what did the others say about me. Axenfeld and De Petrie and Von Slyke?'

'Axenfeld was the one who mentioned you,' I replied. 'He said you and Jeff were lovers in college and remained close thereafter. And that you nursed Jeff during his final illness.'

'To be precise, I was Jeff Weber's first and last heterosexual lay,' Bobbie said. 'We did it twice. It was wonderful for me. So-so for him. I was in love with Jeff then. And forever afterward. That's why I chose to remain his friend after he'd come out, why I put up with all of his shit, and why at the end I saw him out that final doorway.' She paused. 'Some people think I've wasted my life. My family. My friends. Lots of people. What do you think?'

'I'm too inexperienced to make judgments like that.'

'Well, either you're wise beyond your years or shrewdly diplomatic,' she said. 'They call me the Widow Weber behind my back, you know, Von Slyke and Axenfeld. They make fun of me. But I'm proud of it. I mean what else do I have? I used to have a lot more – promise, potential. When we first met, Jeff and I, I was the one with all the talent, I had all the promise. Bet you didn't know that? No, no one does. I had a one-act play put on in high school. By the time I'd graduated college I already had three of my plays produced at the college and one at a local summer stock theater.

'That was how I got to college in the first place, never mind such a fancy one, on a theatrical scholarship. My dad was a worker in an auto-parts plant in Schenectady. There were five kids. He couldn't have sent me to college. I would have worked in the town bakery like my four sisters, icing donuts and marrying some Italian factory worker who cheated on me and kept me pregnant until I was too old and fat for anyone to notice.

'One of my plays was even published. It's over there.' Bobbie nodded in the direction of a bookshelf. 'That was *Painted Ladies and Pretty Men*, my '60s play. Hippies, nudity, free love, political rebellion, women's lib, all rolled up into one. Sort of a mixture of *Oh! Calcutta!* and *A Midsummer Night's Dream* with a touch of Gorky thrown in. It's dated, naturally. But that was how I met Jeff. He showed up at the college theater to audition for a role. Told us he'd been an actor since he was ten. He didn't look like it, but he handled the "sides" we gave him like a pro. Miles beyond anyone else we saw. So we gave him the lead. I was the painted lady; Jeff the pretty man.

'You ever see a picture of Jeff Weber at eighteen? He came from Wyoming, you know. Still dressed country, in shit-kicking boots and skin-tight jeans, with those piping-lined checked shirts and a big wide belt. He still had that West of the Platte River twang to his voice, unless he was acting or public speaking, when he was letter perfect. His eyebrows were blonder than his honey-colored hair and fuzzy, and Jeff learned how to use the muscles in them so they sort of shaded his eyes. And those eyes! Oh, my! Not a photo, not a video exists to tell you how blue Jeff Weber's eyes were. The blue of the first clear sky after a storm, the blue of hope chest panties, the blue of every gift you ever opened as a kid. He would bend one of those eyebrows and twist his mustachioed upper lip and squint one eye so it sort of concentrated the rays it could shoot out, and then he'd laugh, a great big man's laugh, with big white, perfect teeth.

'A laugh bigger than he was physically. Jeff was only five-seven or so and never weighed more than 150 pounds. But he looked big on stage. Had he gone on as an actor, he would have hit the silver screen and looked big there too. Like Dustin Hoffman and Tom Cruise did, despite their height. Sometimes I wish I had pushed him into being a screen actor. He would have done well, he would have played the "I'm straight" game longer and maybe he would have lived longer. That's hindsight, isn't it? I loved him. I wanted him around. Not in Hollywood or Cinecittà, where they didn't want me.

'Then, too, Jeff was a real writer. I knew that the first play he showed me. *Bauxite Flats* it was titled. A Western. Not deep. But real. And strong. Good characters. A few good scenes. Not my kind of thing. He went back to the material again and wrote it as a section of *Cheyenne August*. The part about the cousin who borrows all the money for the mining operation and what happens to him, how he drinks himself to death, when the mine goes dry?'

The dog had crept back into the room. Quietly it had moved up to where Bobbie was sitting, and slowly it had insinuated its head to directly under where her free hand lay. As she was speaking, she was pulling the curled hair on the top of its head, petting it.

'So, I'm the one responsible for Jeff Weber beginning to think of himself as a writer. For switching his major from history and politics to English and theater, for moving to New York City after we graduated, and for getting him his first job at that branch of the Greenwich Savings Bank where I knew the manager. That was when, 1967? We shared an apartment on Hudson Street in the Village long before it was even close to chic. Then we found apartments that we could actually afford in Chelsea, on West 17th Street, long before that was so gay, one flat directly on top of the other.

'In 1974 we started the world's smallest publishing company, Stratospheric Press. First we published my novella *Cayuga Street* and then we published his poems, *Picking Up Men in Lower Manhattan*. In what soon became typical, mine was well reviewed in the *New York Times* and sold ten copies. Jeff's poetry, with its openly gay title, was completely ignored by the media and was bought by half the queers in New York who knew what a sonnet was. It went into three printings, instantly provided him with entreé to *Christopher Street* and *The Advocate*, not to mention bars, baths, parties, gay literary readings, Fire Island and a new pal, Dominic De Petrie, a successfully published author of three books. The rest, as they say, is Purple Circle history.

'Do I sound bitter?' she asked. 'I am bitter,' she answered herself. 'So it would only be natural if I sounded it. Not that I wasn't welcome as Jeff's pal and as a writer myself. Well, some of the time. But it became clear early on that it was after all a boy's club, and a gay boy's club, so women were, how do I put it, just a little *de trop*!

'Okay, okay, you're saying to yourself. Enough already of the *Redbook* article "Hetero Women Who Love Gay Men"! Where's Len Spurgeon in all this? Hold your horses.' Bobbie looked down at the Bedlington. 'What a jerk! This dog. And Len. And Jeff. And me too.'

'Okay, Len Spurgeon. He came along in – what was it – '78, I think. As I said before, Mark Dodge dragged him to one of those parties at the Robert Samuel Gallery the Purple Circle used to frequent. You ever hear of the place? Robert Mapplethorpe and his lover Sam Wagstaff put it together to show gay art and photography. Mostly Robert's photos, but Platt Lynes and I also remember Arthur Tress's work. It was on Lower Broadway, near 11th Street, on the second floor, just opposite that Gothic-style church, I can't remember the name or even its denomination.

'I never "got" Len's looks myself, but he caused a real commotion among the guys. To me he looked cheap, like one of those teenage punks I used to know in Schenectady who hung out behind the high-school gym smoking dope and drinking hooch out of a brown paper bag. You know the type? Long, heavy, straight hair that falls over their face and naturally muscled bodies – don't know whether it's from their working-class genes or from eating so many peanut butter and jelly sandwiches on white bread as a kid. Big biceps and heavy calves on their legs. But otherwise skinny. No hips. Waists you can hardly see. Stomachs you can count the ribs on. Sort of bored expression on their faces, unless they're pissed off, when it gets all scrunched up. A perpetual wooden toothpick wedged between sharp canine teeth, sticking out of scornful fat lips. Stubby noses – bull noses, I called them – wider than usual from the brow down and flat, as though flattened by a board when they were a kid. Surprisingly good complexion. Lazy-looking. Wouldn't move to save your life, but athletic enough when they

wanted to be, active as hell when they needed to be. That was Len
Spurgeon.

'He came from Texas, the Permian Basin, he said. Which I later
found out was central and west oil country. So I guess he and Jeff
had that cowboy shit in common. Len played up his juvenile-
delinquent looks, wearing form-fitting black Ts and the first pair of
coal-colored jeans I ever laid eyes on, along with clunky black engi-
neer's boots and a torn leather bomber jacket. It must have played
into some fantasy image Jeff had, because at dinner that night and
for the next three days he couldn't stop talking about Len, whom, by
the way, I'd barely noticed. Well, Jeff was always having these enthu-
siasms about guys. He'd gone gaga over De Petrie when they'd first
met. So I didn't pay too much attention.

'A week later, Len's sleeping over when I drop down to Jeff's
apartment. And a month later, he's still sleeping over. In fact, he
hasn't left. He's living there, a first for Jeff Weber, who had at least
until then retained that much of his Western propriety not to mention his last shreds of closetedness.'

'All this took place where?' I had to ask.

'Manhattan. The Village. Are you listening or are you playing
with yourself? By this time in our thirteen-year friendship, I'd
learned not to get involved in any way in Jeff's romantic or sex life.
I mean, I knew nothing about it and could know nothing about it
as I was a woman and these were guys and anyway, I'd be jealous,
so what was the use? Even so, I can tell that Len has Jeff spinning
like a top. Part of the idea of Jeff getting the "stupid bank job" is so
that he would have free time and a free mind to do writing before or
after work or maybe on weekends. But he's not finished the essay
that he'd promised some magazine, and the draft of his new story is
just sitting there, untouched, although an actual magazine editor
says he's waiting for it.

'Meanwhile, Jeff and I hardly ever see each other. We used to talk
on the phone twice a day, now I'm lucky if it's twice a week. And
when we do talk it's "Len this" and "Len that". Whenever I try to
broach the subject of writing, or of his future, Jeff avoids comment.
Then one day he tells me they're doing things in bed he didn't think
he was capable of. I reply, "Don't tell me!" but it's clear that Jeff is
beyond infatuated and also that Len Spurgeon, besides being Mr

Venus in Furs, also has a little Freud thrown in too, as he's helping Jeff work out his considerable problems with his fuck of a father and bigoted mother back in Wyoming.

'The next step is, of course, drugs. We're talking about the very same Jeff Weber who signed a pledge when he was fourteen never to drink alcohol, and who would pass a stick of grass, averting his nostrils so he wouldn't have to smell it. Suddenly he and Len are dropping LSD every weekend. Partly, it turns out, this is allegedly "therapeutic" as it allows Jeff to loosen up and experiment more sexually. Partly it's also allegedly "analytical" as it allows Len to fuck with Jeff's until then fairly adamantine mindsets. Jeff assures me that Len knows what he's doing, as he's had plenty of experience with drugs – no shit! – and goes on to tell me that furthermore this will even help his, Jeff's, writing. They are revealing each other's deepest secrets to one another. One of which, I years later figure out to be this piece of manuscript about Len Spurgeon's supposedly unintentional fratricide.

'Who knows what secret Jeff told Len? Probably that he was repeatedly sexually abused by a grown man over a four-year period, this friend of the Weber family who had encouraged Jeff to become a child actor, and used occasions of long solitary drives with the boy to and from rehearsals at a theater in the next county to sodomize Jeff and force him to fellate him. This I discovered only years later when Jeff was dying

'Whatever is going on between Jeff and Len, it's tight, and I'm so far out of the picture that I admit the fact although it pains me incredibly. For months Len and Jeff remain together. Len has no occupation I can figure out, but always seems to have money and always pays his share. The one week I'm home from work sick, I spy on him, but he's not hustling, not seeing other guys. Occasionally he puts on a suit and goes out with an attaché case a few hours at a time.

'This, according to Jeff, is Len's alleged work in "sales". Sales of what neither ever says, and if it's drugs, it's on a small scale. So I say to myself, okay, Jeff's comfortable and you're overreacting; now go get a life. For a few weeks I even believe it. Then it happens. One day the bank branch that Jeff works at is robbed. In fact, Jeff is the teller who is robbed.

'Some of this I discover at three-oh-nine on a Wednesday afternoon, when the bank manager, my old pal remember, calls me to say come get Jeff at work, he's still in shock. Well, that's putting it mildly. Jeff's a basketcase. And while all of us can understand this as a result of having someone put a revolver up to your head and demand money or your life, we don't know all the lurid details.

'Until later. Later, when we get home to Jeff's place and everything is a mess, and it turns out all Len's things are gone. And even later, when Jeff breaks down yet has sense enough to swear me to secrecy before he tells me that in fact Len Spurgeon was the bank robber who put a revolver to his head. And Jeff tells me that this was not a surprise to him, as they had planned the robbery together. Jeff's part was to tell Len what time of what day he believed his till would have the most amount of cash, and his other part was to be too upset to tap the emergency floor button.

'Well, it turns out Jeff told Len when — he had 22,000 dollars in the till when it was robbed – and he did manage to panic enough not to push the emergency floor button, because during the robbery Len Spurgeon clicked off the revolver's safety and scared the everliving shit out of Jeff Weber, threatening to kill him if he wasn't faster, and further whispering that he would find and shoot him if he ever revealed who Len was. This will explain Jeff's lack of surprise when we got home and Len's stuff was gone. And explain Jeff's feeling that he'd been manipulated, preyed on and utterly betrayed by Len Spurgeon.'

Bobbie looked at the dog, who looked up at her. 'So, that's who Len Spurgeon is. Satisfied?'

'And Len vanished,' I asked. 'Just like that?'

'Well, you see, that's exactly the problem. Len didn't just vanish. He turned up a few months later, tanned and cheerful, at a party given by Mitch Leo and Frankie McKewen, who were seeing a lot of Len at the time. And Len went on to become really palsy with Rowland Etheridge and I believe he lived with Axenfeld a short while. I lost track.

'The point is, Len didn't vanish. That at least would have allowed poor Jeff to deal with it all. To come to some sort of closure. Instead, Len stuck around. He never explained to anyone why he suddenly moved out of Jeff's place. And while at the bank no one ever hinted that it was an inside job, partly because of how truly upset Jeff was when it happened, Jeff eventually left and found another job in that dopey little social work agency, where he remained until almost, well, the end. Needless to say, Jeff never took LSD again, did go into real therapy, which sort of helped, and never had another relationship until he was already infected and it was pretty much too late for true love.'

I'd been sitting there with my mouth hanging open. 'Wow!' I finally said. 'Yet you're not sure who wrote the story. Weber or Spurgeon?'

'As I explained before, maybe Len dictated and Jeff wrote. Or Jeff wrote it after Len told him the story. I'm not sure it's true or whether Len Spurgeon just used it to further sucker Jeff into being his accomplice in the bank heist.'

We stared at each other a minute, then Bobbie began petting the Bedlington again. I heard my microcassette shut off inside my pocket. I thought surely she must hear it too. But she didn't. Then, in the sweetest possible voice, she said to the dog, as she caressed it, 'You think you had it bad today! Your suffering has only begun! Tomorrow, I'm going to clip your hair. Yes, I am! Yes! Yes! Yes!'

Book Three

THE DODGE BROTHERS INC.

There are at least three types of betrayal, he found
himself deciding, but probably the worst was the one
where the stupid son-of-a-bitch then spent the rest of
his life explaining to all and sundry (including
naturally yourself) exactly why it was that he'd
screwed you.

Mark Dodge, *We All Drive Fords*

'I DISCOVERED WHO WROTE THE manuscript I found among the Von Slyke papers,' I repeated. 'We won't have to meet after all.'

On the other end of the line, in the background, I heard a baseball game on the radio or TV, and voices, male voices, rooting for a team.

It was mid-afternoon, the day following my visit to Bobbie Bonaventura. I was calling on a cellular phone from the pergola-roofed rearmost garden of Von Slyke's Hollywood home, where I'd retreated with a bottle of papaya-mango iced tea and my laptop, trying to escape the day's intensely hot sunshine and a suddenly sti-fling indoor atmosphere. Given the noise on the other end, it sounded as though I'd reached Thom Dodge in his home, while I'd intended to phone him at his place of work.

'I found it too!' Dodge surprised me by saying. 'The five pages you faxed. And another five. Not a continuation. Another story. Years later, when the boy – what was his name? Paul? – when he's grown up.'

How could the story be by Mark Dodge? Bobbie told me it was by Len Spurgeon?

'I never knew the second piece existed until you faxed what you had,' Thom went on. 'That first part was there, and so were these other pages, in the back of it all this time.'

Had Bobbie lied? Made up all that about Spurgeon? Why? To aggrandize another piece of writing for the Weber estate? Despite how short, sketchy and of not terribly high literary value it might be?

'Are you telling me the story was written by your brother?'

'Why else would it be here?' Thom said. 'It's a hell of a story. I mean, what it says about Mark.'

'You'd read it before,' I tried, 'when you prepared his papers for the collection?'

'I'd be lying if I said I did. There was a whole bunch of papers I

didn't know what in the hell to make of. It's not as though I'm a professor or anything. I'm just an Air Force man. I always felt Mark
had done himself a disservice making me his literary executor. I
looked for what the Timrod Collection asked for. But there was a lot
of loose stuff that hadn't been published. Without titles and all.
Weatherbury looked at all Mark's unpublished works when he put
together the first volume of the *Reader*. I gave him free run. He took
what he wanted. Photocopied it. Left the rest.'

'Did Weatherbury see those pages?'

'If he did, he never said anything. Maybe *he* put them together.
You know because of the same name and all.'

I heard cheering: televised and in the room.

'Prieto just hit a triple for the As,' Dodge explained. 'You have the
Angels there right?'

'And the Dodgers.' I was unnerved. I'd thought it had been settled. It would make a lot more sense that Mark Dodge wrote the
piece. He actually *had* older brothers, unlike only-child Jeff Weber.
Even so, it was confusing.

'So you coming tomorrow?' Dodge asked.

'You found the pieces among what Weatherbury thought was
Mark's unfinished autobiography?'

'That's what he thought,' Thom said. 'I was never all that sure.
And those titles he came up with!'

'*Man in a Jar?*' I asked. '*Framed by Life?*'

'Mark used to fool with titles all the time. He'd make lists of 'em.
I remember one time my mamma telling me she'd visited him in a
hospital out East and he left the room for some tests and he'd been
writing something in a notebook; when she went to pick it up it was
just a list of words. She thought it was a poem, but he told her no.
Sometimes he'd make up a title then write the damn book! That last
one? *We All Drive Fords?* He had that title a dozen years before. I'd
catch him saying it, rolling the words around in his mouth to see
how they sounded.'

Dominic De Petrie wrote the same thing in his journals, how he
and Dodge would make up book titles they never planned to use, for
the hell of it. 'You don't believe those titles are what your brother
was going to use?'

'Worse,' Dodge replied. 'I'm not convinced my brother knew

what in the hell he was writing a lot of the time, especially later on. I don't mean disrespect. But you gotta understand, at the end there he was scattered in his mind.'

'I know he developed dementia,' I said, 'as a result of the HIV virus.'

Both Fleming and Cummings had written that, reproducing in appendices to the group bios Dodge's death certificate showing 'Herpes Triplex' as cause of death: i.e. the disease had passed the blood–brain barrier. Not having experienced anyone with dementia myself I couldn't say how it would manifest precisely.

'Mark'd be talking back to the television set as though the woman giving the nightly news were right there in the hospital room with him and Ma.'

'I see,' I said, horrified.

'But then, very next minute, Ma would ask him something – you know, to check out his attention – and that son of a gun would be sharp as a tack. It was hard to fool him. Even so, he might have been writing a half-dozen books at the end. Not just one. He was that scattered in his head.'

I did understand. But I still couldn't figure out how the manuscript could be Len's, maybe Jeff's – and Mark's too. 'You think I ought to come see for myself?'

'That's what you were planning to do, right?' Then in a quieter tone of voice than he'd so far been using, although not quite a whisper, 'And anyway I wanted to tell you something . . . we'll talk when you get here and there's a bit more privacy.'

I wondered what he meant by that last enigmatic bit. Instead, I said brightly, 'Well, then, see you tomorrow!'

'You know the East Bay? You need directions?'

'I'll phone if I get lost.'

There was a single burst of cheers from the other end, and I was sure it was from people in the room. Obviously a home run, on top of Prieto's triple. Thom hung up.

Two pigeon-like birds I'd not noticed before on the property – perhaps mourning doves, for all I knew lovebirds, their clay-colored feathers dappled with circles of bittersweet chocolate and white, their sleek, nougat-colored heads, marbled tan-black eyes and egg-white beaks – were cooing as they pranced and postured for each other, delicately pirouetting in and out of view among the richly velvet, purple-veined, deep green leaves of vine festooning the arbor above my head. Unexpectedly strong drafts of nearby jasmine and honeysuckle wafted complex attars across my face, strong as animal pheromones, nearly causing me to gag.

Then I saw her, Conchita, some thirty-five feet distant, stepping out of a glass door into the terrace. She was wearing a flimsy, pearl-hued robe with matching sandal-strap heels. A drawstring bag flung over one shoulder.

I was about to call her over, into the shade . . . I already had my hand raised in gesture, when Conchita dropped the bag with a soft smash and spread an eye-hurting white towel I'd not seen her holding across one of the sun chairs always paired at the fountain's edge. She half turned and in a theatrical gesture flung her hands out, angled to let the robe slither off her arms, down her naked body, to gather at her feet. She kicked off the big shoes, gently prodded the clothing with her toes and turned to the fountain, which immediately responded by covering her curved, high-tipped breasts and nubbed hipbones, her held-high face, the tawny skin of her arms and her long legs with spray, dewing her so consistently she might have been a statue in a morning park.

Any earlier thought I might innocently have had of getting her attention and drawing her into the shade died quietly inside me then. I watched as she slowly twisted her slender torso within the fountain's invisible wet penumbra until her entire body shone, aquamarine, violet, chartreuse and magenta: an iridescent glitter in the sun. That moment, the two doves chose to fly out of arboreal shelter and into the open space, circling her head. She swanned a regal hand up to provide a perch and one actually touched down a fraction of a second, before shying off, encircling her head as she cooed back at it, and the two birds fluttered around before alighting on the fountain's edge. Alone, she half turned, still not seeing me in the pergola's obscurity, bent down as though in athletic stretch, lifted her hands high on either side, then let her entire frame collapse, as gradually, as silkily as her robe had a moment before, as she slowly slid onto the warm awaiting chaise.

I felt then as Actaeon must have, chancing upon Artemis bathing in Arcady's woods millennia ago: awestruck, gifted, aware I was

perceiving what no mortal must; overconsciously masculine; awkwardly invasive; human; non-natural, in comparison. I must have
stopped breathing, because when I began again I noticed my lungs,
could hear how labored my respiration was. While unaware of me,
Conchita sighed once, murmured surrender to the sun and in seconds was asleep.

I waited a longish time before picking my way out of the arbor
and quietly getting back to my room, afraid to be discovered, though
I'd done nothing amiss, not been where I shouldn't have. Once safely
indoors, what had seemed so stifling not long before was now
unambiguous warmth. I wasn't sexually aroused, but my nape hurt,
as though I'd slept at an odd angle and awakened with a stiff neck.

The combination of Conchita's appearance and Thom Dodge's
revelation had made me nervous, itchy, I couldn't stay still. So I quietly made my way out of the guest-bedroom suite along the hallway,
past where I knew but couldn't bring myself to stare at Conchita
asleep, upstairs into the library. Maybe a book would distract me.
The first one I laid eyes on was Aaron Axenfeld's very personal
essays and I thought, wait, he must know about Len Spurgeon. I
plopped myself in a chair behind Von Slyke's oversized desk, found
his number on the Rolodex and phoned.

It rang and rang, and I had almost despaired when he picked it
up. A cautious hello: he must have been bothered by telephone sales-
men, I thought. I began to identify myself, when I became aware that
the voice was continuing to speak: a machine-activated message. I
left as brief a message as I could, asking Axenfeld if he knew Len
Spurgeon and, if so, asking him exactly who Len was and what
Len's relationship to Jeff Weber was.

I got up, walked out of the library over to the stairs to where I
could peer out the dining room's high windows to the terrace, to see
if Conchita was still there. She was, flat on her back, the dark V
where her legs met her torso . . . The phone was ringing. Certain it
was Axenfeld calling back with something more concrete, more illu-
minating to tell me, I rushed to pick it up.

'Un-for-tu-nate-ly, I can't speak long nor give details.' It was Irian
St George, sounding very piqued. 'Waterford Machado and his proc-
tor have just posted his doctoral thesis topic, and I thought you'd
want to be amongst the very first to know.'

'Oh?' I replied, wondering what this had to do with me.

'Es-pec-i-al-ly,' St George continued, 'as, ex-as-per-at-ing-ly, the topic is more or less up your chosen *al-lée*!'

'Oh?' I stupidly repeated.

'In fact, the title is "The Re-if-ic-at-ion of the Non-nor-ma-tive: An In-no-va-tive Ap-proach to the Purple Circle". Machado claims to have new Purple Circle material. "New and unpublished primary sources," he noted.'

'Meaning what exactly?'

'Un-for-tun-ate-ly he provided no details, and his advisor ev-id-ent-ly thought not to ask for their inclusion.'

St George sounded amused, which naturally irritated me.

'That gives no idea,' I said. 'It could mean anything! What do you think he's found? Isn't everything the Purple Circle has written already published or catalogued?'

'The dead ones, yes. Pretty much everything. But even my own bit of heaven and trib-u-lat-ion – I mean, of course, Dominic De Petrie – has never chosen to release everything he's written.'

'You mean he tells you he's holding back material?'

'He hints. He prevaricates. He works in great looping figure eights around poor un-sus-pect-ing me. On purpose, I believe. For example, De Petrie has, on more than one oc-cas-ion, released three or four volumes of his journal autographs to the Timrod Collection. Generally it's some months before I receive their Purple Circle Catalogue update and appendix and discover his de-lic-ious per-fi-dy.'

'Maybe he does it for the money?'

'Nat-ur-al-ly, that would be his own ex-plan-at-ion. Dis-in-gen-u-ous in the extreme!' St George sighed. 'On the brighter side, as Machado is not currently sorting out Damon Von Slyke's papers,' St George said, stating the obvious, 'I feel confident in strongly doubt-ing his discovery is the same as what you have found. It's probably something quite minor. Some unknown letters between the Purples perhaps.'

I wasn't ready to let it go yet. 'Even so!'

'Even so it na-tu-ral-ly adds pressure on poor you,' St George sym-pathized. 'But then again, stress is not an entirely unknown sensation among these Pierian groves, is it? Must run.' St George signed off.

'Pierian groves, my ass!' I commented to the walls. But on top of everything else, nevertheless, the phone call had managed to ruin my day.

Once past the tunnel into Contra Costa County the scenery turned almost rural. There were unexpectedly high hills through which I occasionally made out spots of blue from three surrounding reservoirs. I felt like I'd been driving most of the day. In truth it had been more than six hours up through central California from Los Angeles, with another half-hour negotiating San Francisco's urban nightmare of traffic, with a short break while I settled my bags with the concierge at my brother-in-law's fancy apartment building, then almost another hour out of the city's bad-dream traffic and directly west, across the Bay Bridge and into the East Bay area, passing around Oakland and Berkeley. The Orinda Valley I was now driving through wasn't much, but what I could make out of the next two large canyons, Bear Creek and Happy Valley, showed they seemed to retain a bit of original forest. The highway narrowed, and after some dips and rises through a narrow pass I arrived at where it divided, north and south. Walnut Creek, once a 'bedroom community' of San Francisco and Oakland, now its own thriving town, lay dead ahead. I got off where I'd been directed and followed a widely curving main road to another curved road and another and another and another, always headed left, as though in some great maze, until I arrived at my destination.

Oak Grove Estates proved to be a sizable, much-wooded and landscaped private neighborhood, gated with entry post, two armed guards, a sign-in logbook and a good-for-twenty-four-hours electronic decal slapped on the car's windshield. Inside the park were swan ponds, tennis courts and a small 'village' including shops surrounding an administration building, and as I checked the map handed out to me when I entered and drove on, a handful of cedar-sided, enormous-windowed, oddly shaped, Gehry School, two-, three- and four-story *Architectural Digest* houses scattered here and there along the road, each 'sited' and obviously designed to be unique.

Thom Dodge's place sat atop a soft hill surrounded by lawns, one and a half stories tall, a bit less of an architectural 'statement' than its neighbors (most of them hidden from view) yet unquestionably expensive. Definitely not the kind of place an Air Force officer of his rank should be able to afford. I immediately wondered how much money used to buy it came from royalties of his brother's books and concluded most, if not all.

That financial success was one aspect of the Mark Dodge legend. He'd been a golden boy: golden in looks, golden in love, golden in finances, but especially golden in his career and reputation. Which was why, when he'd shown the first symptoms of AIDS, been hospitalized, almost died twice from pneumocystis, recovered twice, rapidly worsened and then did die, so many people had been shocked to their core.

Not merely the other members of the Purple Circle, not merely members of what there was then of the gay literary community, not merely the literary world, but anyone who knew Mark, had read him, or even read of him – since by the 1984 publication of *We All Drive Fords*, articles and interviews had begun flowing. His *New York Times* obituary was an unprecedented four columns across and six inches down, with a photograph: a first for someone openly gay and not yet thirty-seven years old.

Hundreds of mourners had flocked to his Manhattan memorial service, had stood in the rain outside the funeral home. Scores had met his body at the Oakland Amtrak station when it arrived on the West Coast and hundreds had attended the East Bay burial. Later the day of the funeral, one poor soul, claiming to have been one of Mark Dodge's lovers and himself suffering from AIDS dementia, threw himself out the window of the TransAmerica building in downtown San Francisco. Another half-dozen suicide attempts ensued on both coasts, directly attributable to Dodge's death: five gay men and a woman.

Gay politicians still struggling to get the word out on the disease had immediately grasped the advantage of Mark Dodge's very public tragedy, and instantly adopted him as a posthumous Poster Child for the illness. In its first five years of existence, the foundation named after Mark Dodge raised more money faster than any other AIDS organization.

Given the enormous amount of extra-literary attention attached to his work, it was surprising how well Mark Dodge's published writing had stood the test of time. All three of his novels had remained in print since their first publication. The American trade paperback of *Keep Frozen* was by now in its twenty-eighth printing, and also available in a lesbian and gay book series from a book club. *We All Drive Fords* had been an international seller since it had come out, not only in the US but also in Britain, France, Germany, Israel and Japan. His first novel, *Buffalo Nickel*, which was not overtly gay, had been published thirty years ago and was now on reading lists at a score of American universities, including two I'd attended. Unlike Jeff Weber, Mark had lived off his writing from the beginning. Advances, royalties, grants, awards, foreign sales, paperbacks, film options, all had brought it in. It was almost twenty years since he'd died and no diminution of his reputation had occurred, but instead a rather steady line.

I'd myself concluded that Dodge's reputation remained high because he had adroitly limited his books to easily identifiable subject matter. For his debut work, *Buffalo Nickel*, published when he was barely a youth himself, he'd written about the high-school graduation year of four members of a teenaged brass band in a rural-changing-to-suburban setting in central California. Those same kids grown up, returning to the town with families of their own, or having remained there, was the subject of *We All Drive Fords*, his last novel, published nearly a decade later. The title derived from the words written on the doors of the gigantic auto plant which dominated the town they lived in and which had in one way or another become connected to all of their fates. In between the two was *Keep Frozen*, Dodge's artlessly masterful tale of a talented young man from the provinces moving to the big city to become an artist in the late 1960s, a book that delighted straight and gay readers with its deliciously eccentric cast of characters and their madcap lives the protagonist moves in and out of and finally becomes a part of.

Another reason for Dodge's continued popularity was his writing itself. It was never as obviously 'styled' as, say, Axenfeld's or Powers's, never drew attention to itself as Etheridge's and Von Slyke's writing invariably did. It was quiet and precise but never prosaic. Of the Purple Circle members, perhaps only De Petrie could write so 'down'. But unlike De Petrie, with Dodge it wasn't a sign of an author wielding yet another aspect of his astonishing versatility;

it was the only style Dodge possessed, and luckily one perfectly wed to the material.

Mark Dodge's poignancy was nearly not present. His humor was so lightly touched as to be almost evanescent. Yet one didn't come away from the books with the sense he'd reined himself in, calculated that 'restraint' that so many minimalist reviewers had demanded of 1970s and 1980s work before it could be considered literary – and which now dated it so much. It was simply how a boy growing up on a farm overlooking the vast inland sea of the San Francisco Bay would think, would write.

'Not so much major or minor, as perfect,' Irian St George had summed up Mark Dodge's work in his study of Dominic De Petrie, 'with the perfection of a classical odist or pastoral eclogist, not an epic singer of wars and dynasties, nations and heroes. Hesiod rather than Homer.'

Reuben Weatherbury had put it another way. 'When we read De Petrie or Von Slyke, we're lost in admiration and quite often in wonder,' he had written in his intro to the first volume of the *Purple Circle Reader*. 'When we read Dodge, we want to phone him, invite him for a Pepsi and a game of checkers.'

Fleming's study had wondered if 'Dodge's nearly monochromatic gouaches could survive the ultimate competition of time from his more brilliant fellows' murals'. A question I'd answer somewhat in the negative, never having been taken with any of Dodge's novels as many other readers had. While Cummings – concerned with the psychology of the Nine's art – put it biographically: 'It's as though Mark Dodge consciously used language to put himself on a more equal footing with the others; as though he wished to tamp down with words, to modify with sentence structure, the lavish physical gifts he'd received, so he'd be on the same plane. An impossibility, of course.' Cummings had concluded, 'In any group photo one sees Mark Dodge instantly, the eye is drawn, even decades later. So imagine how very much it was drawn when Dodge was still alive.'

Cummings had written of the resonating effect of Dodge's death on his family. Robert Dodge, his father, already suffering from cancer, died six weeks later. Anthea, Mark's mother, followed a year after. The two brothers' lives had both gone into tailspins: Thom divorced and requested a transfer to an overseas posting, from which he'd returned a few years ago. Peter abandoned his wife and children, became a homeless alcoholic, wandering southern California's many beach towns. He'd only just recently gotten back on his feet, partly due to the continued earnings of his brother's books. The self-deprecating, easy to get along with, astonishingly handsome Mark Dodge had turned out not to be the 'interior alien, the outsider who only, and falsely, looked and spoke and acted like the insiders' he had always thought he was and had so often written about. Instead, and all unknowing, he'd been the center around which a half-dozen other lives revolved, upon which in fact they depended. With the stability of his existence gone, the others had crashed, and taken a very long while to recover.

This house, the Mercedes roadster and Mini van in the driveway, the children's bikes thrown slapdash against a retaining wall, the pointed prow of a powder-blue ketch half in a shed, were the most material manifestations of that.

I parked by the bikes and ascended the slate steps embedded in the perfect lawn up to the front door, a slab of burled oak and frosted glass. Paper fluttering in the breeze read: 'I'm in back. In the garden or in the hothouse.'

Both garden and hothouse were unexpectedly large, both were filled with roses. The garden was more like an aboretum for roses. Rows of rose bushes, squares of them, circles within landscaped circles of them, in every size and color possible, on the pathways, along the sides of the house, dropping down a hill, rising up behind a toolshed, surrounding the hothouse itself, three-quarters open. Thom Dodge was wearing huge canvas gloves and a darkly soiled canvas apron over a big T-shirt and stained cargo shorts. He waved a trowel to get my attention. I waved back, threading through thorny-looking tea roses toward him.

'You don't want to shake,' he assured me. 'I'm even dirtier inside the gloves.'

'English tea roses?' I pointed to those behind me.

'Not bad! Actually they're New Delhi's. Based on the English ones. Don't tell me you know roses?'

'A very little. A woman friend gardened.'

'My passion,' he said simply. He nodded toward a shelf on which a dozen minuscule pots each held a single fragile cutting. 'Those are my newest obsession: Andes White. Allegedly first grown by Incas to keep animals out of their cocoa-tree groves. Thorns sharp as shark teeth.'

Explaining the industrial-strength apron and gloves.

'I've got no signs. But I've planted the following: Ring Red, Lucille Balls, Amazing, Ultra-Brites, Tawny, Nightshade Black, Tantalus, Wing of White, Tom-Tom, Shaggy Pink and of course American Beauties. Among the tea roses, dozens more.' He bent to a lower shelf and came up with two beers. I nodded sure, and he popped them open and handed me one. 'The hell of it all is, until five years ago, I never looked at a flower. I'd buy roses for my wife on her birthday. But I never saw the things. Never even smelled one. Then coupla' years ago, when I was posted in Oahu, I was put into a cottage formerly occupied by another officer, with a rose garden already in place out back. Little Hawaiian fellow came to tend them, got to talking about them, showing them to me, naming them. They were like kids to him. Or big-league batters. Must have been the sun, 'cause I got hooked. And once I came back and moved here, well, hell, the place turned out to be perfect for ninety-eight varieties.'

It was Mark Dodge's voice Thom was speaking in, the big broad steady baritone with its inflections like curled-up edges you can hear in the few tapes Mark made of chapters from *Buffalo Nickel* and the talking book of *We All Drive Fords*. As for looks, well, as Thom Dodge would say, 'Hell, they might as well be twins.' Had he lived to the age of fifty-five, which is what I guessed Thom to be, Mark might have been slimmer; he'd still be wide-shouldered and thick-necked, with a long torso and flat hips, well-muscled arms and Sequoia trunk legs. At thirty-two, Mark had been six foot one, weighed 190 pounds, had thick dandelion-yellow hair that whitened in strong sun. He'd probably lighten up along the sides with sketches of gray like Thom had, lose hair at the brow but more at the temples, so the central shock formed a widow's peak. Being gay, Mark would have avoided his brother's beer-gut. But his eyebrows would have shagged up like these, his nose thickened, his skin developed freckles, his brow furrowed twice horizontally, webs of crow's feet detailed his eyes, vertical cuts guarded his thin upper and full lower lip.

Mark Dodge's eyes had been blue, so dark they read black in photos: 'Magnetic, dangerous, enameled eyes,' De Petrie had written in his journals, 'like lakes brooding in the shell of a not quite extinct volcano, so cool, and so capable of being turned into flaming steam at any second'. At the end of their brief affair, De Petrie had written of Mark Dodge's 'Olympian fury' and how Dominic had to put his hands in front of his face so as not to be 'burned to the soul by the electrocuting Dodge eyes'. Mark's younger brother's eyes were brown, but I guessed they could become equally hard.

'Queen Elizabeth,' Thom Dodge said, identifying the variety, a close-fitted purple-red flower, as he passed a pot on the trestle table between us. He'd knock the side of each ceramic pot with the trowel to loosen soil, grab the plant where it entered the dirt, pull it onto the table, vigorously shake dirt off its roots, inspect it, then, satisfied, twist it with a gloved index finger and drive it into an awaiting pot, refill it with dirt, soak with water, move to the next. He did this a dozen times while we talked.

'Now, I don't know you, except what you've told me about yourself. And you don't know me, except about what I've told you,' Thom Dodge began. I nodded agreement, although I knew a lot about him from books about his brother I'd read. 'So don't be offended by anything I say. You with me?'

Not knowing where he was going, I said sure.

'You have brothers? No? I had two. And I was youngest. Peter and Mark and Thomas. The three apostles they called us in Sunday School. Two years apart. Enough years to lead separate lives. Yet close enough to do everything together. That's how it was, growing up. Not far from here, by the way. Elizabeth Taylor,' he interrupted himself to identify the tiny amethyst bloom, the same hue as the septuagenarian movie star's eyes. 'We did everything, went through everything a child or teenage boy could, if not together, then almost together. School, illnesses, fights, drinking, sports, drugs, sex, girls. Grandpa Dodge used to say we pissed in a row. Pete was the boss, Mark was the brains, I was the baby.'

'Baron Girod de l'Ain,' he identified the next plant, which had large blood-red flowers with white edging. 'Our folks had a farm. But it was a big place, with paid help. So while we had chores, they didn't mean for us to be farmers. They encouraged us in school to aim for college and the professions. Pete was going to be a doctor, Mark a lawyer, me an Indian chief – businessman.

'By the time Pete was fourteen, Mark twelve, me ten, it was clear we needed more spending money than we got for farm chores. It was Mark's idea to pool our money and go into business. We unofficially formed Dodge Brothers Inc. Eleven dollars started our first enterprise, selling pumpkins. We bought a patch our neighbor Howell was planning to feed to hogs but mostly let rot. Pure profit for him. We put 'em all in two wheelbarrows and dragged them out to where Highway 80 met San Pablo Avenue on a Saturday morning two weeks before Hallowe'en and put up a big sign, "Pumpkins Ten Cents a Pound". With Dad's borrowed scale. Made twenty-five dollars that weekend. Thirty the next. And fifteen more the two school week evenings before the holiday.

'Seventy bucks!' Thom Dodge exclaimed. 'Big money to a ten-year-old in 1960 I can tell you. We put aside half and spent the rest on crap. This is French too, Charm of Paris,' he identified the next plant, its petals flat yet tightly budded, pale pink streaked white. 'Day after Thanksgiving, Mark looks at Pete and me and says, "Christmas Trees"! This time we gotta go chop 'em down, even though they cost nothing. Then we have to get a truck. We rent one of our Dad's for five dollars, give a sixteen-year-old neighbor five dollars to drive it back and forth to a better corner of the crossroads than before, and set up. Big sign, "Xmas Trees Five and Ten Dollars". We make 300 dollars that Christmas.

'And so it goes. We sell lilies for Easter, assorted flowers at Mother's Day. We sell watermelons throughout summer and tomato plants in July. Then Hallowe'en and pumpkins, Christmas and trees, and we cycle all over again. By the time I'm thirteen years old, Dodge Brothers Inc. has earned maybe six grand. Pete's got one more year in high school and thinks maybe he shouldn't go to the local state college but stay around the farm and turn Dodge Brothers Inc. into a real business. I'm all for it. But Mark, who's fifteen and, let's face it, the brains of the business and does the accounting and pricing and banking, he says no.

'No!' Thom Dodge repeats, showing me a deep-carmine, small, close-petaled flower with lilac fragrance. 'Another Frenchy, called Gloire de Ducher,' he says. 'No!' he repeats yet again. 'And why not? Because Mark has discovered a book. One of a score or so books hanging around in our family's parlor bookshelf – no one ever really figured how they'd been put there, whether as gifts or merely hand-me-downs from our parents and their siblings. Most of the books we know fairly well, as they are typical children's books, *The Jungle Book*, *The Arabian Nights' Tales*, *Black Beauty*, *Tom Sawyer*, *Swiss Family Robinson*. But a few are grown-up books, about medicine, sewing patterns, cooking receipts, farm animal husbandry and agricultural machinery. Naturally there's a big old Bible. And then a half-dozen or so Reader's Digest condensed novels my mother had picked up in an auction and likes to reread on winter's nights.

'But this one's different. This one is oversized with sharp-edged binding in swirling dark blues and blacks, and inside it are dark and brilliant watercolored illustrations we're fascinated by and at the same time we can hardly figure them out. Intriguing sure, but from the opening paragraph it doesn't draw you in, but pushes you away again, since it contains so many long, incomprehensible words, words it would take me another dozen years to understand, but which somehow Mark already knows or is curious enough to look up. He tells us about the book, me and Pete, on more than one occasion, since he reads it again and again. Not for the story, he tells us, but for what he calls the power of the story-telling: the craft and art of the writing. The book is all about sailors and a great storm at sea. It's not until years later that I finally am able to get to it and read it through and I enjoy it, I suppose. But I never see what Mark sees in that book. By the way, it was Joseph Conrad's *Typhoon*. What I read between those two covers is just a sea story. But Mark, he reads his future in that book. And as a result of that book, he's decided he's not going to be a lawyer, or a businessman. He's going to be a writer. He's going to college, but not up to Sacramento or even San Francisco. No, Mark is planning to go East, to some school in New Jersey or Massachusetts. Jasper's Mixed,' he identifies the next one, moving faster now that he's all het up.

'So Dodge Brothers Inc. has only a few more years in business. Our best ever. Pete goes up to State U. Mark and I do the fall and spring part of it, while Pete helps us in the summertime and at Christmas holidays. It turns out Pete's not nuts about college or his possibilities after college. So he's supporting me in trying to convince Mark to stay nearby and keep the firm going. For a while we think our arguments are working.

'Madame X,' he identifies the next, svelte purple-black rose, almost more bud than flower. 'We've already made about ten grand by now. But something else happens. One day Mark comes home from school and says at dinner that he's not only been selected most popular of the senior class, and Prom King, and Most Likely to Succeed, which we all sort of expected, but on top of that a teacher has sent a photo of him to someone she knows at that fancy clothing store in San Francisco, Wilkes-Bashford, and they want Mark to come down to Union Square and be photographed for their next catalogue. He'll be modeling four hours a day for two weeks and earn – are you ready? – 8,000 dollars! Clearly Dodge Brothers Inc. is doomed!

'Picasso,' he somewhat dejectedly identifies the next bloom, an open-hearted scarlet flower with pale yellow at the sepal. 'What we haven't noticed, not any of us in the family is that while we weren't looking, our regular-as-all-hell brother has become special: he's now something none of us could have ever expected. Cathy Grinstead confirms this next day in school when I tell her about Mark's offer from Wilkes. "Oh! Every girl in the county knows your brother," she tells me. "The beautiful Mark Dodge." Up till then I thought only women could be beautiful. And when I look at Mark, he's, well, he's just Mark. But a few months later, when I'm looking at that Wilkes-Bashford catalogue, there he is, my brother Mark, on every other page, wearing tuxedos and bathing suits and you know what? They're right, he's beautiful! He's fucking beautiful!'

Thom is almost in tears. 'Double Delight,' he identifies a white-petaled rose within a carmine one. 'From that minute on, my brother's lost to me, lost to us, lost to himself, I don't know . . . Maybe the word I'm looking for is cursed, if that isn't melodramatic. It gets worse. It turns out that not only is my brother a successful model, he's also a talented writer. All that scribbling he's been doing up in his room when we're trying to drag him out for fun pays off big. He gets offers from Harvard and Yale and in fact every school he's ever dreamed of applying to, not based on his grades, which were a little better than average, but on the basis of the stories and the essays he's already published in the school magazine and local newspaper.

'One day Mark is there, the next he's gone, really gone, physically gone. Dodge Brothers Inc. is nearly over. For one more winter and spring I keep it going alone. When Mark finishes college that first year, he doesn't come home to us for the summer to help me and Pete out. Mark stays on, taking extra-credit summer courses. Same thing the following year, and the following. It gets so we see him at Christmas and Fourth of July, Ma's birthday. Then he's graduated from college and now we see Mark in clothing catalogues, in full-page magazine ads, and finally on sportswear billboards when we're in some big town. He's already published two short stories in real magazines by the time he's out of college, and won some literary award, and a year later he's living in Manhattan and has a book contract.

'Ice Berg,' he identifies the large, loose-petaled white rose. 'Mark sends a check covering my first year's college tuition and expenses. And the second year's worth too. But the next time I actually lay eyes on my brother, it's years later. Not on the farm, but in San Francisco. In a coffee shop in North Beach. I'm indoors with some schoolfriends, and there's a commotion outside, then these two guys come in with their arms around each other. One of them is this Giants pitcher whose photo was just in the sports section of all the papers because he'd relieved and saved the season opener and the other is this famous young author in town on a book tour for his best-selling novel. And they're handsome, and happy together, glowing, and everybody wants to meet them, and be with them, and know them. Everyone but me. I hide so they won't see me. When our group decides to leave, I go out the back way.

'Saint Patrick.' Its flowers thickly clustered, satiny yellow, with a strong perfume. 'It wasn't that I was ashamed of him so much, you understand, though I could never for the life of me figure out how Mark could have become homosexual with girls crawling over him. Pete and I shook our heads over that for years, asking each other, did he ever touch you? No. Did you see that coming? No! Did you? But, hell, it didn't mean our brother was some pansy. I mean, he was going out with athletes, guys we rooted for at Candlestick Park.

'No, the reason I didn't let him see me then – or in fact ever again – is more that I was afraid that if I claimed any kind of relationship to Mark he'd have to somehow explain me. And what could he possibly say? That he used to help me do my division problems and teach me how to brush my teeth the "Army way"? That we'd talk in bed for hours on end as kids those long sweaty August nights when the three of us couldn't get to sleep. Or that we'd hold belching contests, and he'd crack his toebones a half-hour at a time 'cause he knew I hated the sound and that he'd steal my blankets in the winter and try to frighten me by jumping out at me from behind rocks and bushes and bedroom doors? Once my brother left to go to San Francisco to become a model, it was as though he'd stepped onto a different planet, or maybe a better way to put it is into a different dimension, parallel to ours, touching it at a few points, but nothing more. He never really ever came back. Not even when he was stuffed in that coffin on that Amtrak baggage car.'

Thom starts repotting the last rose bush. 'At any rate, that's what I wanted to say. To say to someone who'd understand. There's no one around here who . . . I had a hunch you might . . . Mischief!' Thom identifies the last sexy, perfectly shaped, pink-red rose cutting as he puts it aside, and cleans off his gloves and takes off his apron. 'Now I guess you want to look at those manuscripts.'

The first thing I noticed about the ten-page manuscript was that it had been typed on a different machine than what I found in Von Slyke's house, and different than the IBM Selectric Elite of Jeff Weber's. This typeface was square, sans-serif, so the lower case g and q were dropped halflines, not curved tails.

'It looks like a foreign typewriter was used,' I said.

'Mark's electric Olivetti,' Thom Dodge confirms. 'He bought it with money from that first modeling job. I still have it around here somewhere. He replaced it with a computer a year before he died. Virtually everything he wrote except the final draft of *We All Drive Fords* was done on that Olivetti. It was low and flat, and pale green, the color of olives they put in Martinis. Only other time I saw a machine like his was in some museum: "Masterpieces of Modern Design" was the exhibit. Leave it to Mark to be in style!'

We had moved indoors, to an office on the lower floor of the house open to backyard and rose garden, but apart from the three-car garage by what used to be called a 'mud room', which was where Thom kept rain gear and garden clothing. In the back of a large, well-framed, amateurish painting of (what else?) a rose garden was a sizable wall safe, and within that, in a metal box, Thom kept copies of his brother's published manuscripts, as well as originals of what he'd not sent off to the collection.

This latter consisted, Thom informed me, of personal letters to the family, manuscripts of Mark's early local writing, and less than a handful of short fragments Thom had found in the boxes of his brother's clothing and household goods that had been shipped from his Manhattan apartment after he'd died. All the other stories Mark had written and published were eventually put into his novels, of which they had formed an inextricable part, naturally enough given how 'organically' Dodge wrote.

Across the manuscript top, it read 'For LS'.

Before my mind could take the next leap to whom 'LS' might be, I looked over the first manuscript, which word for word followed the piece about the two kids in the car I'd read before. Then, without a break, on the very next page, the following:

The deep electric blue of the jukebox is the same flashing cobalt of spotlighted metallic wreath hanging over the head of the bartender at the Eagle's Nest. It is also the same deep neon blue of the tight-fitting T-shirt on the raven-haired number Paul has been cruising for the last hour and a half. It's three-fifteen a.m., Christmas Eve, and Paul does not want to go home alone.

It doesn't seem as though the number is ready to leave, however. Now he's talking to friends who've just come into the Nest. The bar is otherwise pretty empty: or just as bad as empty as far as Paul is concerned, since he's either balled with, rejected, or been rejected by everyone else in the place who even vaguely interests him. Paul's a little high from the six Budweisers he's put down since his arrival – with help from two quarters of a Quaalude in between to keep his act calm.

Paul is twenty-six years old and has been living in New York City for two years. He works for a paperback reprint house where he's employed in what's called 'middle management', doing market research – a job he doesn't like and was not hired for originally back in Sacramento. There, when he signed a contract with the employment scout for the publishing house, he thought he'd finally be getting to do something his university studies had prepared him for: editing new books.

Like everything else in his recent life, the job turned out to be delusory and disappointing. Paul's found it hard meeting men in New York; found it equally hard making friends, found it especially difficult getting used to the high-energy activity level and inbred elitist social life of the gays he's met so far. But here at the Eagle's Nest – at least – he can be more himself, more relaxed, slower, more mellow, even if he has to calm down with a Q now and then. Not that it seems to be helping much tonight.

The raven-haired number's friends go to the pool table, chalking their names up on the board for what will probably be the last game of the night. The number looks toward Paul, and Paul makes his move.

His opening line is banal, but so what? An interesting line would only chase the number away. The guy responds with an equally banal follow-up. It's all a code anyway, Paul knows, although he's not always a hundred percent sure he knows what the code is or how exactly it works. They stare at each other, checking out each other's bodies, chests, crotches, etc. then away again. Paul asks how the number's drink is (fine!); says it's slow in the Nest tonight (the number agrees); even goes so far as to compare the number's shirt to the wreath – an offhand compliment that seems to go down nicely (at least the number doesn't look startled and instantly move away). But the chemistry between them is off, and they know it.

So after a few minutes of conversational leads from both ends that go nowhere, the number says 'See you!' meaning more than likely never again, and he saunters over to the pool table to his friends. And that's that. Another connection that never happened.

Paul splits the place. Not even anyone out on West Street in front of the Nest. Cabs waiting, however. A line of them. They know the place will close in a half an hour. Paul stands for a minute, wondering whether he ought to check out Spike

Bar on the next block, or even the Ramrod down in the
Village. There's always the baths, or the Mineshaft: they'll go
on all night, Christmas or not. But it's not sex Paul wants
tonight, it's companionship. And the chances of finding that
in the Tubs or down on his hands and knees on a urine-
stained floor aren't promising.

He gets into the first cab in the line. He doesn't even see
who the driver is until he's halfway home, uptown, along
deserted Tenth Avenue. That's when the cabby stops for a red
light, slides open the little window separating driver and passenger and says something Paul has to lean forward to make
out.

The driver, he sees, is fiftyish, middle-aged, gone to fat,
with a scruffy graying black beard and glasses. Somebody's
father or uncle working a second job for extra income.

'No luck in the Nest?' the driver asks, in a surprisingly
high-pitched voice.

Now Paul wonders if the cabby may be gay himself, or if
not, just making conversation to ensure himself of a tip. 'No,'
he answers.

The light goes green, but there's no other traffic visible
coming or going on the avenue. So the cab remains stationary. The driver suddenly flips on the inside lights so Paul can
see better, and with one hand, the cabby gestures for Paul to
look at something on the front seat. At first Paul doesn't see
anything special. Then he sees: the cabby is holding a fat
hard-on he's taken out his pants, slapping it against the lower
rim of the steering wheel.

'Wanna swing on this a while? I'll pull into a side street.'

Before Paul completely understands what the driver has
said, the cabbie adds, 'It'll pay for your ride home.'

Now Paul understands. And Paul wants to scream. He
wants to just let it all out and holler for all he's worth.
Instead he manages to say, 'No, thanks!' and falls back, away
from the middle window, against the seat. He half wonders if
the cabbie is a psycho and should he get right out here, now.
But what's the chances of finding a cab on Tenth Avenue and
49th Street at this hour of the night? So instead, Paul pops

the last portion of Quaalude he's been holding into his mouth, and looks out the side windows.

When they arrive at Paul's address, the cabbie says, 'Hey, man! No hard feelings?'

'No hard feelings!' Paul echoes him, hurriedly stuffing the fare and a tip into the change box between them.

'I'll go back down to the Nest now,' the driver goes on, in what Paul could only call a leering voice. 'And I'll find me a taker there tonight. You'll see. Never fails. Hey! Thanks! Merry Christmas!'

Paul gets into the building foyer just as the Quaalude really hits him. He gets through the glass doors in time to see the taxi hang a U-turn and drive off. Paul drags himself over to the elevator, spaces out waiting for it to arrive, finally climbs in, gets out at his floor. He manages to fumble his keys into the apartment locks. Entering, he drops his leather coat on the floor, half kicks off his boots, and falls head first onto his bed, more or less fully clothed.

Better than last year, Paul has a few moments to think. Last Christmas, Paul passed out at an orgy in a complete stranger's house. Jesus! How he hates the holidays. Maybe with this Q he'll be able to sleep straight through Christmas Day.

'See what I mean?' Thom Dodge said. 'It's just a fragment. At first I thought it was part of something larger. You know, like a depressing version of that gay book he did.'

'You're sure it's your brother's writing?' I asked.

'Hell! I don't know! You're the expert. I was hoping you'd tell me who wrote it.'

Instead I hit him with a question. 'What your brother wrote here, what do you think this means?'

Thom shrugged.

'Well, you want my opinion?' I asked.

'I'm listening.'

'I think "LS" is Len Spurgeon. And I think Len Spurgeon wrote this. You ever hear of Len Spurgeon?' I asked.

No response.

THE DODGE BROTHERS INC.   135

'Bobbie Bonaventura, Jeff Weber's executor and girlfriend, told me that Jeff and the other members of the Purple Circle met Len through your brother. Mark knew Len before any of them did.'

Thom Dodge shrugged again, then he looked out the window. 'Then maybe it's a good thing I didn't send this off to the Timrod Collection. You still want a copy?'

I told him yes and tried again, 'Who do you think "LS" is?'

'Damned if I know.' He got up and went to a big floor-standing model of a photocopy machine from the 1980s. 'I told you before, I never had anything to do with Mark's gay . . . life. And he kept it all away from us. Here you go.'

Outside the house, kids had gathered. Maybe eight or nine of them. Among them are two of Thom's that he called indoors as I got back into my Celica and drove off.

As I approached the long involved highway corridors a mile from the Oakland Bay Bridge, I suddenly flashed on something that had been tugging just below my subconscious for maybe a half-hour since I'd seen what was written on the manuscript. That note on the yellow foolscap pad I found in Von Slyke's bedside drawer when he had me looking for his lover's telephone address book, the note Von Slyke had written to Dominic De Petrie. I'd have to check it when I got back to Hollywood, but I was sure Von Slyke was writing about me when he'd written to De Petrie that he thought that I looked like L. Meaning that coming across the lawn toward him, I had reminded Von Slyke of L. In other words, I'd reminded Von Slyke of Len Spurgeon. Something made me feel sure of it. Why was that? Whatever the reason, it meant that Len *had* to be the key. Bobbie said they all knew Len. How possible was it that Thom hadn't even heard his name?

From the wrap-around dining-room windows of the penthouse triplex I could see straight ahead to the Golden Gate Bridge, down and ahead, quarter of a mile away. This early evening it appeared to be less a practically usable traffic span than a gigantic pale pink erector set fantastically floating atop the huge field of mist that filled the strait. The mist completely hid the freeway I knew was down below, as well as the toll station, Fort Point, and the strip of park along the shore. Across, where gigantic stone bulwarks seemed to rest on little but smoke, I could make out a few distant stained-brown splotches representing hints of the opposite shore: Fort Baker and, beyond it, the now brown hills of Golden State National Park.

This twenty-story condo, consisting of ten- and twelve-room apartments with 180-degree terraces, had been put up at the spot on Lincoln Boulevard where it would provide the most picturesque views in all of what had been the military installation called the Presidio a few years ago. Naturally, Mr and Mrs Bart Vanuzzi had been given their choice before anyone else. Equally naturally, the residence of the quarterback, the Bay Area's consistently best, and best-known, since the palmy days of the legendary Joe Montana, had drawn in other celebrities, CEOs and assorted high-rollers.

The athletic paragon himself was sitting across the glass-topped table, dressed in a pale yellow crew-neck jersey jogging suit delicately picking at his third steak of the meal, only just delivered by the younger of my two sisters, who had then settled herself not at the table with us but instead in front of the silent but lighted sixty-inch TV, chewing on a celery stick, staring not so much at the screen as seemingly anywhere else but: at us; at two magazines spread on the coffee-table and occasionally out at the spectacular combination of deep sunset and fog.

'You ought to eat more meat,' Bart commanded. Since the day we had met a decade ago, my brother-in-law spoke to me in commands and orders. 'You need more protein!' he added.

'So I can grow up big and strong like you?'

'Boys!' Judy casually warned, used to our quarrels.

'You could do worse than look like me,' Bart concluded, without vanity. Then, 'So tell me,' he asked for the third time, 'what exactly are you doin' here?'

'I'm hunting down the authorship of a particular manuscript I found among the papers of the famous author Damon Von Slyke.'

'Yeah, and?'

'Yeah, and,' I echoed Bart, 'what I'm finding so far is that there are two well-known and one not at all known possible claimants to the piece. So tomorrow I'm seeing the niece and executor of Mitch Leo's estate, at Berkeley, in hopes that maybe she can clear it up for me. Or if not, maybe she'll shed light on this unknown guy.'

'So you're what,' Bart asked, 'a literary detective?'

Bart was by no means stupid, merely closed to just about everything in the universe but the things that interested him. I was
surprised by the new range this question implied.

'You've got it!'

'Sounds fascinating!' Judy said, crunching fiber. Unlike Bart, who
did seem to get bigger and stronger and even handsomer every time
I saw him in an almost cartoony black-curly-hair, five-o'clock-
shadow, generous-featured, dark-eyed, clear-skinned, Sicilian-
American way, my sister seemed to become thinner and frailer and
more ethereal. She'd been a constant eater as a teen, but had the
metabolism of a hummingbird and never gained weight. Now, in her
mid-thirties, the freshness of her prettiness was gone, replaced by
what to me seemed to be high-style elegance. And while she still
seemed to nibble a great deal, it wasn't ever meals, but rice cakes,
carrot sticks, celery stalks, Asian radishes: things that appeared to
have limited nutritive value.

When I'd mentioned this to Dr St George a while back, wondering if hers could possibly be a healthy diet, he'd smiled demurely
then suggested, 'Could it be all that fiber is needed to keep the anal
canal healthy, open and well lub-ri-cat-ed?' We'd both laughed at his
imputation, but I knew better. According to what they'd both hinted
at over the years, and what I'd seen of an amateur sex video of
theirs I'd happened upon the last time I visited, Bart Vanuzzi probably hadn't screwed his wife since their honeymoon. Their sex was
oral, him on his back watching porno movies, she going down on
him and masturbating herself, which seemed to satisfy both of them.

'So this is what? A big deal?' Bart asked.

'Could be.' When dealing with Vanuzzi, the safest route to avoid
withering contempt for anyone not as rich or successful as himself
was to downplay it.

'There are people who actually care about this?' was his next
question. See what I meant?

'Boys!' my sister warned.

It wasn't a bad question. 'Some people do. I care.'

'After hunting around, what's it worth?' he tried.

'Can't say. If it's what I'm looking for it could be worthwhile.
Maybe not so much in financial terms, but it could be the corner-
stone of my book about the Purple Circle. That could lead to me

getting the chair that's just opening up at UCLA, tenure, a house in Holmby Hills. You know.'

'The Purple Circle is that group of gay writers?' Bart asked. So he did listen when I talked. Or had Judy told him?

'Right, the ones who started gay literature. I'm living in one of their houses, getting his papers ready. This big library is buying them. And that's where I first I found it.'

He naturally asked, 'Buying them for how much?'

'I'm not privy to the amount. High six figures.'

That was sure to impress him. Bart tried another line of attack, 'So you're what? Putting out for this old gay?'

'Boys!' my sister warned again.

'Hey?' Bart defended himself. 'It's a natural question. Young guy all alone in a big house with a famous queer and all. Wha? You think I'd hold it against you?'

'He's in Europe. Just me and the housekeeper there.'

'That's different. Honest, Ross, you gotta eat meat!'

'I just ate a six-ounce porterhouse!'

'I saw. I mean, you know, you gotta eat red meat on your own. You can afford it, right?'

'If I can't, you'll keep me?'

'I'm not an old gay. If I did keep you, you'd have to put out regularly.'

'Boys!' my sister warned again.

'C'mon. We're havin' fun,' he said, delicately dissecting the potato with the precision of a brain surgeon. 'All the people you're seeing are queer?' he asked.

'No, and the funny thing is so far no one I've met in connection with this is. In fact the guy today, the brother of Mark Dodge . . .'

'I read Mark Dodge,' my sister interrupted, then asked, '*Buffalo Nickel*? Did he write that?'

'Sure did.'

'In college,' she mused. 'I loved that book.'

I now addressed her rather than Bart. 'Well, listen to this: Mark Dodge's brother is his heir and executor. Lives off the substantial money the books and rights still bring in. Has a big house, a boat, Mercedes. And you know what? He never talked to his brother once he found out he was gay – even though Mark had paid his younger brother's way through college. The brother kept going on to me about how as kids they had this two-bit roadside stand and how Mark ruined it, and ruined this guy's life by going off to Princeton to become a famous author. Like that's an excuse for him being such a bigot. Do you believe that?'

'Older people . . .' Judy began. 'You know, Ross, they're different.'

'Ross is right,' Bart unexpectedly piped up, between sips of his wine. 'If the guy hated his brother for being gay, he shouldn't take the money. He should give it to charity. Hell, I get gifts and things all the time from people and groups I don't care for. You know. It all goes directly to charity. Right, Jude?'

'You're sensible,' my sister said, and looked at him with that same dumb look of love I'd seen on her face when I was twelve years old and she first brought him home.

The phone rang and was automatically answered. Neither Mr nor Mrs Bart Vanuzzi had, to my knowledge, personally answered a phone in years, even if they were inches away when it rang, had nothing else to do and were dying to speak to the person on the other end. I had no concept what the source of this affectation might be and no one had ever thought to enlighten me. I listened to their brief message begin and was surprised to hear Thom Dodge's voice on the other end.

'Speaking of the devil,' I said, and stood to get it. At the receiver, I looked for some way to intercept his call. The receiver was Swedish, lightweight, all curves, no buttons anywhere, more a piece of sculpture than a usable mechanism. 'How do I break in?' I asked. Both of them shrugged. So I let Thom Dodge talk, telling me he had something else, important, to say to me, before he hung up.

'Maybe he's seen the error of his ways and decided to give you all his brother's royalties,' Bart said. For him that constituted sarcasm.

I took another sip of wine, walked to the suite where I was guesting, the one with a slightly less fantabulous – if this evening far clearer – view east toward Russian Hill and the Coit Tower – and dialed Thom Dodge back.

'I heard you,' I explained, 'I just couldn't figure out how to break in to speak to you. You said it was important?'

'I'm sorry you drove all the way out here for nothing.'

'It wasn't for nothing. You told me a great deal about your

brother that might be useful,' I fudged. 'And you gave me the other manuscript and . . .'

'Well, I don't know why I did it,' he interrupted. 'Maybe it was because you were right there and all, but . . . I have to say it, I wasn't completely forthcoming with you.'

'Oh?' I said, surprised by this turn.

'Remember I told you about having no contact with my brother Mark once he'd gone East? That wasn't true.'

I waited for him to say what was evidently very difficult for him to say.

'And remember you asked me about Len Spurgeon and I said I didn't know who he was. That wasn't true, either.'

Now I was waiting eagerly.

'You still there?' Thom asked.

'I'm still here.'

'What would you say if I told you there was a letter from Mark?' he asked.

'Yes, go on.'

'Only one letter. No more. And I never answered it. So he never wrote again. I got the letter a few days after I saw him in that coffee shop with that baseball player. It seems that Mark did notice me there after all, and he wrote to say he was hurt that I'd run out on him, as he put it, and not even stopped to meet his friend. He'd thought I'd be thrilled to meet a major leaguer and the only way he could figure it for himself was that I was too ashamed about them being so obviously and so publicly together, which he said he could sympathize with. Mark tried to explain to me what had happened, how it had come about that he and Len had met. I've got the letter here. I was too upset about it at the time, because it confirmed everything, and drove the wedge between us deeper. I haven't looked at it in years. I only did look at it again because of what you said today when you were here. And of course because I wanted to read it over and check the name of the baseball player.'

My head was swirling. 'The baseball player was named Len? Len Spurgeon?'

'That's right. He played two seasons for the Giants, then something or other happened to him, and he left the game. Come to think of it, maybe it was my brother Mark that happened to him. I never thought of that before! At any rate, I think you're an honest fellow, someone seeking the truth, and I wanted you to see what Mark wrote to explain himself. You have to understand that at the time it cut me deeply. I was young, just starting out in life, just twenty-three, twenty-four, and I didn't really understand what he'd written. Well, I understood the words well enough, I just couldn't understand what he could have meant by it. So I put it all away. The letter. Our brotherly love. All of it. For so long. My brother Mark was good to me. And how did I repay him? . . . Well, maybe now I can repay him. You have a fax machine there?'

They did and luckily I'd already learned how to use it.

'I think it may support your idea that someone other than my brother wrote the two pieces we looked at today. This letter really has Mark's voice the way I recall it and I'm no expert, you understand, but it doesn't seem to be the same as that excerpt you read.'

A few minutes later I received the two-page, handwritten letter. It was dated April 27th, 1974, and the opening paragraphs were exactly as Thom Dodge explained them. Then came the part that I suspected had 'cut deeply' into Thom and which he'd not understood then, and who knew, maybe still could not understand or accept now. Following Mark's line that he'd thought Thom would want to meet a major league baseball player, he went on to write:

Len Spurgeon and I met last October after the Conference playoff games he was out here to pitch for. It was at some party. The minute we looked at each other, I wanted to tear his clothing off him. I did so that night, in his hotel room. I ripped off his clothing but kept him wrapped in it, trapped in sleeves and buttons so I'd be free to kiss his face and neck and body, to lick his chest and front and legs, to suck and bite and tear at every single part of him, both evident and hidden from sight. Len has a taste that is part like those salt-water reeds we used to gather and suck on at the marsh edge but also like what wheat smells like in a barn after spring rains when it goes to black rust, drugging and maddening livestock with ergot.

That first night we spent hours with each other's bodies. I finally let him free, so he could do to me back what I'd done

to him. *I swear we were like animals in rut. We sucked and
fucked for maybe five, six hours, until our peckers and
mouths and assholes were rubbed hot and red and too sore to
touch anymore. Then we got into a bathtub together to cool
down and wouldn't you know instead we continued doing it
there until we fell asleep from exhaustion.*

*Thom, brother, I have had girls. You've seen 'em, you've
even seen me and Pete doing it to them, although you
thought you were completely hidden from view. And I've had
guys. Yeah, queer guys like I am. But I swear to you, I have
never had anyone or anything like this Len Spurgeon. He is
like heroin and LSD and grass and the best Scotch all rolled
into one. I can't get enough of him. I can't separate from him
one second but I don't ache all over needing him. And I can't
go to sleep at night or go to my typewriter unless the smell of
him is on my face and on my hands and in my hair. I'm glad
that he loves me for now and that he will stay close to me,
because if he didn't I swear I'd chain him, tie him, strap him
down. And if he got loose I'd follow him to the end of the
earth and bring him back and if he spit in my face and told
me he hated me, I'd kill the bastard and keep his rotting
corpse in my room so I could be with him always.*

*What I'm saying is, we kids never had any idea – any idea
AT ALL – that life could be this – thrilling . . . terrifying. I
will not ask your forgiveness or even your understanding but
merely say that I am doing what I want to, love to, must do.*

Book Four

THE LEO-MCKEWENS AT TEA, PART 1

He resembled an immense yacht that had seen more
extravagant days, that perhaps had been fractionally
stripped at one point and reappointed with less
enthusiasm—and a good deal less discretion.

Mitchell Leo, *After the Piano Recital*

TANYA CULL HAD MENTIONED TO me on the phone in a final aside that the university – although by no means specifically the Languages Department – had recently received bomb warnings and other related threats from nationalists of some Pacific island – an atoll vaguely related to some financial and scientific interests of the college – demanding their independence. This explained the surprising amount and depth of security around Sproull Square, the metal detectors at Sather Gate, as well as at each building's entrance, each of which now sported a white-armbanded guard, although in the school's tradition some of these security people looked as though they'd only a few days before been hawking nipple rings and tattoos to students and tourists a few yards away on Telegraph Avenue.

I was directed up the hill toward the tower, to what must have been the oldest building on campus, South Hall, a great Victorian object with dormer windows and a dozen chimneypots which looked out of place in the sun-struck East Bay but would have fit in nicely with the rounded hills and flat pastures of western Massachusetts. The sign on it read 'Library Sciences Annex', but that had another, handwritten sign partly atop it, with a stenciled hand pointed in another direction, thus completely confusing me. Tanya would probably not be in till later on, she had told me, but she did give me the name of a colleague, Janet Carstairs, in the next office, who would let me in.

As promised, Janet was in and got me cleared into the Languages building. She was waiting outside the elevator when it opened, a statuesque, dark-skinned Afro-American woman, still talking on a cellular phone as I got off. She signed off and closed the phone to warmly greet me.

'Sorry about all this,' she said referring to the security. 'The times we live in.'

I had the feeling she'd expected someone different, younger or older, or maybe less casually dressed, I couldn't be sure. I wanted to calm her down.

'At UCLA they would try to electronically decal everyone on campus. Right here –' pointing to my forehead.

'Sometimes Tanya and I wonder if America's universities are responsible for propping up every minor dictatorship in the world. She thought she'd be back by five.' Janet led the way, her heels striking the wooden floor like rifle reports.

She unlocked the office door and flipped on the lights, saying, 'Tanya said she left detailed instructions. If you need anything, just knock.'

Once inside Cull's office – one not much bigger or better furnished than those made available for instructors at UCLA, I noticed with satisfaction (although it had a great view of the Berkeley Tower) – I was directed by Tanya's notes to the computer terminal, and a tall file cabinet. Only one drawer was unlocked, marked 'Mitch Leo'. When I opened it, a sheet of instructions for its use lay on top.

All this is available on the computer screen. I trust you know Windows 100. You may access first lines, paragraphs etc. by striking MITCH:MSS and going into Search or Global Search modes. For names, titles etc. do the same thing but go to Direct Search mode. Actual file names for anything on the screen are always in the upper right-hand corner. You may hardcopy anything you want, not to exceed ten pages. Or mark what you want to download with a double dot, and enclose your net or modem address, it will be sent to you directly. But nothing else – and no disks – can either be inserted or physically leave the files or room for computer virus reasons. University rules. Hope you find what you need.

As instructed, I typed in the first line of the manuscript I'd found among Von Slyke's papers, then went into Search mode. 'Not found' was the response. So I tried Global Search mode. 'Not found' was repeated. I then keyboarded in two more lines and tried again. Still nothing. I keyboarded in the first ten lines. Still zilch.

Disheartened, secretly wondering if the system really was as

complete as Tanya Cull claimed it was, I tried the opening lines of
the second manuscript I'd found, the one Thom Dodge had given
me. Search. Nothing. Global Search. Again nothing.

Next I inserted the name 'Paul' – the narrator of the second, and
a character of the first, manuscript – into the system and, following
Tanya's instructions, put it in Direct Search. 'File?' it asked. That
was more like it. I asked it to check 'All files' and waited. To my surprise, it responded.

'Two files found. View #1?'

Absolutely!

I struck 'Access' and was rewarded by having a manuscript
appear on the screen. Or rather the middle of a page of a manuscript, which I immediately recognized as not having anything to do
with the anecdote about the two kids in the cars, as I'd hoped, but
which I did recognize as being from somewhere in the first section of
Mitch Leo's fourth book, *After the Piano Recital*, published in 1983.
The area highlighted by the cursor read, 'We lived first with Tom's
Princeton friend Paul, but discovered him to be pathological in too
many respects – including food, sex, drug use and dress.'

This extremely minor character, Paul, returned once more briefly,
much later in the novel, as I discovered when I asked the machine to
access the next place in the file where the name was mentioned.
That read, 'Around two o'clock in the morning, we heard something
hit our hull, and looked over the side to see Paul in a small boat
shaking hands with its sailors. He came up and asked, "Anyone got
hashish. Mother's brains are simply marinated from being screwed
by the crew all night!"'

And that was it. Unfortunately. As it proved at least that the computer's search mechanism was working. The question now was if it
was working for all the files or only for the files of the published
work. What I needed was to get into something I knew was not published. Not that there was much Mitch Leo had written and not
published. A true follower of the literary aesthetic of Flaubert, Leo
had written little, worked slowly, carefully reworked his writing
many times, and had at last released it only with difficulty. This,
despite the fact that once his 1981 novel, *Refitting Tom Devere*, had
'broken through', Leo had become a regularly published author for
the few remaining years left him.

Wait a minute! There was a possibility. The bulk of Mitch Leo's unpublished work probably lay in his letters to Aaron Axenfeld! They'd known each other for two and a half decades and had lived far enough apart during at least half of that period to have corresponded weekly. Once the Leo–McKewens began making regular spring pilgrimages to Europe – mostly residing for two to three months in Florence – the letters were even more regular. Ditto once the Leo–McKewens would arrive at the Leo family beach house, every August through October. Axenfeld had left Manhattan in 1982, further adding to their distance and need for correspondence.

Those many missives, and their responses, had formed the basis of an entire chapter of Erling Cummings's group biography, focussing as it had on the Leo–McKewens as the gay literary couple of the era, and had in addition provided the meat for that section of Thad Fleming's study of the group in which he'd concentrated on their and the other Purple Circlers' experiences in Europe, which he had titled – felicitously I thought, given their many sexual adventures – 'Tramps Abroad'.

I'd begun typing in Axenfeld's name when I thought, wait, the Leo–McKewens never called Aaron by his real name. They'd never called *any* of the others by their real names either. According to both Cummings and Fleming, they had fabricated 'drag names' for all of the Purple Circle's members. Or more precisely, pet names, since they were seldom female monikers: more like names that were coined as a result of peculiar circumstances or odd personality quirks, or arose who knew how, most of the circumstances being lost in the miasma of the past.

Each other the Leo–McKewens called 'Baby' or 'Babe'. Mark Dodge of course was Marco. Or Marco Polo. Or sometimes the Pole. Odd but understandable enough. As was Rowland Etheridge's nickname of 'Metheridge' or 'Meth' or sometimes 'Drina', the latter two names being short for Methedrine, a recreational amphetamine quite stylish in the 1960s (and the 1990s, although there was no indication that Rowland used or abused the drug in either decade). After that the naming became more complex. Von Slyke's sobriquet of 'Dame' – short for Damon, used by the other Purple Circlers – wasn't enough for the Leo–McKewens, who had changed it to 'Camellia' or, more simply, 'The Lady C', in reference to Dumas fils's novel *La Dame aux camélias*. In a similar bit of legerdemain, Cameron Powers's name had gone from 'Cammy', which the others most often used, to 'Cameron of Sulleyville' – a town not far from where Powers had grown up in Mississippi – to 'Sulley' and via some unknown incident to 'Sulky', with an occasional reference to 'Miss Sulks' or 'The Sulky One'. Dominic De Petrie's name had undergone similar transformations from 'Dom' to 'Dome' to the nearly anagrammatical 'St Peter's Dome', thereafter landing most often on 'Saint Pete' – when, that is, it wasn't 'Sneaky Pete'. But neither biographer had located the exact foci through which the name Aaron Axenfeld had become transformed into 'Glum Gus' or more simply 'Gus'. Cummings had suggested one pathway from the name Axenfeld through Thomas Mann's *Death in Venice* character Von Aschenbach, to that character's first name Gustave, to Gustavus, and finally to Gus – which did make a weird sort of sense. Anyway, Gus was what they called Aaron.

I keyboarded the name Gus and went to Direct Search, All Files. Pay dirt! It listed seventy-five files. Just to make sure, I accessed one and got a letter from Florence dated April 17th, 1976. Okay. This meant the two manuscripts were not on the computer. That was disappointing, if not particularly revelatory. Why should they be here if Len or Mark or Jeff were their author?

I decided to move past Tanya's instructions and went backward, looking for a listing of 'All files' under Mitch Leo to see what of her uncle's work she had listed. This proved to be the titles of his published books, a few book reviews he'd published, a speech he'd given on 'Gay Literature: The Future' for a Midwest university, and the many letters. Nothing else.

Only one more possibility to try. Bobbie Bonaventura had told me that after the bank heist involving Jeff Weber, Len had been hanging around with the Leo–McKewens. While I couldn't completely trust her yet, the other thing she'd said about Len – that he and Mark Dodge had a previous relationship before Len met Jeff Weber – had proved true. Mark Dodge's letter to his brother Thom confirmed that. It didn't prove that Spurgeon was a bank robber. Even so . . . I opened the file for Leo's letters again, went into Direct Search mode and typed in the name Len Spurgeon. I accessed for 'All files' and waited.

Three entries showed up. The first two were dated June and September of 1979, exactly when Bobbie had said Len and the Leo–McKewens were hanging out together. The first, in a letter to Axenfeld, merely mentioned Len Spurgeon as 'an old flame of Marco's whom the Babe is sure he still has La Grandissimo Crusheroo on. And why not? Len is hot as the Fourth itself. One of those muscular, but somehow loosely muscled bodies you seldom see on white boys – which he very definitely is – but more often find on very deeply Southern-raised Afro-Americans. (I know, I know, I'll always be a BlackHawk at heart.) Only medium height, but the languid pose, the downright dirty way he walks and gestures, make him seem a lot taller. Yessiroo, this Len got the old gonads going for *moi-même* not to mention scads others in the room. Waco, on the other hand, hated him at first sight. Must have been a chemical thing.'

Waco – sometimes Wacky-o – the Leo-McKewens' name for Jeff Weber, not inapt, in honor of his Western upbringing. And if Bobbie hadn't been lying to me, I now knew better than Mitch Leo that it hadn't been hate 'at first sight', but exactly the opposite emotion.

The second Mitch Leo letter mentioned Len again, saying 'this time without Marco, Len came over for High Tea yesterday'. Present at the occasion had been the Leo–McKewens' usual assortment of those in the arts, socialites, people with summer houses they wanted invitations to, and Spurgeon, 'dressed in tight-fitting black denims, black T-shirt, silver and ebony vest and excellent hand-made boots from Texas'. One of only two women present, a vacuum-cleaner heiress, had flirted outrageously with Len, who was not amused by her attentions. Frankie McKewen had come upon the two of them smoking cigarettes on the little dining-room balcony, and he'd overheard Len saying, 'Well, I for one damn well know the difference, and I very much prefer having male buttocks bouncing in the palms of my hands, and a male rectum on the head of my cock.' Which had been duly and immediately reported to all present indoors. With the expected, sensational response. According to Leo, 'many were the barks and (masculine) giggles that ensued'.

So far, so good. If not telling. So, I went for Letter Number Three. As soon as it appeared on the screen I knew I had found something of significance. First, because across the top was written, 'Not Mailed? Confirm with AA', which I supposed to be Tanya's note to herself. And beneath the comment, another note: 'Confirmed with AA. This letter was never mailed.'

The letter, in its entirety, read:

La Cittá
October 18th 1983

Caro Gus,

  One hates to be here before the Season has really begun. Yet once it has begun, it's so much better if the weather is boring, which it's been. Even better if one has a new experience to report. A new experience to have experienced. We jaded old Hussies so seldom do have them. And so seldom are they as 'downright ego-satisfying' then as 'purely mortifying!' as what I am about to report. In secret, s.v.p. The Babe is not to hear a word of this except from my own lips, when I choose the time and place.

  Do you remember that divine Len Spurgeon who several years ago came to a few of our Teas on West End Avenue? Did you ever meet him? I think Marco said you eventually did, although he didn't say in what context. Well, said lovely Len vanished from sight and when I severely quizzed Miss Polo about the lad, Marco claimed he knew rien pas. Perhaps he was in Parigi, from which I gathered Marco had 'made the move' and been repulsed. Or, more likely, they'd done the deed and it hadn't worked out as planned. L'amour, L'amour as Mary Boland always said . . .

  Well, the lad resurfaced, with a vengeance. Last Monday night, I was at some stupid quasi-literary shindig at someone's drearily furnished but v. nicely laid out flat at the Parc Vendôme on West 57th Street and I left about midnight. Alone. The Babe was home with La Grippe. Could locate no taxis going uptown. So I wandered around Eighth Avenue and noted right there a place I'd heard about for years but never actually been near, although doubtless the Lady C, not to mention the Sulker know it v. well – I'm writing of that sleazy bar named the Hay Market. Second most famous hustler bar in the città. Since I'd never entered, that oversight had to be immediately rectified. I went in, ordered a drink and looked around. Mostly older gentlemen. As expected. But in the back pool room was all the young meat. And among the young meat, there was one partikularly cherce cut of darkmeat, just the way I like it. 'Wayne' – made-up name, I'm sure. It's probably Cato or Norman. But despite that, v. special. And obviously trade.

There too, leaning on the arm of another piece of trade, after a minute I see, is our old pal Len Spurgeon, also looking pretty damn tasty, in rubbed-raw 501's left unbuttoned at the navel and a T that don't quite meet the pants. He, alas for my interest that soir, was Caucasian and unquestionably 'our age'.

Len, however, does me the kindness of remembering me fondly, is amused when I ask, 'Buying or selling?' and buys me a second beer. He also points out that I'm looking pretty good myself and that one older gent looks v. interested in me. He points out the guy, who is maybe four years older, but v. square and out of town. Actually, handsome face, nice bod. Bad clothes, if not quite polyester. But almost ostentatiously 'out of town'.

I tell Len what I want, and he introduces me to Wayne. I take off my jacket, reveal tight bod beneath, lose a game and a dollar to Wayne playing pool. Afterwards, Len says of Wayne, 'That'll cost you seventy-five bucks the hour.' Well, who has that on me? And anyway, who wants to pay? So I'm glum, until Len suggests the following: he'll introduce me to Mr Out of Town. I'll go trick with him at his hotel, then come back and use the money to buy café au lait Wayne.

I can't believe this is a realistic scenario. But Len does intro me to Herbert WhatsisName from Wherever, Indiana, who's in town for a tool convention if you can dig it and wears a double wedding ring and wants sex bad enough he'll pay me. The only way to be quite such a putana, however, is if Wayne knows about it in advance. So I go up to the pool table and tell him what I'm going to do, asking him to wait for me. He smiles widely and promisingly. And with the excitement potential, I go off.

Halfway down the tackiest part of Eighth Avenue, feeling truly cheap, I wonder how I'm going to pull this off. It's worse in the hotel lobby. And worse in the elevator, where I'm sure everyone is looking at me and thinking the truth. Upstairs, inside the door, I'm about to give Herbert a chance to rethink the scenario, but he's instantly all over me. And he is the Roman candle of all time. Four-time shooter, in short, once against me in his shorts necking at the door, once on top of me, à la frottage, and twice when I've mounted him and am copulating like all get out. Turns out he's nice, he's handsome, he has a nice body and he excites the shit out of me. Terrific sex. So good I almost give back the money.

I don't. I leave when he's half asleep, and I go back to the bar. I see Len and we wink conspiratorially. He connects me up to Wayne and we three laughingly discuss what I just did and after another half-hour or so, Wayne and I leave and we go to some fleabag room he tricks out of, which uses up both my twenty-five-dollar tip from Herbert and my taxi fare home. Wayne prefers posing, being adored, and being caressed. But finally relents and allows a blow job. He's beautiful and it's okay, although truth to tell, if I'd not fucked my brains out earlier, I'd possibly be a wee bit disappointed with how I was spending my money. I get home at three a.m. The Babe, luckily, is dead asleep.

Naturally I keep all this to myself. Then last night, a week later, the Babe and I join La Simplessa (the Ribs Heiress) as her escorts at the Met Opera for a black-tie charity do, a production of La Bohème. V. High Society. Guess who's in the lobby with three or four other tuxedoed to the toes v. attractive guys who all turn out to be A-list gays, but Len Spurgeon? We all meet at the first interval and I like who he's with, and so does the Babe and even La Simplessa. So we all meet again at the second intermission. And we're in a circle, talking, near the big horseshoe bar under the awful Chagall mural. I'm really a little bit getting to know these men, when one of them whom Len and I have moved a little bit away

from the others to talk to – Rick something or other – really
the neatest of them all, asks me what I do for a living. I say
I'm a writer and am about to go on being mock-modest yet
sincere (you know the act: hell, you invented the act!) when
Len turns to Rick and says, 'Of course, Mitch is also a
whore. Aren't you, Mitch?'

Well, Gus, I could have died right on the spot. But I found
that I could not say one word in my defense, and I could feel
my face get deep red, which would have lied for me if I did
try to defend myself. Len goes on to say, 'A hundred dollars a
throw! Isn't that right, Mitch? Or is that only with a tip?'

Rick looked surprised and Len smiled oddly at me, and a
second later we were with the others again. And I knew that
wherever I went from now on, wherever Len Spurgeon or
any of these people said my name or had my name mentioned
to them, one of them would bring up the fact that I was a
hundred-dollar-a-night whore.

It's unbearable. Yet what can I do?

You're so clever. Do you know what? Is there anything at
all?

The 'Doughty Lion' or sometimes just 'Our Lion', Dominic De
Petrie had called Mitch in his own letters to Aaron Axenfeld, and the
name was more than just a play on Mitch's last name. First there
was his gleaming chestnut-brown mane, the beautifully – and expen-
sively – kept hair, shoulder-length since the mid-1960s, and,
according to everyone who met Mitch, the first thing one noticed
about him; and long after his Italian Renaissance *condottiere* good
looks had been absorbed, the last thing one noticed about him.
Additionally, everyone testified that Mitch Leo's character was that
of someone strongly independent, protective, self-sufficient to the
point of arrogance, leading, at times dictatorial, at all times socially
conscious, dignified and, above all, proud. What had happened with
Len Spurgeon must have been beyond mortifying to Mitch Leo. The
fact that he'd never sent the letter attested to that. He'd probably
never even told Frankie.

True, Mitch wasn't perfect. And, in a way, it was a pretty good, if
spontaneously planned, comeuppance that he received. De Petrie

often accused the Leo–McKewens of being unadulterated social climbers, and although he himself attended a half-dozen 'High Teas' at their apartment – a rent-controlled pre-war five-room flat on West End Avenue and 100th Street – when he wrote of it to Axenfeld or to others, invariably it was to make fun of the event and some of the more outré characters to be found there. 'Severely aging heiresses in equally aging satin skirts and bad make-up,' he'd written. And, of some of the artists, 'He derives his iota of fame from having painted a portrait of a Surrealist poet none of us ever heard of about three minutes before the old fraud died.' Even so, the Leo–McKewens often had four or five 'real', i.e. currently successful, authors and composers present along with what De Petrie described as the 'usual crowd of ancient interior decorators, overdressed landscapers and questionably garbed Sotheby's solicitors'.

The monthly social teas had come about for one reason: the Leo–McKewens had run out of money and couldn't afford dinner parties. The afternoon events were accomplished by guests bringing cookies, cakes and candies. Their hosts provided the place, the atmosphere, the tea and the china.

Exactly why the Leo–McKewens had run out of money is a bit more complicated. Cummings had written about it at some length. It mostly had to do with unmet expectations on Mitch's part. The Leo family were successful ethical drug manufacturers, providing among the first so-called 'generic' brands on the market. During Mitch's twenties and thirties, the company money had flowed and had been sufficient not only to buy the family large homes in horsy Montclair County as well as at the Jersey seashore, but also to send the kids to private schools, colleges and to pay an annual stipend to Mitch while he became a writer. Shortly before his fortieth birthday, Mitch's mother died, and on his forty-first birthday, the family birthday card contained a single check for 10,000 dollars – with a note from his father saying this was Mitch's share of what was left of his mother's estate and that, with her death, the annual fund would no longer be continued.

At first, the Leo–McKewens thought all would be well. They would live off their earnings as authors. Hadn't Frankie's last two books gone into hardcover and paperback? His 1978 tome on the 'new sexuality in America', titled *Switch Hitters*, had been reviewed in the Sunday section of the *New York Times*. As had the next book, published a year later, McKewen's first truly gay opus, titled *Whitman's Sons and Sappho's Daughters*, an early study of the roots of gay male and lesbian poetry. Frankie was on something of a roll: working on two autobiographical novels – one about growing up in the Midwest, the second about his adventures as a young man in Europe – as well as another sure-to-be-profitable non-fiction title, a cultural history with lots of character sketches about that most openly homosexual period between ancient Greece and modern times: fifteenth-century Florence, the era of Michelangelo, Leonardo and Pope Leo X.

If Frankie was heading toward a career culmination, with several books behind him and sections of the two novels already being accepted for magazines and anthologies, Mitch Leo's star was only now for the first time seriously on the rise. By comparison with Frankie's, it had been far dimmer for the past decade or more.

In fact, since the two of them had collaborated on their first book, a curious, precocious, partly autobiographical study of UFO sightings and touchdowns, as well as alien abductions and 'definitive' signs of time travel (such as the Nazca carvings), titled *Signals in the Sky*, that book – seldom brought out for guests to inspect at tea, De Petrie acidly noted – had been issued in 1967, when the Leo–McKewens, according to the back-cover photos, were in their young manhood, lavishly coiffed, bearded and mustachioed, tanned, lithe-bodied in their snorkeling gear, and not much different than the Euro-Trash to be found sniffing coke in corners of Regine's and the Peppermint Lounge or in beach-shack bars on Montego Bay. Oddly enough, while the book was remaindered within two years of publication, *Signals* had found fans enough since then: it had sold constantly in a 'special' edition, meaning at about half of its original price, and available in hardcover only from wholesalers, prominently listed in the 'Arcana' or 'Psychic' sections of their widely distributed mail-order book catalogues and flyers.

While Frankie had eventually followed up that volume with another, then another, trendy non-fiction book – rock music and Native American Indians were two subjects, for example – Mitch had returned to his first love, fiction.

That, after all, was what had initially brought the two together at that famous writers' colony deep in the Vermont woods, to which each had received grants upon their college graduation in 1962. It had been there, among the hushed groves of towering alder and birch trees and the tiny hippie-style wood and stained-glass writers' studio cabins that they had first befriended each other; there in clandestine fresh stream beaches and covert clear-as-glass pools, while discussing Fitzgerald and Edith Wharton and critiquing each other's work, that they'd first discovered their shared sexuality. Partly, the Leo–McKewens had fallen in love and begun an affair as an escape from the voraciousness of two older, obviously husband-hunting, women, a poet and a novelist, at the colony. And while it had been touch and go for another two years afterward – as Frankie moved to Manhattan and Mitch returned to Montclair to live – at last they'd both managed to spend time together again in Florence. There, on the sizable outdoor terrazo connected to the seventh-story flat of a nondescript Contessa, amidst abundant springtime flowers and a bevy of tipsy guests, in view of the Duomo and the Ponte Vecchio, as the sun culminated in Gemini, the Leo–McKewens had exchanged gold rings and married for life.

Mitch was himself then a potential heir (along with his two brothers) to a third of what promised to be the nicely sized Leo fortune. He needn't work. He could spend a decade writing what would turn out to be an enigmatic, Jamesian novella, *The Younger*, published in 1977, with a lovely cover wrap and wonderfully apt interior black and white etchings by a dilettante older friend, whose current beau celebrated by throwing Leo a very toney book party in one of the generally unused galleries of the Frick.

No one was more surprised than Mitch himself when, in the wake of the novella's publication, his next book, *Refitting Tom Devere*, more or less 'wrote itself', as he put it in a letter to Axenfeld. No one was more surprised and thrilled when that novel found a good publisher and caught the wave of gay lit hitting the country at the cusp of the 1980s.

It had been terrifically reviewed, had sold well, and in trade paperback had sold even better. Further opening the creative flood gates. Again, before *Tom Devere* was out, Mitch was already working on *After the Piano Recital*, and while that book – odder in content, if very Mitch Leo in its interests – didn't enjoy the same success of its predecessor, it led to an even more easily penned third novel, *Serial Childhood*, which took up the character and life of Tom Devere and which, eventually, outstripped both prior books in both sales and critical acclaim.

It still wasn't enough financially. Partly because Mitch's success turned out to be simultaneous with Frankie's appalling lack of same. The Renaissance study McKewen had labored upon for several years and therefore had counted on to fulfill all, was, when he at last handed it in, sat on for months by his editor before – to the horror of all – being eventually turned down. Although it was subsequently shopped around for the next several years by McKewen's agent, it didn't find another publisher and moreover was never finished.

Frankie's two novels came to more and more occupy his time and mind – it couldn't have escaped him that all the other Purple Circlers were succeeding in the area of fiction – but he found writing them hard-going, especially as he wasn't able to presell either book, which would have provided at least some fiduciary motivation. All those book editors who'd spoken so highly of the published excerpts at lit. conferences and parties now refused to look at his work in progress and demanded to see 'the finished book'. Which only added pressure on Frankie, who, after all, was an essayist, a miniaturist, who believed in 'intuitive' rather than highly crafted writing, and who knew his talents and limitations enough to know he didn't have the narrative sweep and psychological acuity of a novelist.

It could not have been easy on their relationship, this final period of McKewen's non-achievement, coming so directly alongside Leo's sudden success, but the couple did manage to weather it psychologically, which attested to the strength of their bond. Financially, it was a different matter.

Mitch's income, now only advances and royalties (both of which were lower than what McKewen had regularly received for his non-fiction), was not anything like as large or as regular as it had been when his income was a Leo family monthly stipend. On top of that, the Leo–McKewens had developed spending habits over two decades that proved difficult to grow out of. They would primly budget and prudently live a month or two at a time, then one or the other would see something pricey and gorgeous they had to have, and would blow the equivalent of three budgeted months on, say, a Persian turquoise ring or an Erté letter H watercolor or a Portuguese lace tablecloth. After all, it was difficult growing up to believe someone would always be there to pay and at the same time learn to deny yourself anything.

Frankie and Mitch kept up the belief that the Leos' company would get back on its feet and return to its headier profit-making days. If it ever did, his brothers – now managing the company –managed to skim the earnings toward themselves and their families, so Mitch only got it last and least. One could understand the brothers' point of view: they worked in an office nine to five, forty-eight weeks a year; while Mitch sat a few hours a day at a desk, usually in terrific surroundings – in Florence, in Paris, at Fire Island Pines, at the family beach house. Anyway, didn't he now have other sources of income?

Among the other Purple Circlers, however, the truth was more evident: it was clear to those who were better off financially that money to sustain the Leo–McKewen *folie à deux* would have to be loaned to the couple on a more or less regular basis. Axenfeld and De Petrie and Mark Dodge were the usual lenders. One time, finding himself with a windfall, generous Axenfeld had simply, anonymously, paid their Macy's account, knowing the Leo–McKewens depended upon charging at the gourmet basement to food shop when they were in straits. To his great annoyance, the duo were certain the bill had been paid by one of the heiresses they cultivated, and they delightedly speculated for weeks which one it had been – until, and to everyone's embarrassment but his own, De Petrie at last set the two of them straight.

Coming in the midst of all that scrimping, what had happened with Len Spurgeon must have been deeply troubling to Mitch Leo. The fact that he'd never sent the letter to his closest correspondent, to whom he confessed all, attested to exactly how mortifying. I wondered if he'd ever gotten around to telling Frankie what had occurred. Somehow I doubted it.

Another problem that probably added considerably to Leo's troubles at this time concerned health. It's at this exact time, according to Frankie McKewen's journals, that Mitch Leo begins section three of *Serial Childhood*, i.e. begins writing about his narrator Tom

Devere's still-unnamed disease. Cummings believed that Mitch Leo had already been tested for HIV during the summer of 1983, following the hospitalization for pneumonia of David Caspar, a former 'adulterously regular trick' of his, which Mitch reported in a letter to both Von Slyke and Axenfeld. Cummings was certain Mitch had already found out he was HIV positive by August of that year. This naturally would have added to the psychological 'boost' Leo would have received at first in the incident with Herbert from Indiana and Wayne, but which later blew up so disastrously in his face.

To back up Leo's changed health status at this time, Cummings found indications that Mitch was regularly going to a Harlem dermatologist he knew during this year. The biographer was certain the visits were so Mitch could have Karposi's Sarcoma lesions lasered out of existence on his face and limbs. Going so far uptown and out of his usual circles, Cummings speculated, Mitch might be relatively certain people he knew would not discover the visits. Financial records Cummings located showed treatments on each of seventeen dates from April through December. We know how proud and vain Leo was of his looks. It now seems clear that he either knew or strongly suspected he was sick with AIDS by mid-1983 and still hadn't told anyone, not even his old pal and correspondent Aaron Axenfeld.

At the time, of course, Mitch Leo could console himself – as the saying goes – with his reviews. As well as with the fact that the reviews got progressively better right up till the end of his all too short life. Of course, there was the expected critical opposition to Leo's obliquity of angle, as well as to his 'mandarin' style. Yet the middle-aged men and women who most often reviewed his novels in the book pages of the New York and Washington papers found them to be 'balanced portraits of families in crisis with alternative life styles'.

But to younger, more radical, class-conscious gays, the cosmopolitan settings, the *haut-monde* characters, their elaborate social niceties and the sophistication of emotional conflicts Leo delineated so well all seemed to smack more than somewhat of a less contemporary and less interesting kind of gay life. 'Useless except as a memento and then only for retired decorators and beekeepers,' one reviewer had written of *Serial Childhood*. While *The Advocate*'s critic had been even harsher, calling the novel's failure to name AIDS and to deal with it except as in an allegorical mode 'the Damnable Closet, homophobically prevailing even unto sickness and death'. Even so, when Leo died in 1988, he could content himself that he'd opened up new avenues of discussion, especially regarding gays and their families, in literature and that his vision would persist.

Subsequent studies, a decade later, ended up being altogether less certain. Once the issues of 'mainstreaming', 'gay adoptions', 'same-sex marriages' and 'gays in the military' were recognized to be transitory and ultimately peripheral to the true issues of the homosexual liberation movement – i.e. the removal of all sodomy laws and complete equality under governmental law – Mitch Leo's 'breakthrough' was naturally reviewed and re-evaluated as a less crucial position. Dr St George had written, 'The Leo oeuvre will stand the test of time, although it's unclear what ultimate position he will hold among his Purple Circle colleagues. Surely not in the top echelon, as contemporaries assumed during his lifetime, yet not at the bottom either. Possibly he will be in the center, as he was in life, at least socially.'

Erling Cummings had enjoyed writing about the Leo–McKewens because they were such richly detailed characters themselves, as well as because of the romanticism of their 'fated' love story and their early deaths, only months apart. But even he admitted that the couple as authors were 'transitional: like Etheridge and Von Slyke, their coevals, they represented a pre-Stonewall mentality, contrasting with the evidently post-Stonewall mentality of Axenfeld, De Petrie and Dodge, who were writing at the same time. But unlike Etheridge and Von Slyke, who did recognize how their age might hold them back and who did attempt in their subject matter and approaches to keep up with the others, the Leo–McKewens never seemed interested in pushing forward into that Brave New World of topics and experimentation that gay literature had opened up. They held onto ideas regarded by other Purple Circler's like De Petrie as outmoded – Eurocentricism, the class system, the family above all, even religion, i.e. all the traditional, old-style, school-tie values others wanted destroyed.'

Thad Fleming was even more critical, 'In the end, Leo's work stands on that borderline leading to the new. The essential charm of his voice, the pleasure we derive from the stories he tells and how well he tells them do count. The novels are not so much "dated" as they – gently – often require the reader to constantly mentally redate them for him/herself during the reading experience, saying, "But wait, this must be happening in the '60s!" or, "Right! It was different then!" Which seldom happens with the totally contemporary works by other Purple Circlers, written at the same time or earlier.'

Mitch's unsent letter to 'Gus' seemed a perfect example of that much discussed style of writing and thinking: arch and yet direct, 'classicist' yet almost vulgar in its leering. Filled with foreign phrases, yet almost blunt in its other language. As I printed it out for myself, however, on the university bubble jet, I found my thinking revolving back and around to not Mitch Leo but the still-unknown Len Spurgeon. Who was Len? In the words of the Bard, 'What was He/that all our swains commend Him?' Was he sinner, as Bobbie and Leo assumed? Or savior, as Mark Dodge thought? Or both in some combination?

More and more Len Spurgeon seemed to me to be a linchpin among the Purple Circle. Might he possibly be the only outsider all of them had known and – loved? Lusted after? Slept with? Not slept with? What? I wasn't exactly certain. And what of this manuscript I was finding parts of? Would I find more? Was it Len's writing? Or Len's story as written by others? Was it whole? Or merely unrelated fragments? And was it true? Or even supposed to be taken as true?

Perhaps when I met her, Tanya Cull might enlighten me.

'It was on my eleventh birthday that my uncle first made an impression on me. Naturally he'd been there, somewhere in the midst of the big Leo–Manetti family gatherings since I was born. But as he didn't live close by and was often away, out of the country, he never seemed to occupy an important position for me. It was my parents and brother, my Grandma and Grandpa Leo, my uncle Richie Leo, his wife, Cathy, and their two kids, my cousins Richie Jr and Susan, the big Manetti clan. Only then Uncle Mitch. On my eleventh birthday all that changed.'

Tanya Cull was in the driver's seat of a large, off-white, borrowed van. I was in the passenger's seat. We were driving Route 980 headed toward the Bay Bridge, and eventually Holly Park, south of the Mission District, newly gentrified, to where we would be delivering furniture and cardboard boxes intended for the new two-room apartment her eighteen-year-old daughter had just moved into.

'You sure you don't mind doing this?' Tanya asked.

'What choice do I have?' I half joked. 'If I'm going to probe you, I've got to help you.'

Tanya sighed. She was a large woman, not obese but big-boned, large-shouldered, with a leonine head and naturally honey-blond thick-hair worn trendily cut in a fashion not unlike that I'd seen on movie actresses in films of the mid-1950s. This, despite her broadly Calabrian facial features: large soulful black eyes, distinctively outlined lips and eyebrows, almost perfectly aquiline nose. At about forty-two years of age, Tanya looked healthy and strong and at the same time pleasure-loving and sensual. Her face was unquestionably that of a Leo, while her body was quite different than Mitch; he'd been tall, with a slender upper torso, solid almost jutting-out rear end and long strong legs. A contemporary artist had posed Mitch as a centaur for a party invitation drawing at the age of forty, and many photographs confirmed that it was a good likeness: not only his body but also the abundant shoulder-length, carefully, even over-groomed rich brown hair and beard, the classical brow and long nose that had all given Mitch Leo both a naturally aristocratic and a somewhat equine appearance.

'When I tell Jeth you're Bart Vanuzzi's brother-in-law, he'll have a conniption I'm not inviting you to stay.'

'I have a class to teach in LA Monday morning,' I said, then went on, 'You were saying, your eleventh birthday . . .'

'Did you see that lamebrain. He charged into my lane, then slowed. I hate that. I wish I could install a missile launcher on the fender like James Bond had. Where was I?' Tanya asked. 'Right. The lawn of my Grandma Leo's house. My eleventh birthday. About twenty kids. A big table on the lawn. Games. Gifts. A great party. Then my grown-up relatives arrived. Around five or so this silver-blue Corvette drives up, its doors swing open and out steps my uncle Mitch and Frankie. They're dressed unlike the other men. They're not wearing suits, but summer jackets accentuating their figures, with polo shirts and close-fitting denims and fabulous cowboy boots. And as they come to the table, they're happy and smiling and young. Not like kids, but not like parents either. It's like I'm seeing them for the first time.

'They have a gift for me. A grown-up card. Inside the beautifully wrapped package, with paper on it that looked like old buildings, fake marble and all, is this good box and inside the box among tons of white tissue paper is the most beautiful leather purse. Not large, but perfectly made. Solid, thick leather, yet delicate too, and Mitch shows me how to adjust the strap and wear the purse. Well, are you going to move into my lane, lady?' Tanya rhetorically asked the driver ahead, 'or just blink your directionals all day?

'The bag's a Gucci, Mitch tells me, the best in Europe. When I open it, inside isn't more tissue paper, but three very large 10,000 *lire* notes. "It's Italian money. The purse is from Italy. So is the wrapping paper," Mitch says. I notice so is everything he and Frankie are wearing. Which is why it all looks fine. Finer than anything we have despite our money. They sit next to me on either side and tell me about Florence and promise to send me a book about it. They talk to the other kids, my friends, complimenting one on her hair and another on his watch, acting as though they're regular people not kids and it's a different party. Frankie is telling a story about his motorcycle accident on the *autostrada* and all of us kids are listening and lapping it up and asking questions, which Mitch and Frankie answer in great detail, not annoyed, like parents. Mitch makes me serve cake and drinks since he tells me I'm the hostess. It's as though a door opened to another world. Finally, she changes lanes,' Tanya comments. 'Congratulations, lady, you don't need an analyst after all.

'That night, Mitch and Frankie stay for dinner and I notice they sit together, and when my aunt Cathy or my uncle Eugene ask Mitch something, he always says "We". "We went here." Or, "We didn't see her." This is my first indication that Mitch and Frankie are a couple the way my mother and dad and Grandma and Grandpa Leo are couples. They live together, travel together, sometimes work together. There are coins in that little change thingamajig for the toll,' Tanya directs me. 'I'm eleven. I have to go to bed before they leave, but they take me aside, upstairs, and they kiss me and tell me that they think I'm very promising. That's the word they use. I'm the most promising of all the nieces and nephews, they tell me, and they'd like to see me. I'm thrilled to the toes, and dance to my bedroom and don't sleep for hours.'

The toll payment lines are long but not slow. It gives Tanya time to spruce up her face in her mirror. 'A week later the book about Florence arrives. Photos. Art. It's like a magic fairy kingdom. I realize that's where they live when I don't see them! A few weeks later, me and Mom drive to Manhattan to have tea at their apartment with this nice old woman and that's a revelation. First how beautiful yet masculine the place is. The books. Though there are two rooms with beds in them, Frankie tells me that the room with the single bed isn't so much to sleep on at night as to nap on during the day, to help him think when he's writing. He and Mitch sleep together in the big bed.

'Hello,' Tanya greets the toll-taker. 'Can I get a receipt?' She does and puts it in the purse. 'Jeth says to get a receipt for everything! Come on, don't you have third gear?' she says to the driver dawdling ahead. Tanya changes lanes and we take off with squealing tires, headed toward Treasure Island. 'Well, that more or less begins our relationship. Mitch and Frankie call me on the phone, write me letters, send me cards, meet me for lunch at a roadhouse outside of Montclair, then take me into New York for dinner and a musical. They direct my reading. They teach me how to dress. They take me to museums, and jewelry shops, to foreign movies I don't quite get and to clothing boutiques where they show me how to shop. They train my eye and my taste, and when I begin to fall in love with books and reading, they buy books and recommend books. By the time I'm in high school, I realize they're both writers, published writers, who know other writers. I once hear my mother say to my aunt Cathy, "I only gave birth to her. She's Mitch's kid. Mitch and Frankie's." And that's how it is. Any problems with my folks that I may have, Mitch and Frankie enter into the talks as equals.

'You ever been to this park here?' Tanya asks me. 'It used to be a big naval station, I think the mid-'80s. Now it's a theme park. Militaristic theme park!' She sighs. 'When I'm fifteen or so, my Grandma Leo, who is the absolute center of the family, gets sick with cancer. Or at any rate, that's when she becomes too sick to hide it. She moves to the beach house at the New Jersey shore in early May, and Mitch and Frankie move in to help her. My Grandpa Leo lives at the big house with a servant during the week, but by Friday he's down at the beach, and we go there as much as possible too.

'By August, Grandma Leo can't get downstairs. So I go visit her in her bedroom. Look at that asshole, sliding across four lanes going eighty!' Tanya interrupts herself. 'We'll be reading about him in the *Examiner* some day and not because of some good deed! So, after one visit, when I'm very sad about how weak Grandma Leo is, Mitch and Frankie take me for a walk in the dunes. The house is located on an estuary of a river with views all around. In front, on the beach, there are no boardwalks, which is rare for a house on the Jersey shore, and so people lay their catamarans there. It's a beautiful sunset, and we're walking hand in hand, through the dune sedge, all three of us.'

Tanya shakes her head. 'I remember as though it were yesterday. It must have been, what, 1981? Well, the three of us are at the water and Mitch says, "Grandma's dying. If she makes it through the morning, I'd be surprised." It's such a terrible thing to say, such a surprise, I look to Frankie. He says, "If you have anything important to tell Grandma, you'd better do it right away. You'll never have another chance." Now no one in the family has said anything like this, so I'm shocked. I don't believe them. I try arguing, then I get angry with them, and go back to the house alone. Instead of going in, however, I hide in the rose-hip bushes in the back garden. I hear Mitch and Frankie coming, and I peek. They're standing there. Then I see Mitch lean against Frankie, shaking from head to toe, shaking and hiding his head, and I know he's crying his heart out. They aren't lying; it's the others who are lying. Mitch and Frankie are telling the truth. They will always tell me the truth. Do you see that?' Tanya asks, all mistiness suddenly out of her voice. 'That damn construction has been going on six months. They just switch it back and forth across the bridge. Idiots!

'So I go up to Grandma. I tell her it's okay, if she's so very sick, it's okay to die, although I'll miss her and so will everyone else, especially Mitch. And she smiles and says, "Listen to Mitch. And Frankie".'

The traffic slows and begins to snarl on the bridge around the exits to Treasure Island. Tanya is biting her lip. 'She died that night. Who knew then it was just a coming attraction?' she says. 'For a few years all goes well. By the time I'm in college, an honor student, studying literature, I've met – what? – twenty-five, thirty writers at tea. All the Purple Circle members. Dozens of others. They've connected me up with publishing people with whom I can intern in the summer and with professors at Princeton and Yale under whom I can study. They send me to Europe. They connect me up to Jethro, whom I marry. They do everything and anything for me. They are my fairy godparents. And it's true. Unlike any of the other Leo kids, I'm the intellectual, the special one: I'm Mitch's daughter, once removed. You know how it works genetically? I have as many of his genes from my father as if Mitch himself were my parent. This is getting hard.'

Not the traffic, but what she has to say. 'It's 1988 and my life is perfect. I have an honors degree from an Ivy League school, I'm studying for a Master's in literature at another Ivy League school. I've got a husband, a new daughter. I'm content. Then they invite me to the beach house. I've followed Mitch's rise as an author with close scrutiny and with great pride. Meanwhile, I've also become aware that Mitch has taken over my Grandma Leo's role as center in the family. Mitch and Frankie now live several months of the year at the shore. They've redecorated the house and relandscaped it. They have card games for the "boys", which is my Grandpa and uncles Leo and Jeth, and they have afternoon parties for the "girls", my sisters-in-law, me, two aunts. So I'm surprised when I arrived at the beach house and see I'm the only visitor. The house and gardens look more fabulous than ever, thanks to Mitch and Frankie. But that's all that looks good. Frankie is thin as a rail, looks exhausted and has a constant dry cough. Mitch is only a bit less worn-looking, and he's got these awful purple-black spots on his upper arms and neck. The reason they've asked me there, alone, they tell me, is to work out Mitch's will. He wants me to be his literary executor. Uh-oh,' she commented. We were coming to the San Francisco side of the bridge. Downtown and the Financial Section in full view to the near right, Coit Tower even further right of Russian Hill. Then the fog rolling in. Traffic was slowing down now and beginning to look ropy and thick.

'I couldn't believe it,' Tanya went on. 'But of course I gave in and said yes, and we prepared and I signed all the papers in front of a notary public. Another six or eight months go by and I've begun to follow the illness in the papers and magazines and I'm sure that with all the research a cure will be found or at least some treatment. That's when Frankie is hospitalized. Mitch moves into the Manhattan hospice-care unit with him at some posh East Side place. I see Frankie once: he's totally out of it, hallucinating from the pneumonia's ridiculously high fever. Then Frankie's dead and we're burying him and we're all going to a memorial service for him. Jesus! Despite all the construction, this bridge gets worse every week.

'After that I make sure to talk to Mitch every day. But he's disappearing on me more and more. After two months, he can't take care of himself and he moves to the big house in Montclair and one afternoon, waiting in his old bedroom for the maid to bring a bowl of chicken soup, he dies. Sitting up. Just like that. My life is perfect. And they're both dead! Mitch and Frankie. My parents. How could this happen?'

Tears are rolling down Tanya's cheeks as she gets ready to move two lanes to get off the bridge and head south.

'So you can understand how it's been very, very difficult for me to be Mitch's executor. At the same time, it's been an enormous honor. The very least I could do. I still haven't gotten over the shock of it. What is it? Eighteen years? I don't think I ever will. Every once in a while, I'll look at my dad or my cousin Richie and I can see Mitch in the way they roll their eyes, in an unconscious gesture they make, some expression they use. Mitch and Frankie were my first loves. Unattainable, beyond me, as first loves should be. Lovers and teachers. I can never ever forget them until the day I also die. I still hear their words in my mind. Phrases. Comments. Jokes they told. I didn't mind my mother's death as much when that happened.

'Oh, God,' Tanya moans as we exit the bridge, 'this traffic is a mess. I'm looking for what? The 101?'

'The 101 South,' I said. 'Watch out. The road splits.'

An hour later, we were headed back to Berkeley. Tanya meanwhile had been a mother whose first child is leaving home, probably for good: part mother hen, part resigned to it. Coming back she continued talking about Mitch and Frankie with such gusto and in such detail that I suggested she write up a memoir. To which she replied, 'Maybe.'

'I'd read it,' I say. And she took my hand across the space between us and said, 'He would have liked you. Mitch. He liked people who were direct and positive. Also—' one eyebrow raised— 'he would have liked your looks.' She released my hand. 'So who is it you're searching for?'

'Len Spurgeon. He's mentioned three times in Mitch's letters. Twice in 1981, then once in a long, unsent letter to Aaron Axenfeld a few years later.'

'I remember that letter,' Tanya said and her voice was suddenly much smaller. 'I did call Mr. Axenfeld and ask if he'd ever received it. I suspected it would be a great bother to him to look for it...'

I remembered Axenfeld talking to me about his Fibber McGee room of manuscripts. I'll bet it was hard to locate.

'I sent him the letter, finally. Didn't get back a peep. That one really plays it close to the vest.'

'I've found him to be both forthcoming and off-putting. But so far not gloomy.'

'Gloomy Gus!' we both said. Then Tanya was a little girl again. 'Oooh ooh!' She put out a crooked pinky and I did the same and we made a wish.

' "World peace?" Mitch once asked about wishes,' Tanya said, ' "Or the ability to sustain an erection until death? *That* is the question!" '

We laughed. Relaxed, I went on probing. 'So, did Cummings or Fleming ever read that unsent letter?'

'Possible but unlikely. They looked through the mess. The letters weren't keyboarded then and by no means as closely indexed and filed when the two of them were working on their books. I'm still in process, actually. The two scholars concentrated on various years anyway. So...who was this Len Spurgeon, anyway?'

'That's what I'm trying to find out. He was involved with Jeff Weber and Mark Dodge, sexually and romantically. Possibly with Etheridge and maybe even more of the Purple Circle. He was a major league baseball player a few years here in the Bay Area. Who knows what else? There may be a manuscript of his scattered among the Purples' papers. You've not come across anything of Mitch's that doesn't fit or that might be part of Len Spurgeon's story?'

'No. But I'm not sure I have everything, you know.'

'Oh?'

'Well, I don't know if you're aware of this or not, but I thought I was also Uncle Frankie's executor. I was surprised to discover I wasn't. This guy . . . Camden Phoenix he calls himself . . . I'm not even clear what his relationship to Frankie was . . . Well, after Mitch died, everything of Frankie's went to him. He's been unfriendly, difficult to contact, he moves around a great deal, and seems not to be able to settle. Luckily, the collection got its hands on Frankie's major stuff. And a lot of minor stuff too. Cost them plenty. I purposely held off Mitch's stuff and kept my price low so Phoenix would sell as much as possible of Frankie's papers. But he's – I don't even know how to describe him – only peripherally in literature, and who knows what he may still have. Or if any of it's Mitch's. He's down near you, in one of the beach cities. Torrance? Manhattan Beach? At least, he was six months ago. Now, who knows?' She paused. 'So, this Len. Is his stuff any good?'

'It's autobiographical. And I've got two chunks. Don't know what it is. But if he is a link among the Purples, you know, a personal link, then he might be a major influence.'

'You mean in addition to the creation of gay literature as a genre, they also would share experiences with him?'

'*Intense* experiences. For good or bad,' I clarified. 'Maybe Spurgeon's Zelda to their nine F. Scott Fitzgeralds.'

'Great thesis if it works!' she admitted. Coming from someone in her position, it half amounted to a blessing.

'That's what Dr St George thinks.'

She raised the eyebrow again. 'Irian St George. Well, you don't fool around, do you?'

When we parted near the college a few blocks away from Telegraph Avenue, where I'd earlier, finally, located a parking spot. I felt we'd come close enough for us to hug. So did Tanya. She was as tall as I was. And almost as solid.

'Next time I need moving help,' she joked, 'I'll call.'

I was at the door of my rented car when I realized she was

walking back to me. 'By the way, I got this e-mail from someone in your department. I thought maybe he knew you were up here seeing me and was trying to locate you. No message, really, only a name. He wants me to get back to him. Do you know who it is?' She was looking in her pockets, and finally located a shred of pink paper. 'Here it is'.

All the paper held was the name Waterford Machado. And his e-mail address.

What did he want? No way he'd know I was here. He was just trying to get at Tanya for his own reasons. Well, I'd put a stop to that. I took the paper from her hand and crumpled it up. 'He's no one important,' I said. 'In fact, he's something of a crank. I'd avoid him in the future if he contacts you again.'

We smiled and parted. But my stomach had already begun to turn as I got into the car seat, fastened the double seat belt, snapped on the air-bag buttons, turned off the anti-theft device and the electronic locator and finally was able to start the ignition.

Book Five

THE SHORT, HAPPY, POSTHUMOUS LIFE OF CAMERON POWERS III, ESQ.

The Capitoline air was streaked with invisible bars of
heat and cold. Coolness flowed out of shadowed
doorways, and at every transverse street the sun
breathed down fiercely. It was like walking through the
ghost of a zebra, he thought. Three beautiful young
men passed him, talking and laughing together. Like
laughing flowers, like deer, like little horses. He smiled
to himself thinking how deliriously he'd tricked them.
Tricked them all.

Cameron Powers, *'Miss Thing' and the '41 Bugatti*

'OKAY, WE'VE DISCUSSED RACISM AND the Civil War era and twenti-eth-century Southern American ideals and ideas, let's move on to form. What's the first thing you noticed when you read Faulkner's *Go Down Moses*? Ms Tranh?'

It was a gray misty morning, the night before the so-called 'Coastal Eddy' had dove deep into the Los Angeles basin, bringing along with its cold marine layer a heavier than usual summer-night-early-morning fog. Even more odd, it hadn't yet dissipated by the time this class met at eleven a.m. I'd driven to work in mist, which thickened along Sunset Boulevard, turning into a real headlights-on-go-ten-miles-an-hour pea soup from the Beverly Hills Hotel on west. Two drivers hadn't been respectful enough of how rapidly fog could sweep down the furling four-lane road at Stone Canyon. The vehicles were a twisted mass at the southwest corner of Beverly Glen Boulevard, which shouldn't have affected the traffic on the other side going west, but of course did severely, as it allowed An-gelenos to indulge in a favorite pastime: slowly driving by and com-pletely checking out exactly what happened to the other guy's car. Traffic flowed at the rate of old polenta. I just made it to the Eng-lish Department office by minutes before class. Several students were evidently also caught in the traffic as they were late for class, filtering in for a half-hour, which let me notice that all the jocks were unusually garbed in light sweaters, sweatshirts, slacks and denims: very few tank tops and shorts.

'The first thing I noticed,' Kathy Tranh began in her precise alto voice, 'was that the book is in seven unequal parts. And the second thing is that they aren't exactly chapters, nor are they exactly inde-pendent stories.'

'Good! Anyone else? Mr Rice? As there's no louche sexuality in this volume, I trust you read it.'

He'd come into the class on time, looking sleepy, his thick head of jet hair tousled, clothing seemingly thrown on, soiled, ripped denims, thong sandals, a parka-like shirt-sweater, as though he'd spent the night on the beach.

'Well?' I asked. 'What did you notice about it?'

'The same as Kathy did. It's all in pieces. As though Faulkner didn't mean for us to exactly figure out who all the characters were and what their relationships to each other were.'

'That was exactly his intention. Anything else?'

'Yeah. The time-frame of the book is all freaked out.' Ray Rice uncharacteristically went on, 'At the beginning Ike McCaslin is old. Faulkner says he's almost eighty years old. But a few stories later he's a young man. And in the middle of the book, in "The Bear", he's a boy. In another place he's not yet born, and in another he's already dead.'

'You all read this book.' I didn't hide how astonished I was, and pleased. 'Not only did you read it, but you seem to have understood what Faulkner was aiming for. Can anyone sum up Faulkner's formal achievement here? Ms Agosian?'

But it was Ray Rice who had his hand up and that was so extra-ordinary, I said, 'Mr Rice? You have something else to offer?'

'Time.' He simply said. And for a moment I was thrown off kilter. Did he mean the time was up? I peeked a look at my watch. No, not yet. Then Rice spoke yet again. 'Time's Faulkner's subject in this book. How flexible time can be depending upon where you happen to be standing relative to some particular incident or to some other person. That's why it's put together the way it is.'

'I couldn't have said it better than Mr Rice did. Let's all recall that Albert Einstein's world-shattering Special Theory of Relativity was new during the years Faulkner was a young man. The effect of that theory upon not only science but upon the philosophy and art of the era was profound. Every thinker, every writer of the period, was somewhat shaken. Ms Agosian?'

Pamela had tied her golden tresses in a double braid and tossed it over one shoulder today. She was wearing a surprisingly deep-purple school sweatshirt, the first dark-colored piece of clothing I'd seen on her so far.

'Wasn't Einstein's theory already in the air in the arts before he published it? I'm thinking of the work of Proust and his search for lost time?'

'Yes. Henri Bergson, a French philosopher was writing about the subjectivity of time in France, as had Nietzsche in Germany a few decades earlier, and of course at this time Lyell in geology was coming up with his own theory of Deep Time to explain such major anomalies of nature as the Grand Canyon and the cliffs of Dover. Time as a theme becomes the pre-eminent subject of the most widely read authors of the first half of the twentieth century. How time flows, if indeed it does flow, if indeed it actually does exist, and if not then the question of how it actually does move and especially how it affects our lives.'

'But –' This time it was Ben-Torres amazing me by speaking for the first time aloud in class. 'But don't other writers do this before? I remember Miss Havisham, in that Dickens book *Great Expectations*. She's lives at the moment the clock struck when she was left at the altar. She's stuck in the past.'

'Exactly,' I agreed. 'While the protagonist of that book, Pip, lives entirely in the future. In fact a future that will never become what he hopes.'

Just then the bell rang and I looked at my watch. It had stopped. Now I could see why. The watch crystal appeared to be shattered and a small piece pushed in, touching the face, keeping the minute hand from moving. When had I done that? In my sleep? So, Ray Rice *had* been warning me about class time. I looked at him for confirmation. But his head of dark hair was angled down, as he searched through his backpack.

'I want you all to think about this topic when you're reading the next title on our list *Black Elk Speaks*. This book was published in 1929, at the same time as Faulkner and Hemingway and Fitzgerald were putting out their best-known work. Think about that fact for our next class.'

As they were leaving the room, Kathy Tranh was at my desk. She looked around and then said, 'We're having this sort of birthday party for Pamela in a few days. Nothing big really, just a dinner at an inexpensive Thai place in Hollywood. We wondered if . . . well, you know, because I think Pamela would be pleased and we'd sort of like it too . . .'

I kept waiting for the subject of her question. It was like hearing someone imperfectly speaking German, the many qualifications of

noun and adverb waiting for the damned verb to arrive at the end of
the sentence.

'You're inviting me, I take it?'

'I mean, I know it's unusual for students to . . . and all?'

'Fine. Thanks. I'd be happy to. When? Where?'

Surprise on her face, which would have been even more
attractively Eurasian without the yellow-tinted dreadlocks and
bubblegum-pink lipstick that was so trendy. 'You'll come? I didn't
think you would. Danielle said you would. Wow! Pam will be
thrilled, I think. Well, okay then, day after tomorrow and . . .' She
pulled out a brightly neon-colored invitation with place and time on
it for a 'Pamelicious Birthday Dude and Dudettes Night'.

She all but floated out of the classroom. Outside, the mist had
broken very little. I was dreading another bumper to bumper drive
home. Maybe I'd hang out in the faculty dining hall for a while. Or
go to the Armand Hammer on Wilshire. A big photo show titled 'Big
Bad Fags, Tiny Sincere Dykes and Crazed Hetero Perverts' opened
last week: 1970s to 1990s artists, consisting of photos by those
dethroned giants Cindy Sherman and Robert Mapplethorpe, but
with Joel Peter Witkin work I was dying to see.

Out the English Department office windows, which unlike my
classroom faced east, I could see the fog was almost totally shredded
toward Hollywood and Downtown. It might last all day here. I
could go home and work. The photos could wait.

Irian St George had left a note in my mail-box telling me to drop
by his office sometime today. I'd already tried to beard him in his
den earlier, though I'd only had a few minutes before my class. He'd
been in conference.

We'd not spoken since I'd returned from my trip to the Bay Area,
not since I'd come back with the second piece of 'unknown' manuscript in hand. He'd have a surprise coming his way. The new MS,
Mark Dodge's letter detailing his passion for Len Spurgeon, as well
as Mitchell Leo's never-sent letter to Aaron Axenfeld.

All growing proof not only of the existence and importance of
Len Spurgeon to the Purple Circle members, but also of something
else, I wasn't quite certain yet what. I had to remind myself I was
way ahead of St George on all this material. He was still at the
point where he thought the piece I'd discovered in Von Slyke's

papers could be his – an experiment, juvenilia. Or by another Purple. I knew he was secretly hoping its author was De Petrie.

How could I forget St George's wounded admission over our tofu burgers and quesadillas at Hamburger Hamlet: 'He keeps things from me!'? Things, including, one had to assume from his tone of voice, manuscripts. It had been several years since De Petrie had published his memoir, *Death and Art in Greenwich Village*, a volume with such an autumnal, valedictory atmosphere to it, such a feeling not so much of 'summing up' as 'letting go', that I was by no means the only reader to feel it would be wiser to expect nothing more to emerge from De Petrie's study while he lived. And with that foreboding, at least among my peers whenever we discussed De Petrie, was another, less definable feeling: a sense that the author was consciously holding back something. Some large, wondrous, absolutely crucial book that lay finished (perhaps long finished) in a library drawer, in a manuscript box long ago sealed and addressed to his agent or publisher. We didn't say what form it would take, whether epic poem or Gothic novel trilogy – De Petrie seemed to master genre so easily, to throw off whatever he wished, whenever he wished, however he wished. But we had no doubt that whatever its form, it would be the book that would complete the great edifice he'd built – sometimes slapdashedly, sometimes carefully – over three decades; complete it, crown it and polish that crown with a flourish.

It was almost, we told ourselves and each other, as though De Petrie were holding back for a reason, almost as though he were letting the grass grow under his own reputation so Von Slyke could come forward more completely, to become Purple Circler Supreme; at least take the role of grand old fag of American literature. Despite other contenders scrambling for places around that throne, the only other real competition Von Slyke might possibly accept besides De Petrie was Aaron Axenfeld, and he'd dropped out of the race years ago, decades ago, perhaps before there was a race.

I couldn't get over an associated feeling that Von Slyke also knew, indeed all too well realized, De Petrie was holding back something and allowing Von Slyke to pull into the lead. And while he must have secretly feared when that held-back masterwork would be released, Von Slyke was intelligent and ambitious enough not to let anxiety stop him from moving forward toward and up onto the throne his fellow Purples seemed to either disdain or ignore. Doubtless, as he'd done so, Von Slyke must have come to increasingly worry that because it had been ignored or disdained by the only competitors who in his mind really counted for anything, it was therefore a somehow false eminence he was clambering onto, a height his pals Axenfeld and De Petrie had in effect and for their own reasons abandoned to him. That could do nothing but rankle, no matter how high his status rose: the sense that he dominated because Axenfeld had far too little self-esteem to dream of such a place for himself, and because De Petrie had another aim, one possibly higher or more tuned to immortality, to attend to.

I'd have to proceed slowly with St George. Let him into the information I'd already gathered about Spurgeon slowly enough so that he might for himself see how important he was, despite seeming to be a side issue to the Purple Circle. Tanya Cull had instantly grasped the beauty of my growing discovery of Len's *vita et opera*. She'd quickly grasped their psychological validity as they referred to her famous uncle, and sensed their criticality beyond Leo's life's and their relationships. If she could, with, her own necessarily biased perspective, see their scholarly importance, surely the equally slanted St George might too.

Once again, St George was in conference, so I opened his letter and read:

> *Reuben Weatherbury is teaching in the area this fall term. He has already arrived at the U Cal Campus at Irvine, has settled into a place in nearby Contra Mesa, and is even proctoring a seminar there during the summer session. His phone numbers are enclosed. It's a half-hour away via the Hollywood Freeway to the 5 to the 65 to the 405. Call him immediately. We've spoken by phone. He's expecting you.*

I was startled, and a bit taken off guard. I knew that eventually I'd have to see Weatherbury if I were to make anything of my thesis. He was one of the experts on the Purple Circle I could not choose to ignore. I'd need if not his blessing then at least not his enmity if the project were to get off the ground. Among the other experts,

Fleming was in England these days, at Manchester University, and, according to my Internet sources, deeply involved editing the letters of Oscar Wilde's lover Bosie, following the discovery of a batch of them in an old scullery of a small estate being converted into luxury flats in Kent. Cummings was still in Gainesville, Florida, where he was allegedly editing what he believed would become standardized volumes of Rowland Etheridge's works. He was known to be a sweet old man, delighted anyone would share his interest in queer writers of the past, only truly testy (if passionate) about nineteenth-century Italian opera. But Weatherbury, well, he was anything but sweet-tempered, and while he was still in Austin, Texas, I'd thought it prudent to keep a distance, until it proved absolutely necessary to enlist his aid.

I couldn't forget that encounter at the MLA conference a few years back at Columbia. I was asking him something quite innocuous about the Purple Circle's period and he'd suddenly sputtered out, 'Why ask me? There are texts that tell all that. Dozens and dozens of texts!' As he'd stormed off, two other grad students had told me of their own, not dissimilar, run-ins with him. Not that I expected to gain much from him anyway. Even so, like St George, Weatherbury not only met the fabled Nine, he'd staked out his claim to one of them early on, Cameron Powers, whom in Weatherbury's brilliant doctoral thesis emerged from obscurity to stand in some relief.

Of all of the Purples, Cameron Powers's life and work was undoubtedly the tiniest of fields to claim, but it turned out to be a half-acre Weatherbury so prudently farmed as to gather for himself most of the other Purple Circlers too. No wonder then that he'd quietly taken on the job of editing the *Reader* of their works, and when that proved to be a much class-adopted text, that he'd edited a second volume. The publicity the second volume received in the media had come at a key moment in the rediscovery of the Purples and had pushed their fame. Almost at the same time Weatherbury's 'discovery' (there for the discovering all the while) of Cameron Powers's posthumous stories was published. Together they were responsible for whatever scholarly status he'd achieved.

Still, if St George said to call him, I'd call. Who knew if Weatherbury would remember me.

Thus was I musing when my attention was grabbed by another summer-session substitute lecturer who had a question about some paperwork we had to cope with. As she kept repeating the question I'd already answered, and I grew bored, I began edging out of the office and into the corridor, attempting to make good my escape.

We'd gotten so far down the hall, in fact, that I was able to notice Irian St George's outer office door open and a tall, lanky, dark-haired young man step out. At first I thought he might be one of my students as he had a vaguely jock look, but as he came closer to where we were, I noticed he was too old to be an undergrad, early to mid-twenties, with a striking yet not handsome face: long, filled with planes of relief; sharp cheekbones; overhung brow; big, triangular, bony nose; a rather unendearing dimpled chin. I could barely make out the color of his slitted eyes, but I suspected they were brown or dark blue. He'd dressed to be stared at in a shaggy palomino vest with western-style long-sleeved shirt, close-fitting jeans cut cowboy style, and overdecorated, steel-tipped Western boots. He seemed deep in thought as he passed us, yet when my companion said hello, he nodded before throwing me the oddest look.

After he'd gone into the English Department, I asked who he was.

'I thought all of us PhD candidates had met,' she said. 'That's Waterford Machado.' And when I looked stunned, she went on, 'He's striking enough, but he plays up the Native American bit a little much, the way he dresses and all.' And when I still must have looked baffled, she went on, 'You know, Water Ford!'

'Oh!' I replied, and got out of there before I could show how disturbed I was by seeing him exiting St George's office.

An hour later, I was calmer. There were a dozen perfectly logical, departmental-related reasons why Machado had been in St George's office, and I'd found them all. Even so, I was still a little shaky, sitting in the garden, at my favorite spot under the pergola, in the strangely moist heat and humidity of the afternoon, clad in only a baggy light pair of Egyptian cotton shorts, drinking a Mocha something or other that Conchita had thoughtfully whipped up for me, when I picked up the phone to dial Reuben Weatherbury's number.

I was immediately shocked not to get a dialtone. I checked the buttons. No, everything was tuned correctly. What now? I began pressing them again. Oh, great, the phone was dead! I went inside again to see if the problem was only with the cellular or if the entire house was out. As I arrived in the library, the desktop computer was signaling that it had incoming e-mail. I moved the icon to display what was being received and read:

> Regarding the little manuscript. I won't help you. But I won't stand in your way, if that's why you've phoned me and what you're asking of me. I believe I know whom the author may be. Also I believe there are more little manuscripts floating around in Axenfeld's Fibber McGee room, among Cameron Powers's unsorted papers, and among Camden Phoenix's stuff.

The icon on the upper left said the caller was 'DDPet', whom I immediately assumed was De Petrie, and the next icon said that he was currently on-line. I activated a 'flash session' to talk to him in 'real time' but held off a bit, waiting to see what else he would write.

Nothing for a second. He must be aware I was on-line. So I typed in:

> I think I have a pretty good idea of the author myself.

> Really?

> Yes. And while I don't know your own relationship to the author, since it appears all of you had some kind or other of relationship to him, still I think you won't be surprised or even too displeased to hear that he's going to be the nub, the core, the very center of my PhD thesis on the Purple Circle.

> We-ell-lllll.

> Will you help me? Support my . . . thesis?

I can't say I will do anything for or against your thesis. What do scholarly pursuits have to do with me? Or I with them?

Before I could reply, he added:

What – exactly – is your request? What – precisely – is it you want? That any of you wants from us. Can you tell me that?

More than you want to give. And not because we're so selfish, but because we need someone to look up to, someone to admire.

Ahhh! I wish I could even remember what it was like to look up to another.

So you'll consider seeing me? Talking with me.

About the past? The past is another country, someone said. L. P. Hartley to be exact. But it's worse than that. The past is . . . if there weren't all those journals of mine in the collection, I would have no proof at all that it even happened. Everyone dead. Everything changed. All of us altered. No proof at all, you see. That's what the past is. And what it's worth.

But you *do* have proof. You have all your journals as proof.

And that's the very, very worst of it.

I couldn't think of any rejoinder.

Dame said you were good-looking. If you really want to meet me, send me something to look at.

Like what? A photo?

Or nude photo?

Or nude video? I had to wonder.

In my youth, I used to see this written on men's lavatory walls all the time – 'Show hard, make date!'

De Petrie clicked off.

Around me the entire cast of the day had altered. Where there had been almost oppressive heat, a brilliantly sun-glinting garden, was now clammy cold grayness. I recognized this as the marine layer that caused the strong morning fog moving back unexpectedly early. In the few minutes required for me to go back outside to gather my laptop, notes and coffee mug together, I discovered I was shivering uncontrollably. And even after I was inside, windows closed, me wrapped in a sweater and sweat workout pants, I still found myself chilled, and I huddled on my bed with a blanket cover for a surprisingly long while, watching mist filter into the central court looking like stage fog in a theater, appearing oddly, depressingly appropriate.

I found myself returning to De Petrie's last words, after I'd said to him that having his journals he had the proof of the past, and of his response: 'And that's the very, very worst of it.' What had he meant by that? Shouldn't it have been a triumph that he had proof that their glorious past existed? Wasn't that the entire idea of art? To exist beyond time? As the Purple Circle's best books did continue to exist and to communicate, decades after they were written. Why then did he see it as a defeat? It reminded me of what had happened the last time I'd spoken to Axenfeld on the phone and he'd remembered in such detail that snowy night at Etheridge's flat. That had left a bitter, frozen feeling behind. Why?

It began to depress me so much that I forced myself up and out of the bedroom, along the corridor, past the kitchen and into the dining room. More than half of those lines of MSS I'd laid out weeks ago were picked up, packed away: proof of the work I'd already done on the morass of Von Slyke's papers. Why not do more now? In fact, why not put a little fire in the huge fireplace to heat the place up. There were logs, kindling.

A half-hour later, a fire was roaring, and I was comfortably sorting and filing away, sitting Indian fashion on the now warmed blood-red tiles, when Conchita looked over the balcony. 'It's Mr Von

Slyke.' She held up a phone receiver. 'You look warm! It's like January out there!'

'Come join me. It's great here.'

She did in a few minutes, carrying sewing and a mug of herbal tea. Von Slyke was still going on about an outdoor production of *The Abduction from the Seraglio* he and Puddles had seen the previous night in some Hamburg *platz*. 'It was the Goosemarket Theater's production, but all but one of the cast members were American, which neither of us could figure out, until he said maybe they were summer replacements, but no, the program claimed they were regulars. The soprano's *"Marten alle Marten"* was stratospheric. She sounded like Caballé in her heyday, although of course I was a mere child at the time.'

He went on for the longest time, until I was convinced he had no real reason for calling. When he provided a minute break in the endless chitchat, I managed to tell him the work was going well, and being there doing it, I could be both truthful and precise.

'And how's your love life going?' he suddenly asked me. 'Did you make it with that cute boy chasing you? You know,' he prodded, 'the one in your class?'

I waffled so much in not answering Von Slyke that he finally said, 'You know of course that there's a historic erotic legacy to the house. You've got a responsibility . . .'

'You told me. George Peppard . . .'

'And it's up to all of us to make sure we make some erotic history there. No arguments. Get laid! That's an order.'

'Yes, sir!' I replied, with mock obeisance. But while he was in this playful mood, I decided to try something.

'My thesis is moving along well too. But you know I've come across somebody I wasn't aware of before. Maybe you'll be able to tell me more about him. Guy named . . . where is it . . .?' I play-acted looking for the name, all the while aware Conchita was watching me. 'Here we go! Len Spurgeon. His name seems to keep coming up. You must have known him.'

'A little. Long time ago. He knew the others better than me. Rowland before he met Chris. I think Dom after that. Axey a bit. He's dead, right? What is it, fifteen, sixteen years?'

'Something like that. From what I gathered, he and Mark Dodge dated, then he and Jeff Weber, and then he and the Leo–McKewens were tight. Cameron Powers too?'

'I think they dated a while. Or . . . I don't know how long. It was before whatshisname, that little English lit. professor, moved in with Cammy. Weatherbug or . . .'

'Reuben Weatherbury?' I asked. 'He lived with Powers?'

'That's why he got all of Cammy's papers,' he said casually. 'Look, I just wanted to check in and . . .'

I wasn't ready to let him go yet, long-distance or not. 'So tell me, Mr Von Slyke, who was this guy? This Len Spurgeon?'

'A number. A Woman of No Importance, as Wilde put it.'

'How come his name keeps coming up? In letters, diaries?'

'Does it? I wasn't aware . . .'

'It comes up constantly. According to my calculations, all of you knew him.'

'He was a *very* hot number, if you must know.'

'Did you have an affair with him?'

'No. Of course not.'

'But you slept with him?'

'Well . . . it wasn't like that. It was . . . how can I put it, a lot less romantic than it was . . . sleazy, if you know what I mean. I was in my experimental phase and he was known as top . . . Why don't I tell you this when I'm back?'

'Yeah, sure, okay,' I said.

We ended the link a few seconds later. I closed the phone and sat back on my haunches. I couldn't help but think Von Slyke was hiding something, or at least not telling me something important about Len. How quickly his tone had altered from the casual to the studied-casual-but-in-reality-defensive had given the fact away. What he'd let slip already about Reuben and Cameron Powers was a choice enough item to allow unexpected leverage when I met with the scholar. But I now knew Len Spurgeon and Powers had had an affair, and that Len and Von Slyke had been into S/M practices. That only left out . . . whom? Frankie McKewen? Well, maybe not. Rowland? The more I probed, the more it was beginning to look like Len Spurgeon was involved with all of them, every single one. My thesis was going to be great!

I dialed Reuben Weatherbury and although he seemed distracted, he agreed to see me two days later, at his school office. He gave

elaborate directions I carefully copied. When I hung up, I couldn't
help noticing Conchita looking at me. With a question or . . .

'Yes? What is it?'

'I'm confused,' she shrugged. 'I thought you were like . . . a librar-
ian. But the way you're looking for this guy and the way you
sounded on the phone, it's more like you're a detective.'

'A little of both,' I admitted, not for one instant liking her question.

The following morning's mail contained a standard-sized business
envelope from Aaron Axenfeld, stuffed to bursting. The cover page
in his rather elegant handwriting said, 'I found this in my Fibber
McGee room last year while looking for something else. I don't
remember it. But if I didn't, then . . . [eerie Celesta music on the
soundtrack] who did? It's doing me no good. You might find it
amusing. If you're still thinking of visiting, bear in mind that the
hurricane season has already begun.'

That was it. Of course he'd scribbled a signature. But not a hint,
not a clue further as to its authorship. I calmed myself, then began
to scan the pages in my hands. Not the same typewriter font – an
IBM Selectric Elite – as the cover letter: this was an older strike
ribbon. But in only a paragraph the style was definitely not
Axenfeld's. I sat back in the big library chair and read:

We'd arrived several days ago, and were already a little bored
with the gorgeous Caribbean weather, the cerulean skies, the
aquamarine waters, the hot days, the cool nights, the teeming
sudden downpours, the swaying palms, the hordes of mosqui-
toes, mercifully kept at bay by screened windows and doors.
But our absent hostess had foreseen everything, so we weren't
at all surprised the fourth morning when an old Jeep
Wrangler drove up to the house and a tall, whiplash-thin,
colorfully garbed native man stepped out and greeted us. His
skin was so dark it shone in the mid-morning sunglare. He
looked to be in his mid-thirties and spoke English with the
usual Islands lilt and a few odd accentuations and pronuncia-
tions of his own.

'Captain Tommy' he told us his name was, and he showed
us a very curled-up letter he'd been left by the owners of the

wonderful house we were vacationing in, mentioning us. Jim
remembered who he was instantly. Chiara had said he'd come
by the house and check it out. Captain Tommy pointed to the
boat that lay anchored at the little back-deck dock, a glamorous red and silver 'cigarette boat' speedster right out of
some episode of *Miami Vice*. He told us he'd take us wherever we wanted. Fishing, touring the islands, to distant white
beaches, where we'd have privacy. We could even go to a
shipwreck if we wanted to dive, but he'd have to warn us,
there were barracuda around those wrecks.

So, for the next few days we became not merely house-
guests, we became boatguests. We actively and lazily trawled
off the back of the boat, fishing for the little clawless, sweet
lobster of the area, for skate and yellowback and the unbe-
lievably rich grouper we'd wrap in tin foil and cook on the
side-deck barbecue. Captain Tommy took us to all the places
he'd told us about that first morning, and then since we
enjoyed it so much, and liked him so much, he took us to
more. One all-day trip to faraway Turk Island, once inhab-
ited by pirates and although tiny compared to any of the
others in the chain, both historical, colorful and festive.
Another time he took us to a resort on Pine Cay, where he
dropped us off on the dock and said something to a man
awaiting us there, who then took us on a single horse shay
into the little private town, consisting of a dozen houses
stretched out along a single road, and a Tudor-style inn-
restaurant, which might have been a thousand miles away in
upstate New York or outside London, where we had cock-
tails, an excellent British Sunday dinner of roast beef with all
the fixings.

Our final trip with Captain Tommy, however, was to be
the biggest surprise of all. It occurred a few days later, our
penultimate day at Sapodilla Bay. I spent much of the morning hunting down the completely transparent and logy
scorpions that invaded the house so regularly, finding shelter
in odd places like where toilet paper was stored under the
bathroom cabinets and suchlike spots, causing Jim to skittle
out of the john, gasping 'Paul!' and pointing indoors

wordlessly, fearfully. I saw no reason to harm them: after all, they lived there, while we only visited. So I'd grab hold of the barbecue tongs and carefully locate and lift out the poor, stupid arthropodic things from their dens and toss them into the scrub and cactus gardens surrounding the house.

Usually Captain Tommy would tell us where we were going the day before, but this time he didn't, and when we kept asking him where we were going and whether we should bring fishing tackle or snorkeling masks, he just said, 'Bring whatever you be wanting. But today, I's taking you to a special lunch. Very special. At my friend's in Grand Caicos.'

We'd tipped him well after each of our trips, and we'd always given him the bulk of whatever seafood we'd caught for himself and his girlfriend, Juanita, to take home to his place or to her family's house at Blue Hills. Even so we were surprised by this offer. After all, every native to this island was poor, although its tourism board encouraged visitors, builders, and becoming an 'expat', i.e. buying land and settling there as a tax shelter, it would be (thankfully to us) years, maybe decades, hopefully never before the place ever caught on. We'd no need for any gift from Captain Tommy. Hadn't he shown us beaches so pure-sanded white, so vacant we'd not seen another person all day? Hadn't he shown us the sunken British fort from the seventeenth century we'd dove around in for hours? Hadn't he shown us how to net a conch, carve it open, scoop out the vanilla-custard center and eat it right there, while we cut up the harder-meat 'foot' and sprinkled it with lime juice, which would 'cook' it, à la ceviche, in two hours? Hadn't he shown us more good sights and more wonderful and adventuresome days than either of us had experienced since we'd been pre-adolescents?

He had. So it was as little kids, not knowing what to expect, that we changed into bathing shorts, big-brimmed sunhats, and long-sleeved white T-shirts against the strong sun and leapt into the boat he'd already revved up.

An hour later we stopped seemingly nowhere on the northwestern side of Grand Caicos Island. Originally settled by Tories who'd been on the losing side of the American

Revolution, the entire chain had been handed to them as a
freehold by a grateful if bitter British government. After New
England the land was poor and weather was terribly hot and
it was too far off the much-plied sugar and rum shipping
lanes to be of much use for trade, if indeed anything on the
island could be found to trade. In fifty years, most of the
white farm owners had abandoned their plots to their slaves,
who then had been freed anyway, so they became the
landowners. Being African-American they were less bothered
by the weather than Nordic types, and they were able to fish
and farm sufficient to their needs, if they kept their families
small and their ambitions low. Of all the islands, Grand
Caicos had the most and greatest extent of more or less
arable soil.

We landed on the jetty, tied up the boat and waited for a
man with a late '40s vintage Dodge pickup truck. Jim and I
bounced twenty minutes to a crossroads where we all got out.
We walked to a long cinder-block building, a sign on it read
'Antonio's Café and Club'.

A more sorry place in a more godforsaken spot you'd
never dream to see. Jim and I looked at each other in astonishment. A big rectangular room, containing a half-dozen
trestle tables, and a long, deal wood bar. An adjoining
kitchen. A man and a woman were working there. No customers but us. Captain Tommy was already inside, greeting
them warmly. Cold beer bottles with lime wedges were put
on the counter, and throughout the introductions and banter
between them our lunch agreed upon.

It was airless indoors, so Jim and I stayed outside, on a
little cement terrace set amidst a totally undistinguished bit of
yard. There was an unexpected view of a landscape brown
and scrubby with no sense of glamour. The land sloped down
all before us into a depression that eventually became a large,
maybe mile-wide lake. A strangely deep blue-tinted, still-
watered lake. The closest arm of it lay maybe a quarter-mile
away. But given the flatness of the landscape, all of it was
quite visible from this little rise.

Food arrived: typical Islands sandwiches, French rolls with

a tasty, hot-flavored, tomatoey, fishy-fillet mass, accompanied by thick-cut greasy potato fries and some turmeric-flavored rice concoction. But we were hungry and all five of us, hosts and guests, slopped it down and washed it down with more beer. We continued to sit at the little table.

Time dragged on. Captain Tommy and Antonio went back indoors drinking. Jim and I remained outside, quietly disappointed, and a little annoyed. I was full and hot and tired, and I was about to lay my head down on the table and sleep, when I noticed a distant pink streak across the pale blue sky. It seemed to hover over the most distant point of the lake, then settle down. We drank and mused over the messy cheap china a while. Another, then another pink distant object wheeled and dropped onto the lake. Jim and I got to talking about some upcoming party back in New York City. All the while we talked, more pink objects hove into view, and around us began a distant clamor, difficult to assess as to its precise source or significance.

The sky became filled – no, let me say saturated with, then supersaturated with – more of the pink objects, until there were so very many of them we could hardly make out any sky at all. And of course, now that they were closer, we could see what they were: flamingos, big pink flamingos. And all of them wheeled in, circled the lake and dropped to its surface, until the sky, the air, the lake, all of it was covered with pink flamingos. Thousands of them, then tens of thousands of them. All dipping their heads in for shrimp or algae and lifting their long necks and stepping forward. A sea of pink so constantly in motion, a sky of pink so filled with the sound of wings and feathers rustling and honking and calling out, that we sat there absolutely stunned, believing that soon every inch of land as well as sky and water would be covered with them, the noise so infernal and constant and overwhelming a din, we couldn't speak or be heard.

I don't remember when exactly it was later on that Captain Tommy came to lift us away from the sight and drag us back to the crossroads.

After we arrived back at Sapodilla Bay, Jim and I never

spoke about it. We left at noon two days later. I never figured out what that experience meant. Only that it was overwhelming.

I guess we all need to be overwhelmed every once in a while.

Reuben Weatherbury's elaborate directions seemed to be important only once I'd gotten off the 405 Highway. Then, I had to look sharp to find my way. During most of the drive down to Irvine, I remained so nervous about the upcoming meeting that I tried to focus on anything but what might occur. Luckily, I had exactly what I needed to do it: I mean – besides the typically cowboy and Indians southern California midday freeway traffic – the fragment Axenfeld had sent.

No question about it, of all three pieces, it was the most unusual. Possibly the most purely 'literary'. Unlike the others, it might even stand on its own. That it was the work of the same author as the fragment about the kids in the car and the one about Paul and the cabdriver, I had little doubt, even if the syntax and language were more elaborate. But if those two had appeared to be progressive, in at least a chronological sense, this piece didn't fit into that chronology so much as stand outside it. Leading me to a few speculations. Most prominent among them was that what I had was either truly a trio of unrelated fragments, essays into fiction, experiments in writing even, that Len Spurgeon had written because he had somehow fallen under the influence of various Purple Circlers he'd befriended or been befriended by at various times in the late 1970s or early 1980s, or – conversely – that it was a much larger, more thought-out book, possibly autobiographical, possibly a novel.

There existed considerable pros and cons to this last theory: the biggest pro so far was that the more I looked, the more I found fragments. The second biggest was that I'd expressed this to Dominic De Petrie on-line yesterday and he'd done nothing, said nothing, to bar it. Indeed, he'd led me directly to the next manuscript. Of course, the biggest con was that the fragments didn't fit together – and, more importantly, none of them fit what I knew so far about Len Spurgeon. But then I knew so very little about him. And the remaining Purples, for whatever reason, were each keeping mum about him. I know, I know, Von Slyke had told me that he and Len had

had some sort of S/M relationship. The problem was I wasn't sure I believed him. Even so, he'd been the first of the three survivors I'd outright asked about Len. Why not try the other two? Why not? Because I was sure Axenfeld would weasel out of it somehow and I was sure that De Petrie would tell me off.

A right-hand sign listing my exit as the third of three suddenly showed up, and I began the task of changing lanes from the fastest to the exit ramp. Not long after I'd gotten where I wanted to, the exit sign itself appeared. As I slowed down along the long curving rampway, I hit the Celica's brain button and its onboard computer projected the next steps across the windshield. I was to turn right, go along for three traffic lights then turn left.

Another half-dozen turns and more instructions later, I realized that I was driving along a road that encircled the U-Cal Irvine campus. My directions were for a right to a particular road, which I at last arrived at, and thence to a chain of medium-sized parking lots. I was to find a spot among the visitors' row in the faculty parking. I did so, then got out of the car and looked around. From what he'd said on the phone, I guessed that behind, up that hill and through those single-story buildings, I'd find the English Department. Yes, there was the little campus radio station.

Students – or at least younger people wearing shorts and thin tops – began to appear in ones and twos as I got up one paved path and into a sort of woodsy area of buildings. This campus seemed to be typically late-twentieth-century SoCal in that, unlike earlier colleges like Stanford and Occidental, and unlike virtually all eastern and Midwestern campuses, it hadn't been designed and laid out for pedestrians, strollers to class, but for cars and drivers. A ring road opening out at points to parking lots that gave onto each distinct area: sciences there, humanities here, etc. Sure enough, as I gazed back I saw a small electric bus pull up, disgorge a few passengers and take one on. Those busses must circulate the campus for those without cars or those who didn't care to drive from class to class.

Unlike the single-story buildings I'd first passed among, which housed administrative and student-organization offices and appeared from their slapdash architecture to have been put up temporarily if still not replaced after some decades, the two main buildings attached by a common courtyard looked to be staunch and foursquare in their permanence. Built in the late 1960s or early 1970s, they were once-white cast concrete, identical to the least attractive housing projects of the day with their great swaths of pitted ramps and stony balconies. Despite that, the buildings had managed to age far more gracefully than anyone might have expected. This was due to the sylvan setting, the tall straight trees which rose seventy and eighty feet close around the buildings, casting them into a dark green shade flecked with hot sunlight, dropping tendrils of creepers to nearly hide in ivy curlicues the otherwise dreary giant concrete posts, suspending great twisted lianas of black-brown bark and mossy greens covering and cascading down the edges of each dreadful concrete balcony, the entire ensemble softened and glamorized by the constant birdsong and the sudden eruptions of bright fuchsia and hot honey-orange hibiscus flowers that seemed to bud and bloom out of every possible chink and crack of the crumbling old stone. What must have been industrial-complex monstrosities when erected on this hillside was now a grand old city abandoned to picturesque rot in a jungle.

Indoors, it was basic college building style. I located Weatherbury's office, knocked and steeled myself before entering. No answer. My guts churned. I knocked again.

The door opened: a middle-aged, heavy-set man with tons of gray-flecked hair in a tank top, running shorts and air shoes.

'You're Ross!' He all but pumped my hand in greeting. 'C'mon in. Or rather, why not just drop your things? You have any trouble getting here? You thirsty? Hungry? I was about ready to go for my run. You're dressed to run too. Do you want to wait around here in the office, or wouldn't you rather join me? C'mon, join me. It'll be fun! Just drop your stuff. It'll be safe. I'll lock up. I'm glad you got here. This is so great!'

Minutes later, I was astonished to find myself jogging alongside Reuben Weatherbury down the ramp of this building, out and around the single-story offices, through the linked parking lots, down and around the gently curving double-lane tarmac road that dropped onto the ring road. Once there, we kept to the right-hand painted-lane bicycle path, along with a few passing bikers and a few other joggers we pretty quickly surpassed.

'Isn't this a great afternoon?' Weatherbury enthused. 'Don't you

love this place? God! I'm so glad to get out of Texas and into southern California. It was so fucking brown there! You were grateful for
a sod of grass and a few straggly cottonwood! You're even better-
looking than St George said you were. Great physical shape. You an
athlete? Or just work out? Where we're headed to is the faculty gym.
Got a big weights room. You can work out with me. Or just spot
me. I'm on a routine. Gotta lose some of this.' He slapped his
abdomen. 'How is the old man, anyway? St George, I mean. God, I
love the guy. No one like him in the world! You should have seen
him at the Queer Studies bash the MLA threw in Seattle last April.
Someone said he looked like a pawnbroker, spoke like Somerset
Maugham and acted like King Farouk! You weren't there, right? I
would have remembered.'

I kept looking at him, nodding, not even trying to answer the constant barrage of his questions, trying to connect this heavy-set,
tanned, sporty-looking, suburban hale-fellow-well-met with the nervous, thin Weatherbury I remembered from only a few years back.
The thick, kept long in the front and top hair in TV-commentator
style and the square face with its slightly pug nose and bushy eyebrows over pale brown eyes set deep in chubby surrounding cheeks
seemed undoubtedly to be the same as the man I remembered. And
even the old-style brightly metallic, square aviator glasses he was
wearing were identical. But everything else was altered. Well, not so
much altered as developed in a totally different direction than I
would have expected. Not to mention the change in his personality.
Then he'd been aloof and unfriendly, taciturn and sarcastic. Now he
was almost bubbly.

He veered off onto another rising road and we were soon within
the Phys. Ed. complex. Weatherbury headed us into a doorway and
we jogged through a long, narrow corridor that seemed to go on a
half-mile, before he turned up an internal ramp and from there into
the faculty gym and through, to get to a locker room.

'Okay.' He was barely panting. 'Time out. I gotta shoot up.' He
opened a locker and took out a hypodermic needle and something
else. 'It's kosher! I'm diabetic.'

I watched as he prepared the needle and injected himself.

'Three and a half years ago, I passed out getting off a bus in
Chicago. Best thing that could have ever happened to me. I found

out I was diabetic. Never had a clue. According to people I've known, in the years just before the discovery I was a real downer, a complete schmuck. I blame it on being sick and not knowing I was. Now . . . well, now I guess I don't have any more excuses, do I? Don't look so serious!' He slapped my arm.

He laughed, cleaned up and slammed shut the locker. We got a fresh grass juice each from the university-operated business, then went into the nearly vacant, well-equipped gym, where he selected a machine and routine and began it, asking me to either join him or stay nearby and spot him on the various machines. I chose that.

'So, tell me –' Weatherbury at last got around to the subject of my visit – 'what St George only hinted at so tantalizingly?'

He seemed so open, I could have just spilled it all. Instead I said, 'He told you that I've been getting Von Slyke's papers organized to go to the Timrod Collection?'

'And that you'd found a suspect manuscript.'

'Well, I've got two more, what you call suspect manuscripts. And I'm beginning to suspect who wrote them. If I'm right, and in truth I'm really only partway there right now – well, it might be a considerable addition or new path in Purple Circle studies.'

'Three manuscripts?' he gushed. 'Wow!'

'All fragments. I'm not sure yet what they're fragments of.'

'Sounds intriguing,' he grunted. 'More! More!'

'Well, that's why I'm here. Von Slyke told me you knew Cameron Powers personally . . .'

'He did?!'

For a second I wondered if I'd been led astray. 'I'm terribly sorry if I'm wrong. Only yesterday, he told me on the phone . . .'

'I'm kidding! I'm kidding!' Weatherbury assured me. 'I thought everyone knew I was Cameron Powers's catamite.'

'Catamite?'

'We lived together and he porked me regularly and paid my bills for nearly two years. What would you call it? Come on. Don't act shocked. Minute I laid eyes on Powers, I told my best friend I was going to get him in the sack no matter what it took. It turned out it didn't take much. I was just an undergrad at the time: and the cutest I've ever looked in my life. He was on the skimpiest of book tours for the paperback version of his one published book. How he managed to arrive in New Haven, I'll never know. But all of us in school were reading the other Purples and we all knew he'd been Von Slyke's lover and that he knew the others, so we showed up at the reading. There must have been six of us, including the bookstore manager, one woman from a local gay rag and a guy taking notes for a term paper. Afterwards me and my best friend invited Powers out for a drink at a local gay-friendly bar. To our amazement he accepted. And to my amazement afterward, Powers took me to his hotel room and screwed the bejesus out of me. Never having been so expertly or assiduously analized before, I naturally fell in love. I visited him a dozen times that summer and when I graduated and moved to Manhattan to go to Columbia Grad School, I haunted his doorstep till he let me in. I moved out of the dorm and into his apartment in January for the spring term. I stayed there, till he kicked me out.'

During the remainder of his physical routine, Weatherbury told me the rest of the story. They argued so badly, they'd come to blows. It wasn't until Powers was hospitalized and in the last stages of a massive pancreatic degeneration as a result of HIV infection that they'd seen each other again. He phoned Weatherbury out of the blue, told him he was dying, and that he didn't trust any of the people who'd begun hovering around him like vultures. Reuben had dropped everything and flown to his side. No tearful farewells, but he'd taken over the remaining three months of Powers's life, arranged for a will to be written, arranged the burial and memorial services, found and fed him cocaine when he was asked to do so, and watched Powers sink daily until he reached first coma then oblivion. No one was more surprised than Weatherbury when the will was read and he was made literary executor. The other Purples weren't in the least surprised: Cameron had intended to do it for years.

'So!' Reuben concluded. 'That's how I became the main Cameron Powers scholar. Sort of reminds me of what Mae West used to say.'

'What's that?' I asked.

'She used to say, keep a diary when you're young. When you're old it'll keep you,' Weatherbury laughed. 'In my case, it was keeping Powers happy when I was young that's going to keep me when I'm old.'

He was finished. We hit the juice stand, this time for some carrot-ginger concoction, then we jogged back out of the Phys. Ed. building and back to the English Department.

Reuben changed shirts and threw me a towel.

'So? How can I help you?'

'Well, I guess for starters, you could help me locate any possible references to Len Spurgeon in any files or letters you may have that belonged to Cameron Powers.'

'Len Spurgeon? Yeah, I remember the name.' He hit some buttons on his computer screen and said, 'Okay. We've got thirteen minor references. Citations by name only. That sort of stuff. Then we have two full pages. I'll bring that up, okay?'

'What is that anyway? Powers's letters? His journals? Or what?'

'Who told you Powers wrote letters or kept journals?'

'No one. I just guessed.'

'Guess again. What we're looking at is whatever *I* wrote. Either at the time I was living with Cameron. Or later on, after everything had come to me.'

'I don't get it,' I said, as the computer screen opened the file, which he was blocking from view.

'How do I put this?' Reuben began. 'Well, there's no way but one way to say it: Cameron Powers wrote virtually nothing himself. Whatever you're seeing was written by someone else. Most of it is my notes for a sort of biography or book about Powers and the others. You see, Ross, Powers was dyslexic.'

'Dyslexic? How can that be? He was a writer? A senior book editor for a major publisher? If he couldn't read and write . . .'

'He could read. Up to a point. Never too fast, of course. But enough for letters and memos and suchlike. He'd taught himself enough tricks by then to read okay. As for longer things. Well, he'd scan them and work from reader's reports. But his writing was com-pletely . . . He'd dictate everything . . . I see you don't believe me. Look at this!' He hit another button, opened another file in a window over this one and showed me.

That winter Dame got a big enough advance that we were able to move down to this wonderful second-story apartment on Duval Street in the Old City of Key West. It was located just off Darkie Town, so we heard roosters crowing every morning, the same fowl that were sacrificed at night in Macumba ceremonies we'd recognize from all the drumming and strange shrieks. By day we'd leisurely lunch, bicycle down to the local beach, come back home and nap, have a cocktail, and join friends for dinner until long past midnight. One day, however, Dame said, 'We've been here a month and haven't done a stitch of work. Time – not to mention my cash advance – is a wasting. We've got to get to work, boy!' So we did. In the morning, he'd write in bed, on a pad of yellow foolscap, while I slept or tried to get him to play with me. But after lunch, or on rainy afternoons, we'd work on Via Appia *together, we managed to get parts one and two of it done then.*

'That was in the winter of 1979,' Weatherbury said. 'I arrived on the scene 1981. He'd not done anything further in the book. I myself helped Cammy with parts two and three. One section from the latter chapter, retitled 'The Pines – and Pimps – of Rome' – was cobbled together by the two of us and appeared in the Fall 1981 issue of the *Sewanee Review*. After that, the MS sat. Until, that is, Len moved in. What follows Cameron told me during those daily work sessions we had when he was at St Vincent's Hospital.'

Reuben closed that window and opened another windowed file. He scanned it a minute, until the cursor began to be underlined black, then said, 'Here goes!'

I met Len for about the third time at one of the Leo– McKewens' famous tea parties uptown. I'd arrived late, and he was about to leave, having just had some kind of a tiff with the Fried Chicken heiress. I complimented him on his boots, never mind what else he was wearing, and for some reason he didn't bite my head off, but instead talked with me a while. We left the place together and headed for a local Chinese restaurant. Over Prawns from Lo Mountain he found out I was living alone, and that I had a spare room. He needed a place and said he'd help with the rent. Len moved in a few days later, and I soon discovered that he was a lot more fun in my own bed than on that single mattress in the so-

called den. About a month or so after he'd moved in, he somehow or other found the MS of Along the Via Appia *or at least as much of it as I'd done, and read it and said, why the hell didn't I finish it? And I said, why the hell don't you help me? So he did. We did not only parts four and five. But revised the whole thing. He was awfully smart at editing, suggesting words, choosing syntax. He had a natural sense of how words flow and how they denote and connote. I couldn't have done the book without him. And I wanted to dedicate it to him or at least acknowledge his help, but he said no. So I didn't. Whatever happened to him? Last I heard he was hanging around with Dom De Petrie. God, was he beautiful! I can remember waking up from a nap one afternoon and watching him sleeping, laying on his back, and I thought, I'm not crazy about this man, but I surely could be.*

I suppose I must have looked surprised, because Reuben said, 'What? What is it?'

I didn't want to immediately respond to the De Petrie connection, so instead I asked, 'I suppose I'm surprised by how, you know, flip, unserious he sounds when talking about his writing.'

'All of them. All the Purples. I'm not kidding. De Petrie once wrote under the title page of Mark Dodge's *Keep Frozen* – 'Semen on Board'. And they were always changing the names of each other's books in letters. You know *Irrigations* for *Instigations*, that kind of thing. But, of course, Cameron was almost the worst.'

I'd been thinking. Now I had to ask. 'If you and Von Slyke and Len Spurgeon wrote Cameron Powers's first book, then who . . .'

'Wrote the stories in the second book?' Reuben finished for me. 'I did. Mostly while he was in the hospital. He had notes. God, he had entire sections of them written down. After a fashion.'

'He wasn't in terrible pain? I heard pancreatic cancer . . .'

'He wasn't in pain whenever I brought him cocaine. Which, yes, I did regularly. Which he took regularly. Then I couldn't keep him in bed, or shut him up. De Petrie came to visit and forgot his little microcassette recorder. I arrived maybe a half-hour later and Cameron was moaning and carrying on. Once he'd snorted, however, he all but leapt out of bed, and began telling me the story about the drag queen Jackie Von Vetch, you know, "Miss Thing" in the story. I just grabbed the microcassette and began recording it. I used it for the next two months. Only after Cameron died did I return it to De Petrie. At the memorial service I handed it to him as he came in the door. He looked at me and said, "I knew I'd left it there, but Cammy said no".'

While I was absorbing that information, Reuben asked 'So? Is this guy Len the one you're interested in?'

'He seems to pop up in all of their lives. I'm working on a sort of theory . . . it's not developed yet. You don't have anything else, do you? On Len?'

'Only an anecdote that Cameron told me. Let me see –' he turned back to the computer and brought up yet another window, searched through that and said, 'Okay, here it is.'

Len had been living with me for about three months when one night, maybe four o'clock in the morning, the phone rings. I pick it up and a very official voice on the other end asks to speak to him. It's four o'clock in the morning. We've just gone to bed – what? – two hours before. Len's out like a light. I try to wake him up. Get nowhere. So I ask the man who he is and what it's all about. He tells me he's from the INS, Immigration Service, and that he's got a Leonard Spurgeon Junior in custody, directly arrived on a flight from El Salvador and he can't allow him through customs until one of his parents comes to get him.

As you can imagine, I wake right up at this news. But despite my efforts, when I shake Len and tell him all this, he sort of murmurs, 'Yeah. Yeah. Tell him we're coming.' Which I do. Then when I hang up the phone and ask him what in the hell that was all about, he says to me, 'Call Haifa car service. We need a limo to go to the airport.' Which I also do.

Well, you can imagine my continued surprise and annoyance as we dress and go down to the rented limo and drive all the hell to JFK airport and Len – who takes even longer than I do to wake up as a rule – sleepily murmurs nothing like an acceptable answer to my eleven hundred questions.

We get to the INS office and there, sleeping in a bassinet, is the cutest, brownest-skinned, blackest-haired, three-months-old baby boy you've ever seen. No way this is Len's baby. But Len signs all the papers, and they give us the baby. Who gurgles and coos in his sleep and holds my finger with his hand in the back-seat of the limo all the hell back to East 24th Street in Manhattan.

We go back to sleep, all three of us, and the next day, as casual as possible, Len wakes up, has breakfast and phones some lawyer who arrives that afternoon, with this very handsome Jewish couple in their early forties who, it seems, are going to adopt the baby. All the papers are signed and passed over and the Salvadoran baby is out of the apartment by eight o'clock that night.

Turns out that Len was down there, in El Salvador, when he was in college or shortly after on some student exchange program, and he either had an affair with or became close friends with (it's not too clear) this woman who it turns out is part of the intellectual leftist organization fighting our CIA-supported right-wing government. Her job is to manage to get the small children of leftists who are arrested and executed in the middle of the night by right-wing death squads out of the country by bribing the maids to say the kids are their own and to hide them in their rooms when the parents are dragged away. The children are then put on a plane and secreted into the US, where adoptive parents are all lined up waiting for them. It's an underground railroad for these poor kids, and Len is a crucial link. Everyone, including the INS, knows what's going on. He's down there at that JFK shed once every month or so. It's all a charade. Yet . . . He's a fabulous man, isn't he?

'Do you think you could print that out for me?' I asked.

Reuben not only printed it out, he also gave me a disk copy of the two pieces of Cameron Powers's papers to contain long references to Len. 'So, you going to meet with the surviving Purples?' he asked, as we headed out of his office and toward the parking lot.

'I've already met with Damon Von Slyke, naturally, and I've spoken on the phone with Aaron Axenfeld,' I said.

'Well, you saved the real treat for last, didn't you?'

'You mean De Petrie? I don't get it. In all the articles and biographies about the nine of them, De Petrie comes off as the easiest-going, the most fun-loving of them all. How did he become . . . I mean he's a recluse, doesn't write, or at least doesn't publish. Have you heard his phone message?'

We'd arrived at my car in the parking lot. Reuben leaned against it to retie his sneakers 'You'll have to ask the others what happened to him. I don't know. I always deal with him – when I'm absolutely forced to do so – by letter. Usually certified or registered mail. Since that's the only kind he doesn't send back. You wouldn't want to stick around and join me and my lover for dinner? We're meeting up with another gay couple. From the Math Department, believe it or not.'

I pleaded a previous engagement and we shook hands.

'Tell St George I'm coming up there soon,' Reuben signed off.

As I drove back to Los Angeles, I smiled. Not only had I made an important new ally, not only had I found out a crucial secret about Cameron Powers, but I'd also come closer to getting a more rounded picture of Len Spurgeon. Not only a sexy guy, a wit, a tease, a game player, a lover, but also a humane man, saving people's lives. No wonder the Purples were so interested in him. Who wouldn't be?

The restaurant where I was supposed to meet the students was located in the middle of a newish mall area along Yucca Avenue off Vine: a recent redevelopment turning the half-century-old Capitol Records Tower into a historical landmark and music industry theme park, complete with do-it-yourself recording studios, the Hollywood and Vine Michael Jackson Museum, and five new 'official' restaurants, each with its own individual topic, area and era: Adagio for the Classics (Italian-Asian cuisine); Beale Street for Jazz and Blues (Southern home cooking); La Bamba for Latino and Salsa (Tex-Mex cooking); Rockin' Robin for Golden Oldies (standard burgers, fries and sodas); and the Flaming Needle for contemporary-post-alternative-new age-neo-funk (the menu as eclectic and changeable as the music itself). This time-evoking was of course carefully laid out among Disneyesque plazas, fountains and huge banks of flowering trees and bushes, and all of it was encircled by and ramped up to

and away from the *raison d'être* of the entire thing: the four enormous shops – Virgin, Tower, HMV and DreamworksSKG – each
within its own multistory glass tower, devoted to differing kinds of
music, all of them more or less directly influenced in architectural
and interior-decorating style by the presiding Capitol Records
Tower. The idea, indeed the advertised guarantee, was that upon
entering Hollywood–Vine Music City, you would be able to locate
any piece of music – a dueling banjos tune, the 1905 De Reszke aria
from *Manon Lescaut*, a never-released cut from the Bangles' *My
Boyfriend's Back* album, the CD, videoptape, laserdisc, red-vinyl
45-rpm record, beta-max, 8-track, the original goddamn Edison
cylinder if need be – of whatever you happened to crave to hear.
Connecting chutes among the shops and related warehouses, as well
as all the other, more specialized music boutiques in the three-block
complex, would locate and deliver your choice to you before you
drove out of the vast underground parking space, sometimes while
you were sitting drinking a margarita at a terrace.

Among all of this, the Thai restaurant listed on the birthday invitation was an old-timer. Established way back in 1985, the plaque
attached to the black marble façade of the building boasted. Given
the changing, the almost immorally changing tastes and fads of Los
Angeles eateries in the several decades since then, Chaya Dan was
truly a monument of stability. Indeed part of its fun, it later turned
out, was to look at those old photos and holographs on corridor
walls near the men's, ladies' and 'whatever' restroom, showing the
place in earlier times. Flanked by a Domestic Help Office on one
side, a Medical Prosthetics shop on the other, during its first decade
in business; the entire open front area, now garden and outdoors
dining, had been given over then to being a small, surpassingly unattractive parking lot; the blocks surrounding the place dreary and
utterly pedestrianless, with only an old Nissan 300Z parked in view.
Or, a decade later, once the restaurant had taken over its neighbors'
space and it had become for a while a hot biz (i.e. film and TV business) hangout, the surrounding area even less frequented, with
nothing but the BMWs and Rolls-Corniches of the agents, stars and
other players filling the front parking lot. And finally, a few years
ago, when Music City had just opened.

The food, however, was said to be virtually unchanged, or only a bit updated to reflect new diet beliefs. It smelled great and looked wonderful on diners' plates as I entered, a bit later than the invitation had called for.

I was directed up a flight of stairs all but wrapped in an aluminum sculpture titled *Anaconda* to a balcony where several booths and tables had been moved about to form a single large table.

Luckily, people were just arriving or standing around or sipping aperitifs and nibbling at appetizers. So I wasn't too late.

Bev Grigio noticed me first. 'You made it! Great!'

'Where do the gifts go?' I'd wrapped a first edition of Damon Von Slyke's *The Japonica Tree*, certain that it wouldn't be missed among the dozen or more of the books I'd found huddled in a lower shelf of the library subcloset.

She pointed to a pile of packages on the floor. 'Just put it there. Don't you look handsome, all dressed up,' Bev said, and blushed at the same time.

Before I could say anything, she added, 'All the guys do, tonight. That's one of the nice things about LA weather. No matter how hot it gets by day, you can still wear a jacket at night and look formal.'

'You a native?' I asked, less out of interest than to make small talk and meanwhile look around us.

'Oh, no! I'm from Hawaii. Big Island.'

'Hilo?' I asked.

'Actually Pahoa.'

As we spoke, a waiter offered me drinks. I took a white wine spritzer and what looked to be lightly floured, sautéed zucchini.

Pamela Agosian was in the corner, by her gifts now. She wore a metallic teal-colored single-piece sheath of a dress. Very appropriately Asian-looking. Her thick blonde hair was up on her head, wrapped in some sort of European-looking-style bun I didn't know what to call. It was held in place by a jeweled pin the size of her hand, composed of a dozen or more green and blue gemstones. It made her look elegant and grown-up.

Talking to Pamela were Danielle Tsieh, her twin Michelle, Kathy Tranh and another young woman not in my class. Already sitting down were Perry Valentine and Cheryl Taylor, two other classmates who were what passed for African-American in southern California, i.e. not very. Ben-Torres, in an expensive sport coat and slacks, was standing at the top of the stairs talking to the Samoan linebacker Taponaupoa, also wearing a sport coat but with shorts and sandaled sockless feet. And behind them was Ray Rice in a similar-looking outfit, except his jacket was a navy blazer. He stepped aside to let two more younger women come upstairs, both obviously Pamela's sisters, Tanya and Tonya, which Bev confirmed. A minute later we were all seated.

Pamela claimed to be thrilled to have me attend, as had been predicted, and made sure I sat on her right. I couldn't help but notice Ray Rice placed himself among males opposite, all the jocks in a row.

The dinner was in the form of a Thai banquet, the dishes brought out two or three at a time in great metal-covered salvers, their lids removed with a flourish for us to ooh and ahh over before they were served. Since we all more or less faced each other, it wasn't difficult to see the various interchanges between diners. I'd only been out of undergrad classes a few years and though I was now their teacher, it was obvious that little had changed in those few years. The young women were trying to be dignified yet light-hearted. They were flirting with myself and the other four younger men, without making too much of it, at the same time that they were checking out the lie of the land to truly assess any serious interest among us.

Ben-Torres, Perry, Ray and Taponaupoa, on the other hand, were about ninety-five percent oblivious to what was going on, not only between themselves and the women, but among the women themselves. Indeed, if I was a bit more conscious of it, it was not because I was so much older or more worldly-wise, it was more because 1) as a teacher I was in the somewhat more aloof position of being an observer and 2) not too long ago, a woman had gone out of her way to point out my own general ignorance in these matters and had attempted to if not quite correct them, then at least lead me into a general area where some repair might take place.

Thus I could see that Danielle, Michelle and Kathy Tranh all 'liked' Ben-Torres, but were all afraid of him a little, mostly given his general lack of communicativeness and more specifically his opacity about feelings and emotions. As obvious to me was Bev Grigio's amused interest in the gigunda Samoan linebacker: an interest she kept going by managing to needle him whenever possible – in the gentlest of manners. Equally clear, Cheryl Taylor had no interest at all in Perry Valentine besides student camaraderie – an attitude he was only partly aware of.

Among the other women present, only Pamela was a mystery to me. She treated all four men students with the sort of slightly patronizing interest one uses to deal with people one is forced together with on a much-delayed, long and not especially interesting plane ride. Toward me she was less constant. In class she was usually 'Junior Miss' – perfect in behavior and attitude. But then I'd come across her on campus, or in the library or in some shop in nearby Westwood Village, and she would look momentarily uncomfortable, as though unprepared for me outside of the formal situation she'd consigned me to. Of course that could be the entire answer. Undergrads had plenty on their minds. She probably did pigeonhole me, as she did her other summer-session teachers. And it was true that she usually regained her class composure quickly enough. Why, then, did I intuit that within her gape-mouthed surprise at those unexpected encounters along Bruin Walk or along Broxton Avenue was some other even more salubrious sensation: a sheer pleasure, lighting up her face, and especially her large pale eyes, and animating her to an altogether higher pitch of both alertness and intelligence? Was I utterly vain in thinking she had something of a crush on me? An interest in me less overt than, say, Ray Rice's more disturbing interest; one she'd probably never make a move on; and thus one I had to admit I unaccountably much preferred.

Before dessert – and I assumed some sort of cake – a break was called. The tables were cleared. We stood up and milled about. Ben-Torres and Ray Rice approached me. Taponaupoa hovering just behind them.

'So, Professor Ohrenstedt!' Ray waved me closer into their tall trinity. 'Settle a question for us.'

'What question?' I asked warily. As I joined them I noticed the group shifting ever so slightly, with the big Samoan blocking us from the others. What was going on?

'Well, Ben and Tappy and me are curious about this ghost-dance business.'

I looked up at Taponaupoa. 'You read *Black Elk Speaks* too?' I couldn't believe it. He wasn't even in our class.

'I can read, you know?'

'He read the section about the ghost-dancing,' Ray Rice clarified. 'We got to talking about it, trying to figure out what it meant. Tappy here comes from a sort of tribal society, so we thought he might have something like it back home.'

'Do you?' I asked.

'Hell, no! That stuff is weird, man.'

'Yeah?' Perry had joined our group. 'What exactly were they all doing?'

'Well, you understand that by 1885, any Native American of any intelligence and foresight saw the writing on the wall and knew that their life as they'd lived it was over.'

'Right!'

'Check!'

'Go on.'

'Black Elk was already in training from the time he was a small boy to become a great medicine man,' I added.

'At seven years old he knew,' Ben-Torres said.

'Right. Well, at twenty or so, he was already pretty high in the many-nationed congress of chiefs and medicine men. So he was there when they decided to initiate the ghost dances.'

'But what were they?' Ben-Torres asked.

'He tells you what they were. All-day and all-night dance sessions of all of the most important braves and chiefs of all of the remaining tribes. Two or three days on end. Until they all dropped. They did – what? – a hundred ghost dances over four years. All over what was left of their homelands in the West.'

'We know. We know, but why did they do them?' Ray asked.

'He tells you that too,' I replied. 'They all painted themselves white to look like ghosts. And they danced until the noise they made attracted their future people. Their grandchildren and great-grandchildren.'

'You mean the Native Americans of a hundred years later?' Ben-Torres was getting it.

'And of 2085 and 2185. They believed time is a continuum. It isn't as solid as, say, space is, it has points where it can be crossed. If you did some extraordinary act, that would cross time. Maybe forever. That's what they did. They danced and sang until they had effected a rip in time. They brought their life and times and troubles into the future.'

'They thought they did,' Perry said.

'No,' I said, 'they actually did it. By a hundred years later, their grandchildren and great-grandchildren were suing the American and Canadian governments and getting their land back, and getting reparations. As well as having books, TV shows, movies all being sent out to revive their people and their time. To revive them not only in their own minds, but in the minds and culture of other Americans.'

'But they thought they would come back too?'

'Maybe they did. Maybe they were reincarnated in that post-World War II baby boom. My parents' generation. Look how tribal they all were? How they gathered at what amounted to being huge music and dance powwows days on end. At Woodstock. At Monterey. At Altamont. Then, too, look at Dominic De Petrie and Aaron Axenfeld's stories and novels about the '70s and early '80s disco-dance era. How they too believed they were the old tribes come alive again. Look at that poem where De Petrie writes, "We are the Paiutes, the Dakotas, the Perce-Nez/ and ours the dance eternal atop/ mountains, in tented cities, in caves/ below the ground where we return/ to dance again. This time in triumph!"'

'So they did cross time,' Ben-Torres mused.

'They knew they were lost in their own time. They had no choice but to cross out of their time. Not that Native Americans will ever be fully compensated. But they sure are in a better position today than they have been for more than a century. In terms of land ownership, financially through oil and mines and casinos on their land. In terms of freedom from government interference. In terms of outside interest and respect for their culture.'

'We thought it was like a metaphor,' Ray Rice said. 'We didn't know they expected it to really work.'

'Can a female enter this conversation?'

We all turned. Bev Grigio. 'Cake and presents!' she announced.

'No metaphor,' I said when she was gone. 'They expected it to really work.'

A half-hour later, people were still in an up mood, but the restaurant was undoubtedly finished with us, even if we were upstairs and out of their way. Bev and Taponaupoa were two-stepping.

Pamela and Ray were arguing over where to take the party next, as no one seemed to want it to end yet. There were clubs nearby and cafés with recorded and live music. But everyone agreed they were too touristy. If we were going somewhere to dance, we should head to the Sunset Strip. Or to one of the nameless places around the area. But this led to some of the women deciding that it was getting a bit late: tomorrow was after all a school day.

I wasn't precisely aware when and how it was that Ray Rice said, 'Hey! Professor! You live near here, don't you? I hear it's a big place. Maybe we could drop by there?'

Expecting one of the women to shoot down the idea, I didn't instantly protest.

'Is it nearby?' Pamela asked.

How could I lie? 'A mile or so. Just off Franklin Avenue.'

'But where would we all park?' Kathy Tranh asked. 'We've got – what – a dozen cars among us.'

I heard myself saying, 'It's got a big circular driveway.'

Fifteen minutes later, as I dialed open the gate to Casa Herrera y Lopez, I received the first hesitancy from, of all people, Pamela, in the passenger seat of my Celica. 'You're sure we're not imposing on you?'

Behind us a row of cars all the way back to Outpost Road told me I'd not been able to lose the others despite my fast driving. I shrugged and mumbled something and drove into the gate. I parked in the *porte-cochère* and guided the other vehicles in and to parking spots: two canvas-sided Wranglers (Perry and Ben-Torres), one 1976 Buick Electra (Taponaupoa, natch), a Beemer Micro-Sport (Cheryl), a shiny new dark pickup truck (Ray Rice, who else?), and assorted Asian marque coupés (the women).

'This place is huge!' Michelle Tsieh said.

I managed to herd all of them into the partly roofed-over front patio, and into the house through the double front doors. Milling about in the corridor the group looked larger than it had in the restaurant. I must be out of my mind!

'Mr Ohrenstedt!' Kathy Tranh raised her hand, looking apologetic. 'I need the ladies' room.'

'Me too!' Bev Grigio agreed. Cheryl seconded her.

I guided the group into the living room, which I'd never even sat in, not once in the time I'd lived here. Then said, 'Those for the ladies' room follow me.'

'I could use ice for this,' Taponaupoa held up a soft drink in a crush tube.

'Okay, and anyone else want a drink? Three, four. Tappy, follow me.'

I led a half-dozen of them toward 'my' wing of the house.

'Is that the dining room?' Pamela asked. We were now peering through the adobe-wall opening down into the high-ceilinged room.

'Looks big enough to hold twenty people,' Danielle said.

'Is this someone famous's house?' Perry Valentine asked.

'Damon Von Slyke,' I replied.

'No. I meant someone famous before him.'

'The actor George Peppard lived here in the '60s.'

'Who? Petard?'

'It was supposedly built for a famous Latina courtesan in the '20s.

'Courtesan?' Tappy asked.

'Prostitute,' Kathy dead-panned.

'Really?' the linebacker asked, evidently impressed.

'A high-faluting, evidently very well-kept prostitute,' I agreed. Then, 'Ladies! There's a lav off the library. And another downstairs way over there, next to my bedroom, if two of you are desperate.'

I didn't particularly want any students down there, but I wasn't sure if Conchita was sleeping over in her maid's room. Hers was the only other bathroom on this side of the house besides the two I'd already mentioned.

'Right here!' I showed them the library powder room.

'Jeez. Look at all the books!'

'Is this Von Slyke's library?'

'Sure is. *Do not touch a thing*!' I was strict. 'Got it?'

'We can look, can't we?' Kathy asked.

'Look. But do not touch.'

I left Kathy and Danielle there and led Perry, Cheryl, Pamela and Taponaupoa downstairs. As we passed the balcony giving onto the dining room, Pamela asked what all that on the dining-room floor was.

'Manuscripts!' I explained. 'Von Slyke's papers. I'm getting them ready for the Timrod Collection.'

Past the door to Conchita's room, down the stairs. 'Here's the kitchen! Stick around and help me get soft drinks.' I left Cheryl, Pamela and Tappy there and led Perry further along the hall to my bedroom bathroom.

When I got back to the kitchen only Cheryl was there. I noticed the kitchen door to the courtyard was ajar. Pamela was standing at the fountain. The Samoan was not in view.

I located and flipped on courtyard lights: pale green and blue and fawn.

Pamela gasped.

Tappy hove into view. 'This place is something. Hey, Pam! There's a huge hot tub back there. Big enough for six people.'

I'd only lighted up this garden once before at night. I had to admit it looked wonderful. Pamela was twirling around in a slow arabesque; her shimmering metallic teal dress caught and reflected light and shadow.

'What's that you're humming?' Taponaupoa asked her.

'"Nights in the Gardens of Spain", Manuel de Falla.' She continued to twirl, now iridescent as a goldfish: he partnered her, with that light grace of the big-bodied.

'Way cool!' It was Perry now, in the garden too.

'Hey, Per. There's an orgy-sized hot tub over that way!' Tappy directed

'Perry! Will you give me a hand in the kitchen?' I asked.

'Yes, Mastuh!'

Kathy and Danielle found their way down the stairs and outside too.

'Why don't we stay here?' Kathy suggested. 'It's warm enough outdoors.'

'Mr Ohrenstedt?' Tappy asked.

'Oh, okay. I'll go get the others.' This way we wouldn't have to troop everything upstairs.

'I'll go get them,' Perry offered. Bowing repeatedly at me until I swatted him with a dish towel. I then laid it across one arm like a French waiter, and went out to where Kathy and Danielle had sat at the little table. 'Zee kitchen, she is open! Your wish?'

Pamela, I noticed, was still doing slow rotations, her Ginger Rogers being partnered now by Perry and the Samoan.

'Mademoiselle,' I asked her, 'your order?'

'Champagne,' she added, 'What else?'

'Perry, I thought you were getting Ben-Torres and the others?'

'In a minute.'

'Here we are!' Ben-Torres announced from the kitchen doorway, looking out. With him, Ray Rice, Bev Grigio, and Pamela's sisters. 'Uh, we found a wet bar in the living room and helped ourselves. Is that okay?'

So the party moved into the courtyard.

Several people besides the linebacker turned out to be interested in the hot tub. And since I'd found the lights for its little niche area, they listened in disbelief as I told them that not only had I not used it, but that I didn't even know how to use it.

'You're kidding?' Tappy declared. 'This is a babe-attractor supreme!'

Someone had brought out the little kitchen radio tuner, some '80s and '90s oldies station was playing sequential cuts from REM's 'Automatic for the People'.

'You press this button,' Ray Rice showed me, 'and the pump goes on. *Voilà*! Then this button and the heater for the hot water goes on.'

Instantly, it began to make noise.

'Have to take the cover off,' he continued to explain, all the while illustrating his words. 'Otherwise you may harm yourself when entering.'

'Don't be such a jerk!' Cheryl warned.

The entire tub was now a seething mass of bubbling water. I tried it out with a hand. Still cool.

'Takes a few minutes to warm up,' Ray said.

'Doesn't it have to cleaned?' I asked. 'The water changed?'

'The water circulates in and out of a filtered pump. It's self-cleaning.'

'We'll need towels!' One of Pamela's sisters was saying. Tanya or Tonya, I didn't remember which. 'In the bedroom?'

'You're not going in?' I asked in disbelief.

'Sure am.'

'Me too!' her sister agreed. As did the Samoan, Ray Rice and Ben-Torres.

So I had to show them to the two adjoining bedrooms and get them bath towels.

'We're going naked,' the Samoan called to the girls in the other room.

'We're wearing bras and panties,' one girl declared.

'All right. All right. We'll keep ours on too.'

'Worse,' Perry was saying in an exaggeratedly Belgravia accent, 'than the worst excesses of the French Revolution. And we know what that unfortunate incident led to.'

'Yeah! Hot tubs!' Tanya Agosian responded. She led them out into the tub. The others followed. Soon there was a happily splashing party there too. When I left them to return to the fountain area, I thought I saw a couple being furtive under the vines of the pergola. Who was it? Oh, to hell with them, I thought. Let them have fun. I'm not playing house mother. I'm going to enjoy myself too.

Despite the group and the possibilities, it all turned out to be pleasant and well behaved. Pamela found me in the kitchen. 'Imagine living in a place like this,' she enthused.

'Actually I do. Or at any rate, I have been.'

'It's so . . . old Hollywood! You know? Not the fake new glitter and glamour.'

'But instead, the fake *old* glitter and glamour?' I asked.

She laughed. 'But it seems more real when it's older.'

'I suppose.'

'Doesn't it?' she asked, sincerely now.

'I suppose. I suppose that's one of the things that attracts us to the past, to old houses, to classic movies and books. That they've somehow withstood the ravages of time and taste and fads and other human silliness. We all wrinkle and sag and get smaller or fatter, and they remain as they were. It's a sort of perfection. Immortality.' I caught myself. 'Sorry, I didn't mean to lecture. It's just been on my mind a lot lately.'

'Thanks a lot, Mr Ohrenstedt. This really crowns my birthday. Oh, and the book. A first edition! It's fabulous.'

She leaned over the counter to where I was cutting limes for drinks and bussed my cheek. Smelling of some unknown but musky perfume. For a second it seemed as though she might linger. Then that second was over and she was gone again, in a silvery blue-green rustle of dress, like a prize carp slipping out of a seine.

At about one o'clock, people began to leave. I was in the middle of a conversation with Cheryl Taylor and Michelle Tsieh about the early women's movement, when I became aware of the general dispersal.

Ten minutes later, I was standing at the circular driveway, watching the last Miata pull out through the gates, then all of them were gone. As I went back through the house, closing and locking doors and opened windows, picking up the odd gum wrapper and emptied glass, turning off lights, going from the living room to the library to the kitchen and courtyard, the place all seemed for the first time since I'd moved in not old and lovely and glamorous, but instead huge and empty and hollow. Friendless. As indeed I was.

Lying on my bed in my undershorts, I thought about what we'd talked about at the restaurant earlier. The phenomenon of the ghost dance Black Elk had written about, that had swept the northern plains and Rocky Mountain river valleys so long ago. How they'd danced, hundreds of them, thousands of them, all night long, painted white, dressed in white. And how a century later, according to Jeff Weber and Mark Dodge and Axenfeld and De Petrie, thousands of gay men had crowded into dance clubs, also dressed all in white, at 'White Parties' celebrating their tribe, themselves, and what else? Their survival, their renascence. A brief one it had turned out to be. Scores of thousands of them dead by AIDS not long after. What must it have been like to be alive then? In 1985? In 1885? To have watched your tribal brothers die? To have watched your gay brothers die? This, I knew, was the key to the Purple Circle. They had not only written of the renascence, they'd not only lived through it, they'd then suffered and died of it, or suffered and survived a new massive die-off of their people: their lovers, their friends, their soulmates. Every one of their biographies therefore was a tragedy, no matter how ultimately triumphant it turned out. Tanya Cull at twenty-four losing her Uncle Mitch and today, decades later, crying, 'How could this happen to me?' Reuben Weatherbury's wry, ironic smile as he told me how very much he had benefited through AIDS: how his entire career and life had been decided because HIV had stalked and claimed Cameron Powers, forever altering their two lives. Death dancing like a partner through all those lives, AIDS like the matching, twisting, other coil of a DNA chain. Dominic De Petrie telling me that the survival of his diaries containing the proof of his past was the worst blow of all. The triumph he had poeticized too soon, so soon over. The past a hot wire in the veins years later.

Although I'd been exhausted only a few moments before, now I couldn't sleep. Couldn't even remain flat on my back in bed. I was too restless, had to move around.

I got up, thinking I'd get a light sedative from the bathroom cabinet. Instead I heard another sound in the garden. Not just the fountain, no, that was now ingrained in the diurnal and nocturnal sound-wave pattern of my life. No, another sound.

I searched for its source in the courtyard, but couldn't . . . Wait! There it was! The hot tub! Still turned on. I almost shut it off when I thought, wait! Why not try it myself? It's supposed to be better than a valium for relaxation. I dipped my hand in. It felt good. I dropped my undershorts and stepped in.

Aaah! Perfect temperature. Perfect everything!

I leaned back, looked up at the dusky satin-black of the post-midnight Los Angeles sky through which one or two tiny flickers of starlight sparkled. And I sighed. Then I relaxed completely, chiding myself for never having done this before.

I don't know how long I lay there. It was a while, because I'd relaxed pretty completely. I may've even nodded off once or twice because suddenly I came to with a start and thought I'd heard an odd sort of gurgling in the surrounding foliage. I listened carefully. There it was again, from within the pergola. After a minute or so of listening, I recognized it as the call of a nightingale. Jug, jug, the poets had imitated it in their work: Keats, Shelley. But they'd either not gotten it accurately, or California nightingales sounded different than those in England and Italy. Or maybe it wasn't a nightingale at all, but instead a nightjar. What in the hell was a nightjar? I'd have to go look it up in the library. That could wait till later. Right now I wanted to just softly ooze here. Like some sea slug. I was reminded of those incredibly hot vents that deep diving submersibles had located at the bottom of the ocean, boiling and bubbling away, thousands of miles deep in some ever-nightbound trench, surrounded by the most alien-looking life, great tube worms, eyeless bony fish, blinded crabs. Then I thought about Pamela Agosian in her shimmering-scaled fish-like dress tonight, twirling in the blue-green light of the courtyard, iridescent and covered with fountain spray, twisting out of my arms and slithering outside. No wait, kissing me first, leaning over for that lightest of touches across my cheek, just long enough for the perfume she was wearing to permeate the air all around us in the kitchen, then slipping out of my grip . . . What the!

I opened my eyes. Looked into the eye of what? A cat? Or . . .

They were gone now, below the rim of the hot tub opposite me. Was I dreaming? Seeing things?

With some difficulty, I stood up, moving toward the far end to look over the side of the hot tub.

A figure leapt up at me from below and lifted me off my feet.

What the!

I fell back in the water, trying to grab at the wooden sides to regain balance and to keep from swallowing water. Suddenly someone or something else was in the tub with me. A pair of hands had my shoulders, and was holding me, half lifting me up, up, out of the water until I was almost on my feet. At the same time a head was sliding along my body, my torso as I rose. Now I could make out a dark head, a head of dark hair. A second later, I felt myself engulfed in warmth and another kind of wetness.

I'd grabbed hold of both sides of the tub for balance. I let go of the right side and used that hand to jerk up the head to look at the face which had engulfed my penis.

Ray Rice! I should have known!

'How the hell did you get in?' I tried sounding angry, not frightened. I was both.

He released me with his lips, still held me with one hand, slowly pushing me back against and then right into the hot-tub seat.

'I parked behind your car and waited, then jumped over the fence. In the garageway.' He nodded toward the fence between the motor court and the garden. 'Don't be pissed. Anyway, you were already good and stiff before I decided to jump in. Looks like you could use some . . . C'mon, man, I'm stronger than you are. Might as well let me have what I want.'

I held his head away. 'What if I don't want you to?'

'I'll do it anyway.' He kept trying to get nearer me with his mouth. 'Oh, you're really mean!' he said in another tone of voice. 'I like mean men! Want me to beg for it, huh? Please, sir,' he mewled. 'More please, sir, please!'

'If I do let you I'm just encouraging you,' I argued.

'Too late to discourage me. I'm already a dick sucker!'

As we'd been talking, he'd managed to get my hand on his head off and now he grabbed at my other hand, the one holding the side of the hot tub. He pushed the two of them down into the water, and held them on either side of my body on the hot-tub seat.

'Haah!' he said in triumph. 'Now I've got you where I want you.'

I struggled. But he had me. I tried one last argument: 'Technically, this could be considered rape, you know!'

He ran the tip of his tongue alongside of it then looked up as though suddenly distracted. 'Don't give me any more ideas, Prof. Okay? I'm settling for dick tonight. Now you gonna get blown or what? Looks like Mr Pecker here is waiting for you to make up your mind. He already knows what he wants!'

He was right. I felt betrayed by my body. Betrayed and angry. No matter. It seemed to have a life and wishes of its own.

I didn't answer. So Ray did what he wanted. I came. When he was done he let go of me and we got out of the hot tub. He climbed into his clothing and before I got out of the bathroom, where I'd gone to wash up with hot water and soap, he was vanished. I went back in and checked for any apparent damage, broken skin, bites, whatever. I found nothing. Now I really was exhausted. Even so I wondered if he'd return and make good his threat. All I could do was make sure all of the windows and doors were locked, although anyone with any strength could have forced them easily enough.

I fell asleep surprisingly fast and slept surprisingly deeply.

Book Six

The Secret of Rowland Etheridge

W̲hat was needed, indeed what absolutely required
if they were going to go on at all in any fashion
whatsoever, was precisely that brand of honesty he'd
spent most of his life eluding. He'd turned the aversion,
the avoidance, almost into an art. A minor art, true; or
was it merely a craft? Whichever it was, like so much
he'd produced it had proven only strong and good
enough to ensnare him all the more deeply within his
own overweening sensibility.

Rowland Etheridge, *On Buzzard's Bay*

MY LAPTOP'S E-MAIL HAD A message from Tanya Cull. She must have left it overnight.

This Machado person from UCLA keeps bugging me. Who is he anyway? What does he want? Is he really crazed?

I've located Camden Phoenix's address. You know, the executor and heir of Uncle Frankie McKewen's estate? Camden moves around a lot, as I told you, but for some reason he always sends me a change of address. This one is 18820 Burbank Blvd. Encino, Ca. 91356. Do you know where it is? A colleague from your area says it's in the San Fernando Valley. Not far from where you live.

As I was saving that and looking through Von Slyke's enormous leather-bound, laminated-page *Thomas Guide* to the city for the address Tanya had given me, my e-mail flasher came on, telling me I'd just received another piece of mail. I turned to this, hoping it might be Tanya, on-line, and I could warn her of Machado.

What I read was:

Mmmm. Slurp. Mmm. Yummmy. Yummy!

What?
I typed question marks in response. It was on-line and I got back:

Mmm! Slurp! Mmm! More please, sir!

Damn that Ray Rice! How did he get my e-mail address? Probably lied to someone at UCLA for it. Bastard. I typed back:

Pop quiz tomorrow on everything we read so far!

And got no smartass answer in return. Show him who's boss!

The phone rang and for a second I thought it might be Ray in person. I was letting the machine pick it up when I interfered and grabbed it myself.

'Oh?' A surprised answer to my rather vehement hello. Then, 'This is . . . umm. Umm . . . is this Ross Oh . . . ren . . .'

'Ohrenstedt.' I said. Not Ray but a stranger. 'Can I help you?'

'Yes . . . umm. Ummm . . . well I'm not sure how to begin.'

'Why not tell me who you are?' I suggested.

'Yes . . . umm. Ummm . . . okay, you won't know who I am.'

'Try me.'

'Ummm . . . ummmm . . . Chris . . . tian . . . To . . . ber . . . mann!'

The last almost spit out. Funny accent too. Unplaceable.

'I hope you won't be too disappointed,' I said. 'But I do know who you are. You are, rather, were – Rowland Etheridge's life partner.'

'Why that's rr-rrr-right!' he sputtered. So he had a stammer.

'How can I help you, Mr Tobermann?'

'Well . . . ummm. Ummm . . . Aaron . . . Axenfeld . . . he told me that maybe I could help you.'

'Did he? Did Mr Axenfeld tell you that I'm writing my doctoral thesis on the Purple Circle, and that I'm trying to locate the author of certain fragments? Or those fragments themselves?'

'Why, yes . . . ummm. Ummm . . . he said maybe I've got some . . . umm. Ummmm you know, among Rowland's pages and things. Ummm . . . he said you might want to come look for yourself.'

'I would. Very much so. Thanks. When is convenient?'

'Anytime . . . umm. Ummm . . . I don't work. I'm here a lot.'

At which point I wondered if he were Australian.

'Mr Axenfeld told you I'd found other fragments. Maybe you've got copies. Should I fax them to check if you may have doubles?'

'Umm . . . no fax.' Nervously said.

'E-mail?' I tried. 'On-line chat?'

'Umm . . . umm.' Very agitated now. 'Nn-o. Nn-one of that! You can drive up. It's not too far.'

Three and a half to four hours by car, actually, it would turn out to be. A small beach town just south of San Simeon. He stammered out directions too. Simple ones they seemed to be. Luckily they'd turn out to be. And he really was so insistent that was the only way, I agreed to drive up on Friday.

Again I checked my e-mail. Then sent back a message to Tanya Cull:

I've found fragment #3 – of Len's work? It's terrific.
   I'm seeing Etheridge's lover. Maybe he'll have more.
   Thanks for the address. It's not far away. As for Machado. You're a big girl now. Do whatever you think. But I'd avoid him.

And saved the entire morning's messages.

Conchita chose then to come into the library. She was holding up two long thin dark-plastic tubes, each ending in bright orange fluffs. Pulling along a light plastic wheeled cart filled with her cleaning materials. For the first time since we'd all arrived last night I wondered if she'd been in the house. There was no way I could have checked without disturbing her, as she always kept her maid's room door closed.

'I won't be too much longer in here,' I told her.

'I'll leave all this stuff out here and come back,' she said, standing the space-age dustmops up in a corner made by two bookshelves. She was clad in her usual sweater and tights get-up.

'I slept late,' I fished, pulling her back into the doorway. 'Didn't hear you drive up this morning.'

In fact, I'd awakened early. Strangely refreshed despite how late I'd been up last night. And I hadn't remembered seeing her old Corolla sedan in the *porte-cochère* or in the motor court last night.

'I didn't. I slept over.' she said.

'But your car wasn't . . .'

'My sister needed it today to go to Burbank Ikea-Town for some shopping. She dropped me off last night.'

'Then I hope we didn't disturb you when we all came in. My guests and all. Did we disturb you?'

'I heard a little when you first came in. But then the sleeping pill took. So I don't, you know . . .'

She stood there still.

'Some of my students. From class,' I added stupidly. 'One was having a birthday, you see.' It came awkwardly. 'I'm sorry if we disturbed you.'

And now I felt my face redden with a thought: what if she'd been awake and had seen Ray Rice and me in the hot tub?

'Like I said,' she said, 'no problem.'

'Sure. Mr Von Slyke said I could have occasional guests.'

'I don't doubt that,' she said, which sounded as though she did.

'You know, as long as we weren't too noisy, he told me,' I went on. 'I figured that they wouldn't be too noisy. I'm their teacher, you see. At school. UCLA,' I added lamely.

'Let me know when you're done here,' Conchita winked.

I don't know, maybe it was that wink, but I reddened all over again, I mean what was I thinking of last night, when I let that stupid boy . . .? Wait a minute! Damon Von Slyke and his lover lived here. If Conchita saw anything last night, which I doubted, it probably wouldn't be the first time she'd seen it. After all, the hot tub was right off their room and bath. They must use it all the time, no? Must cavort at night. Cavort. Was that what we were doing? Cavorting? Jesus. I was trying to get him off me. Away from me. But of course to an onlooker, that wouldn't be obvious, would it? No, probably not. But then she would have had to have awfully good eyesight to see anything from the kitchen-corridor window doors. She'd really have to be standing close to see anything going on at all in the darkness. So, no, she couldn't have. She mustn't have. God, I hoped not!

I dialed information for the San Fernando Valley exchange and did locate a phone number for Camden Phoenix. That seemed too easy. I dialed and was told the phone number had been changed. To a 714 exchange. That meant what? Orange Country? Reuben Weatherbury down in Irvine had that prefix. So I dialed and of course that number had changed to – you guessed it – another 818 prefix number for the Valley. Okay! Let me try that one.

It rang. Actually rang. Did not switch me to another number. Was picked up. A very affected-sounding, perhaps British West Indies-inflected voice said, 'You've reached the Harmonious Fist Martial Arts Academy and Meditation Center. We can't pick up the phone, but if you leave a message, we'll get you! Ha ha . . . Peace. Ommm.'

I managed to hang on long enough to give my name and phone number and what I hoped would sound like a message filled with potential dollar signs. Even so, I had to wonder, really wonder if I'd reached Camden. What had Tanya said about him? He moved around a lot. Held a variety of jobs. He was 'more or less' literary. What did that mean? Could aikido and jujitsu be in the realm of the possible? I suspected even if this was his number, it still might be a while before I actually made contact.

Conchita arrived back at the library door and despite her once again saying she didn't want to bother me, I figured she wanted me out so she wouldn't have to alter her cleaning routine schedule. I took the laptop and cellular phone to the breakfast room. I would have preferred being out of doors, but the marine layer was a thick mist in the courtyard and garden. From the breakfast nook, I could see both inner garden and outside to the little dining terrace partly blocked by a fence of screen. A few ringdoves were on the grass, pecking what? Seeds? Shoots? Insects? I couldn't tell. I decided to try Irian St George again, despite my poor luck in reaching him lately.

My luck held. He was in conference, his secretary told me. I wondered if he could be avoiding me. Why? He had led me to Reuben Weatherbury. What a find that had turned out to be – a storehouse of stuff about Len Spurgeon.

Maybe I was being unduly sensitive today. Because of last night. Because of Ray Rice. Damn. It had been such a great night before he showed up again. I felt I needed positive reinforcement, so I dialed Aaron Axenfeld's number in Florida. I owed him a thank-you anyway.

'It's a terrific piece of writing you sent me!' I enthused.

'Do you think?' he asked in such a sincere tone of voice I had to wonder if he were the real author of the piece.

'Don't you?' I asked back.

'It's different,' he allowed.

'Different from the other fragments Len wrote, perhaps. More of an evolution, I think, than a radical break. Wouldn't you say?'

'If you put it that way . . .' he hedged. Then suddenly, 'I'm not definitely saying it's by Len. It's not signed. It has no byline on it.'

He was right of course.

'But it's not yours?' I asked.

'Mine? No!'

Said so definitively, I quickly replied, 'I mean clearly it's not like any of the Axenfeld work ever published. Not nearly as styled or as individual or . . . Tell me, though, how did you happen upon it? De Petrie never told me the exact circumstances.'

'So you did speak?' Axenfeld asked. He had the most irritating way of answering one's question with one of his own.

'We did. By e-mail. I was frightened nearly to death when I realized it was Mr De Petrie live, on-line,' I said, deciding a not far from true statement would melt further ice. 'I was De Petrified,' I joshed. 'But he wasn't at all the ogre he pretends to be.'

Axenfeld laughed. 'Wait until you know him better.' He laughed again, then added, 'I'm kidding, of course. But he has been rendered tragic. And while some us all but thrill to wear the ebony of mourning, others, I'm afraid, were meant for brighter hues and resent their lot.'

I tried to recall what specific tragedy and mourning De Petrie had undergone. I really ought to reread some of the group biographies. I remembered. It wasn't one death; De Petrie suffered through a chain of deaths. A favorite brother died in a motorcycle accident. His mother died of a sudden heart attack. A beloved sister-in-law lingered for years with non-Hodgkin's lymphoma. All the while those were going on, De Petrie lost friend after friend to the AIDS epidemic. Including Mark Dodge, Jeff Weber, Cameron Powers, Mitch Leo and Frankie McKewen. And when that seemed over and the endless hospital visits and memorial services done with, his closest pal, his oldest and longest friend in Manhattan, Rowland Etheridge, committed suicide. A remarkably bad run of luck. No wonder De Petrie was bitter and isolated. No wonder he'd dropped out of the book tour circuit, out of book reviewing and article writing, the publishing world altogether. No wonder he'd stopped writing. Or at least stopped publishing books. It would have taken far less than that to stop me.

'I'm not sure,' I began in a somber tone, 'whether I'm more sorry for Mr De Petrie or for all of us he's left behind.'

'I suppose he has left us behind,' Axenfeld agreed.

'And the manuscript fragment,' I gently nudged, 'was among some papers? Other manuscripts?'

'What happened was a very nice woman from some British periodical had written asking for one of those essays I used to toss off on
a monthly basis in the '80s. She had three in mind for this anthology
she's putting together. I went looking for them. After about two
days of the usual madness, I at last located two. Lo and behold,
stuck to them was "The Flamingos".'

'"The Flamingos"? Is that the title?'

'Who knows? I sent it to you as is. Who had any idea what it
was? But I was speaking on the phone to Dominic not ten minutes
after I found it. We thought it might be the kind of thing you'd
want to see.'

I tried another tack. 'Can you think whom else might have written it? Say, Mr De Petrie or . . .'

'I was still in Manhattan much of the period. On the other hand,
this particular batch of manuscripts was under a copy of *Tales of the
Offeekenofee*. Which meant it's been here in this room a while.'

'Because . . .'

'Because that was my father's book and he used to refer to it and
periodically tell me to read something in it. He's been dead
since . . . well, a long time. Dominic and I tried to figure out who'd
been here in this house. You see, the little manuscript was typed on
my old Remington manual. That old machine hasn't been out of
the house.'

'That left . . .'

'In our little group, Cammy – Cameron Powers. He was here a
weekend or so in 1979. Finishing off some research on an article on
St Petersburg he ended up never publishing, I don't think, and he
phoned out of the blue and came by. A few years later, Dom stayed
a week. But he carried his own little laptop computer with him even
back then. When was that? 1989? 1990? Far too late for this to go
under *Tales of the Offeekenofee*. None of the others visited. I mean,
it's just a bungalow.'

'But Len Spurgeon did stay there?' I interrupted. 'Which is why
you and Mr De Petrie think he may have left it.'

'He did visit. He did stay here.'

'Before you left Manhattan for good.' I tried to clarify it. 'In what
year was that, 1982?'

'It was in November, I remember. The three of us lived here

together. My father. Len. Myself. They got along well. Better than my father and I ever did, really. He was housebound by then. A first stroke had limited his range. I thought, why not keep Father and Len together. Len had nowhere to go.'

'This was when, exactly – '78? He'd just moved out of Jeff Weber's apartment in the Village?'

'How do you know that?' Axenfeld asked.

'Bobbie Bonaventura told me that when he moved out, Len "vanished" several months. People don't usually "vanish" within New York City. And Mitch Leo's niece showed me Mitch's letters. According to both Bobbie and Mitch, Len reappeared and the Leo–McKewens invited him to their teas.'

Axenfeld didn't contradict this, so I went on, 'Unless, of course, this was in the winter of '81-2, when Len moved in with Cameron Powers for close to a year, helping him finish writing *Along the Via Appia*. But you already knew that.'

'Reuben confided in you,' Axenfeld said rather than asked, confirming for me that he had already known.

'He sure did. And it wasn't until somewhat later that Len and Damon Von Slyke began their S/M affair. That would have been when, 1985, 1986? Mark Dodge and Len were together first. Before the rest. In what, 1976?'

When Axenfeld didn't reply, I prodded. 'Mr Axenfeld, look, I know I must sound terrible to you . . .'

He sighed. 'No. No. It's your job to get it all down right.'

'I'm afraid to ask the next question, but exactly what was Len to you? To any of you?'

I expected Axenfeld to answer me with a question. He did, but not any question I expected. 'What about the others? What did they call Len?'

That was a loaded question. 'Mitch Leo said he was merely an attraction. Len did something pretty cruel to Mitch.'

'Yes, the scene at the opera,' Axenfeld murmured.

'I thought he didn't send you the letter about that?'

'He didn't. He told Rowland. The first time Frankie was so ill.'

'When Len moved into Rowland's place? In, what was it, 1983?'

'I don't know for sure. Mitch did warn Rowland. Of course, Rowland didn't take it to heart. Who would?'

They all had stories of Len. How could I get Axenfeld to talk?

'They weren't lovers, Len and Rowland?'

'They were . . . whatever Len wanted. He took what he wanted. Gave what he wanted. For some it was enough. For others not.'

'But he never ever defined the relationship?' I asked.

'Why should he have to?' Axenfeld asked back.

'For clarity. For peace of mind,' I answered. 'Because calling someone a lover implies that love is the emotion involved. And if not reciprocated by both parties, then at least acknowledged.'

'Oh, Len acknowledged!' Axenfeld burst out in what for him was passion. 'He acknowledged all the time. Acknowledged beautifully, and usually without words. That was his virtue, don't you see? How beautifully he acknowledged and reflected back at one the clearest, the least distorted of images. Who could resist it? In a world of such astonishing egos as ours, who could possibly say no to his least disfiguring of looking glasses?'

As he spoke, some things were forming in my mind. 'During the time Len was living with you and your father . . . what were you working on?'

The passion was gone from Axenfeld's voice, the friendly diffidence back. 'This and that! A lot of false starts.' As I'd expected him to answer.

'The reason I'm asking is that in an interview you gave when your *From the Icelandic* was published, you said, and I'm quoting from memory so correct me, "I actually began this book ten years before. But it was all so fresh and unformed, too close to the original all of it, it had to be put aside." Is it possible that your character, Laurence Grace, is actually Len Spurgeon?'

The slightest voice possible to hear over a phone wire asked, 'Whatever would make you think that?'

This time I held my words and let him stew in both questions.

'Thanks again for sending "The Flamingos". I think it's really important. I hope you don't take my prying as gossip-mongering.'

'I don't at all,' he replied, once more all sincerity. 'I respect the fact that you've got such an overwhelming interest in it all. Really. It's only that . . . well, you know, it could turn out to be such a quagmire, all this business.'

'A quagmire?'

'Exactly, dear, and I wouldn't want to see poor, serious, intelligent you sink into it, without leaving a trace.'

If he'd meant to dishearten me, he'd succeeded. 'You think that's likely?' I asked.

'Not yet "likely". Certainly "possible".'

On the lawn now more than a dozen, maybe a score, of birds, ringdoves as well as the large local bluebirds, all with their heads down, were assiduously and methodically pecking the grass, moving forward in almost perfect, even synchronized, rows like little machines of death.

After Axenfeld and I disconnected, I scanned the rough sketch I'd put together on the computer screen while talking to him. It read:

LEN SPURGEON AND THE PURPLE CIRCLE
(AND THE WORKS HE INFLUENCED)

1976–7	Lover of Mark Dodge – SF & NYC – *Keep Frozen*	
1978–9	Lover of Jeff Weber – NYC – Story 'In the Tree Museum'	
1980–1	Lives with Axenfeld – Florida – *From the Icelandic*	
1981–2	Lives with Powers – NYC – writes last parts of *Via Appia*	
1982–3	Lives with Rowland Etheridge – NYC – ???	
1983–5	Tea with Leo–McKewens – NYC – ???	

One name was not to be found on that list: Dominic De Petrie's. I wondered why not. I still had no clue if Len's relationships to the others were as I'd had them. Even so, it was beginning to look to me, in the words of Irian St George, 'Aw-ful-ly damn sug-ges-tive!'

Ray Rice didn't show up in class, which calmed me a little. I didn't know how I'd lecture with his smirk before me. Instead the class was filled with faces of newly minted young friends: Danielle and Michelle Tsieh, Bev Grigio, Kathy Tranh, Ben-Torres, Pam Agosian, Perry Valentine, Cheryl Taylor. As the lesson was on *Black Elk Speaks*, our Bruin linebacker pal had also come: Taponaupoa's girth filled out the back row of the usual jocks.

Once again the ghost dances came up. I told them what I'd told the young men the previous night. Kathy Tranh had heard her grandfather tell stories of time-crossing rituals of the Montagnard tribesmen in Vietnam. Hector Chuevo talked about a book *The Teachings of Don Juan*, where time and space could be crossed by sorcerers and initiates after much training, by eating datura plant seeds. Jane Hirschorn spoke of the sixteenth-century Hassidic 'Saint' Baal Shem Tov's trances across time, allowing him to converse directly with patriarchs of the Pentateuch. When the period bell rang, a few students actually said 'Aww!', unhappy for it to be over. I reminded them to read Capote's *In Cold Blood* over the weekend. I promised a scary read.

A group of ten or so continued to hang on as I tried to get out of the room, asking questions as I led them downstairs and out.

I lost half at the door. I headed to the parking garage at Westholme and Hilgard, and I'd crossed Dickson Plaza and already started down the ramping sidewalk and still had students for company. Perry and Ben-Torres turned off, headed to the men's gym. Pamela and Kathy broke next, to the Luis Alfaro Student Center. I still had the Tsieh twins, Jane Hirschorn and Kathy Tranh arguing over the efficaciousness of Native American rights efforts of recent years as we came into view of the faculty center down a sloping road.

My mood had improved so significantly, first as a result of the phone conversation with Aaron Axenfeld (despite his final warning), then as a result of the class, that I almost didn't register what my eyes were seeing. When the appropriate connection was made to my brain, I still chatted about Wounded Knee Two and the Devil's Tower Incident before I actually comprehended what I was seeing: St George, in his usual sport coat and tan chinos, under the faculty lounge access, nonchalantly speaking with Waterford Machado.

I couldn't tell if they'd come out of the building together, were going in together, whether Machado had accosted the English Department chairman and St George was being too much of a gentleman to walk away.

Whatever it was, the meeting agitated me.

I excused myself from the students, telling them I'd see them again Tuesday. Then strolled, almost broke into a run really, to get to the faculty lounge and interfere. I'd just turned on to the brick footpath to the building, when Machado saw me coming, said something to

St George and stepped indoors. St George turned to leave and I all but crashed into him.

'Nat-u-ral-ly you'd appear!' he greeted, ever on the offensive.

'You've been in conference forever!' I defended myself.

'For-ever indeed!' he agreed. 'Are you going in to eat?'

'If you are, I'll join you.'

'No. Walk me to the gar-age.'

He led the way. Hands behind his back. How was it, I once more wondered, that he never carried anything: not a briefcase, not a book, not a sheaf of papers? My arms were always full on campus.

'I see you were speaking with my competition,' I tried.

The famous eyebrow arched. 'His thesis topic was approved.'

Before I could offer a word of protest he went on, 'It's all ter-r-ib-ly po-li-ti-cal, of course. But so it was.'

Before he had told me that Machado had no strong departmental backing. What had changed?

'Un-for-tun-ate-ly,' St George went on, 'he defended his choice well. It's drab stuff, compared to your own sure to be bril-liant ex-e-ge-sis!' Again before I could reply, he asked, 'The work goes well?'

'Fine. Very well. I've already met with Reuben Weatherbury. Thanks to you. He turned out to be delightful. I really was surprised.'

'A de-li-cious lad a few years back,' St George said, his eyes gliding aside in what I supposed was fond memory. 'One of those un-der-grads who are at their phy-si-cal prime, ne-ver a-gain to be surpassed.'

'He sure used it to his benefit,' and when St George looked startled, I added, 'Weatherbury himself told me how he seduced Powers. Which feathered his future nest,' I hoped to imitate St George's archness a bit.

'Op-por-tun-is-tic,' he agreed. 'But smart and per-se-ver-ing. And?'

'And, you mean the other Purples? I've spoken to Axenfeld several times. Only yesterday. And I had an e-mail talk with De Petrie,' I added offhandedly.

It had a different effect than the intended cheering one. St George looked morose as he tramped up the concrete parking ramp.

'Who didn't frighten me as much as I thought he would,' I added.

'He will! He will!' St George predicted so bleakly I stopped.

'Is there a problem with De Petrie?' I had to ask.

'The Oscar Wilde Award for Lifetime Achievement in Literature. De Petrie will not accept it.'

Instituted only a few years ago by the LesBiGay Caucus at the MLA, the Oscar Wilde was granted every three years with a sizable amount of prestige and cash attached. That and its wellspring was one reason why it had been played up a great deal in the straight and gay press. Damon Von Slyke had received the first one.

'He won't go to the ceremony to address the caucus?' I asked.

'He won't go. He won't take their quote, fucking filthy money, unquote. He'd rather, quote, eat ground glass off roof tiles, unquote, before stepping foot anywhere near that, quote, bunch of parasitical assholes, unquote. I, of course, have been angling for the award since the last caucus at Kenyon College. Years of effort down the drain. I told him I'd write the acceptance speech. I told him I'd give the acceptance speech. All he need do is show up. I'd say he had laryngitis and all he need do was sit. He laughed and told me he'd rather quote, blow all those fucking literary leeches to the hell they crawled out of, unquote.'

We'd reached St George's BMW 950, a sleek, metallic-green guided missile pretending to be an automobile. It chirped happily twice in response to the presence of the keypad in St George's pocket, unlocking its doors, starting up its engine, readying his favorite CD, and for all I knew also priming its back-seat high colonic tubes.

Poor St George seemed so dejected.

'Is there anything I can do?' I offered. 'Talk to him or . . .'

'I only wish there were,' St George said.

The car door slid up. Inside it looked like a British men's club of the last century, lacking only vast mahogany bookcases. The compliant leather bucket seat angled for him to sit, then soundlessly spun back to face the steering wheel. Looking up at me, he smiled feebly. 'So you see, it's a joy to me, if a minor joy, that your work is going along so well on all this . . .' St George gestured.

'It is! It is,' I replied. I'd wanted to tell him how far I'd gotten with the Len Spurgeon business. Now seemed the very worst time to do so. Instead, I said, 'I'm driving up to see Rowland Etheridge's widower.'

'Good. Go to it!'

The car door slid shut. I waited until he'd purred out of the garage before I headed for the rented Celica hidden somewhere on a lower, far more plebeian, level of the garage.

The Reseda Avenue exit had looked on the map to be the one closest to the address Tanya had given me. I'd not yet familiarized myself with any of the San Fernando Valley since I'd arrived at UCLA, mostly because I hadn't needed to. I'd heard various disparaging remarks about this large northern section of Los Angeles – separated from the more notable areas of Beverly Hills and Brentwood and Hollywood by the considerable bulk of the Santa Lucia Mountains – among the students, but like other comments they often made about each other's clothing, sanitary habits and computer skills, it seemed something too 'local' to pay attention to. From what I could see exiting the freeway, the area was typical southern California suburb: few buildings higher than a single story, whether shops or homes. Some larger avenue corners were guarded by diagonal strip malls of maybe two and three floors high. It was verdant and at this time of day, i.e. one o'clock in the afternoon, very quiet. A few people on lunch hour walking dogs, Latino carpenters hammering away at a site, women with purple hair unloading groceries from Mini vans.

The address I'd been given turned out to be on a corner, completing another line of single-story shops: printing and photocopying, insurance office, small-children's clothing, two boarded-up stores and a mini-grocery with a Middle Eastern name. The final store had floor-to-ceiling windows, and two doors, one opening on the avenue, the other on a side street. Dozens of giant plants lazed in the oversized windows, saguaro cacti taller than I, python-sized snake plants, a jade tree of such amazing girth and complexity I could understand why they were called 'heaven trees' in parts of Asia. All in large vats. Behind were forest-green-colored shades pulled shut, blocking everything within from view. The place looked closed, despite the listing of hours on the front door that said it was open noon to midnight. Other, more discreet, signage in the windows included a small plaque identifying the place as home to the Harmonious Fist Martial Arts Academy and Meditation Center. I kept wondering where I knew that name from. Whatever it was, it confirmed the connection with Camden Phoenix. I decided to leave a note under the door saying I'd try him later. Meanwhile I'd drive directly up the coast to Ventura and Tobermann, Rowland Etheridge's heir.

The first time I'd heard the name Rowland Etheridge was years ago, in undergrad physics. Our professor, a stout woman with little charm and a thick MittelEuropean accent difficult to follow, was discussing the structure of space and time and other matters of cosmology. She said – and I'd never forgotten – 'It was an American writer, Rowland Etheridge, who when he read that ours might be only one of a chain of many possible universes that had come into existence over unimaginable stretches of time, replied, "Just my luck to have been born in a Bad-Hair Universe."'

I'd of course copied down both his name and his witticism. Then I'd done what any other interested undergrad would do: I'd gone looking for something he'd written. Without luck. By the end of the twentieth century, not a single Etheridge book was in print. Most had been mass-market paperbacks with short shelf lives. I finally located his 1992 novel, *On Buzzard's Bay*, in the library stacks and read it with surprise and pleasure.

Pleasure, because by then I'd already read a few books by Mark Dodge and Dominic De Petrie and, putting together the back-cover squibs about Etheridge's novel being a *roman-à-clef* with the little bio under his photo saying he'd been a member of the famous literary group the Purple Circle, I rather queasily came up with portraits of those authors who appeared thinly disguised in Etheridge's book. Surprise, because of the uncomfortable combination of high satire and affection with which Etheridge had written of the two men – and of others I didn't know.

The result was confusion. Not quite knowing what to do, I'd put aside Etheridge's work, not writing it off so much as filing it away into a question-mark bin. Then, during my junior summer, Erling Cummings's *Nine Lives* was published. The first group study and biography of the Purple Circle, it received acclaim, and by the holidays of that year I, along with 20,000 other readers, was immersed in his lively resuscitation of the group. By then I'd decided American lit. was my field of study, the recent past my concentration. So

Cummings's book led to me locating and reading others: St George's scholarly *On the Edge of the New: Dominic De Petrie and the Purple Circle*, Thaddeus Fleming's earlier *Gauntlet to the Ground: The Purple Circle 1978–1982* and Reuben Weatherbury's two volumes of the *Reader*.

In the latter tomes I once again read Etheridge: an excerpt from his 1981 novel *Desperately, Yours* and his 1979 one-act play, *Singular Sensation*. Those interested me enough to search for more. I got my hands on more plays, available in 'stage editions' stapled together with flimsy paper covers, in a drama bookstore: *Beauregard in Brooklyn Heights* and *Mustang Sally*. Those intrigued enough to search for the novel Weatherbury excerpted. I went back and read up on Etheridge in Fleming's biography.

It was then that his statement, 'Just my luck to have been born in a Bad-Hair Universe', made sense. Because while Mark Dodge had lived gloriously but briefly, and while Jeff Weber had succeeded on his deathbed, while Cameron Powers had been dyslexic and needed others to actually write his books for him, Etheridge suffered a far worse fate as a writer than any of them: he'd begun with great promise and not lived up to it.

Born in 1938, in Richmond, into a family of old Virginia gentry that had gracefully decayed since its glamorous antebellum years, an only child of aging parents, Rowland Etheridge began life with the unfortunate combination of being coddled and at the same time expected to carry the splendid tatters of the family name. A precocious child, he was struck by polio at the age of seven, and for several years lost the use of both legs, forced to move around in a wheelchair. His family's name, position and connections rather than what remained of their fortune got him up-to-date medical care. Rowland's polio was arrested and, following a decade of experiments in orthopody, banished, leaving behind a left-side partially fused hip socket and a left leg that neither bent at the knee nor could be relied upon for support or strength.

As a teenager and adult, Etheridge remained extremely sensitive about this 'deformity'; at the same time he'd done marvels to make certain no one noticed it. It had depressed him to have lost those years of childhood play, and especially as a result of the hipbone fusion to have lost forever the ability to ride a bicycle. He'd spoken movingly about this to his two closest friends among the other Purples, Damon Von Slyke and Dominic De Petrie. Both mentioned it, either in their journals or in letters to others. Both had been amazed at Etheridge's resiliency and courage. Because at the same time as he did whatever he could to hide his physical problem, he went out of his way to make certain people would see him as a fully physical person. From his prep school years through college and later on, he'd appear on stage, in plays. Always in roles that required if not athletic skills, at least a great deal of action. De Petrie wondered whether Rowland was guided to the stage by a helpful counselor, or whether he'd seen it himself as a way to overcome his disability, gain confidence and fulfill a lifelong passion for getting others' attention.

Whichever, the strategy worked. By the time he graduated Yale, Etheridge had appeared in a half-dozen of the much noticed Yale Drama School productions, gotten excellent reviews (as a result of his 'forcefulness, concentration and odd, always clear diction,' said one critic), had one play put on at a small New Haven theater and a story published in the *Yale Review*.

Rowland was twenty-one when he came into his not-very-big-but-after-all-for-a-young man-on-the-rise sufficient trust fund. He moved to New York City, where he joined three pals from the Drama School and Stillman Hall in what was a not quite cold-water three-bedroom flat – in view of, though admittedly without the key privileges to – nearby Grammercy Park. There he settled into a routine of mornings at the typewriter, afternoons outdoors getting to know Manhattan, and evenings at parties, either at their own place, which became popular among the actors/playwrights set, or at local clubs and bars.

During his first year on his own, Rowland had two short stories politely declined by the *New Yorker* and the *Saturday Evening Post*. He also had two full-length plays nicely declined by the six theater companies he'd submitted them to. That was almost expected, everyone around him told Rowland. So he charged on. During his second year out, he had four stories declined, not only by those two august periodicals but also by several others. By now his two completed plays had gone the rounds of every theater company in town without having found a taker. No matter. He'd found a literary agent to handle the rejections. Someone who believed in Etheridge's work and talent. And the increasingly personal and gracious declines from magazines had, after all, not been in vain: they'd led to offers of freelance work, including one from the *New Yorker* itself to (in the words of a subeditor) 'help us' with these little pieces for 'Talk of the Town'.

A job. An honest to God job in publishing!

That called for another party. Rowland's routine altered again. He was now one of many daily denizens of those famously labyrinthine, warren-like, closet-studded, book-filled offices of the magazine, then on East 43rd Street. Not quite an editor, not quite a gofer, not quite a volunteer, paid and part of the grand thing, with people like Alexander King and S. J. Perelman occasionally wandering into his hole in the wall, albeit always looking for someone else. And of course it was more money, so even though Rowland no longer had his mornings at the typewriter, he could usually find an hour or two most afternoons to work at his short stories and plays.

Eventually one story was published – in a rival magazine, barbarously edited, almost entirely, Rowland later suspected, due to the fact that his third roommate was sleeping with the fiction editor. Eventually a play was produced, although in the smallest theater he'd ever laid eyes on, down in some hotel off the Bowery, in a production that cost so little, opening night receipts, while not high, must have recouped. Still, he was young and it was a start.

Almost a finish. Those high points in his literary career occurred in 1962. For another half-dozen years, there was nothing.

Nothing literary that was. His personal life was interesting enough. One of his roommates – not the one Rowland had a silent crush on since the first day of college – announced to all and sundry at one of their rowdier parties that he was homosexual, and the next day moved out of their group apartment and into one with two other men no one seemed to know. Meanwhile, the roommate Rowland had a long-time crush on, a young man of good family, carefree disposition and dissolute habits who'd slutted around with any female under the age of fifty and had oddly (and Rowland thought quite unfairly) grown more handsome and thus more desirable with every new depravity, suddenly announced he was in love; deeply, seriously in love, with Cathy Someone or Other. Taking advantage of the new space in their flat, he moved her in, which, while it gave Rowland an 'office', otherwise reconfigured the ménage and daily discommoded him.

His drinking and partying increased. Conversely the time he spent writing decreased. After a few more years, his agent tactfully pointed this out to Rowland. He in turn diplomatically pointed out that she'd gotten no sales of his work in a very long time. They compromised by blaming it all on the Death of Theater and the Literary Magazines. By the end of their meeting they were once more bosom buddies, off to lunch. By the end of their lunch, they'd hit on a plan: why shouldn't Rowland take advantage of circumstances and write up his own story, that of young Manhattan singles on the prowl, living in group bliss and group despair? It was after all, the 1960s. And while Rowland's connection to the counterculture as it was being lived in Lower Manhattan and San Francisco was virtually nil, still it was all sufficiently 'in the air' and he was no dummy.

A play, he thought. Months were misspent trying the material in that form. Then, since neither he nor his agent could miss the very evident proliferation of paperback books in airports, in Woolworths, on newspaper stands, virtually everywhere one looked, Rowland decided he might try writing the recalcitrant material as a novel. His agent agreed and began talking it up to people in publishing. Rowland set to work.

Etheridge's first novel was published in the summer of 1968. By then his adored roommate had moved out of the flat, on his way to Los Angeles, not to marry Junior Miss but with a woman of forty named Claire – to act in the movies. His second roommate, gone a few years, had still not settled which of the two men he wanted and so he continued to live with both. However, he'd appeared in character parts in so many Off-Broadway plays, everyone said it was only a matter of time before he caught a major Broadway role himself. That happened the spring Rowland bid adieu to his remaining roommate and former college pal, a droll fellow who'd failed at acting and been dragged into the family business and now worked very profitably in commodity futures on The Street.

Rowland moved into his own far smaller, one-bedroom place in the West Village. There he met other, younger, more easygoing, marijuana-smoking, sexually available young men. He himself 'came out of the closet'. An act he made much of but which his former roommates looked surprised at, the stockbroker commenting, 'I thought you were queer the day I met you. In fact all of us have been waiting for you to realize it yourself.'

The Love Tribe was bought not by Knopf or Viking or Farrar, Straus, the houses his agent first sent the manuscript to; not by Simon and Schuster, New Directions, Morrow or Grove Press, the second batch to see it (considered hipper, more open to new authors); not even by smaller presses in all of whose offices the manuscript had languished for so very many months. Instead Rowland Etheridge's first novel appeared as a 'Dell Paperback Original'. With the expected tawdry cover art, graced as it was by an illustration of hippie headbands and love beads, grass pipes and tambourines. Other books have, of course, survived worse beginnings, and Rowland remained hopeful that if it didn't have, in his own words, 'class', at least it would have 'exposure'.

Unfortunately for Rowland, someone in the marketing division read his manuscript after it had been purchased. The backcover copy read, promisingly, 'An in-depth look into today's wildest, most beautiful, and boldest young people. Over-privileged and over-pampered, they indulge themselves and each other in every excess, every depravity, every possible combination of dope-smoking, alcohol-drinking and sexual experimentation!' Despite this, someone had come to the realization that this book was too good, too honest, to appeal to the crowd who preferred the moralizing trash of Jacqueline Susann and Rona Jaffee. As a result, The Love Tribe was released in a first printing of only 20,000 copies. Not nothing, true, but not nearly enough to require those all-important cardboard box 'dumps' to be set up with nothing but his novel in them in the front of book racks in the explosively expanding book-chain shops. Indeed the printing wasn't even enough to require more than one 'pocket' of airport and newspaper-stand racks. Rowland's novel was seen around a few months, and when it didn't require instant reprintings, vanished from sight.

I'd come across a copy of The Love Tribe with its dated cover art a few years back at a yard sale in Cambridge, Mass. 'Arcane, huh?' the girl selling it had said. 'My mother's book! Very "with it" in its time!' she added. I'd paid a dollar for a book that had listed when new for $1.95 and I enjoyed reading it more than I would have thought. The story of four young Ivy League college graduates who moved to New York, the book was as autobiographical as anything the other Purples had written. According to St George, it was 'sincere in its depiction of young men trying to "find themselves" at the same time they are simultaneously hiding and revealing themselves to each other'. Given the year of publication and what else was being written at the time (only Rechy's *City of Night!*), it was astonishingly open in its manner of dealing with 'sexual experimentation'. Cummings pointed out, 'The narrator's one gay experience is charmingly funny in its depiction if ultimately irrelevant to both character and book. While another character, the extremely handsome actor Jed Thomas [obviously based on the adored roommate], ends up a closet homosexual, marrying for his career then hustling skid-row bums for sex in his Lincoln Continental'. Fleming, who knew better than I ever would, wrote, 'The scenes allegedly set in the East Village seem based more on what Etheridge had read in the *East Village Other* than what he'd experienced, sort of a Cook's tour of the hippie scene. But the ambience of young people in a big city feels unforced, and the easy, disorganized way the young characters have among themselves seems accurate. It's probably as incisive a glimpse into those lives as anything written at the time or since.' Reuben Weatherbury summed up in the intro to his second *Reader*, 'All in all, as a debut, while breaking no formal or stylistic ground, *The Love Tribe* was fresh, and entertaining.'

It was about the time of the book's publication that Etheridge met both Dominic De Petrie and the young man who was to become his first lover. De Petrie was a neighbor on far west Charles Street in Greenwich Village, at that time a low-rent neighborhood. He and Rowland had met once before. Now they began socializing. Older, more accomplished and more settled, Etheridge must have seemed a model for the six years younger De Petrie. And indeed, a few years later, De Petrie gave a copy of the manuscript of his first novel to the elder to read, and it was Etheridge's strong positive reinforcement which encouraged De Petrie to continue as a writer despite little immediate success anywhere else. Damon Von Slyke also enters the picture at this time. He'd already had a play produced in the Village several years previously, and we may assume Von Slyke and

Etheridge knew of each other by name and reputation. In his journals, De Petrie mentions both present at a holiday party. His description of their meeting was: 'Although I felt sure they'd be friends since they share so much in common in terms of background and attitude, Dame and Rowland were very cool to each other. The time I dragged them into discussion they went at each other like cats: swift, vicious, indifferent to the destruction they caused.'

But De Petrie's instinct was right. In later years, the two became closer, if never intimate. It was De Petrie who later complained of the two of them at one particular Purple Circle reading session, 'They're like two old Southern biddies in not sufficiently silent conspiracy: they constantly take the High Road in any argument, declaring we'd better get out of the gutter, if we mean to be anyone in the future. As though only they know the correct path for us all. This only irritates me, but Jeff Weber was deeply incensed by it, and swore a deep and lasting oath against especially poor Rowland. Nor was Frankie McKewen amused when the two of them chose the occasion of his reading from *Whitman's Sons* to make disparaging comments about "some people's unconscious constant misuse of certain grammatical tropes".'

If getting Etheridge's first novel published was difficult, getting the second out proved far more difficult. More than seven years would pass, before Etheridge's agent was able to place a manuscript. The Timrod collection lists a dozen MSS from this era by title and form and number of pages, but gives no clue otherwise as to what they are. Thaddeus Fleming read, or at least scanned, most of them and reached this conclusion: 'Not quite literature, not quite genre. One might charitably call them "experiments".' Irian St George had been less charitable in his study of De Petrie and his colleagues. He'd pointed out how Etheridge's fellow Purple Circle members had taken current genres and had "not only fulfilled their readers' expectations as well as any contemporary on the best-seller list, but had deepened them with instinctively serious use of character and choice of "fable", then lifted them to a far higher realm altogether'. Of the unpublished Etheridge MSS, St George wrote, 'They reek of cleverness, they fairly drip with the author's patronizing toward a genre he could not possibly succeed in. He'd have done better to leave off these attempts altogether.'

This is not absolutely fair, however, as it leaves out of the picture what authors actually have to go through not only to have writing careers but also to eat and pay rent and live. But then most critics would say that's none of their concern. By the time Rowland Etheridge's second novel, *The Eleventh Commandment*, was published, another paperback original, from Avon Books, not only had he been out of college fifteen years, not only had he gotten virtually nowhere with his playwriting and not far with his fiction writing career, but also – tellingly – others had succeeded. Damon Von Slyke's *Systems for Approaching Emmeline*, for example, had been published by the most prestigious publisher of the day and garnered marvelous reviews and not bad sales. Mark Dodge's first novel, *Buffalo Nickel* and Dominic De Petrie's first, *Who is Christopher Darling*, were both published the same year, and nominated for that year's Hemingway Award as best first novel. Worse, each followed those books with better sellers, De Petrie's *Singles* and Dodge's *Keep Frozen*. No surprise, then, that Rowland was feeling pinched, in need of success, no matter how literary or commercial it might prove to be.

The Eleventh Commandment would provide little. Set in the revived New York art scene in the new and chic downtown area of SoHo, the book was a mystery novel. With one novelty: the detective was a middle-aged woman, a socialite, who gets drawn into murder and mayhem via her patronage of the arts and her willingness to serve on various committees given to artistic causes. A post-Stonewall-era book, Etheridge's new novel had one openly gay and one lesbian character. Even more 'current', its villain turned out to be a hell and brimstone televangelist minister.

About the novel, Purple Circle critics are almost taciturn: 'Pleasant, well wrought, with an unusual and artfully drawn sleuth,' commented St George. The others agreed, Fleming adding, 'This light entertainment had but one longer-lasting value, an unfortunate one for the author: while not terrifically successful, it was successful enough that the editor requested a sequel.'

The Thirteenth Trump is Death came out two years later, an Avon paperback. This time the setting was the hip art scene even further downtown, in Tribeca and the ghettos of the South Bronx. The scene was again the art world, but also the world of the professional

occult, from new-age astrologers to Spanish-speaking sorcerers oper-
ating out of street-corner bodegas. Another mystery, it was again
light and entertaining, but this time the middle-aged sleuth was
accompanied by her newly divorced daughter, making it more 'feminist'. About this book, the critics have even less to say. Only
Cummings remarks: 'Etheridge's decline into commerciality reaches
its nadir. Unluckily for the author, but luckily for posterity, the book
didn't sell as well as its predecessor and instead of a contract for a
new mystery, Etheridge received a royalty statement showing a large
unearned advance.'

To say this caused a crisis is an understatement. Because by now
not only Von Slyke but other of Etheridge's juniors were obviously
way past merely nipping at his heels, they were surpassing him.
Both Mark Dodge and De Petrie had successfully launched careers.
Then Aaron Axenfeld burst onto the scene with *Second Star from
the Right*, both openly gay and a commercial success. Mitch Leo had
already released *The Younger* as sections from his autobiographical
gay novel came out in *Christopher Street*. This was more successful
in praise and sales than Rowland's book, and also in effect. He
could only wonder at the injustice of it all.

The result of this crisis turned out to be one of the most rapidly
written of all of this usually very slow writer's works, and possibly
the one for which he will be known in the future. *Desperately, Yours*
was intended to be a send-up of the kind of gay novel Etheridge's
pals had written. His intention was to make fun of them. Instead, it
ended up being his most sincere work, not only because of the (unintentional?) openness of its narrator, but because of the revelations
accorded by the use of this specific authorial voice. De Petrie writes
in his journals of the surprise with which all the other members of
the Purple Circle greeted Etheridge's reading of the first chapter of
the novel at their meeting in the Leo–McKewens' living room. And
despite what Von Slyke had told me of De Petrie's put-down of the
novel's opening line, his journal entry is filled with respect, even a
little awe at what his old friend had produced. 'We've all been so
careful so far not to "overburden" each other at these readings,' De
Petrie wrote, 'and so we've generally held back our important stuff
and only read each other short stories or works we're not sure are
yet in progress. Thus it was a great shock to have old Rowland

come up to bat last night and knock our socks off with his new novel. He doesn't have a title for it yet, but it's his first openly gay work, contains his own extremely Etheridgean voice, with all of its peculiar inflections and affectations intact, and we sat open-mouthed, gape-mouthed, stunned, as he read us the madcap opening scene. Afterwards,' De Petrie concluded, 'we were a lot quieter than we usually are at the finales of these get-togethers. Damon, never one to mince words, said to Rowland, "Roll, you finish the book as well as you've begun it and we'll be forced to take turns knifing you in the Senate antechamber." Roland couldn't have been more pleased.'

He did go on to finish the book, if not quite as well as he'd opened it, then not too far off the mark he'd set. De Petrie and Von Slyke went out of their way to get the editor of a good hardcover publisher they knew to take it. *Desperately, Yours* was published in 1981, and it is clear from the author's letters, as well as from McKewen's and De Petrie's journal entries of the time, that Rowland was not only pleased with the book and felt equal to the rest of the other Purples for the first time in years, but that he expected it to make his name once and for all.

As we now know, it didn't. It's difficult to say why. True, it was published at the same time as some of the other Purple Circle members' best-known novels. Yet the simultaneous publication didn't seem to get in each other's way. Damon Von Slyke's *Instigations* sold almost as many copies as Mitch Leo's *Refitting Tom Devere* and De Petrie's romantic idyll *A Summer's Lease*. And all three were well reviewed in the nascent gay press and even in the mainstream press. So what happened to Etheridge's *chef d'ouevre*? Why did it sink from sight so quickly, while the other titles went on to multiple reprintings, paperbacks and long shelf lives? Certainly all three of his fellow Purple Circlers promoted the book and Rowland in the many interviews they did. They made certain it was placed next to their titles on bookshelves and in bookstore windows. One has to assume that people read it and that a few even liked it. Yet there is barely a stir of wind compared to the hurricanes of hosannas that accompanied the other three titles' publication. *Desperately, Yours* arrived and left bookstores with the most minor of flurries. Not even enough copies were printed for it to have an afterlife as a remainder.

De Petrie fulminated about this in his letters to the others. Closer to the author than the others, he was able to see its effects on Etheridge. 'Brave, and silent and absolutely steadfast, yet looking as though someone had from out of nowhere punched him very hard in the solar plexus,' is how De Petrie described Rowland in a letter to Aaron Axenfeld, who was in Sanibel Island at the time. 'Whenever I see him, I want to scream, "Be angry! Please! You have every right!"' For his part, Axenfeld wrote to Etheridge, detailing his own manifold joys in his friend's novel, predicting, 'This is your best work. Don't be too discouraged by the reaction of the gay hoi polloi.'

Unfortunately, the gay hoi polloi was exactly the group that Etheridge had hoped to attract with the book. His long-term 'steadfastness' now began to dissolve. Without telling either his agent or the other Purples, he gave up fiction writing and returned to his first love, the theater. The next decade would be given over to plays, with some minor successes, especially once he'd left Manhattan and established himself as a playwright-in-residence at several New England universities.

Fleming sees *Desperately, Yours* as 'something of an aberration in Etheridge's oeuvre'. He goes on to claim that it was only his friendship with the others, possibly his proximity to De Petrie, that's responsible for Rowland's connection to the other Purples. Cummings is more generous: 'We wonder today what it is about Rowland Etheridge's two gay-themed novels that so escaped his contemporaries. They seem so much a part of the gestalt of the time, so in tune, at one, with the works of, say, Axenfeld and Weber, as to be inseparable. But apparently in that era itself, they stood apart just enough to become pariahs.'

The critics agree that *Desperately, Yours* is Etheridge's best gay-themed work. Cummings likes the two plays Etheridge managed to get written and produced over the following decade. But both Fleming and Weatherbury see in *Mustang Sally* and *Beauregard in Brooklyn Heights* a return to the old try-anything-if-it-works Etheridge credo of literary art: the first play, 'a very slight effort, an obvious rip-off of Sam Shepard and Lanford Wilson'; the second a 'bisexual boulevard comedy with Neil Simon ambitions'. Still, the plays were produced at college drama departments and *Beauregard* even had a brief run at an Off-Broadway theater, while *Sally* was optioned for film. And the two plays kept Etheridge working, busy, among young people, providing local fame and folding money. They also had the considerable side benefit of introducing him to his second, longest-lasting romantic partner. At the time Etheridge was cutting a somewhat glamorous figure on campus, Christian Tobermann, twenty-five years his junior, was a PhD candidate in the School of Physical Sciences at the University of Massachusetts at Amherst, completing his thesis on 'Insular BioDiversity in New World Reforestation Projects'. They met at a party after the UMASS premiere of *Beauregard* and returned to Etheridge's off-campus apartment. Tobermann moved in the following week.

And while their relationship held fast, nothing else seemed to in Etheridge's life. The college connections ended, as they had to, and Rowland returned to Manhattan, to the thankless chore of once more trying to get productions of his plays put on, to write screenplays for producers without sense or cash, to lose one agent, gain another, to try his hand at fiction writing again. All of this activity accompanied by far tighter finances, as his trust fund no longer matched inflation and his royalties slowly petered out. All of it accompanied by less socializing, greater dependence on alcohol and more time spent alone or with only very old friends – including the college roommates, married men (including the avowed homosexual) with families and successful careers. Only one bright spot stands out in this period: a commission for a new novel arranged by De Petrie, who by that time, i.e. the early 1990s, had successfully launched his small press, Casement Books (named after Roger Casement), and done so well with the first twenty titles published that he was looking for new work.

According to the De Petrie journals, Damon Von Slyke confided in him that their old friend Rowland was 'fooling around with the idea of a satirical novel about the New York literary scene'. Sensitive to the many personal and professional complications inherent in their by now much altered positions, De Petrie moved with extraordinary caution. First he'd approached Tobermann, who agreed to quietly slip him a few chapters of the book on the sly. Liking what he read, De Petrie then accepted a grant from a state agency that had been hoping to include his publishing company on their list for years. He used that grant money to open up a competition for new work, to be called the Symonds Award, and made certain Etheridge received an invitation by hand over dinner in a local restaurant. A year later, the Casement Press catalogue announced the winner of the Symonds Award, and publication of what would turn out to be Rowland Etheridge's last finished work.

Titled *On Buzzard's Bay*, the novel – or novella, as it was barely 60,000 words long – was the story of a group of homosexual writers at a New England summer resort who have gathered for a decade to estivate, carry on romantic affairs and sexual escapades with each other's lovers, and with various young and older locals, and, when all else fails, to write. What makes this summer different from previous ones is that one of their number has died, of an unspecified disease (perhaps AIDS), and following the instructions of his will, they've agreed to hold a reading of his final play as a memorial. The play, naturally enough, highlights each of their personal foibles and how badly each one has treated the dead author while he was still alive. The play-reading erupts into mutual recriminations among them and an intense awareness of their loss now that their friend is dead.

By the time the book was published, Mark Dodge, Jeff Weber, Mitch Leo, Frankie McKewen and Cameron Powers were all dead as a result of AIDS. Even so, the dead member who allegedly dominates the group's consciousness and consciences is clearly not based on any of them, but is rather an idealized version of Rowland Etheridge himself. Among the other writers, all are subject to his sting. Worst treated are the surviving three, Axenfeld, De Petrie and Von Slyke, all of whom in real life not only stood by Etheridge but aided him, indeed got him published.

Looking back, one can only wonder at the three of them being so open and accepting of their colleague's caustic portraits. Axenfeld fares best. He's merely selfish and peace-loving; so aloof he can hardly bring himself to engage in sex lest it cause a 'relationship' to blossom and drive him out of his narcissism. The character based on Von Slyke is pictured as nakedly ambitious. Not only does he invite three Nobel Prize-winners into the group's little summer community, he goes out of his way to fawn upon one of them, a bad-smelling, unpleasant old lady novelist, and it's even hinted at that he has sex (of an unspecified kind) with her, thus ensuring for himself a complimentary blurb (which he himself will actually pen) for his next novel. Perhaps worst of all is the De Petrie figure, who in the novella not only manages to sleep with every half-attractive man of any sexual persuasion on Cape Cod, but then makes certain they're all brought together in the most embarrassing circumstances. If he's not pictured as openly brown-nosing, it's because he's too busy screwing around to have time to do the dirty work himself. He merely holds on very tightly to the Von Slyke character's coat-tails and is content with the substantial crumbs that come his way. Needless to say, the dead author, based on Etheridge, is a saint, with no apparent flaws save for his excessive love and forgiveness of these insalubrious pals.

When published, *On Buzzard's Bay* received what would have to be considered 'mixed notices'. It was widely reviewed in the gay media, possibly as a result of having won the 'competition' De Petrie set up, possibly as a result of it being published by the company responsible for much that was new and intriguing in lesbian and gay lit. of the time. Only a few reviewers knew what to make of it. Those who realized exactly who was under attack either hated the book or overpraised it. *The Advocate*'s reviewer wrote that it was 'a necessary corrective to the cult of personality of certain gay authors', then complained that 'the book's provenance throws the question of exactly whom these targets are'.

Among the remaining Purple Circlers, the book's targets were obvious, and generally more openhandedly received. De Petrie's own press release called the book 'chastening and hilarious. So on the dot as to cause instant reform.' After reading the book, Axenfeld wrote to De Petrie, 'It's awfully funny. He's pinned me, at least, into the specimen book with the most secure of clasps. I do think either you've lied to him a great deal or he's fantasizing your sex life if he really thinks you're that promiscuous.' Von Slyke too was delighted. His note to Etheridge read, 'Great comic characters. I laughed and laughed. You make so much more of me than I am, I'm planning to study your character to learn how to really do it right, to be more myself than the vague sketch I've foolishly settled for.'

Subsequent critics have been less fond of the book. St George called it 'a piece of out and out spite. The work of a failure against those he knew who hadn't failed. The only good that could possibly be said to come out of the entire distasteful book and surroundings must be our renewed love and greater respect for Etheridge's unwitting, accommodating targets.' Fleming had to agree, finding the book 'unkind, ungenerous, after Larry Kramer's execrable *Faggots*, this is possibly the most purely evil production of the first quarter-century of gay literature.' Cummings suggests 'extenuating circumstances may exist to explicate this unfortunate work.' He goes on to suggest that Etheridge's alcohol consumption had by this time already caused 'severe physical and unconscious mental duress'. Investigating the last years of Etheridge's life, the group biographer finds 'circumstances during the composition of the book suggesting to those familiar with early stages of disease that the author may already have been suffering from the effects of the cancer that ultimately led to his demise'.

Despite his remaining friends' aid and good wishes, *On Buzzard's Bay* succeeded no better than any of its predecessors. Its initial sales were not enough to put it into a second printing. Although in later years De Petrie claimed that all the Casement Books were successes, when asked about this particular title, all he would admit to was that it had 'sold its initial printing over the years and earned out its advance for the author'. Given that was true of less than a quarter of the company's titles (most did far better) it was an admission of if not failure, then at least not great success. The book remained in print until Etheridge's death in 1995. Along with remaining titles, it fell out of print when De Petrie officially disincorporated his press a year later.

After the novel, Etheridge continued to write: screenplays (including one about a vampiric baseball team, wonderfully titled *Bats*), stage plays and teleplays. To Axenfeld he even wrote that he'd begun a 'new book project. Very feminist, with much promise.' It's likely he was sounding out De Petrie's interest in it as a future publication. When asked by Von Slyke, then residing in Europe, De Petrie wrote to his colleague that Etheridge's new book project had 'all sorts of wonderful possibilities. It's about a young woman of the Confederacy who passed for a man, becoming a noted colonel and helping to win a battle. She might even have been a distant relative of his.' Among the Purple Circle critics, only Reuben Weatherbury seems to have bothered to look up what existed of this final Etheridge work in the Timrod Collection. What he found, according to his introduction to the second *Reader* of 1999, was 'sketches, notes, several outlines for a book, a few newspaper reports of the time, including one rewritten, with some embellishments, in Etheridge's hand, and a letter from one of his forebears to his grandmother, telling the story. An unfinished chapter, possibly to be inserted somewhere in the middle, is written in language of the time, and details the capture and hanging of a Union spy by the observant, intrepid woman. Unfortunately,' Weatherbury concluded ambiguously, 'while the chapter hangs together, it's somewhat outside the purview of this volume.'

It was Dominic De Petrie, still partly living in Manhattan at the time, who ended up seeing and continuing to encourage Rowland in his final years. And writing about him in letters to the other remaining Purples. Etheridge had never left the rent-controlled, one-bedroom flat on West Charles Street he shared with his lover. But De Petrie's own fortunes had gone so much further up and down by then, he'd ended up residing nearby instead of around the corner as in the past. And following the deaths of those close to him, De Petrie had begun spending longer and longer periods outside of New York: entire summers in Cape Cod, all winter in California. Even so, whenever he was in Manhattan, the old friends met, lunched, commiserated. It is De Petrie's mentions of Etheridge's terrible pain, depressions and difficulties with chemotherapy and surgery we turn to for details of his last days.

Not one of the three – not De Petrie, Axenfeld nor Von Slyke – were at Etheridge's memorial service, as all three were by then living miles away. Yet all sent words to be read at the ceremony. On the other hand, all three of Etheridge's former Stillman Hall, Yale Drama School, and Grammercy Park apartment roommates were present, to mourn and remember the old Eli. Yet it was De Petrie's words about Etheridge that everyone remembered afterwards: 'Whatever one wants to say about him, one thing is apparent: Rowland was the last Virginia Gentleman. That most unlikely of creatures, an Etheridge in Manhattan.'

The rented ranch house with its pale yellow siding and gray slate roof was at the very end of the long, twisting, indifferently packed-down dirt road, fairly high on a rise above thick foliage. I parked the

Celica next to a beat-up-looking Jeep Wrangler that sported the identical burled-edge, extra-thick tires and canvas siding of my students' off-track vehicles. Unlike their toney urban transports, however, this one actually looked as if it were used off track, the wheels and sides sporting overlapping, differing shades of yellowing mudsplashes, the canvas sides dotted with rips and tears only partly duck-taped over. Inside, it was far from the vacuumed Brentwood and Van Nuys Jeeps of my acquaintance: the front seat covered with clothing, notebooks, an old laptop, uncomfortable back seat rigged to hold wood cages.

I checked the view. Down several ridges left, the roofs of the small town. Everywhere else green with splashes of beachplum and chokecherry. The ocean's steel blue. The closest house must be miles away.

'You made it!' Christian Tobermann stepped out of his garage carrying traps. 'Any trouble?' and when I said none, he said, 'Why not go on in and use the john if you have to and get something to drink. If it's okay with you, I thought you'd like a break from doing the driving.'

'Where we going?'

'I'm a field biologist,' he said, as he wangled the cages into the back seat. 'Headed to the field. Have to check my area.'

Tobermann was tall, narrow-waisted and narrow-shouldered, but sturdy-looking despite that, with long knotty arms. His unbrushed, abundant hair had once been blond and was now going gray. His face was surprisingly unlined, although loose-skinned and jowelly, like one of those men Peter Bruegel the Elder paints carrying pheasants in a cage across the foreground of an autumn landscape. He wore a wrinkled long-sleeved shirt over a warm undershirt, thick twill bush shorts with lots of pockets, canvas belt with gadgets on strings and leather thongs, knee-high boots covered with the same three-toned mudsplatter as the Jeep.

I got my bottled water in the Celica. 'High-tops okay for where we're going?'

'No problem.' He whistled and a large, fluffy, tortoiseshell-colored tomcat sidled around the corner of the house. 'I'll be back before dinner,' Tobermann announced and the cat mewled, then sat down where it was and began grooming its ears. Among the many objects on the floor and in the semi-open glove department of his Jeep was a plastic tube he tossed into my lap. It read 'Blood Protection Unit. People's Republic of China.'

'No saying what's biting today. I'm used to it all, but . . .'

The Jeep started after a strangled ignition. We backed out of the garageway at thirty miles an hour, swung a down-angled reverse arc, stopped for him to shove into first with a multitoned complaint from the gearbox, and chuttered forward in three distinct, equally nasty-sounding gear-changes. 'If it don't die the first mile, it'll carry you to Alaska,' he explained cheerfully in response to my unspoken but all too-obvious concern.

We got back on the freeway for several exits north and ramped onto a coast road that changed direction, size and paving every half-mile. Just before the road committed suicide by diving back into the freeway, we swung onto an official looking dirt road which ascended higher and deeper into pine scrub wood. This became more rugged as the surroundings developed into taller, mixed forest, ponderosa and looselodge pine. A few miles of twisting ascents and we reached a summit, and stopped.

We faced miles of woods in all directions. I could make out an occasional shimmer of afternoon sun off ocean water, but it was far off.

'What I'm doing,' he explained as I helped him take traps out the back of the Wrangler, 'is a population viability analysis on two particular local small rodents in the area. One's indigenous. The other exotic. Exotic not in the sense that it's from Burma or New Guinea, but that it's not native here. Found mostly in the upper Midwestern plains states and wheat-growing areas of Canada. No clue how the exotic got here. Maybe among someone's belongings when a moving van was forced off the freeway for repairs. Maybe someone's pet. Once the back-door was open Mr Fieldmouse from somewhere else escaped. Rather Mrs Fieldmouse. Already pregnant. All I know is that her great-great-grandchildren settled and made a good living. At times, however, they've done so by filling identical environmental niches as Mr and Mrs Local Fieldmouse and their progeny, who've lived here during most of the Holocene, possibly earlier.' He'd slung his laptop over his shoulder via a triply thick strap, and we took off, loping down through man-enchanced paths.

'So what I'm trying to find out is, will the exotic drive out the indigenous rodent, which while not precisely endangered has a small population to begin with, is only found locally, and doesn't appear to be as adaptive as the exotic? If it does drive it to extinction, then how quickly?'

The air was fresh, the day warm yet breezy, the walking stimulating, the forest interesting. Tobermann stopped to point out amphibians, birds, small mammals, insects, or to drop the cages, which it turned out were not baited for fieldmice of any kind but instead for local wild dogs and snakes, their predators. For the next two hours I was assistant to a field biologist, as he went about doing a population viability analysis of whatever the field mouse's official name was.

I quickly realized two things. What I'd thought from our brief telephone conversation was a stammer or stutter was instead a startling physiological tic Tobermann occasionally manifested. Its source obviously neurological in origin. Its manifestation a sudden turn of the neck and head, accompanied by a shudder or flutter of the hands no matter what they might be doing. The first time it happened, I was looking at something else and noticed it peripherally, unsure of what I'd witnessed. The second time, after ten minutes or so, I was looking at Tobermann and I not only saw the two-part physical tic, I also heard him stop in midsentence for the tic and go '. . . umm. Umm . . .' just as he had done several times on the phone earlier.

No matter, because by then I'd fallen under his absolutely indifferent, noncommittal spell. We might have been kids, he fourteen, I ten, he showing me how the world worked, how nature worked around us. It was a perfectly adolescent, unsexual enchantment I felt, not important, except I realized it at the same time he did and he was evidently enough used to it (from students?) to feel comfortable and slowly open up about his years with Etheridge. Not his relationship to Etheridge exactly. That he said little about. But almost anything else . . . all I need do was ask.

I told him the first of his lover's books I'd read was *On Buzzard's Bay*. Had he read it?

'Read 'em all,' he said. 'Not when they were published. Usually a while after. When Roll didn't expect me to. He was always surprised. Because, you know, I was the practical one. The scientist. But sure, I read it. And I recognized the others. Is that why you're asking?'

'You associated with the other Purple Circlers?'

'Not as much as Roll.'

'What did you think of the book? How it treated them?'

'Like shit. I told Roll. We both knew why. Didn't have to say it. He did ask once out of the blue, "Do you think they'll ever forgive me?" I told him they already had. He felt it was his last chance to make his mark. He never understood how it happened.'

'How what happened?'

'You know, that he was so blue-blooded and well brought up and Ivy League and all that, yet when he sat down to write, none of that came across on the page. Instead, it was that farmboy Dodge whose sense of being American and all of the good and bad that meant was in every sentence. Instead, it was De Petrie, who'd come from an immigrant family and had to put himself through City College at night, who wrote like a nobleman. It killed Roll. He'd read every Mark Dodge and Dominic De Petrie book as they came out, and I'd come home and find him staring out the window, and I'd know he'd been standing staring there for hours. When I'd try to get him to have a cocktail or make dinner, he'd ask, "Why was I led up the garden path all these years, only to find out the garden would never be mine?"'

'It disturbed him that Dodge and De Petrie were fine writers?'

'And that he was a mediocre writer,' Tobermann said with startling honesty. 'It gnawed at him. He'd forget for months, then . . . and it wasn't just Dodge or even De Petrie, although because they were close . . . With Von Slyke, for example . . . umm. Umm . . . Roll could at least say, well, he's like me, from a good WASP American background, from expensive prep schools and good universities . . . But they all moved ahead of Roll. Everyone knew it. He'd critique the hell out of their books to their face, tell them how upset he'd been by what he, not they or their editors, considered grammatical errors, lapses of taste. You know, the old schoolmarm. It didn't make any difference. He'd end up standing at the window, and his fists would ball up, and he'd ask, "Why do you think I've been cursed like this?"'

Etheridge had known he was unable to write that well himself. 'Wasn't that difficult for you?' I asked. 'Didn't that put a strain on your relationship?'

'It helped it. Because I was so outside it all, he could always find refuge with me. And because what I was doing was on a less intense level. The worst thing that ever happens in my field is you don't get project funding. It was a relief for him . . . umm. Umm . . .' Tobermann ticced. 'It kept us balanced, equal.'

'Which you weren't when you first met,' I said, seeing it, 'because he was an established author while you were only a graduate student?'

'Which was at first an advantage for me. Like this exotic field-mouse arriving in this new environment. Because of my youth, and my distance from his set, my distance from the literary world, I was able to be protected by Roll while I developed. He nurtured me. I was able to observe it and learn how to behave. Until I was ready to go out on my own. Even then, Roll aided me. Because he loved nature and hiked with me on field trips. They were fairly local as we were still living in Manhattan.'

'So you were put in a position to return the favor later.'

'Right. By the time Roll's . . . umm. Umm . . . cancer was diagnosed, we'd already passed the crossover mark. We were already headed in the opposite direction. It was only natural I became the care giver. Now,' Tobermann said in a more official voice, thus changing the subject. 'Look! This is the local fieldmouse's scat.' He pointed to four little striated brown pebbles left in the middle of a dirt path. 'Fecal droppings. Probably adult.' He pulled a camera film case out of his pocket, scooped up the scat, closed it, covered it with white matt tape and marked date and place, then attached it to a clip thonged to his belt. He opened the laptop, snapped it on, brought up some schedule, hit a few keys, closed it again. 'Scat locates them better than anything. They're too small to see. Back in the lab, I'll do analysis, find out where they've been, what they're eating. How good their health is.'

I was able to point out three more examples for Tobermann. Luckily from a 'doe' of the exotic species. He avidly collected and marked and put it away and tapped out something on the laptop. I kept thinking about what he'd said about his and Etheridge's

THE SECRET OF ROWLAND ETHERIDGE 259

relationship. Something else wasn't yet clear. 'I don't mean to pry,'
I said a bit later, 'but you live alone?'

'And Homer, the cat. You mean people? Yes, alone.'

'Since Rowland Etheridge died?' I asked.

'If you're thinking I'm broken-hearted and all, try again.'

'Because?'

'Because while, sure, I miss him and all, we were always more,
you know, roommates, friends, fuck buddies, than romantic. Fine
with me. It turned out fine with Roll. When we met, he told me he'd
had enough of all that with Norman to last a lifetime.'

'His first lover?' I asked. 'You two met in – what? – '83?'

'Year after. At UMASS, Amherst.'

'He'd broken up with Norman earlier. In '76 or so. Wasn't someone in between? Maybe he meant that other fellow?'

'No. No one in between.'

'What about Len Spurgeon? Roll tell you about him?'

'Oh, sure. But Len just lived there. Roll took care of him.'

'Took care of him?'

'The way you take care of someone sick.'

'Len was sick?' I asked. 'In – when was it? – 1982 or so?'

'Roll helped nurse him back to health.'

For a second I thought maybe Len had contracted AIDS and that
was why . . . now I was stymied. 'Sick with what?'

'At first amebiasis. Some kind of cryptospiridium he'd picked up in
the Caribbean. But the treatment sickened him worse. It turned out
Len was allergic to Flagyl, the usual treatment for intestinal parasites.
So he went to this specialist, who gave Len something new. Diotiquin.
It killed the parasites in Len's digestive tract okay, but contained traces
of arsenic in it, and it turned out Len was even more allergic to that
than to the Flagyl. His body couldn't shake the arsenic for a long time.
He remained poisoned months. Sick to his stomach, like being seasick.
Occasional worse bouts of nausea and vomiting. Roll wrote about it
to the others. Dom, I think. I could find the letters back at the house
if you gave me a few minutes. Stop. Absolutely still.' His voice turned
into a whisper. 'Turn right. Look down ten degrees.'

I did as instructed, and at first saw what looked like a few fallen
logs, and around them large fungi. Then something moved and I
realized it was a fieldmouse. No, two. Wait, three, more, maybe

five or six little ones surrounding a larger one. 'Local or exotic?' I whispered.

'Local. With a new litter.' I could feel thrill in his voice. Although we were quiet, the rodents stopped and faced our direction. Their ears went up. Their pointed noses twitched. A second later they were gone. So fast, so noiseless, I'd not seen it.

We waited a minute, then Tobermann went to where they'd been. We hunkered down on the uncomfortable angle of dirt and log and he checked. He began scooping up half-bitten seeds and pine nuts; I pointed out the edge of a mushroom which was chewed and Tobermann broke it off, included that too in a film case.

'You're not half bad at this,' he said, once we were hiking back up to the Jeep. 'Observant. Logical. You ever consider going into science?'

'I'm having a hard enough time with people.'

'Don't think dealing with animals is all fun and games. For example, if for some reason in the future I deem this local rodent endangered, say because I notice smaller or fewer litters, or because of substantially fewer actual sightings, well then, by law, I have to report it immediately to the appropriate state and federal wildlife protection agencies. I have to prepare a feasibility study on the rodents' survival under various intervention and non-intervention scenarios. I have to make recommendations for what kind of intervention should be used, whether a captive-breeding program or "thinning" the exotic rodent population. Maybe translocation of the local species to another habitat. It's complex. The ethical issues aren't easy or clear.'

'Jesus! And I thought I was organized!'

My expostulation was in response to having returned to the rented house via another fast, jolting drive in the Jeep, taken off muddy high-tops, been brought into a bedroom now office, though not Tobermann's lab, where I faced a wall of foot-square cubbyholes ten feet wide and eight high.

'I didn't know how else to arrange them,' Tobermann explained. 'You know. For the Timrod Collection and . . . umm. Umm . . . for Mr Weatherbury, who needed things for the two volumes he edited. I thought, maybe . . . umm. Umm . . . someone else would come. I tried to figure out how, and all I could settle on was . . . umm.

Umm . . . chronological. From the top and going down. Thirty-six
boxes. From 1959 to 1995.'

I couldn't help but notice how his tic worsened now that he was
out of the field and indoors. Or was it because he was dealing with
an area of expertise he wasn't familiar with? Whichever, he was tic-
cing all the time now. I tried to calm him.

'It's terrific! You've done a great job! I don't know that I could
have done it any more simply or elegantly.'

'You think? It just seemed, you know, logical.'

I looked at the top shelf cubbyholes. Each held loosebound plays.
The plays produced at Yale, I supposed. And down at the last few
cubbyholes, which contained a transparent-covered sheaf of what I
took at first glance to be the unfinished Civil War novel. There was
something else in that shelf, a pale-blue-covered claspleaf. I bent to
look more closely.

'May I?' I asked, reading 'Excerpts – Sophonisba Peabody Smith –
Confederate Colonel'. I'd just glimpsed the other enough to see it
had a different title.

'Sure. Whatever. I'll get Roll's letters. That's where the references
to Len are. Something to drink? Coffee? Tea?'

The tea would be in a bag, the coffee instant. I said coffee.

'Here we go.' Tobermann removed three paper accordion files out
of a lower drawer of a large, old-fashioned roll-top desk. He put two
away, pulled out the third and laid it on the desk. It was '1980–85.
Carbons of letters.' Five pockets, labeled by year. At 1982, I pulled
out a packet neatly clasped on three sides, wound with a thick
rubber band.

'You're a bibliographer's dream! Most people hand you a wad of
crap!'

I thought Tobermann was going to blush, but he ticced once in
evident discomfort and left the room, I guessed to the kitchen to
make us coffee.

Once he was gone I turned to the wall bookshelf for Etheridge's
final year. As I'd thought, the other MS that caught my eye was not
the novel fragment. I read on the cover page, 'Teenbeat and Other
Poems' and below that, 'A private edition especially prepared for
DDP by his old friend and admirer REE'.

Poems! Who knew Etheridge wrote poems? I was certain the

others never mentioned it. Not Fleming. Not Cummings. I'd remember if they had.

The first page was not a table of contents, as I'd expected, but the title poem. The next twenty pages were poetry, closely printed. Most a page long, one poem several pages long. The final page was verso, and had a postcard pasted to the recto, an inner sheet of the same construction paper as the pamphlet's cover. A postcard of a black and white photograph had been glued in as a sort of envoi. It pictured three nude pre-adolescent boys, one leaning against, one standing athwart, the third upon and partly within a tall old wooden dory shelved upon a beach. The boys' heads looked round and vulnerable as a result of being closely cut. Their figures looked both babylike and adult, boyish yet girlish too. Their buttocks looked as soft and lightly furred as ripe apricots. All three had been photographed faced away from the viewer, looking to sea. I turned back to the MS. A fast scan of the text brought to light lines confirming the content. Let these serve as example: 'I fear that life is like a passing boy/ Who, followed block on block to some dark door/ Will pause at last to talk and then to toy.'

Footsteps. Guiltily, I put the manuscript back, thinking, 'Rowland Etheridge was a boy lover! A boy lover! How does that fit with anything?'

Back at the desk, accordion file on the floor, I rapidly began shuffling through the letters, all neatly typed, looking for references to Len Spurgeon, all the while unable to stop thinking, 'Etheridge was a boy lover. That throws it into a new light. But if that's true, then where does Len or, for that matter, where does Tobermann come into the picture?'

'Coffee'll be ready in a minute. Drip okay?'

'Sounds great. Thanks. It'll take me a while . . . Would you mind . . . I feel I understand someone better if I can see their face. And I'm just totally blanking on Rowland Etheridge's face. You wouldn't have a photo album or something? Photos of maybe the two of you, when you first met. From the time the letters I'm reading were written?'

Tobermann looked startled, ticced extravagantly, then said, 'Oh, sure! I can understand why you need that.'

A few minutes later I'd separated the year's many letters into piles. One of Etheridge's letters to Dominic de Petrie (the DDP of the poetry chapbook dedication, I was sure); another, far smaller one of Etheridge's letters to Damon Von Slyke and Aaron Axenfeld; a third of his letters to everyone else, which I put back.

Scanning the second batch I arrived at several mentions of Len Spurgeon's name to Axenfeld. Len had moved in with Etheridge in April of 1982. 'You were absolutely right about Len. At times I scarcely know he's here,' he wrote to Axenfeld. And in another letter, 'He's now taking some new medicine called Zantac that costs a dollar a pill! He must take a minimum of three per day, directly after each meal.' A third letter added, 'Len said we didn't have to eat together, or even in the same room. The reason of course is that he belches so often, then reddens terribly afterward. I try to tell him it's all right. That I know he can't control it and that I'm not offended. I even once told him that when he does it, I'll simply fantasize he's my Hell's Angel biker lover. Poor thing, he only blushes more.'

To Von Slyke, Etheridge writes little about Len, until a June 1982 letter in which he says, 'Poor thing. He's ailing virtually all the time! Perhaps an hour or two will go by when he's not ashen or pale green in facial color, but then I can see it all change, actually watch his visage alter, become constricted-looking, and he has to get up and leave the room.' And in a later letter, 'The other day, poor Len was so very weak, he barely could bring himself to crawl up to the *chaise-longue* where I'd settled to read over what I'd written earlier that afternoon, and he just lay his head on my leg. And not the good leg either. But you know, it really didn't bother me in the least.' And again, 'I remember how ill I used to be when I was a child. Feeling just terrible all day, days on end, weeks on end. I know what Len's going through. As God is my witness, Dame, if I ever have to be as endlessly ill as I was again, I won't go through it. I'll end it all and kill myself.'

'Which is exactly what he did,' I said to myself. Or rather not quite to myself. Tobermann was in the doorway again, holding open a forest-green naugahyde photo album. 'You ever read these letters?' I asked.

'I used to. When Roll first died. And when I was getting everything ready for the collection. Maureen, was that her name? She asked me to separate out letters to and from the other Purples.' He dropped the photo album onto the desk. 'This what you want?'

I recognized the long modern red-brick exterior and interior of the UMASS, Amherst, drama building from productions I'd attended there. The main entrance, and lobby, with a large placard announcing the premiere of *Beauregard in Brooklyn Heights*. The next photo showed the placard with a mustachioed Rowland Etheridge next to it. Either an effect of the overhead lights or something making his hair look red. I asked Tobermann about that. 'It was chestnut. But at sunset and on the beach it often took on red highlights.' Other photos on this page were of the cast, the stage crew, the theater company. In a few, in a back row, looking over someone's shoulder, was a tall, butter-yellow-haired boy. He looked familiar, but then no. But wait, wasn't he . . .

'That's you!' I pointed Tobermann out.

'We'd met maybe five minutes before the photos were taken. Roll wouldn't let go of me. He invited me to the cast party afterward at the Lord Jeff Inn.'

Tobermann turned the album to the next page and the next. More photos of him and Rowland Etheridge. And now I think I was getting at the source of the relationship.

'How old were you then? You look maybe ten!'

'Twenty. No, I'd just turned twenty-one, that May.'

'You look like a kid,' I said, which was true. Not only looked like it, but seemed to act like a kid in the photos. Not in any way a contemporary of the other students in the cast.

'I looked like a kid until two years ago,' Tobermann admitted. 'Now I look like an old man. The coffee must be ready. What do you take?'

'Black. Two sugars.'

While he was gone I looked through the next few pages of the photo album. Manhattan. Summer. Or spring. Rowland and Christian along the Hudson River piers. The old giant metal-sheet and wood-frame piers still mostly standing, a few looking punched in at their sides, falling apart. Axenfeld had written about those piers. De Petrie and Von Slyke had set scenes in novels there. Now the photos changed to autumn in what I knew was Manhattan's Abingdon Square Park, at what looked to be an autumn festival. Or was it the Saturday morning greenmarket De Petrie had written of? There, could that be, in a photo with Rowland, De Petrie?

The coffee arrived in a mug, thick, black, steaming.

'Is this who I think it is?' I pointed.

'Dom.'

'He looks very attractive.'

'He was very attractive. If you like that dark, bearded, muscular, clone-dressed look. Which millions did.'

'Which you didn't?'

'Dom never looked at me. He moved in higher circles.'

'Other authors, you mean?'

'Male models and Fire Island Pines beauties, I mean.'

'I don't get it,' I said. 'None of the other Purples write about his looks. I've seen maybe a dozen or more photos of him. But he himself complained he never photographed well. And the other Purples write about each other. Axenfeld about how many people fell over themselves for Mitch Leo and Von Slyke and he about how gorgeous Mark Dodge was, what a beautiful face Jeff Weber had. But no one wrote about De Petrie.'

'Roll didn't care for Dom's looks. Too ethnic, he said. But no one could figure whether that ethnic look was Greek? Syrian? Italian? Spanish? Or Arabic? If you liked dark men, which many people did and do, but which Roll didn't particularly, you'd like De Petrie. All I knew of his private life was the talk and that plenty!'

'And . . .'

'The talk went that De Petrie slept with anyone and everyone he wanted. He had the handsomest boyfriends the most consistently of all the Purples. But no one accused him of being vain. He seemed not to pay much attention to his looks. He dressed simply. Tight-fitting denims with a button open, close-fitting T-shirt and polos, leather bomber jacket. Clone look, but hot. He never made a thing about it. But we three would sometimes be walking down a West Village street together, me and Roll and Dom, and I could see guys' heads just lock onto him and then swivel watching him pass. They wouldn't even see us but their eyes would all but rip off Dom's clothing. You . . . umm. Umm . . . find what you're looking for?'

'Some,' I admitted. I pulled out the MSS I had brought of the Len Spurgeon fragments and showed them to Tobermann. 'If you have doubles of any of these or something of Rowland's that's unmarked, that you're not sure he wrote, say, from 1982 to 1985?'

'When I sent it to the Timrod Collection, I went through it all. Everything had a byline.'

Tobermann took the papers I had and began to peruse them. I now turned to the Etheridge to De Petrie letters. These were sent from Manhattan to Fire Island Pines, where De Petrie resided all summer. The fifth, dated late June 1982, was pay dirt:

> . . . *woke up from a sweet nice little dream only to hear some remarkably odd noises from the living room. When I'd managed to stagger out of bed and get there, I discovered Len in his undershorts with a pan of sudsing hot water and several dish towels, down on his knees. He was washing the carpet in great circles all around the day bed.*
>
> *'I think it'll be okay,' he said, continuing to lave it. He wasn't wearing any kind of top, no undershirt or nightshirt. In the lamplight from the old Tiffany shade, he appeared as white as a ghost. I thought, the boy's gone loony on me.*
>
> *'Get up,' I insisted, and I grabbed an antimacassar from off the sofa and threw it over his icy shoulders. I could see goosebumps on his skin. 'Leave all that alone.'*
>
> *He continued to seem very upset. 'I don't know what happened,' he attempted to explain. 'I woke up ten minutes ago. I was cold and clammy at the same time. I sat up in bed and my stomach was growling something terrible and then I retched and . . . it just shot out of me. Up and across the bed and onto the floor. Like in some horror movie. But I think I've mopped it all.'*
>
> *Now I could see that the bedcover was wet, I had to assume from where he'd washed vomit off.*
>
> *'I'll launder it,' Len said, 'tomorrow morning, first thing. Or if you want, I'll take it to the cleaners. Don't know why that happened.'*
>
> *He was shivering quite badly. So, I hushed him and turned off the lamp and took him into my bedroom, and put him next to me in bed. He kept on apologizing but I was so beat I'm afraid I dropped off in a few minutes. But when I*

*awakened again, not an hour later, he wasn't in bed with me.
Once again, I got up and went looking for him. It was almost
dawn, the sky outside on Washington Street was still thick
and wet. I found him in the living room, sitting up in one
corner of my big old horsehair couch. He was completely if
inexpertly wrapped in a blanket, with several pillows behind
and thus holding vertically his head. It turned out he was
only half asleep. He woke up instantly and told me that he'd
felt it all coming on again, and had become frightened he'd
ruin my bed and bedroom carpet and so he'd gotten up and
managed to catch it in time. He'd vomited in the bathroom,
he told me, and cleaned up as best he could. Then he'd
remained out here, afraid it would happen a third time. As he
spoke, he picked up a plastic refrigerator bag in which he'd
put ice cubes, most of them melted by now. He'd had a
pounding headache after he'd upchucked that second time,
Len told me. He couldn't think of taking anything for it since
he found out that even sipping water would nauseate him.
That's why, you see, he'd settled on the ice at his temples to
help ease the pain. And he'd also discovered that lying down
only made him retch. Thus the awkward, uncomfortable,
upright position he'd adopted to sleep. After a while, I realized there was nothing I could do to help the poor lad and so
I went back to bed. I found him exactly the same way, only
not quite so nauseated, when I awakened again at eight
thirty.*

*This, with minor variations, has now occurred three nights
running. Finally last night, Len more or less slept through,
without incident.*

*Do you think he could be suffering from something else,
worse, than what they say it is? Meningitis or . . . I dread to
even wonder what? I'm terribly worried.*

I could picture the scene all too easily. Another few letters, during
July and August showed a one-night revival of the projectile vomiting. Then from early September this account:

Len's diet consists of 1) Rice boiled, with a pat of butter. A

pinch of salt. 2) Pastina or Orzo, again boiled, served with a
little butter and salt. 3) Bread. White and sourdough. Again
with a little butter. Len loves black bread, but the one
attempt at pumpernickel failed. He almost fell to the floor
with cramps. Even with all the blandness, he continues to
belch. But it's now so quietly I barely hear him. He does,
however, complain about belching afterward. Even so, he's
eating, putting on weight again – he was really looking bad.
In short, my little patient is on the mend.

Three weeks later, the letters to De Petrie stopped; ostensibly
because the addressee moved back to Manhattan. By the following
year, when De Petrie once more moved out to the Pines, Len was no
longer living with Etheridge, and Etheridge himself was no longer in
the Charles Street flat, but instead already beginning his summer
term as playwright-in-residence at UMASS, Amherst. Naturally, his
letters are all about the school, the personalities in the Drama
Department, the students, rehearsals, the premiere of *Beauregard*.
Not a word about Len, who is obviously out of Rowland's life.
Wait! A mention. July 21st, 1983.

I'm enjoying such good health, good spirits, just good every-
thing this year, I can't help but think that it's somehow all
connected to, even a result of, what happened last summer.
With Len, I mean. How, by allowing me to help him regain
his physical health, he somehow or other helped me to regain
my psychic health again. I have, you know. I'm not depressed
at all, ever. I look forward to every evening, every morning.
It's fine now. All of it. Does what I'm saying make any sense
at all? Oh, shit! I actually only just now realized what I AM
saying! That Len Spurgeon is some kind of . . . what? Angel?!
Dom. Slap my face hard until I come to my senses. Ow!
OWW! . . . Thanks. I needed that.

I was about to turn to Tobermann and ask if he'd read this letter.
But I realized he'd already told me he had. He'd read all of the let-
ters. However, he now handed back the MS fragments.
'Sorry. Never saw any of these before. Not one.'

I located one more Etheridge letter to De Petrie exulting over the 'week of love' with Christian Tobermann. Rowland added, 'Now don't think me unduly sentimental or spacey, but I really do believe this is Len's doing. He always told me I deserved love. I'm absolutely certain he did something wonderful for me!'

I finished the coffee, leafed through more letters, none of which mentioned Len, and put aside those I needed copies of. Tobermann had a photocopier in the house, a single page at a time copier attached to an old, *circa* 1990, fax machine that no longer telemitted. This was good enough, however, and I got copies of what I wanted. What I really wanted, naturally, was a copy of Etheridge's little poetry MS. But maybe I could get that later. If I spoke of it now, he'd know I'd been sneaking around. But if I said something like that Reuben Weatherbury mentioned it. Or Maureen . . .

Outdoors, the sky was already streaking gray and pink to the west. Sunset? Was it that late? No, only six. Must be signaling a change of general weather for the area. Maybe a low front moving in. The cat came out of hiding to say goodbye. I thanked Tobermann and he said he'd keep a look out for anything else I might need. As I drove off, I remember thinking, even with fast clean traffic, I won't get back home till nine at night. But I was wide awake from the caffeine, so my next thought was, since I was going through the San Fernando Valley on my way home anyway, maybe I could try Phoenix's shop again. I pulled out my *Thomas Guide* and checked. Sure, easy. And there even appeared to be a short cut from Ventura Boulevard down to Franklin Avenue, not far from the Casa Herrera y Lopez: via Laurel Canyon Avenue. That should save time.

Of course, I kept thinking of what Rowland Etheridge had written about Len Spurgeon. I was half willing to bet that when I looked at my copy of *Beauregard in Brooklyn Heights*, I'd recognize Len Spurgeon as the title character. Of course, Etheridge's Beauregard, with that almost ostentatiously antebellum name, had been Southern, which suggested a self-portrait. But he'd also been stunningly good-looking. And he'd been a shrewd operator, using his Virginian drawl and extra-fine manners to lure men and women into his varied schemes and scams. The more I came to know of Len, the more he seemed to have been a sort of litmus test for each member of the Purple Circle he'd become involved with. He'd been a passion pit for Mark Dodge, a mind-fucker for Jeff Weber, merely a polite house guest who'd entertained Aaron Axenfeld's infirm old father, yet amanuensis, goad, indeed a co-author to Cameron Powers. Most extremely, he'd been a little devil to Mitch Leo and now a kind of angel to Rowland Etheridge. Everywhere I turned I found contradictions.

The Harmonious Fist Martial Arts Academy and Meditation Center looked closed at nearly nine-thirty at night as I circled the block. There appeared to be a party going on at what seemed to be a pop-ular Italian restaurant ('Mamma Laura and Lil' Joe' according to the rose-red neon sign) across Burbank Boulevard. I could hear a great deal of party noise only partly blocked and filtered by windows and walls. Cars were still pulling up to the door and dropping off guests, who then gave the keys to two small men in dark blue uniforms: valet parking, I guessed. Whomever they were, they'd already done a pretty complete job of filling up several blocks of Burbank parking space in either direction and on both sides of the street. I had to drive around several times before I at last located a spot inside one of the residential streets.

The Harmonious Fist looked closed and unlighted from up close. Even so, I went to the front door. Knocked. Nothing. Went around, trying to see if the interior shades reached the floor and if not if I could make out any light behind them. I couldn't. Should I leave a note? In addition to the phone message I'd already left? I decided not.

I got back to where I'd parked the Celica, got in, started it up and decided to make a U-turn back to Burbank, going the other way. Rather than getting on the freeway again, I'd take the Ventura Boulevard route I'd seen on the map. Just as I was pulling away, a small dark-haired young woman in shorts and halter top ran out into the street in front of the Celica's headlights. I slammed on the brakes and she came to the driver's-side window. In her hand some kind of paper fluttering. She was shouting, 'You can't park there!' pointing to across the street where I had just been parked 'Why not?' I asked. 'The signs said it's okay.'

'That's my spot!' she said, thrusting the paper into the car window. I could see it was handwritten, though I pushed it back without reading it. 'I called to have you towed away,' she added.

'Your what? Your spot? What are you talking about? This is a public street. I don't see your name stenciled on the curb. Besides which, I was parked there maybe three minutes, tops!'

'You can't park there even one minute! It's my spot.' she insisted, stamping her foot in the middle of the street, looking as though she were about eight years old. 'I park there every day. All the time! I live right there. It's my parking spot. Everyone on the block knows that.'

'Well, I'm not from this block. But you know what, I'll try to remember that fact the very next time I want to park here, lady, Okay? Want to get away from the car now? I'm going,' I said and gunned it. She was still running after the Celica, waving her piece of paper and yelling when I reached Burbank and turned off.

I found Ventura Boulevard a bit later and as I drove along it, I recognized various parts, especially around the crossing of the 405 as familiar, probably because it was a much cinematographed place in various films and television movies. I almost shot past my turn-off at Laurel Canyon, and all the while I was thinking, Jesus, what lunatics lived around the Harmonious Fist! Maybe Phoenix should keep the place open longer. This young woman seemed paranoiac and or deluded enough to require the benefits allegedly brought about by extensive meditation.

The four-lane road I was driving on ascended smoothly, suddenly veered into a turn left, veered even more suddenly right, then right even more sharply, rising all the while. Despite the hour – nearly ten at night – the traffic was moderately thick around me and surpassingly fast. I could make out Beemers, Vitechs, a Tiburon, a Firebird, Camaros. I hurled ass up and around another turn arriving at a streetlight signed Mulholland Drive, but it was green and I sped across it onto what had now unexpectedly become a narrow, double-lane road with a variable, barely visible, yellow line divider. Furthermore, it was a double-lane road that twisted even more sharply than a minute before, into smaller and smaller Ss, still rising, and at one time startlingly opening out from around a left-side cliff face onto an expanse through which I could see distant lights from what must be the end of a steep and quite high rock gorge. As I completed the turn and immediately had to counter it with a right-hand turn, I realized I was driving on what was essentially a country road, a mountain road, deep in the, rather high up in the, Santa Monica Mountains, at the same time that I was also in the very center of a city of close to nine million people. I didn't have time to ponder this enigma. The road swung downhill, continuing to curl itself into tighter and tighter S-turns around which the cars in the sometimes far but sometimes amazingly close opposite lane almost hurled themselves directly at me, their headlights shining directly in my eyes one second, flashing along my side windows and vanishing, only to be replaced by another pair of headlights coming at me from an extreme right angle, blinding me, before vanishing. Meanwhile the road spun and twirled, rose briefly up to another stoplight, green flashing red, and since the Beemer was right on my tail I couldn't even think of stopping or even slowing down but instead leapt through the intersection, picking up even more speed as I flew down in a shallow S that ended suddenly at another stoplight, also green, which I shot through like a bullet, and despite the fact that I'd picked up speed, I could see the line of car headlights behind me beginning only inches from my rear fender spoiler, a whole line of cars behind it, also curving, also speeding up, although I was going maybe fifty miles an hour, while in front of me approaching headlights would flash into existence from around another bend, blind me, swerve across my view as the road continued to drop and curl up on itself, before unfurling into a sudden straightaway and I felt like I was flying down it, until there was another tight curve and as the rental car was a sporty vehicle with good steering and great weight ratios, it just gobbled up the turn, really ate up the road, stroked like a scared cat along the straightaway. I'd never felt anything like it, the exhilaration of having a car this fast, this supple, not merely bend to my will but anticipate it, drive better than I wanted or knew to want to drive. I could feel my adrenalin rising as the road curved yet again, this time extravagantly, opened out into two lanes per side as suddenly as it had closed down into one before, and meanwhile kept swiveling to the right, going straight, curving, straight, corkscrewing down at an incredible angle, and I was in the middle of thick traffic with roads opening out on either side, and I could make out what I knew was my turn-off to Hollywood Boulevard on the left, but how the hell could I get to it from here, so I continued hurtling down, fitting in with all the other fast-moving, tightly spaced cars, around two more bends, wondering where in the hell I would end up, until there, directly in front of me, was the Sunset Strip at the Wolfgang Puck Dining Center, and I was choice-less, moved along as though the car's wheels were in slots, as I crossed over Sunset, suddenly freed of all that traffic that had turned off either side, gliding along now, having hit the rise and gone over with a deep V view through the side of the street trees of what had to be all of Los Angeles before me, the famous street-pattern-lighted gridwork directly in front as I hurtled down Crescent Heights Boulevard, diving into the city's yellow-stained, night-lighted heart.

Somewhere around Melrose Boulevard, I regained my wits, turned, turned again and at last found my way toward familiar streets that I knew were heading home. But my pulses were still scudding and my heart was racing from the well-oiled speed, smooth as glass, mechanical yet effortless, the feeling of it as good at least, at least as good, as the best sex I'd ever had, and without having stopped once since I'd turned off Ventura fifteen minutes of time and what seemed a half-lifetime of experience earlier, I pulled up to the huge gate of the house, thrilled, excited, coming down, spent, utterly exhausted.

Book Seven

The Leo-McKewens at Tea, Part 2

In fact, the Master is defined by his very acceptance of
being finite, and the limits the Master dictates then
become the limits of the agreed upon obsession. By
setting up rules and acting as constant enforcer, the
Master transforms himself from the lowly
distinctiveness of person into the world-arcing
cruciality of totem, indeed, into a symbol of the Slave's
obsession.

Frankie McKewen, *Switch Hitters*

'I FOUND THIS IN THE GARDEN,' Conchita said, holding something in her hand. She dropped it on Von Slyke's desk next to my laptop for me to inspect: a small white Gund teddy bear, maybe ten inches tall, wearing a Dodgers baseball hat, a pair of Virgin Airlines earphones, and RayBan sunglasses. 'I thought maybe one of your students left it. You know, when they were all here the other night,' she added.

'Maybe,' I said. 'Thanks! I'll bring it to class and see.'

'It's cute,' she added.

She was right. It was cute. Adorable. Serious yet warm somehow. And now, looking at the bear and its odd get-up, I immediately thought: Ray Rice. This is his sense of humor. He put it here. Came last night and put it here for me to find. I hadn't seen it anywhere in the courtyard yesterday when I'd been out there. And only now did I remember that I'd awakened in the middle of the night last night, maybe one or two in the morning, thinking I heard someone out there. Completely fatigued as I'd been from a terrifically busy day of working here at the Casa Herrera, then teaching, then driving up past Cambria, then hiking around with Christian Tobermann, then driving back, I'd been really more asleep than awake as I'd gotten up and gone to the bedroom door leading to the courtyard and checked to make sure it was locked, and to the next bedroom door, and the doors adjoining the breakfast room and kitchen. Satisfied, I'd peered into the empty courtyard, the inexorably splashing fountain, and had almost fallen asleep on my feet before I'd padded back to bed and slept deeply. Ray must have left it as a peace offering? Okay. If he contacted me, I'd be nice to him. Or at least not mean. After all, mean was what he wanted; wasn't that what he'd told me?

Conchita returned with more coffee but had to relocate me in the dining room where I'd moved to complete the cataloguing. I was now up to the very last, or rather the most recent, manuscripts of Damon Von Slyke's works – the 'millennial novel' *Canticle to the*

Sun was put out in 2001 to respectful reviews and his most recently published book; the far more interesting and better-selling novella, *Epistle to Albinoni*, a return to his earlier, intricate style and subject matter. In addition there were a half-dozen essays created for various magazines. His own brief, modest prefatory contribution to the printed program of the Von Slyke *Festschrift*; a special issue of *Figaro Littéraire*, in which he'd penned a post-post-Stonewall summing up of the Gay Movement as an ongoing political entity; a devastating attack titled 'Follies of the MLA', in reviewing for the London *Times* the latest volume of fatuities published by a famously self-promoting heterosexual American woman scholar who called herself 'The Doyenne of Queer Studies'; and lastly, from just this year, Von Slyke's brief 'appreciation' of the life and works of Mark Dodge, written for a famous rock music magazine. It had rediscovered the Purple Circle author, dead now twenty years, and had decided to revive him as a 'famous progenitor of our time who will live on forever', i.e. a sort of latter-day literary James Dean. It had accomplished this by going all out with nearly nude poster-sized inside and cover photos of Dodge, an astonishing four-page layout including substantial use of his professional modeling shoots, not to mention many photos of Dodge with friends and co-authors and, last and almost least, 'boxed' paragraphs from his books.

Now, with all of Von Slykeana catalogued on the laptop and backed up two or three times, including once in a cyber space 'locked office storeroom', I had to decide what next. Obviously the papers had to be photocopied. His old copier in the library wasn't equal to the job; I'd have to take the papers out to do it. It would all have to be wrapped and labeled by year, put in boxes to be labeled and taped up, before the Timrod Collection was contacted and told me how it was to be shipped cross-country. I estimated roughly a dozen boxes would be going.

While I was refolding the rock magazine I stopped and went back to the layout on Mark Dodge. For a second, I thought I'd seen a photo of him with a baseball player. No: other Purples, other folks. I rummaged through the magazine and found the picture of the ball player. An advertisement.

But it was enough. Because now I realized two things: 1) there might be a picture of Dodge and Len Spurgeon somewhere, and 2)

I knew nothing about Spurgeon except what I'd found out in the
past few weeks. I didn't know his date or place of birth, when or
even whether he had died. I knew nothing, and the few times I'd
thought that before, I'd always gone on to think, 'and I never will
know!' This time I went in another direction. Spurgeon had been a
professional baseball player in the major leagues. There must be
data on him. Not comprehensive, but more than I possessed.

I closed the Von Slyke files on the laptop and opened one containing what I already had on Len. Nothing but his connection to
the Purples, plus some childhood possibilities. And three fragments
I'd scanned in. Not a thing more. I opened another window and
tapped into the Internet. Began scanning for general information,
found SPORTS, moved to 'Baseball', shot past 'history of, Worlds
Series Games, statistics' and arrived at 'Players'. I limited that to
'fourth quarter of 20th century'. It seemed a book-long list, so I limited it to S, and when that was too long did a search. There!

SPURGEON LEONARD, Pitcher, Relief pitcher, Prof. career
1968–76. Minor league teams: '68–9, Davenport Beavers,
'69–72, Detroit Redwings. Major league teams: '72–3,
Oakland Athletics, '74–6, San Francisco Giants. Maj league
stats: H. 2.42, RBA 3.22, ERA 0.52, Strikeout Games 4,
Saves 12, Opp. Avge 5.

That looked right. Even so, I needed personal info. So, while
saving and underlining the entry, I used a sidebar menu to ask for
more. I got these categories: 'Stats', 'Specific Games Played', 'League
and Series Games', 'Awards', 'Biography', 'Contemporary
Evaluation Comments', and 'Professional Critique'. I settled for the
bio. It turned out I needed a password for what was called 'In-depth
on-line', for which they would bill me. That took a few minutes to
locate. I keyboarded what was needed, stroked the mouse, and
waited.

This is what came up:

Leonard Paul Spurgeon, born October 20, 1943, Davenport,
Iowa. Parents: Herbert Alan Spurgeon, Martha Barnes. Attd
Davenport Elementary and High School, Bettendorf Junior

College, University Iowa. Grad. 1965, BA. No info re marriage or children. Died Sept 17, 1991, North Truro, Mass.

So he *was* dead! I was sufficiently excited to find anything at all
that I didn't immediately realize all the information actually in front
of me. I saved what I'd found to the appropriate document file,
leapt up and ran to the library. Because while I hadn't immediately
seen all the implications of what I'd found, I did see two things
quite clearly. Len's middle name, Paul, the name used for the narrator in two of the three MS fragments I had in hand. And the place of
Spurgeon's birth, Davenport, Iowa, which I was certain was one
of the cities that figured in the title of Frankie McKewen's posthumous autobiographical novel, *A Boy from Quad Cities*. The year of
birth also seemed close to McKewen's. I thought McKewen was
born in '42. What if they'd known each other earlier? First? Before
Mark Dodge and Len met?

I raced into the library, took down the big *Dictionary of Lesbian
and Gay Authors*, and located McKewen. Sure enough, he'd been
born July 15th, 1943, in Davenport, Iowa, and attended Davenport
Elementary and High before shifting to Bettendorf. Furthermore,
he'd graduated in 1965 from the University of Iowa, although unlike
Spurgeon, who had gone to the minor leagues to play ball,
McKewen had taken a two-year course at the Iowa Writers' School,
where he'd met Mitch Leo, they'd become lovers, and as a result the
nucleus of the Purple Circle had been formed.

Now I had something. But did it signify merely contiguity while
growing up and then meeting later on and becoming friends (or
whatever) because they'd lived so close as children, or more? A lot
more? It depended upon Frankie McKewen now. More specifically
upon his journals of those early years, housed now in the Timrod
Collection. When had McKewen begun his journals? I went to the
collection's catalogue and was disappointed to see they were later,
briefer, less inclusive than the De Petrie journals, which had been
continuous since 1972. McKewen's only ranged from 1984 to
1988, i.e. just before he'd died: eight volumes of octavo notebook
of 150 pages each. I'd have to read them for any references to Len.
As well as his letters to the other Purples in the mid-1980s, when
Spurgeon was attending the Leo–McKewen 'Teas'. Still, it was a

strong connection between Len and the group. I had to wonder about Len and Mitch Leo, to wonder if the animosity that erupted between them at the Metropolitan Opera House might have had earlier origins – say, in the relationship between Spurgeon and Mitch Leo's lover, Frankie McKewen.

Who could tell me? Axenfeld maybe. He often gave information he didn't know he was giving. Or . . .

The house phone rang and Conchita came to tell me it was Von Slyke.

'I was about to call you,' I told him. 'I just finished the cataloguing. I want to photocopy everything.'

He was delighted and we spent some minutes discussing details of where and how. As for the shipping, he thought the Timrod Collection would take care of it all. But when I began asking specific questions, he sighed and said, 'Would you be a dear and go over it all, after them? You're so reliable and I don't really know anyone there but Maureen.'

'Who's not there this month,' I answered.

After that was settled, Von Slyke said, in a lower tone of voice, 'Ross, one reason I called is to tell you I've written to you about Len, you know, Len and myself, way back when. Remember what I told you? But I don't want Puddles to know about this. He gets sensitive about the oddest things lately. I'm going to mail the pages to you. Okay? I'm doing it by overnight mail from the concierge's desk at the hotel. Oh, and Ross, dear? We're off to Majorca tomorrow. I've put the address and phone number of the house where we're staying on the bottom sheet. Now remember what I said, these pages are "For Your Eyes Only", you understand!' With that Mata Hari sign-off, Von Slyke hung up.

Axenfeld wasn't in or wasn't answering the phone. I called and left another message at the Harmonious Fist (once again pondering how I knew that name) and that discouraged me so much I have to admit I sat a minute at Von Slyke's big library desk and despaired. I suddenly pictured my mentor, Irian St George, and how he had sighed yesterday when he'd spoken of Dominic De Petrie's treachery. Before I could change my mind or really think what I was doing, I hit the speed dial for De Petrie's number. And was blessed with the same rude message I'd heard before about not leaving my name and number unless I had a large amount of money to deposit. Something about that message on top of De Petrie's perfidy got me and when it ended and message recording began, I identified myself and added, 'I suggest you make a new phone message. This one's a lie.'

The phone was picked up. 'What do you mean it's a lie?'

I was startled by De Petrie's voice in person, but not startled enough to back down. 'Dr St George has a check which you refuse to accept.'

'I assume you're referring to the MLA pelf? What exactly is your interest in that hypocritical treasure?'

'None! That is, none beyond its effect upon a man whom I esteem and admire.' Before he could answer. 'Who worked quite long and hard and no doubt against opposition to obtain that treasure on your behalf. Who doesn't deserve such a poor payback.'

'Loyalty and ethics at the same time! Imagine? Whatever is academia coming to these days?'

'Go ahead and laugh.'

'I'm not laughing. I really was not aware that St George went so much out of his way in the matter. You're right to chastise me on his behalf. As you are to point out that he doubtless faced enormous opposition in the matter. What do you want me to do?'

'He did go out of his way,' I insisted. 'Although I don't know if the opposition was all that –'

'You needn't downplay it,' De Petrie interrupted. 'I've no doubt the opposition he faced was vicious *and* prolonged. I may not be in academia, but I do have a few spies in those currently leafless groves.'

'What should you do? Well . . . you know, take the award. The honor. The money. Dr St George said he'd write and deliver the acceptance speech himself. All you'd have to do is sit there.'

'He confides in you that much?' De Petrie asked 'I'm both surprised and glad to hear of it. But if I am going to appear in the bailiwick of the enemy, I think I ought to dress myself in the finest chain-mail verbiage I can muster. Complete with the usual anachronistic, scholarly adverbisms like "the commodification of such and such" and "the reification of such and other". Not to mention a liberal sprinkling of their typical velleities such as "heuristic" and

"textist". Wait a minute! I've got it! Ross, what if I titled my accep-
tance speech "The De-reification of Heuristic Non-gendered
Inter-verbal Texts Qua Commodities in a Pre-discoursist
Climatology"? How does that grab you?'

'I think it would be hysterical,' I said

'I can already see the opening line,' he mused. 'First, naturally, I'll
take an epigraph from something popular yet also somewhat arcane.
Say a line spoken inside a balloon by Sluggo from the late '50s
comic strip *Little Lulu*? I open punchily, saying something like, 'We
know now, of course, the reason Little Lulu's beautiful Aunt Fritzi
spent all her days at home primping and bathing and dressing, and
all her nights going out with different men, is because she was an
independent and highly paid sex-worker. But more than merely
an independent and highly paid sex-worker, Aunt Fritzi emblemized
a topological phenomenon in early post-World War II capitalist society's underlying anxiety, in which American gender values were
undergoing their most salient, albeit non-persevering, transmogrifi-
cations. It is impossible not to see in this hermeneutical
superfetation, an attempt to reduce the dialectic of diurnal cultural
artifacts to a level where even neo-Freudian influences are forced to
confront symbolical allusions in the most primitively anti-aesthetic
Antikweltanschauung! Moreoever . . .'

But by now both De Petrie and I were in stitches, he laughing too
hard to go on. When I finally caught my breath, I said, 'You would-
n't?'

'Don't dare me,' he warned.

'I won't. But Mr De Petrie, if you do go, please don't say anything
to Dr St George about this phone call.'

'He hides his light under a bushel too! You're beginning to seem
as extraordinary as poor Axey thinks you are. What?' he asked in
mock disbelief, 'Have I let the panther out of the purse? Surely you
know he dotes on you. He's awaiting your arrival at the Refugio de
Isla Sanibel with the most acute anticipation. Indeed, he has even
threatened to . . . are you ready? . . . neaten and clean up the house
if you arrive.'

'Not the Fibber McGee room?' My horror apparent.

'You know about that, do you? Why, you are the slyest of pusses,
if even Axey confides in you. I mean, St George is a bit circumspect

284 THE BOOK OF LIES

but, as we all know, easily influenced by even the possibility of obtaining the favors of a handsome young man, which you evidently are. Whereas Dame is a total whore who'll put out for anyone. But Axey, our beloved Axey, well, he's quite another genera in the piscine world altogether. Far harder to get to nibble anywhere near the dangling worm, never mind actually land.'

'Mr Axenfeld has been very kind.'

'Then I suggest you repay his kindness by visiting him.'

'But he never . . .'

'No, and he never will,' De Petrie said. 'You must insist. He'll spend days looking for and finding dozens of reasons why you can't go there. But eventually he'll relent. Anyway, it's not such a bad place as all that, unless of course you're allergic to breezes from the Gulf and occasional Spanish moss and azaleas the size and, who knows, perhaps the colors of an ancient iguanodon.'

'I'll get to see what's in the Fibber McGee room.'

'Perhaps you will.'

'Have you ever been in there?'

'At the threshold. But then I never had an impelling reason to want to.'

'Would I presume by asking if you have a similar place?'

He was silent for too long a time. But before I could rephrase my question or take it back, De Petrie said, 'No, Ross, my life is . . . how do they put it? . . . an open book?'

De Petrie was too clever by half for me to get anywhere with. So I asked him once again not to tell St George that we'd spoken of the award, and this time he promised. As we were saying our goodbyes, I slipped in, 'And maybe sometime I can visit you, where you live?'

I was surprised to receive this answer: 'Maybe sometime you can. And then you may discover that I do, after all, have a special room. Although perhaps not special in any way you're currently aware of.'

I let that mystery hang for the time being, but as we signed off I immediately looked for, located and dialed the Timrod Collection. Was put through to Christopher Kovack, the same lockjaw-accented minion I'd reached before, and began speaking in my official capacity as Von Slyke's bibliographer about how to get the papers East. He was surprisingly pleasant this time, helpful, and even suggested that if I was all that concerned about the papers arriving intact, I arrange to be at the Sikorsky Memorial Airport to meet the cartons when they emerged out of the cargo plane. He would arrange for a van and driver to pick them up anyway, and I could accompany them to the collection, go over and confirm them as they arrived and were unpacked. I told him I'd have to speak with Von Slyke about these plans (because I suddenly realized it would cost money flying East) as they sounded a bit much. But I was pleased when he told me he could also arrange to have a check cut for the total amount and handed to me upon receipt of the papers. Von Slyke might pay my airfare if he knew I'd get money fast.

Kovack offered further news. He'd found a few minutes (i.e. one of his assistants had been talked into it) and he'd managed to locate the MSS I'd requested a few weeks ago in the Purple Circle collection. These were the pieces I thought might be the same as the earliest fragment of what I'd now come to believe was Len Spurgeon's scattered, possibly unfinished, novel. I'd more or less written off actually seeing them as a wash. He was willing to fax the pages, right after we hung up the phone.

I said, fine, great, let's go. A few minutes later, I was looking at the new fragments. The first was titled 'To the Solano County Fair' and was typed so obviously on what I by now recognized as Mark Dodge's electric Olivetti that I knew what it was before I saw the Timrod Collection's label, 'from unfin. MSS #6, *Man in a Jar*'. It wasn't at all the same as the car ride in which Paul shoves his brother out, but about three brothers whom I now recognized as the Dodge kids, traveling with their grandparents.

The next piece was labeled as Jeff Weber's 'What Occurred on Route 90' and was another car ride, although this one turned out to be six pages of action and dialogue between a boy named Tray and an older man, Carl, on what seems to be a biweekly evening drive to Cheyenne, where the two are actors in the local theater company's newest production. Carl stops to pick up a down-on-his-luck cowpoke named Hy, who's just been sacked from an 'outfit' of cattle herders, and who's planning to drink and whore his sorrows away with his final paycheck. The dialogue consists of Hy's sad tale, followed by Carl's attempts to get Hy to allow them to stop, so the hitchhiker can be orally serviced by the unwilling, silent boy in the back seat. The piece ends with Hy: 'I ain't never said no to a pretty boy, but I think if you're fixin' to look at us all the while, then you'll probably have ta . . .'

The third set of pages faxed to me was a remarkably inconsistently spelled few pages about a late at night drive in a gigantic rattling old Hispano-Suiza 'cabriolet' convertible through the streets of downtown Mobile, Alabama, by two characters, the narrator alternately named Louie and Lewie, and a great flaming black queen usually called Miss Rich or Miss Bitch-to-You, Boy. This I supposed to be an early draft or perhaps even the primal nugget out of which eventually had grown the eponymous tale, '"Miss Thing" and the '41 Bugatti' of Cameron Powers's posthumous collection, completed by Reuben Weatherbury. Three down. None to go.

I was just biting down on that good-news/bad-news when Conchita appeared in the library doorway.

'Did he say when they're coming back?' she asked.

That surprised me a little. I thought she already knew.

'Not for a while. They're going to Majorca today. Was there something you wanted to tell Mr Von Slyke.'

'No. Nothing,' she said, which sounded lame to me. She left the doorway and, a second later, was back. 'By the way . . . what happened to your car?'

'Nothing! Why?'

'It looks all screwed up. You know, like someone keyed it? I noticed when I drove in this morning.'

'Keyed it?'

By this time, I was up and moving. I ran to my room and grabbed the car keys and hurried out through the courtyard to the motor court. At first I noticed nothing. The car looked fine. From what she'd said, I expected great swaths of damage. From what, I couldn't begin to think. Had I inadvertently come too close to something last night while driving along Laurel Canyon Boulevard? And if so, wouldn't I have heard something? Noise of the damage as it was being made? As I got closer to the car, it suddenly appeared, became unmistakable: as though someone had used black chalk to make big lines and swirls and curlicues all along the pale blue side fenders, hood, trunk. Lines of it everywhere. Only when I touched it, it didn't rub off. And when I spit in a tissue and rubbed at it it didn't erase or smudge. It hadn't been penned on, it had been gouged out of the carpaint itself. Now I understood why Conchita had used the words 'keyed it': someone had used a metal key to do this. Someone had deliberately done this. I circled the car and began to notice oddly placed and scuffed dents where each door reached the top fender trim: near each door handle, scuff marks as though from shoes. As though someone had kicked the car in anger. Who would do such a thing? . . . Ray Rice jumped into my mind. But why would he do this and then leave the teddy bear? If he had done it? If he had left the bear? But I also thought of that crazy woman in Encino last night with her paper note fluttering, shouting about how I'd taken her parking spot. She'd even had keys in her hand.

'S'a shame,' Conchita commiserated, 'a nice-looking car like this!'

'It's a rental car. I'd better call this in.'

'You'll have to pay something,' she said with such assurance in her voice that for a second I wondered if she'd done it.

An hour later, I'd discovered I would have to pay something, but not the entire cost of the repainting the car would require. As I'd taken a long lease on the car, I'd received the maximum liability insurance. I'd have to come up with a secondary payment to extend it, two hundred dollars. That stunk. But when I left the house later on that day, bringing one box of the Von Slyke papers to be photocopied at a place he'd recommended, and looked at the poor marred convertible in which I'd only last night had such a wonderful experience, I felt sad, the same way I would have felt if someone attractive I'd slept with had been discovered beaten, requiring hospitalization, stitches.

While I was outside looking at the car, Camden Phoenix of all people phoned and left a return call, in which he'd pointedly mentioned the fact that he was currently only partly employed. This was clearly a message about him needing, indeed requiring, money, for which Tanya Cull had already prepared me. So when I called back and actually got him on the phone, I said, 'About money, you realize that I'm not a publisher. Not an editor. I'm a graduate student at UCLA, doing my thesis on the Purple Circle. I don't come equipped with much of a budget.'

Silence greeted that. Then in that accent which by now I was sure was phoney, he testily asked, 'Then why are you bothering me?'

'Not that money can't be found, if it turns out that you have in your possession something I can use,' I quickly replied. 'And, in fact, should my thesis be published in book form, as it probably will be, there could be reprint-rights money in the picture. Not a lot, naturally, since it will be a university press . . . but something.'

'Well,' less testily, 'perhaps we can do business,' he replied. 'I'm not, after all, a foundation for college students . . . yet!' he added.

We made plans to get together at his address that night at six-thirty. Just before we disconnected, I wondered whether to ask if he thought his neighbor might have vandalized my car. But it had already been such a mixed morning, I didn't dare risk it.

'Higher!' Camden Phoenix insisted.

'This is as high as I reach,' I insisted back.

'Okay! Hold that frame piece still.'

'I am holding it still,' I protested.

'No, you're not. You're wiggling it.'

He finally found it motionless enough to mark the wall with a pencil point. My arms were killing me from holding up for so long the large, weighty, green graphite blackboard while he took his sweet time to mark off spots where he would insert butterfly screws. Having at last mastered the arcane art of marking off spots, Camden now sailed into the equally complicated task of hammering a nail into the plasterboard wall, not a half-inch, not a quarter of an inch, but three-sixteenths of an inch deep. That done, he took up his automatic drill. The screwholes were relatively quickly made, but then he had me hold it all up again while he engaged in the elaborate chore of emplacing butterfly screws. I was made to heft the graphite board yet again, while he used a contrasted attachment to the drill to tediously drive the screws home. Satisfied, he stood away from the wall and looked it over.

'Not bad,' he declared. 'Now for the next one.'

'Carpenter's journeymen hire out at ten dollars an hour, you know,' I said.

'What's that supposed to mean?' he asked, an edge of menace in his voice.

I wasn't to be cowed. 'It means that I didn't come here to help you build your martial arts studio,' I said. 'I came here to interview you.

Perhaps to find out something about Frankie McKewen and the other Purple Circle members.'

'I know that,' he growled. 'I also know this work isn't going to do itself. And I also know that you have nothing to offer in return for my knowledge except pie in the sky promises about some future possible publication. Which doesn't do me a shitload of good now, does it? Does it?' he repeated.

'So you're saying that in return for helping you here, you'll tell me what I want to know? Is that the deal?'

'What else you have to offer?' He looked me up and down and his face said as much as his words. 'Forget that I asked. The very last thing I need in my fool life at this moment is a piece of young ass. What I need is a second pair of hands to get this work done. C'mon now, youngblood, lift the sign!'

I was going to ask if it had ever crossed his mind that people did things without pay, did things without requiring that you do something in return? However, it was crystal clear that in Camden Phoenix's universe they didn't. So I hefted the next object, a slightly less heavy framed sign to go into the front window, and held it up, staggering from the weight, until he'd arrived at the end of his time to mark and drill and insert and drill again.

He was right about one thing: the space needed work before it could open. Even though once complete, it probably wouldn't include more than a bare parquet floor with a few canvas-covered mats, a brace of wooden folding chairs, the sign and hanging blackboard – the last I assumed for him to draw strategy diagrams. The ceiling was a chalky-white patterned tin – painted before he'd moved in but still clean. The floor had apparently been swabbed, sanded for smoothness, then waxed to a high, even slippery, gloss. The windows appeared newly washed. The ample window ledges looked recently painted. The colossal houseplants set upon them that I'd seen when peeking in the day before seemed well cared for: trimmed and watered, they'd even had their leaves shined. Even the rolls of dark green construction paper that I assumed had found their way here from some photographer's studio were newish and unsoiled.

Only in the small chamber behind this public one, in the room labeled 'office' that appeared to be anything but – its door quickly

closed when I'd first been admitted a half-hour ago – was it unmistakable that someone was also living here. A brief peek had enabled
me to see dozens of messily stacked, miscellaneously sized cardboard boxes, a low-built, poorly made, planked bookshelf atop
which sat a flat-screened TV and a superannuated phone-answering
fax/printer/copier. A double futon lay more or less flat on the floor,
partially obstructed from view by a transportable, upright, canvas-
sided wardrobe and what had to be a truly ancient artifact: a
naugahyde-covered bean bag from the 1960s in an exceptionally
putrid tinge of mustard that suggested it might have initially have
been either canary yellow or ivory-colored.

'You're damned useful,' Camden said, 'when you keep your
mouth shut.'

'I'm not going to much longer,' I said. 'What else do you need me
to do?'

I couldn't see anything more, but he could. He needed a writing
desk from the back room carried out, and he required me to hold up
a large, slender-framed (and thus over-flexible) poster taken from a
martial arts festival in Seoul, so he could tell where it would look
best. Then, of course, hang it.

I took advantage of a microscopic break to say, 'I take it that you
and Professor Cull don't get along all that well.'

'Professor Who?'

'Cull. Tanya Cull.'

'Oh! Her!'

'The two of us had a long talk,' I said. 'A few long talks. But
somehow or other, I never managed to figure out your exact relationship to Frankie McKewen.'

'That's because she didn't want you to figure it out. I was his
boyfriend the last five years of his life. You get it? The reason she's
not letting you know?'

'You mean because she's so busy projecting her own fantasy about
her uncle, Mitch Leo, and Frankie McKewen that she can't accept
the possibility that their relationship wasn't as conventionally happy
as she'd prefer to present it?'

'You just said a mouthful. 'Course, all that might have been different if I weren't black,' he added.

'You're not black. You're whiter than I am.' Which was true. His

skin color was so milky, with ruddy cheeks and abundant freckling
all over, that my own – now aided by a fresh tan – looked in comparison swarthy. His eyes were green. His hair was strawberry
blond. Yet it was also true that his hair, while fair, was curly enough
to be considered 'kinky', while his smooth, handsome facial features
could have signified one of a dozen differing genetic combinations of
Caucasian, Native American, Mongoloid and Negroid.

'Tech-nic-ally speaking, that's so,' he admitted. 'But when I'm
with white folks, they always wonder what in the hell I am. When
I'm with black folks, I'm considered a "brother". You know, sort of
a High Yaller.'

'Nowadays though it's all so mixed up. Half the students in my
class at UCLA are of mixed-race parents. Nobody cares.'

'They're fortunate. They sure enough did care when I was a kid.'

Along with his unusual physical characteristics I'd also been
trying to gauge his age. I had figured no more than forty. Though
that made little sense in my Purple Circle chronology. The way he
was talking, he was far older.

'You mean you were a kid in the '60s? During the Civil Rights
marches and all?' I asked, daring him to confirm it.

'I was born in '67. But don't think I didn't come in for my share!
You kids today have it easy, you know.'

As he spoke I began calculating. 'Then you were sixteen when you
met Frankie McKewen?' I found that hard to believe.

'Sixteen. And he was forty years old. Older than my daddy.
Though at the time I was sure he was only thirty-five or so. You
shocked?' And before I could answer, he went on, 'He didn't know
I was only sixteen. I was already this big. I'd shot up at fourteen.
Never grew an inch after. And because of where we all met. He
later told me he thought I was under twenty-one, which was how
old I told him I was. But it was only when he caught me with my
algebra textbook that he found out I was still in high school. Of
course, among the Other Countries and Blackheart Collectives, I
was always the baby and more a guest than full member. You ever
hear of those?'

I did, a bit. I remembered reading about them in Erling
Cummings's book on the Purples. 'Donald Woods, Assotto Saint,' I
hazarded. 'They met at the Twelfth Street Center in New York . . .'

Camden brightened up. 'Well, you aren't completely stupid!'

'They evolved out of two previous groups that got going in the '70s. Black and White Men Together and Men of All Colors?' I hazarded. 'Is that your connection with Frankie McKewen?'

'That's right. Frankie and I think maybe Dominic De Petrie too were in those early groups, doing readings and fund-raisers and I don't know, maybe also in demonstrations. It was a tough thing, a really tough thing to even admit being African-American and gay in those times. The political brothers were always down on you, calling you a sister-boy, saying that homosexuality was "the white man's disease" and all that shit. It was hard. The black gay brothers needed whatever help they could get and they took it wherever they believed it was given honestly. They got it at last, and then they demanded respect and they got that too. But it was a long struggle. Hard to explain to kids nowadays, how long, how hard!'

'"The Second Harlem Renaissance",' I offered. 'That's how Dr St George characterized those writers. He also mentioned that almost none of the members of the gay group lived in Harlem.'

'Some did. Roy Gonsalves and Joe Beam. Ron Dildy. They also lived in Chelsea and the Village – Isaac Jackson and Dave Frechette. Yves and Jan. And a lot of them in Brooklyn, because rents were cheaper. Suggs. But that's what it was all right, a renaissance. A brief flowering, all too soon over. By 1995, all but a few were dead. But it was glorious while it lasted. Every year there was another anthology: *Black and Queer*, *In the Life*, *The Road Before Us*, *Here to Dare*, with new discoveries galore. And it seemed that every few months another black gay man would emerge as a writer with his book of poetry, or his novel, or his new play, as though out of some underground cocoon! It was fabulous. And I was there. Sitting at their feet. Knowing I'd never be as good a poet as Yves or Donald. Never be as angrily eloquent as Essex or Marlon. Never be as committed to being "black" as Melvin. But you know what? They listened to my third-rate efforts with respect and every one of them encouraged me. It was a beautiful time to be young. New York was a beautiful place too, even with all the dirt and the noise and the prejudice. My! The people! The places! The Sound Factory! The Nickel Bar! Paradise Garage with Junior as DJ!'

'You met Frankie McKewen at a reading?'

'Actually, I met him at a party. I can't remember where exactly. It wasn't given by any of the major players of the group. Some hanger-on had thrown it. But I do remember it was summertime and, despite the air conditioning, I was still quite warm. I was wearing a rayon shirt, you know, one of those Hawaiian numbers. Gigunda yellow hibiscus on a field of black. I kept all the buttons opened. By then Frankie had been writing his column "Off Amsterdam Avenue" for several years. So when someone mentioned he was at the party and asked did I want to meet him, I said sure. Well, my mouth almost fell open when I was introduced to him. Not because he was the only white man there, you understand. He wasn't. In fact his lover, Mitch Leo, was there. Of course, James Turcotte was always hanging around the group, wanting to be a part of it. There were a few other white guys too. But it was because Frankie wrote that column from so inside being a brother, you know what I'm saying? Casual, informal yet cool . . . it was so much the way I always thought a real sophisticated brother would write that I'd just always assumed McKewen was black. So I stood there meeting him, look-ing like some farmboy fresh out of cotton country, saying something stupid about how thrilled I was. But I wasn't, you know, because I felt . . . well, how do I explain it, deceived? I guess you'd say. And I could tell that Frankie understood everything going on in my mind as I was thinking it. He was wearing this sort of sly yet understand-ing smile. Finally I tried to get away, saying something like "see you later", and he took my arm lightly at the elbow and he said, "Okay, later. It's a promise. Right?" I didn't know what he was talking about. I pulled loose even though I wanted to stay next to him, just be near him, since I was attracted at the same time I was repulsed. He let go of me and then he said, "By the way, don't button that shirt for the next ten years!" Someone laughed. I knew it was a ter-rific compliment, and I blushed like crazy. Did all I could to stay away from him at that party. I was that interested. My pecker was especially interested in him. Even with all the complications. Someone pointed out Frankie's lover, who was handsome, and I saw that they left together, and I thought well, honey, that's it! You just forget that white man.'

'But you didn't.'

'I didn't. And he didn't either. There was this reading I went to a week or two later at the Gay Community Center on West 12th Street in the Village. Essex Hemphill had come up from DC. The gang was all there. It was on the first floor in that place. You know, the building was still being converted from an old elementary school and there was construction stuff everywhere: bundles of wires twice your size in one corner, wooden lathing and plasterboard, and even water piping. Cement dust covered everything. Even so, it was the main floor of the place, which our group hadn't even had to demand – it had been offered – and Essex was still doing his fire and brimstone act, as a hundred people had come out for it, and not only brothers either. It helped that it was an unexpectedly cold night. And there was Frankie McKewen. Without Mitch. This time the reception was held right there, it being too cold outside, where they'd originally planned it. Frankie got me alone fast, and he asked me if I was "jailbait" and we teased around, but I took him back to my room and once I had that man in my arms no other would do.

'He told me that first night that he and Mitch had been together since college days, but that they both slept around outside of the relationship. They both had boyfriends. They were both what he called "Blackhawks", a term I'd never heard before. Mitch himself had had a boyfriend for almost a decade, but Frankie hadn't had one in a few years. Now he was ready. Was I?

'It all happened so fast, there seemed to be no way to stop it. He insisted on using condoms from the beginning. I didn't find out he was HIV positive till a few months later. I never went to one of their teas, although I was invited several times. I did meet several brothers who'd gone out with either Mitch or Frankie and who told me I was in "good hands". These were good people. They stood by you. I was surprised by how many of the group had slept with them. How beloved Frankie was as a buddy long after the sex was over with. All of which recommended him to me. Once Frankie started getting sick, which he did really sudden, Mitch kept me informed of what was going on. He had me up to Frankie's hospital room, allowed me to stay there as long as I wanted. He asked my opinion in all medical treatment matters. He treated me like family. He made sure I got to speak my piece at Frankie's memorial service, although I was pretty stunned, out of it, by then, never having lost anyone but one distant old grandpa before in my young life.

'I guess it was Mitch's doing that got all of Frankie's papers to me a month later, and before Mitch himself died. Frankie hadn't made a will. But it was Frankie's wish and Mitch let everyone know that. By that time Mitch had already spoken to someone at the Timrod Collection and he believed they would probably approach me about buying them. Mitch told me, "You made Frankie so happy. Now it's time for him to do you some good." That was nice of him, don't you think? 'Course, it took another ten, fifteen years to get it all settled.'

We'd stopped work and were standing, half sitting on the edge of the work desk. Camden had opened a fruit juice for each of us and we'd sipped at them until they were empty. All earlier hostility was gone. As he'd spoken about the past, Camden himself had somehow altered, to become that naïve young man of sixteen Frankie McKewen had met. It was easy to see the attraction. He must have been delightful, so full of life, so filled with promise, before the multiple deaths and the drab reality had set in and it was all over and never again would be so glorious.

He was calmer now. So much so, that I felt able to say, 'That was eighteen years ago. Surely a great deal has happened since then?'

Camden sighed. 'A great deal and not much of it good. I sometimes think that if Frankie came back and saw me now, he'd be real disappointed. But then, you see, it's not all my fault. It seems to be my fate to get involved with things and people, projects and groups, just as they're ending . . . falling apart . . . dissolving. The Black Poets in New York. A theater group in Philly after that. A black arts project in Oakland. A film production company in Ladera Hills. Seems whenever I get involved in something, it's about over. You could say I'm the finishing man.'

'You're making a start now,' I argued. 'By the way, I've been racking my brains about something. The name of this place. Where did you get it?'

'The Boxer Rebellion,' he said. 'The Chinese who tried to get the foreigners out of their country in the nineteenth century called themselves "The Righteous and Harmonious Fist of the People".'

'Of course!'

Since we were getting along so well, I told Camden what it was I was looking for. He listened carefully. I knew it might be difficult to get him to admit to me that he'd held stuff back from the Timrod Collection. But I had to know. I kept asking about diaries, letters, journals, rather than fiction or non-fiction manuscripts, stressing that I was really interested in any material from McKewen's early days, hoping that as that would predate the Purple Circle's existence, he might have felt justified in holding it back from them, salting it away while awaiting a future Frankie McKewen revival.

Unlike the other heirs and executors of the Purples, Camden had not put anything on computer, he told me, never mind organize it by page number and number of mentions. He said he did have a few hard-copy lists of MSS and he'd kept photocopies of everything he'd given to the collection – presumably that was what was in those cardboard boxes encircling his futon. Nor did he seem to be as up on the material as some others. Perhaps he'd never even read it all through. Perhaps that would explain why Len Spurgeon's name elicited not a glimmer of a response from him. He seemed extremely hesitant before he finally said, 'Whatever it is, this has to be between the two of us, you understand.'

'Meaning if I publish it, I can't mention the source in my attributions?'

'You can,' Camden said, 'But only if you say a "family member" or a "former friend or lover".'

'That can be done,' I agreed.

'And you have to evaluate it, tell me how much you think I could get to have it published.'

'I'm not a book editor,' I said, 'but I'll try.'

'Also you have to agree to get someone who is a book editor to look at it for possible publication. And you have to agree to provide or to find someone else even more appropriate than yourself to provide a – what do you call it? – a preface? Or an introduction.'

'Is it a Frankie McKewen book? An early, unpublished book?'

'It's –' Camden Phoenix smiled and his eyes looked to be the color of old hundred-dollar bills – 'Frankie McKewen's "Berlin Diaries", which,' he quickly added, 'you've never heard of. Because no one has. He wrote them in the early '70s in Europe. I found them by chance, inside a box that contained an early draft of *Whitman's Sons*. So? Are we agreed?' he asked.

'Agreed,' I said.

We shook hands then high-fived our palms.

I waited nervously for the next ten minutes it took him to locate and get the MS. Before he handed it over, he said, 'Maybe we should put this in writing?' He took another ten minutes to locate an old Brother Word Processor, a glorified typewriter, to have me keyboard and then have him read over and approve a written agreement between us. He asked me to add in a clause in which I relinquished any and all future monies connected to publication in any medium.

'Now you've got to leave. My aikido class begins in five minutes.'

I was so astounded by this news, I let him thrust the MS into my arms.

'There's a Denny's up the street on Ventura Boulevard,' Camden said. 'You can take it there and read it through. The class lasts an hour and a half. That should be enough time. Bring it back when you're done.'

Naturally I would have preferred it if Frankie McKewen's 'Berlin Diaries' was an unexpected masterpiece suddenly come to light. What literary scholar wouldn't have wanted to be connected to such a discovery? And McKewen's reputation could have used a shot in the arm. None of his books were in print. Only two of his titles had been available at the time of his death, the perennially titillating 1978 *Switch-Hitters*, McKewen's study of the leather scene – gay, straight and bisexual – and the 1971 *Signals in the Sky*, the book on UFOs and other strange phenomena he'd co-written with Mitch Leo, a book by then already two decades old and for which neither they, their agent nor lawyer could ever obtain a sales statement for its very long run of being 'remaindered'. Of the nine Purple Circlers, Frankie McKewen was the one today most ignored and forgotten, except maybe for Rowland Etheridge, and like Etheridge this was sad because he'd begun with so much promise: following the UFO book, another four non-fiction titles out of two publishers in less than a decade. Even more sadly, Frankie's books had been reviewed in the major media, had gotten attention outside the book world, and he and Mitch and all their friends had believed he was headed toward long-term literary fame, and they all behaved as though this were so.

That, of course, only made it all the more sad, strangely sad, when

Frankie's career seemed to come to a full stop in the same year that Mitch Leo, his lover's, began to rocket up. 'It was as though,' Reuben Weatherbury had written in the intro to the second *Reader*, 'there was a large talent between the Leo–McKewens, but alas only enough talent for one to enjoy at a time.' Irian St George in his book on De Petrie speculated further, wondering if 'this *folie à deux* wasn't indeed something more, a vampiric relationship, à la Scott and Zelda Fitzgerald, where the energy, talent, ability, the life-force itself, was sucked out of one by the other, taking turns at varying times'.

True, there had been a brief flurry of excitement surrounding the publication of McKewen's posthumous novel *A Boy From Quad Cities* two years after his death. But that was in 1991. A lifetime ago in the publishing world, not to mention in gay literature, with its more than usual share of meteoric ascents – and fizzling crashes. And, as Erling Cummings had pointed out in his own book, McKewen's novel might not have gotten the attention it did if it hadn't coincided with the publication of Reuben Weatherbury's well-reviewed first volume of *The Purple Circle Reader*. The novel hadn't sold more than 5,000 copies, hardcover and trade paperback, and a few years later it too was gone. And while that first volume of the *Reader* had also never been a best-seller, it had become a steady one, eventually adopted for college use in the many lesbian and gay lit. courses that had popped up in the late 1990s. Cummings had openly wondered why McKewen's own study of lesbian and gay literary precursors, *Whitman's Sons and Sappho's Daughters*, wasn't also kept in print, or reprinted and used for courses. The critic/biographer thought it 'good enough in its insights, wide-ranging in its allusions and references, if lacking the usual scholarly graces'.

Both he and Fleming had also mentioned McKewen's *In the Spirit of Chief Pontiac* as a potential reprint. That 1976 study of how several once rich and powerful Native American cultures had or – more often – had not managed to survive the twentieth century was not only ahead of its time as a sociological study, it was also one of the earliest representations of 'successful Indians', including the Lenape-Sonorans, a southern California tribe that held onto traditional oil-rich lands and never lost wealth or power.

The book on S/M life was one Frankie McKewen had been planning to write for some time and one reason he'd ended up in

Germany in the spring of 1974, and come to pen a diary. The more specific reason for being there was research he needed for the book he had already half written, his 1975, *I am You and You are Me*. McKewen's story of the rise of British rock music of the 1960s and its enormous influence on the American public and on American musical artists would become his best-selling title, coming out in four hardcover and two mass-market paperback editions, totaling 300,000 copies. It was this book and those on Native Americans and the S/M world that were responsible for him always seeming to have a book contract. That book's title, taken from a Beatles' song, gave precedence to the Fab Four. McKewen had come to believe that it was in Hamburg and Prague and Berlin, in small, smoky dive-like clubs, that the quartet had spent years perfecting their songs, their ensemble, their act, before they – and the Stones and the Who and the Animals – exploded first on the British, then the American (and world) publics. Frankie felt he had to be on the spot, to interview club managers and hangers-on, once contemporary groups still playing the venues, people who'd seen and heard them, the girls (sometimes the boys) members of the various rock bands had picked up, to get a sense of what had really been going on a decade before.

The original plan was for Mitch to join Frankie for three months in Germany. After all, they lived and traveled together. But the money somehow failed to materialize. Mitch's favorite aunt was diagnosed with leukemia. The trip was reduced to a month and a half, and Mitch stayed home.

Unfortunately for Phoenix, and for me, Frankie McKewen's 'Berlin Diaries' wasn't anything more than working journals about the vagaries and obstacles and wrong turns in his travels, the slow-downs and about-faces and dead ends of his research, his sometimes – usually not – successful attempts to connect up with the people the Beatles or Stones had known, and the people he was meeting in the clubs, most of whom were destined to never rise above this local fame. McKewen's descriptions of characters and places weren't more than utilitarian, his grasp of what was happening in central Europe not sophisticated in politics or sociology, and when he did get someone interesting to interview, he didn't dig deep, possibly afraid he would scare off the interviewee. So while I wouldn't be able to tell Camden Phoenix that he'd been stashing

something worthwhile all these years, someone at some future date
might well edit it, issue the little book out of some university press.
I'd try to interest Weatherbury in having it done.

More crucial to my own purposes, the journals, which went along
for some fifty-three pages without an enormous amount of interest,
suddenly at page fifty-five contained this:

> . . . one of those allegedly outré leather parties common here
> in Berlin, where everyone gets together in some odd, large,
> unheated, unair-conditioned, temporarily unused formerly
> commercial structure – an old bakery, or recent pig slaughter-
> house, cleaned up, still somehow redolent of their recent
> unsavory past. Karla had invited me and told me I'd meet her
> closest friends, Hei-ko and Hei-jo and Hei-pe. Japanese gen-
> tlemen, I assumed from their names. Wouldn't you? But it
> turned out that they were merely hip young Berliners, their
> names short for Heinz-Konrad, Heinz-Joachim, and Heinz-
> Peter! We were all dancing in a circle, the three Heis, Karla,
> some older women with hennaed hair and kohl-smeared eyes,
> when I suddenly felt someone looking. The feeling went on
> for another ten minutes, so I could no longer deny it. I
> excused myself from the group, went over to the side of the
> huge, cool space where Pilsner in litre-sized bottles was sell-
> ing, got one, sipped and looked around myself, trying to
> determine where the odd feeling was coming from.
>
> There he was. Directly in front of me. Wearing a black
> leather vest over his shirtless, blond-tufted chest. A black
> motorcycle cap askew over one eye, and the tightest black
> denims I've ever seen. Yummy. It took me maybe one minute
> to remember him. We'd first and last met on the athletic
> grounds of Bettendorf High. Two or three classes as well as
> one or two teams had been out that afternoon when one of
> those astonishing Midwestern squalls had arisen as though
> out of nowhere at all. As these sometimes were accompanied
> by tornadoes, we'd been advised to seek shelter. When the sky
> darkened and the apple-sized hail began pelting, the only
> shelter I could see around was a half-underground athletic
> equipment shed. I ran for it.

Inside, already soaking wet when I arrived, was this boy, someone on the track and field team practicing long jumps in the center of the oval around which I'd been running twenty laps of punishment thanks to that fuck Coach Jugend, who complained during our practice scrimmage that as his lead running back, I needed to 'get the lead out of my ass'.

We slammed the slanted door shut, then because the wind was grabbing so hard, bolted it shut. We peered together out the little window at the storm lancing the ground, listened to the noise of hail pelting from above, and suddenly – I didn't know how – we had our hands all over each other and were pulling our soaked clothing off and he was on his knees, blowing me, then I did the same, and then we took turns screwing each other, all in the fifteen minutes it took for the storm to arrive, cause havoc in the stadium area, and leave.

'Ken?' I asked last night, not sure of his name. 'Len,' he said. 'Len Spurgeon. You're from Iowa? Right?' I said right. We shook hands. Stood next to each other, sipping Pilsner. 'You still in track and field?' I asked. 'No.' he said. 'I'm a professional baseball player. But I still suck dick and fuck guys. See that –' pointing out this big Teutonic Adonis dancing in front of us – 'he's my boy!'

We jawed a bit more. Len was in Germany since last year's off-season. He wasn't happy with his league contract offer, so he'd come to work for the government, helping the US Air Force set up baseball programs at their bases in Nuremberg and Pennemunde. He knew a lot about Germany and especially Berlin, as he was currently working out of the air base at Tempelhof, if I needed tips. Said he'd show me around if I wanted. He had plenty of spare time. I said sure. So we exchanged phone numbers. For a second I thought maybe we'd get a replay of that afternoon in the equipment shed, then Adonis showed up and made it clear that Len was all his.

The next week of journals contained nothing about Len. Then there's an account of a political demonstration of students, post-graduates and punks at the Marianneplatz, a popular hangout in

302 THE BOOK OF LIES

Kreuzberg, where many younger West Germans had moved in, becoming squatters in apartments emptied in 1960 because they were so close to, indeed faced the narrow-at-that-point no man's land on either side of the omnipresent Berlin Wall. McKewen can't figure out the reason for the demonstration or the protests that have been going on for a week already, centering on nearby Yorckstrasse. Something to do with a Berlin newspaper publisher. Or a new residence law. He's not sure. Although it is clear that the West Berlin police will soon move in on the crowd as they've done before. During the demonstration/picnic/music festival, Len Spurgeon makes a sudden appearance, dressed casually rather than formally in black leather, but without his Adonis, and finding the whole thing boring, says 'This Oranienstrasse scene is so yesterday, don't you think?' He drags Frankie off in his shiny new Opel coupé and deposits McKewen and himself inside a large, old-fashioned, mahogany, mirror and chandeliered coffee house close to the toney Kurfürstendamm. There, amidst watercress and schnitzel sandwiches and huge glasses of Viennese coffee mounded *mit Schlag*, Len asks Frankie if he would like to accompany him to his tailor, a Franco-White Russian named Gyoetz who does superb work and doesn't charge that much. Not only does Frankie go along with Len, but he ends up ordering his very first 'bespoke' suit, which Len arranges to get him at a good price. Furthermore, they'll meet in two weeks to pick the suits up and then they'll celebrate not at Café Einstein but at the even more famous Krantzler for nesselrode pie.

Another week of McKewens' cultural lapping-up journal entries about visiting Baroque palaces like Schloss Charlottenburg, as well as a night at the Deutsche Oper (Peter Schreier and Edith Mathis in *Mignon*) and an afternoon amidst ten centuries of artistic glories at the huge Kunst Galerie down at Dahlem, then this appears on the travelogue like a dark stain:

> . . . at this little dive named Buddy's Bar off the Kantstrasse
> with Hei-ko when who should show up but Len Spurgeon,
> looking very hot and with him a very handsome black-
> skinned gentleman, a corporal in the American Air Force
> named Hiram something. Both in leathers. Both with so
> much attitude, the usual crowd of skinny boys for hire and

older gentleman with two hairs plastered across their bald
spots made way and even bought them drinks. Len said they
were going afterward to a private party up in Wedding near
the Berlin Grossmarkt, where there would be other 'leather-
men' and a lot of 'good-looking, bad-tempered Negro
gentlemen looking for white boys to piss on before fucking.
Interested? You should be.'

I had to admit that if Hot Hot Hiram were any indication
of the guys, I actually might be interested, although I'd never
really done anything S/M, he should understand. To which
Len replied, 'Don't be a pussy. Have yourself a life. You'll
have plenty of time to become a suburban matron when
you're back in the States.'

So the three of us drove to this I mean beyond nowhere
area around the docks at the Spee River, where there was
nothing but factories. Sure enough, in the middle of this big
empty-looking building, there's a party going on, very hush-
hush, look through a peephole at you when you ring the bell.
Inside there's a small, rather middle-class decorated apartment, with maybe fifty guys, all in jeans or leathers, most
without shirts, a few only in jockstraps and obvious orgies
going on all over the place, as well as spot S/M demonstrations of bootlicking and one guy being spanked over
another's knee and a more formal-looking flogging. I'm
already tanked on beer, and the hashish we smoked on the
way over, and once we got here, and it's all very hot. I figured
that Hiram was Len's date, but once we're inside, Len vanished, and after I'm wandering a bit, I come onto Hiram
being sucked off by some German guy and he pulls me over
to play with my nipples which I don't usually like, but when I
pull back from his fingers, Hiram slaps my face hard, and
says, 'Stand still.' And I say, 'I don't like it when anyone does
that.' And he says, 'You'll like when *I* do it.' And now the
German guy takes my dick out and he sucks us both at the
same time, then takes us in turn and meanwhile Hiram plays
with my nipples, twisting them, and pulling, and kneading
and it no longer hurts, in fact it's wonderful, wonderful, I'm
about to come and I say so and he pulls the German guys'

head away from me and onto himself, and keeps playing with my nipples, and we do this maybe through five or six rounds, until I'm about to collapse with the plain/pleasure, and then Hiram lets me come and tongue-kisses me while I do, never once letting go of my nipples. And when I'm done, he makes me bite his nipples, saying, 'Harder! Harder!' while the German guy brings him off. And afterward I fall on someone's sofa, and just black out. Someone manages to get me home, and the following afternoon, I wake up at maybe ten past one and it's Len on the phone and he says, 'I knew you for a Blackhawk the minute I laid eyes on you,' and I say, 'A what?' and Len says, 'A Blackhawk! A dinge queen! A nigger-lover! Stick with me I'll bring you places you never dreamed of.'

Another few days pass with nothing. There's a brief, intriguing entry the following Saturday at the morning open-air food market at the KarlAugustplatz on Schillerstrasse where Frankie thinks he's seen Hiram walking with another black man. When he tries to catch up to them through the crowds, they're gone. He bumps into Hiram again that night, at a leather bar in Schöneberg, however, and meets the other fellow, also Air Force, stationed at Nuremberg, named David. For a few minutes its looks as though they might even have a three-way. Then something unclear happens and the two leave without him, headed somewhere else. The very next night, however, Frankie encounters David at a music club he's doing research on, and this time they do go home together. Frankie is enchanted. His journal entry for the next day goes on at embarrassing length about David's body, his penis, the softness and different brown shades of his skin, his hair etc. David leaves on Monday morning but McKewen is hooked on black men now, himself using the name 'Blackhawk' that Len gave him, and suddenly seeing African-American men all around Berlin, on the *U-Bahn* subway, among the soldiers stationed at Checkpoint Charlie, restaurants and clubs on the Kurfürstendamm. One time someone he approaches turns out to be Nigerian, and although they converse, McKewen figures out the man doesn't exude the same appeal. 'They have to be American!' he concludes.

This will become a major theme in Frankie McKewen's life and later on in his work, playing as it does into some fantasy image he has of himself as a child growing up along the Mississippi River (which he did) and having a black friend/lover/playmate (which he probably didn't).

The next entry that interested me occurs the morning McKewen is to pick up his 'bespoke' suit. He and Len meet at the large open-air flea market that has sprouted along the north side of the Strassse des 17 Juni, alongside the Technisches Universitaat in Charlotten-burg. McKewen goes on at some length about the goods at the stalls, vendors and passers-by, then notes,

Among all the strangely sized hardcovers in German, most of which Len told me were school texts and the kind of books teenagers read, was a copy in English of Ackerly's *Hindoo Holiday*, a book I've been trying to find for the longest time. In a solid-looking 'pocket-sized' British version. Only prob-lem was the price: DM35.00. Far too much for the book or for my own pocketbook, which was about to be crashed into later on today when I paid for the suit and Dutch treat at Krantzler.

I was about to move to the next table but kept coming back to the book. Len couldn't help but notice and he asked whether I was going to buy it. I told him it was too much and that I couldn't, wouldn't pay for it. 'No trouble,' he said, and looked at where the blowzy stall vendor was bad-naturedly haggling with another middle-aged woman. As I watched he slipped it off the table and into the pocket of his corduroy jacket in a single, graceful movement. He moved onto the next table, and the next. I was astounded by the casualness and by the deftness of his larceny. Both convinced me this was by no means the first time he'd stolen something from under the eyes of its owner.

Even though I wanted the book, after we'd left the market Len had to force it on me. I relented, of course, feeling per-haps he'd stolen it, i.e. put himself into jeopardy, because of me.

The little incident cast a pall on the rest of their relationship. McKewen refers to it several times in the journal. He also mentions one further incident, later that afternoon, after the two had not only tried on but decided to wear their new suits. They've just spent a wonderful hour walking together along the Kurfürstendamm, another hour in Krantzler, they've paid the bill and stood up to leave. McKewen goes on in this entry about how the suits make him and Len look 'handsome as gods, rich as Rockefeller, manly and exciting as prizefighters'. When they pass through the restaurant's narrow foyer, two attractive, well-dressed German women pass by speaking to each other constantly through the half-veils of their hats, noticing Len and Frankie. McKewen thinks the women are attracted to them, and he turns to follow them with his eyes. One woman has just spoken to the maître d'. The two then half turn to look at Frankie, who bows in their direction. '*Zwei Schwüle*,' he hears the woman say to the other woman, without breaking step, without any emotion, as they are led to their interior booth. 'Two faggots!' McKewen is embarrassed; no, he is mortified. But Len only laughs. And when they get outside it has begun to mist suddenly. '*Schüle für Schwüle!*' Len quips, (dampness for faggots) and whoops in laughter as they run for separate taxis. Frankie will never forgive him for that.

When I arrived at the Casa Herrera y Lopez that night I was surprised to find a note flutteringly attached to the gate. Thinking it might represent some domestic emergency, I got out of the car and took it down.

Scribbled in a handwriting I didn't recognize was the message, 'I Know All About You! Everything.' No signature. No identification. I crumpled it and was about to litter the street with it when I thought, wait, what if it was Ray Rice's doing? I'd save it to compare to some future handwriting he did for class. A test or something. Instead of ditching it, I threw it in the backseat.

I slept easily and deeply. I was awakened at what the digital clock told me was 5:45 a.m. by an insistent ringing of the bell on the outside gate. Evidently Conchita had not slept over. I dragged myself out of bed, put on a bathrobe and answered. A few minutes later, a Federal Express truck pulled around the circular driveway and stopped at the front of the house and a package was thrust into my hands. One glance was enough to tell me it was the promised overnight package from Von Slyke. I signed for it, saw the truck out the gate, locked up, threw the package on Von Slyke's library desk without inspecting its contents and dragged myself back to bed.

Once again I fell asleep surprisingly fast and slept deeply. This time, however, I had a dream. In the dream, the bell was once again ringing. I got out of bed and at the front entry let into the yard another Fed Ex truck. Only this time the deliveryman was Ray Rice. And the package in his hand was filled with something alive. Alive and squirming. Squirming so hard it all but leapt from his hands. I kept trying to look and see whom it was from, by reading the return address. When I'd just managed to do so, the package split open and a large eyeless pink snake jumped out at me. I fell back against the double doors as it writhed around at my feet and raised its head, cobra-like, hissing and spitting. Only at that moment did I realize that I'd forgotten my bathrobe and was naked, and tried to cover myself up.

I awoke from the dream to hear the phone. Grabbed it.

'Dear boy! I apologize for ringing you so early. But I have the best news. I ab-so-lute-ly must share it with some-one.' Irian St George, breathless with excitement.

'What do you think?' he went on. 'He's done a complete volte-face and said "yes". He'll come to the Oscar Wildes. He'll write an acceptance speech. All I need do is in-tro-duce him.'

'Did he tell you why he'd changed his mind?'

'Not a bit of it. Which makes it all the more de-lic-ious! You know, of course, he's not been photographed, not allowed an inter-view, in nearly a decade. This will be the first time De Petrie's been seen in public since he shot up the bank at OutWrite in Seattle. Of course you're too young to know about that *scandale*, but you may have heard about it.'

Even in my slumberous state, I recalled something in Cummings's book about how De Petrie, as introductory keynote speaker to the literary weekend, had told the audience they were all wasting their time and they ought not have wasted their money but that it wasn't too late and they should go home immediately, before they further corrupted each other.

'Not that I give two damns what he says to offend at the Oscar

Wildes,' St George beat me in saying. 'Just so long as he shows up and says some-thing! I will be for-ev-er grat-i-fied! By the way, he ac-tu-al-ly men-tioned your name. Said some-thing or other about you and your thesis. Yes, I recall. He said he wants to talk to you in person about it.'

'Really!' That was news.

'I know you contacted him at the be-gin-ning. Still, I'm aw-ful-ly sur-prised he's going this far,' St George said. 'You must have some-what piqued his in-ter-est to gain such lar-gesse.'

'I have been speaking to Mr Axenfeld, who's been very helpful,' I said. 'I believe they speak regularly. Which might explain it. Of course, I won't be able to see either of the two in person, as I'd hoped to . . .'

'Why not?'

'The expense. I couldn't possibly afford it. Nor the time.'

'Time ought not be a prob-lem! The sum-mer ses-sion midterm is upon us next week. Sure-ly in the five days you can man-age to get to Florida and Cape Cod? As for the expense –' he headed me off before I could interrupt – 'make your plans, then call my office. We'll arrange it.'

'You've already been so kind,' I began. 'How can I ever hope to compensate you for –'

'You can't. You won't. We'll both sim-ply have to ac-cept that,' he said. Then, in a less peremptory tone of voice, 'Re-garding your the-sis. As your proc-tor, we ought to be meet-ing for an up-date.'

'I'd been hoping you'd find some time,' I quickly said. 'It's really progressed a great deal since we last spoke. Developed richly in some unexpected areas. But you've been so busy lately whenever I've attempted to see you and you've had so many other, far more impor-tant, things on your mind that it seemed difficult to –'

'Make an ap-point-ment to see me when you re-turn. We'll dis-cuss it then . . . Just think of it, my boy! De Pet-rie at the MLA awards! It fair-ly gives me shud-ders! The Lord a-lone can fore-tell what great swatches of de-light-ful mis-chief he shall dream up for the oc-cas-ion.'

St George tittered, as though he were holding an especially dis-solute pornographic glossy, then signed off.

I brewed myself a pot of coffee, then wandered back to the

library and pulled open the Fed Ex package, trying not to think too much about the all too transparent symbolism of that tiresome dream about Ray Rice and the snake. I did for one second speculate upon what exactly I might and might not be apprehensive of. I concluded it was senseless and split open the package.

I'm not sure what I'd expected from Damon Von Slyke. Whatever it could have been, what I received wasn't it, but instead a decided curiosity. It was a photocopy of a short story titled 'Master and Man' from his collection of tales *The Japonica Tree*, a story I'd read years ago and which, despite the Tolstoy rip-off title, was rather more in the vein of Tennessee Williams's almost equally famous tale 'Death and the Black Masseur'. In Von Slyke's opus, a young man fresh out of college in the Midwest finds himself living in Brooklyn Heights, and completely by chance encounters a stunningly attractive character named Harold, known to his louche companions as 'Horsemeat Harry', due to his massive genital endowment, with whom the narrator has at first a spoken, then a sexual relationship. Harry teaches the narrator a variety of nuances concerning Sado/Masochism, a service for which the narrator pays handsomely. At the end, the tables are suddenly turned and Horsemeat Harry begs to be humiliated. The narrator, irritated and irked, abandons him to his depressing milieu.

What Damon Von Slyke had sent me was this not-up-to-snuff story (according to Fleming, the 'feeblest and most unwholesome of the collection') with the name Harold crossed out wherever it appeared and the name 'Leonard' drafted in by hand. I reread the story, but when I was finished I found that I didn't believe a word of it. That is to say, I didn't believe that Len Spurgeon was Horsemeat Harry. Or that Damon and Len had this particular kind of relationship. I couldn't precisely say why I didn't believe it. What I knew about Len so far from all the other Purple Circle sources was so varicolored and at times so morally and ethically indefensible that this specific relationship would not have been far off the mark. Yet, in my heart, it felt off. I put it away, drank my coffee and pondered.

First was my absolute certainty that Damon Von Slyke was inventing in attempting to pass off the story as a bona fide account of what had transpired between himself and Len. The one thing I was sure about was that whatever relationship any of the Purples had with Len had been unusual, unexpected, in some way unprecedented. This yarn, with its bullshit O'Henry ironic reversal, seemed too glib, too expected.

The second thing I pondered evolved out of an unanticipated memory that arose while I was reading the story, a detail in that dream I'd been rudely awakened out of this morning. The Fed Ex package with the Freudian, attacking, hissing, orgasmically discharging penis-snake had not – like the real parcel – originated from Von Slyke, and despite Ray Rice being its means of conveyance, he hadn't instigated it either. The name on the package had consisted of two capital letters 'LS'! I couldn't possibly deceive myself that they stood for anyone else but Len Spurgeon. That perception was so unlikely, so disquieting, I didn't have any idea what to do with it. What did it signify? I was terrified of being sexually penetrated by someone long dead?

I decided to move on. I opened my laptop and began searching the Web for airline reservations, looking for flights to Fort Myers, Florida, for the following day. From there, I settled a flight a day later to Boston connecting to Provincetown, and a connection from P-Town to Boston back to Los Angeles. Those accomplished, I arranged for car rentals at both destinations, utilizing the same firm I was using long-term in LA so as to retain all insurance benefits. Only then did I dial Aaron Axenfeld.

'Family business,' I prevaricated, 'brings me unexpectedly to the Fort Myers area this coming weekend. I was hoping you might discover an hour to give me. I'll drive over from the mainland. It'll be my one retreat from all my humdrum family. Please don't say no. I couldn't bear it. I'll only take an hour of your time. I'll stay in a hotel. I promise to limit my bothering of you.'

As De Petrie predicted, Axenfeld unearthed a dozen excuses why he couldn't possibly see me, but I wore him down; he had no choice but to eventually relent. We settled on three p.m. tea.

Feeling I was on something of a roll, I instantly phoned Dominic De Petrie, got his off-putting phone-answering message, assumed he was eavesdropping, and said, 'St George was so ecstatic about your appearance, he's fronting my trip East. I'll be in P-Town staying at some dive called the New Crown and Anchor on Saturday and Sunday. Can I drive to your place one afternoon? From the

computer's map it's only a distance of a few miles. Oh, by the
way, thanks for not telling him of my involvement!'

He picked up the phone at that moment and, surprisingly excus-
ing himself, said, 'Some half-witted bitch who calls herself the
books editor of what claims to be the world's best newspaper has
been badgering me with phone calls for a week. Those jackasses at
that rag spent the first thirty years of my career denigrating my
work. Now, without any warning at all, they can't exist without
me. I'd sooner have bamboo shoots hammered under my toenails
on an hourly schedule than be subjected to her. So, you're coming,
are you? Not scared of encountering me in the Old Dark House?
You know, I've not been seen in public since plesiosaurs hunted
Triassic oceans.'

'At Tobermann's I saw photos of you and Etheridge.'

That aroused De Petrie's attention.

'You were handsome,' I ventured. 'He said you were.'

'That poor boy is so deluded he'd think anyone or anything neither a Rowland Etheridge nor a mole-rat was handsome.'

'I'm not deluded,' I said. 'I know what I saw.'

'Perhaps, but I'm a ghastly phantom today. In fact, whenever I
unawares pass by a windowpane and catch an inadvertent glimpse
of myself, I can't help but instinctively think, "Quick! Kill it with a
stick!"'

'I'll bet you're handsome and distinguished!'

'God, anything but "distinguished"!' he shot back.

'Well, I'm coming. Ready or not,' I replied. 'I'll be seeing Mr
Axenfeld too. But of course you already know that, don't you?'

'What was it they called Louis Treize? The Universal Spider!
That's me. Spinning, ever so gently testing my guy line for any con-
ceivable quarry.'

I laughed and said, 'Maybe you can help me with something? Mr
Von Slyke told me he was going to send me a story about himself
and Len Spurgeon. He was very furtive about it. What I received,
however, was merely a story already long published, which he had
defaced to alter a name.'

'"Master and Man",' De Petrie said.

'That's right.'

'For years now he's been retailing that fabrication.'

'But I don't believe it's about them at all.'

'Why not?' De Petrie asked.

'I don't know . . . It's not how Len would act.'

'How do you know how Len would act? You never met him. He's been defunct half your life.'

'True, but I still feel he wouldn't . . . the story is bogus.'

Silence, then, 'You are astute, aren't you? Or perhaps you've achieved a preternatural link? Yes, the yarn is – as you so ungently put it – bogus. It didn't betide Dame at all, but Mark Dodge. And, as you also correctly guessed, did not concern Len, but instead a model-slash-hustler named Larry Kalani from Maui.'

'Then why would Von Slyke . . .?' I couldn't finish.

'Because he's a fabulist,' De Petrie said, adding, 'A fabricator! A falsifier! A perjurer! A foreswearer! A counterfeiter! A deceiver! An impostor! A storyteller! A yarn spinner! A teller of tales! A false witness! A pathological liar! He's incorrigible. He'll stop at nothing! Example! I was sitting once with half of the Purples, Dame and Aaron and Cammy, and who else was it? Oh, right! Jeff Weber. It was at the Bethesda Fountain in New York City. Central Park. At that time there was a rather okay outdoor café beneath and surrounding where that oversized cement staircase debouches from the 72nd Street pass-through and they served a not too shabby brunch. On fair weekend days all the most fashionable young queenlets of the late '70s could be found putting in an appearance. We'd proceed there many a spring and summer Sunday just past noon, sporting our latest Ron Chereskin sweaters and Nino Cerrutti jackets and of course our most elaborate footwear. During one such *déjeuner sur le pavement*, Dame began relating to us an amusing little incident that he prefaced by claiming it had happened to himself. He was diverting. His details were delightfully telling. His rendition was *non pareil*. Perfect. Save for the insistently irritating fact that what he'd just related to us had actually happened to Cammy, not to Dame, and that Dame knew that all at the table knew it had happened to Cammy, not Dame. When Dame had completed his tale, there was this long and utter stillness. Then Aaron uttered, ". . . Nevertheless!"

'You know the old joke? An English garden party. Very chi-chi. The hostess, Lady Fitzroy, introduces to the assemblage the cast of the tableau vivant about to commence. In doing so she mentions the name of Mabel Hatter-Krone. Forthwith a voice from the crowd pipes up, "Mabel Hatter-Krone sucks cock!" The most absolute cessation of sound in the garden among them all for the longest second in recorded history. Then Lady Fitzroy goes on gamely, "Nevertheless"!'

De Petrie laughed and laughed until I thought I really do appreciate this man. I wondered whether to inquire of him if Len Spurgeon had possessed a hissing, spitting, pink-colored snake-like penis like the one in my dream, because if he did I was certain De Petrie would tell me. But I didn't. Instead we confirmed my arrival time in North Truro, said goodbye, hung up.

I had one final task. I phoned Camden Phoenix and got his answering machine. No surprise. I hadn't expected him to be awake so prematurely in the day, or if conscious answering his phone. I left the following message:

I'm still searching for a document among Frankie McKewen's papers I have reason to think is in your possession and are holding back for very good reasons of your own. A composition that may be a short story or an anecdote or even a fragment of something larger. If you have what I'm looking for, I'll pay for it. I can offer up to fifteen hundred dollars. But of course I'll retain rights to first publication. Search for something that has 'Paul' as character or narrator. Something unsigned, undated, in a different typeface than most of Frankie's other material. Anything that when you first came upon it you said to yourself, 'Is this Frankie's or not?' and couldn't decide.

When I returned back home to the Casa Herrera y Lopez from my class, there was a message on my e-mail from Camden Phoenix. It read:

Three-page single-spaced manuscript, typed on Frankie's Royal electric portable typewriter but with typing errors different than Frankie's usual mistakes and therefore I think written by someone else. It's a story about three guys taking a cable-tram ride up a mountain outside of Palm Springs, California.

Theo, Harve and Paul. Very exciting. No title page. No date.
No byline. Wire my bank a check for fifteen hundred dollars
and it's all yours.

Followed by his bank branch and a direct-deposit number.

I held my breath a half a minute, dialed my sister Judy in San
Francisco, naturally was connected to her answering machine, and
without preamble asked for a loan. That night she returned my call
and without asking why I needed the money, used her computer to
transfer it to my bank account. Her husband, Bart Vanuzzi, was in
summer training camp in Florida, not far from Fort Myers. I ought
to stop by and see him.

I pretended this was news to me. Instead it had been a stand-by.
If she wouldn't give me the money, I'd try hitting him up.

'Oh, sure!' I said. 'That's all the country's greatest quarterback
needs, surrounded by reporters and coaches and other overpaid
jocks! To have his intellectual nerd brother-in-law hanging around!'

'You're not a nerd. Anyway, Bart is proud of you,' Judy said,
loyal sister that she was. I could hear her munching rice cakes as we
spoke. 'You should have heard Bart talking about you to his family
at Sunday dinner after you visited us. He made you sound like
Oliver Wendell Holmes.'

'You're kidding.'

'Or Ralph Waldo Emerson. Someone great!' she added.

It would be something to tell the jocks in my class when I
returned after midterm. 'Give me his address and number. Thanks
for the money.'

'No problem. I really don't know how you exist on so little. What
do you use when you want to go shopping? Do you even have a
credit card?'

We jawed on a while, Judy amusing me with stories of Bart's
family, and the big Italian-American Sunday dinners at which
everyone tried to feed her something besides her usual super-
high-cellulose celery and fennel from the antipasto plates. Their
failures – and their distress.

When we disconnected it was already nearly midnight. I looked
over the pop quizzes I had surprised the class with this afternoon
and unearthed Ray Rice's page. He'd been there today, silent,

incommunicado, frowning, occasionally growling, ignoring everyone: in short, as customary in class. He'd acted as amazed as
everyone else when I'd sprung the exam on them, despite the e-mail
warning. Had he forgotten my threat? Or could that not have been
him on my e-mail? No, it had to be him. He didn't perform badly
on the test, scoring eight out of twelve questions, which was equivalent to the Tsieh twins and Pamela Agosian, the other high-scorers
in the class. So I gave him an 'A', writing on top, 'Nobly done, Mr
Rice.' And just to bother him, I appended, 'We'll make a *littérateur*
out of you yet!' But I was disappointed to see that his handwriting
was in no way similar to the shape of characters on the bewildering
letter I'd retrieved from the house gate.

To hell with it! It probably wasn't intended for me in any case.
Besides which, I had my thesis developing quite nicely. I was about
to obtain another fragment of Len Spurgeon's book. I was on my
way to the East Coast to encounter two living legends, the other two
remaining Purple Circlers, Aaron Axenfeld and Dominic De Petrie.
At Axenfeld's I would attempt to gain entrance somehow into his
Fibber McGee room and see for myself what he had stashed away
there. As for De Petrie, I was to beard him in his own den on his
own invitation. Doubtless this rendezvous was to some extent
intended for him to check me over and determine if I indeed resembled Len Spurgeon as Von Slyke had written. But it was for some
still-arcane reason of his own. Was I mistaken? Imprudent to believe
De Petrie and I were getting along well? I remembered how Dr St
George's voice had subtly altered on the phone earlier when discussing De Petrie's interest in me: he'd been a little envious, even
grudging. More than that, he'd been very inquisitive.

Generally, I believed as I began packing for the next morning's
eight a.m. flight that I was aimed not merely toward Florida, but
rather toward some majestic expanse of rich and grassy plateau,
both a resting place on my ascent but also a springboard from which
I would soon soar to even more empyrean heights. The more fool I.

Book Eight

IN THE FIBBER MCGEE ROOM

'That's the definition of culture—knowing and thinking about things that have absolutely nothing to do with us,' Janus said, between inhalations of the most crystalline Andean cocaine we'd ever laid eyes on. 'About those abandoned Anasazi cities, for example; or poetic meters during the Southern Sung dynasty; or...' he paused for one more sniff, 'the metaphysical significance of Jeff Stryker's penis.'

Aaron Axenfeld, *At Imperial Point*

THE ONLY TRULY PROMINENT CITIZEN of Fort Myers, Florida, in its short otherwise, lusterless history appears to have been a doozy, Thomas Alva Edison, and the constituents of the town made certain that even the most transient visitor never lost sight of this dazzling fact. There was a Thomas Edison Drive and a Thomas Edison Boulevard, a Thomas Edison Memorial High School and a Thomas Edison Community College, the Edison movie theater, and the Edison–Flagler Bank, Edison hardware, stationery, and book stores, an Edison card 'n' things shop, and numerous elementary schools, post offices, grocery stores and superettes bearing the magical name. Naturally there was also the inventor's winter headquarters, a substantial Spanish-style house fronted by a palm-lined boulevard on plentifully landscaped grounds, now a museum, and the inventor's multi-building laboratories, retained as they'd been left the day Edison had failed his civic duty and died. The most recent addition to the long list of Alvaic fame was a prodigious new Thomas Edison Entertainment Complex and Outlet Mall placed within the confines of an eighteen-hole golf course-cum-retirement village of separate and attached condominiums, able to hold 60,000 people.

In the hour or so I was turned around, bewildered and downright lost in the confines of the city and its environs, I managed to pretty much hit every one of these sites once before a pre-adolescent took pity on me and directed me to Highway 41.

From there, a sign led me to a faster, four-laned thoroughfare. Either 287 or 86. Perhaps both at the same time, I was never certain, given the whimsical signage. This avenue, however, successfully brought me to a bridge that crossed Pine Island Sound and set me onto the island where Aaron Axenfeld lived in a family-owned once vacation-only now year-round home.

Sanibel Island was traversed by an extension of this concourse, transformed into a sometimes four-laned, more often two-laned, thoroughfare running from the southern, lighthouse-dominated, tip

320 TH E BOOK OF LIES

to its north end, where it crossed Blind Pass to smaller Captiva Island. Because Sanibel had been settled late in Florida's history, and by the Gulf Coast's more affluent middle class rather than by the wealthy northerners who'd populated and so defined the state's other cities, it wasn't a resort but a vacation spot, far less built up. Besides the lighthouse with its restored 'whaling village mini-mall' only a mid-island guesthouse, Bayley's Conch Hotel, pretended to any pre-twentieth-century flavor, and thɑt because it was the oldest edifice. Other motels, hotels and eateries were confined to the main road and three narrower parallel lanes. The beaches that girdled the island were thus conserved from commercialization. The many-leveled Gulf of Mexico aquamarine waters were fronted by wide strands ornamented by palm trees, garnished by bougainvillaea and set-back houses subject to severe zoning, rendering them widely spaced and architecturally unadventurous. The less desirable – less breezy – Pine Island Sound side was more closely controlled due to its two serenely beautiful wildlife preserves.

A few small tarmac roads ran crosswise, including one I'd been guided to turn onto. It passed a stone gate flanked by Washingtonia palms curving onto a small spit of land with access to a dozen homes, none very visible through the foliage that made the area seem older, more established, and exclusive.

The seventh house was sheltered by two huge live oak trees, festooned with masses of Spanish moss. A question mark of a path led to a carport where a late-model Toyota sedan the shape and colors of a Japanese beetle was parked. I pulled my rented car alongside it. An implausible proliferation of azaleas and begonias both in soil and set about in pots of differing sizes confirmed I'd arrived at the right place. Axenfeld had confided he was an indifferent gardener but the strong sun, constant breezes and gulf moisture ensured botanical achievement.

The single-story, wooden-sided ranch with angled roof appeared locked, the window screens shut. But a note fluttering on a pushpin wedged into the front door read 'Sur la plage' with an arrow. Following it, I saw the azure horizon and headed that way. A minute later I'd reached the backyard, sparsely cultivated by low bushes that gave onto sand. Taking off my sandals, I went in search of my host.

Fifty yards away, an immense, sun-faded striped umbrella had been wedged at a shallow angle into the sand. As I neared, I saw that someone within was stretched upon a legless beach chair. He was barefoot, in sun-bleached trousers and a long-sleeved shirt out of which long, beautifully shaped hands protruded. His gaunt, motionless head led me to assume he was sleeping with his eyes open, an assumption confirmed by his stillness, and by the fashion magazine that lay on the sand only inches from his outstretched index finger, its cover bent back as though abruptly let drop. In that light, his head looked like one of those watercolor portraits John Singer Sargent created late in his career: bony planes of cheek and nose and forehead, except where immutably worn sunglasses left a sallower complexion. His grizzled hair, close to his skull, was iron-gray except around his temples, where it was so short as to be nonexistent. The eyes in that owlish countenance were the same unflinching gray.

For the briefest of moments I felt I'd so much intruded that I ought to pull back, perhaps drive away. The fingers of one hand moved. Gesturing me nearer?

'Is it three o'clock already?' he asked in that pleading tone, in that young voice, with which I was already familiar.

'I really didn't mean to . . . I ought to come back later.'

'No. It means I've been sitting here for hours. That I've wasted another afternoon.' He drew himself up, threw back the umbrella and stood. I'd expected him to be small and mousy, possibly because of how unprepossessing he'd always been on the phone, possibly because of his decades-long association with a particular insurance company where he'd quietly toiled, in the process becoming to some of the less conventional Purple Circle members the image of a colorless little man, a sort of Bartleby Scrivener. He revealed himself as over medium height, lean, fairly well muscled for his sixty odd years, still agile, if a bit maladroit.

'Tell me,' I said. 'Do I look like him at all?'

'Like . . .? Like Len? Yes, you do! Then again, no! Upon more inspection, you do, yes!'

'You must think me both impertinent and very vain.'

'Not impertinent. And as you're very handsome, vanity seems only natural. If you weren't vain, I'd think you weren't being forthright. But if you were even more vain, well, then you'd even more resemble him!'

He closed the oversized umbrella, gathered the beach gear, and, ignoring my offers of assistance, stowed it under one arm while we trod back though the sands. All but the magazine was abandoned upon the backyard flagstones. We went to the front of the house, where he looked over my rented car.

'Dom said he knew I'd been irretrievably suburbanized when I began checking out people's cars,' Axenfeld half snorted as he laughed at himself. 'And worse, when I began talking about them. This is a Tiburon convertible? That midnight-purple paint!'

'At night, it looks almost black.' I repeated what the youth at the airport car rental desk had told me.

Axenfeld gathered mail from the post box and threw it onto an already mail-strewn telephone table in the foyer. Indoors the house was as middlebrow as out, overfurnished with forty-year-old living- and dining-room 'sets' his parents evidently purchased, which he'd done much in the way of wood care to keep up.

'Why not get your bags?' Axenfeld suggested. 'You're staying over, of course. Don't protest. I've got extra room and you can't stay in any of the local fleabags. My cooking is drab, but you'll survive.'

The dining-room table was covered with folders of what looked to be official papers. He pushed them into two neat files, brushing the table surface. I was made to sit while he served lemonade out of a classic Kool Aid carafe into tall glasses. He put plates, a bowlful of taut-skinned Valencia oranges and a salver of store-bought pecan sandies upon a paper napkin.

I found I was hungry and thirsty. I wolfed down the cookies and drank the lemonade like someone left to die in the Gobi. I was smearily eating the juice-spurting orange, trying without success to keep my face from being a mess, aware that by making myself look unkempt I was making myself younger and more vulnerable, hoping to bring down Axenfeld's guard, when he suddenly said, 'This reminds me of that telling scene about Potiphar's wife from Thomas Mann's *Joseph* tetralogy. You don't know it? It's marvelous. She invites over for an afternoon party the cream of Egyptian high-society women. They disdain her because by now her admiration for the young Hebrew slave Joseph has become the very essence of court gossip. Yet because of her husband's position and power, they daren't refuse her invitation. While they are sitting around the garden, she has the beautiful Joseph in his scantiest outfit go to each of the women, serving ripe fruit and sharp little knives. In minutes all the distracted women are cut and bleeding. When they hold out their lacerated fingers and mutilated hands complaining to Potiphar's wife, she sends them home, saying, 'Now perhaps you'll understand how I bleed every day of my unhappy life.'

We were both silent. I said something stupid like, 'Wonderful!'

He seemed to ignore me, then uttered, as though alone in the room, speaking to himself, 'Joseph may be the first man in the Old Testament to be called beautiful. I wonder what the original word is? For that matter, he's the first person in history or literature to be called beautiful. We don't have a clue what Adam looked like, or Gilgamesh or Noah, or Abraham and Isaac. Never mind the women. We're not told that Joseph's mother, Rachel, was beautiful, only that Jacob loved her much more than Leah and took fourteen years' servitude to win her. We assume she was beautiful because her son was. I don't think women are called beautiful in the Bible – or indeed in literature – until after the beauty of men has been established. Is Bathsheba the first? In the story of David? Possibly. In Homer, there are few beautiful mortal women. Helen. Not Andromache or even Penelope. While most of the men are, including the dishonorable and deceitful ones, all 'godlike', i.e. hunks. So the question is, what happened to consciousness around 1500 BCE that people began to discriminate in terms of comeliness? And why were men recognized first as being good-looking?'

'Perhaps because women were considered inferior.'

'Yes. But you see this is such a change of awareness that it must go beyond mere social standards.'

'Maybe the women were veiled. As they are in the Middle East today.'

'That could be it,' he agreed. 'It still doesn't explain . . .'

'Maybe people became better-looking. Maybe because of the agricultural revolution they were able to settle down, live more comfortably, eat meat and milk and bread more regularly. Even nomads would benefit via trade. As a result, they'd get larger, more muscular, have better complexions. Literally look better.'

'Aren't you clever!' he said. 'That must be it!'

We returned to munching oranges and pecan sandies. At last, I ventured, 'By the way, I'm expecting a long fax. I asked to have it sent here. I hope I wasn't presumptuous.' When he said no, and his intelligent gray eyes slid left toward the window, as though it were no concern of his, I felt compelled to add, 'The fax is from Camden Phoenix.'

His ears perked up. 'The young fellow who spoke at Frankie's memorial?'

'Frankie's boyfriend. Only not young anymore. Still in pretty good shape.' I went on to speak of him a bit more, looking for any sign of Axenfeld's interest. When none seemed forthcoming, I added, 'The fax I'm expecting is a large fragment of the Len Spurgeon work. Or at least I'm hoping that's what it will prove to be.' Still nothing. 'You weren't able to find anything else here? In your Fibber McGee room? Not that I don't appreciate "The Flamingos", of course.'

'I haven't looked,' he admitted.

The phone rang, saving us from ensuing awkwardness.

Axenfeld took it and dragged it via its long cord into a far room so I couldn't hear him. I looked around. Clerestory windows above the longest dining-room wall and part of the parlor-room wall let in dappled sunlight, I supposed from the attached sunporch I'd noticed when I headed to the beach. Axenfeld was back, previous blankness replaced by minor irritation.

'My up the street neighbor. Actually a fairly nice man. I swear, these queens who try to be do-it-your-selfers! I'm always bailing him out of one fix or another.'

'You think I'm out of my mind, don't you?' I asked him. 'Chasing after all of this material.'

Axenfeld's mouth fell open and he stared at me. This was the visual correlative to his long phone silences.

'You probably think I have no life myself and I'm trying to live through the members of the Purple Circle,' I went on.

'Why would you choose to do that? The real question, one I never get, although patient Dame and Dom often try to explain, is why anyone would spend that much time on our stupid gatherings of so long ago. On us.'

'We're scholars. We study great writers of the past.'

A sudden intake of breath through his nearly closed teeth.

'Of the present too,' I added. 'But it's accomplishments in the past, your solid achievements, that make it viable.'

'But you see, dear boy, that's precisely where I run headlong into the wall of your assumption. It's not as though we consciously set out to do anything. We were just writing what we could and . . .'

'I don't mean to contradict you, Mr Axenfeld. But facts defy that. It's precisely because you, out of many other homosexual writers, actually did set out to do something organized and with goals that we do study you. Perhaps you, yourself, weren't particularly activist, but others most definitely were. That letter of Mr De Petrie to Mark Dodge after the vicious *Washington Post Book World* review of Von Slyke's *Instigations*, for example, where he quotes Benjamin Franklin, saying, "We must all hang together, or we will certainly all be hanged separately." If that isn't a conscious act of revolution, what is?' Before he could respond, I went on, 'You did all hang together. You and Dodge, and De Petrie and Rowland Etheridge signed a letter of protest to the paper. Followed it up with attacks on literary homophobia in a half-dozen mainstream and gay magazines and newspapers. That concerted action does constitute a movement. The way you came together at conferences and began giving book-store readings all over the country. No one had read fiction since the Beats. You were the first in decades.' He'd begun to say something, but I held him back. 'The proof of your activism is that you inspired others to emulate you and attack you. People saw you as a group with a point of focus. Straights, closeted gays and open gays. They recognized you nine as an active, often an effective force.'

'All that may be so. It doesn't count if the work isn't good.' As soon as he said it, Axenfeld closed his mouth. 'I didn't mean to sound immodest.'

'That's just it, the work was good. Not all. But enough to still be in print decades later, when most of your contemporaries are kaput, bibliographic history. It's the love of those books that drives us. I won't embarrass you personally, but if *Instigations* and *Keep Frozen* and *The Adventures of Marty* aren't masterpieces, then no books of the past fifty years are. That's what pulls in people like me in the first place. We stick around hoping to learn more, to find out what's hidden. In my own case, not only what but also who may have been inadvertently hidden.'

'Your theorem, if I have it correct, is what? That Len Spurgeon was someone who has been hidden. Someone important? Crucial?'

'Is your character Laurence Grace in *From the Icelandic* Len Spurgeon?' I asked. 'Based on him? Something like him? A homage to him?'

'I haven't a clue how to answer that,' Axenfeld said.

'That's why I'm here. To find out for myself. Not because you're consciously hiding the fact. But because you may not know. Mr Von Slyke does know. Bobbie Bonaventura and Thomas Dodge and a few others do know Len was crucial to their particular Purple Circle member's life. They may not understand how exactly. They may be way off . . .'

He considered. 'I'll grant you Len never stepped into a room but he didn't cause some kind of stir . . . Unless he chose not to.' Axenfeld stood. 'For the rest . . . I don't know. I'd better get over to McCadden's. Let me show you your room.'

He walked me into an L-shaped corridor. One open door led to a television room, five closed doors he said were his bedroom, a bath, two linen closets, and the room in which I would sleep. I joined him outside. While I pulled my bag and laptop out of the car trunk, he fooled around with a large toolchest and cabinet on one side of the carport. He put on a beaked painter's cap, industrial-looking gloves, and was wielding a handful of wrenches when he called out that I should make myself comfortable. He loped down the path toward his neighbor's house.

I went in, dropped my bags on the bed. I was alone in Axenfeld's house.

I was alone in Axenfeld's house. Alone for how long I couldn't tell. I opened my bag, hung a few pieces of my clothing in the closet, put away a few pieces in the drawer he'd marked with a yellow Post-it note saying 'Use these'. It was warm and muggy, so I put on shorts and a guinea-T.

The bedroom doubtless had originally been master bedroom in the house, where Axenfeld's father lay ill many months, where before that his mother and father had slept. The furniture was

blond, of some wood I couldn't determine; the bed covering a finely
made aged chenille, yellow-white like clotted cream, with a beige-
brown, lightweight, waffle-weave blanket beneath it, and faded
canary yellow sheets in a rose and thorn pattern. A blond-wood
armchair and small bedtable gave a surprising amount of space, so
unlike the overfurnished outer rooms I was convinced others once
jostled each other on these ecru tile floors but had been removed
after one, maybe the second parent's death. The small wooden-
framed watercolors hung on wood paneling seemed a smidgen more
accomplished than amateur, but not by much. Possibly done by a
relative or friend of the family. They hadn't been hung to compete
with the many-hued blue-green prospect of the gulf waters through
the triptych of windows opposite the double bed.

Framed photos of Axenfeld's parents, separate and together,
existed, deep within shelves of the commanding dining-room cabinet.
Among them were photos of young Aaron receiving confirmation,
young Aaron graduating from high school and college, and a slightly
older Aaron with two female friends, all three in beach togs, wielding oars twice as tall as they, joshing next to a beached canoe at what
might have been a prelude to a clambake. Another snapshot of prom
night instantly dated Axenfeld by fashions of formal wear and hair-
cuts. It also signaled the viewer that he and the red-haired girl in pale
blue chiffon were pals not sweethearts, friends who shared books,
music, even crushes on class jocks. The photos contained no other
young men, no siblings; though there were a few older women who
might be aunts. I could only find one photo of Axenfeld Senior solo,
out of doors, in the stern of an outboard fishing yacht, half standing
at a chair-like console, wrangling some off-camara colossal fish. The
Axenfelds had been a small, tight-knit family.

Where was his Fibber McGee room? The television room/study
was more sparsely furnished than the master bedroom. The only other
room in the house was Axenfeld's bedroom. I stood on the door sill,
disinclined to enter, peering in; the same blond-wood furnishings. The
bed was a single with yellow-green curtains, peppermint-crème chenille spread, a motley of darker greens in an oval rag rug. One
chiffonier's mirror was blocked from reflection by tiers of books
stacked in front of its glass, most oversized paperbacks, a small
number of hardcover biographies. Was this Axenfeld's entire library?

I didn't find a doorway leading to a downstairs. Few Florida homes possessed basements, never mind cottages on islands. I did locate the furnace and air-conditioning units behind a clever swing-out cupboard built into the larger linen closet. Could the Fibber McGee room be outside? Beyond the carport? Behind that plywood toolshed kept secured by a giant padlock?

I had another worry. Where in the hell were the promised pages from Camden Phoenix? The money had been wired to his bank account yesterday. What if he didn't send them? What if he stiffed me? What would be my recourse? Did I have anything legal to stand on? My brother-in-law Bart Vanuzzi would know. But even though he was less than an hour away on the mainland, in a team-owned condo somewhere in North Fort Myers, and I had his phone number, I was reluctant to use it unless I absolutely had to, despite what my sister said about how much he respected me.

I checked Axenfeld's quiescent fax machine once again, then thought the hell with it, grabbed the beachiest-looking large towel I could find and a few magazines I'd retrieved from atop the old Trinitron, changed into my bathing suit and headed out to soak up rays. The light was strong, despite the sun's descending angle, but ameliorating gulf breezes seemed concentrated upon a square yard of flagstones directly in front of the louvered sunroom, so that's where I settled, in the half-chair Axenfeld used on the beach earlier. After a while, the combination of hot sun and cooling breeze was so seductive, I dropped my magazine and simply stared, gape-mouthed ahead.

Of all the Purple Circle members, Aaron Axenfeld remained the most enigmatic, his life, even his work, mysterious. Yet, when one investigated what was written about the group, it was all there: his ordinary origins, his humdrum central Ohio upbringing, his unremarkable early life, except perhaps for a certain curiosity about other people's more gratifying life stories which led him briefly, unspectacularly, to become cub reporter for his high-school newspaper, dabbling in interviews of senior classmates. His reliable though not top-notch grades and these extracurricular activities probably conspired with his father's high income in getting him accepted into an Ivy League college. He passed an undistinguished four years, stamped only by his late, sudden preoccupation with the college's mediocre literary quarterly, for which he began to write fiction and non-fiction, and which he ended up editing in his senior year, thereby elevating both it and its on-campus reputation. Despite this marked literary interest, and despite his acceptance at the Iowa Writers' School, Axenfeld remained at the college and the following year entered a pre-med course, and the following year the first year of medical school. He remained barely a year. While he didn't exactly flunk out, he did leave with less than stellar grades and it was evident he'd found the course unsympathetic, his professors and fellow students too vulgarly competitive for his own unassuming tastes and manner.

Axenfeld next surfaced a decade later, laboring for the midtown insurance firm within which he'd early on located a well-sheltered niche where he might lick his wounds after his flight from medical school. Of all the Purple Circle scholars, Fleming delved most into this prolonged occupation, yet even he failed to bring forth much beyond the mundane. The job supplied Axenfeld with enough income to live comfortably, sharing a small apartment south of Murray Hill. Presumably, his salary rose by larger increments over those years than his controlled rent so he could take vacations, as well as joining those earliest of all-gay-owned private dance clubs in Lower Manhattan and regularly frequenting the local gay bathhouses. The latter two sites became the focus of three seasons of his urban life. As his income rose, Axenfeld also began to assemble with other young men sharing summer-long beach houses at Fire Island Pines. Along with the baths and discos, this became not only the social center of his life but also the locus around which he would inscribe the life of all the characters in his startlingly successful first published novel.

Weatherbury, in his intro to the first *Reader,* characterized Axenfeld's 1978 novel, *Second Star from the Right,* as 'a comet in the literary firmament, totally unheralded, brilliantly generative, astonishingly liberating to an entire generation in its effect'. The book, with its delightfully high style and its detailed depiction of life in the brand-new mid-1970s gay 'fast lane' of discotheques and bathhouses, beach resorts and penthouse parties, theatre openings and vernissages, received a highly unusual auspicious review in the *Sunday Times* book supplement. This in an era where the more standard procedure for that ambivalent review organ was to hire closeted gay writers to rough up any book daring enough to be positively gay-themed. Before this remarkable review, however, both Mark Dodge and Dominic De Petrie had already befriended the first-time author. They'd received bound galleys for pre-publication quotes, read the explosive new novel and highly endorsed it. Within weeks, the two had introduced him to their own literary circles, which by that time already included Rowland Etheridge and Jeff Weber.

Axenfeld already knew the Leo–McKewens. Mitch Leo had not only attended that Ivy League school along with Axenfeld, but he'd been published in the last few issues of the literary magazine. In the years since school, the two young promising writers had sustained a desultory correspondence. This had become more intense when Mitch wrote about his falling in love with Frankie McKewen, and more intense when Aaron had himself come out of the closet to Mitch. Axenfeld brought the literary duo into the gay lit. set upon the occasion of his book-publication party, an overcrowded fete at the Fifth Avenue apartment of one of the Leo–McKewens' uptown art cronies. Only Von Slyke remained outside Axenfeld's ambit. Fleming believed it was Mark Dodge who at last brought the two writers together. But as Cummings and St George both discovered within the voluminous journals at the Timrod Collection, it was actually De Petrie who did so. The circumstance was a 'morning party' at the Pines, a private affair, harbinger of, if not officially precursor to, the later, more massive, fund-raising events. The encounter of the two was, according to De Petrie's chronicle, 'cordial, at times spirited, even snippy, definitely of two distinct and not easily shaken biases'. But if Axenfeld and Von Slyke kept their association within sharp limits, they did provide the foundation others in the group believed needed to be authoritatively launched.

The first meeting of the Purple Circle took place at Mark Dodge's capacious new Washington Square North townhouse. At that gathering, four read new work: De Petrie the opening chapter of what would become his novella, *A Summer's Lease*; Mitch Leo a central portion of *Refitting Tom Devere*; Jeff Weber one of the stories from his collection *Slights and Offenses*; and Aaron Axenfeld a twelve-page section he prefaced by saying, 'This is all probably worthless

but bear with me if you can,' of his second novel, *Different in Kind*.
Neither that 1982 publication nor his non-fiction collection of
three years later. *Envoi to Obscurity*, would receive a twentieth of
the attention, never mind the glory, lavished upon *Second Star from
the Right*. In fact, looking back on Axenfeld's subsequent career,
Fleming could maintain, 'None of the others, not even Mark Dodge,
could be said to have been so defined by, so described by, and later
on so circumscribed by, a single volume as was Axenfeld for two
decades.' In his study of De Petrie, St George wrote, 'The enormous
success of *Second Star* was nearly transmogrified into a débâcle.
Not only because anything Axenfeld wrote thereafter was held up to
its perfection and found wanting, but because Axenfeld himself
came to believe he would never again, could never again achieve the
level of artistry and entertainment of his first published novel.'

There would, of course, eventually be more Axenfeld books. Each
released following the greatest hesitation, often at the urging of his
friends and editor and agent. Neither his 1995 novel, *At Imperial
Point*, nor his 1999 collection of stories, *Plaid Flannel*, would, naturally enough, repeat the tremendous acclaim that had greeted *Second
Star*. Neither, however, would they be met with the disappointment
and left-handed compliments of other volumes. Another factor
entered in: time was on Axenfeld's side. By the time his third novel
was published, five of the Purples were dead. By the time his stories
came out, only himself, De Petrie and Von Slyke of them had survived; and increasingly they were being recognized as the core of a
canon of gay male literature. For the first time, Axenfeld went on
a book tour. And he was gratified to find people wanted to meet
him, to hear him speak and read, to know his opinions on matters
literary or not. That generation of readers he'd first electrified was
by now mostly dead as a result of AIDS. This newer age group had
read not just *Second Star* but all of his books, sometimes in reverse
order from that in which they'd been written. His newer contemporaries followed his essays, kept track of his stories in anthologies,
were often more widely read, if shallower in their understanding of
his actual accomplishments.

By then, Axenfeld had at last retired from Turtle Bay Prudential
and moved out of New York City. He'd, of course, returned at once
to his office position following the ten-month sabbatical caring for

332 THE BOOK OF LIES

his father. The Sanibel Island home had lain vacant over the years, except for his winter vacations and occasional loans of the house to family and friends. Pensioned off, Axenfeld returned to the family place and, as he told De Petrie (and De Petrie retold in his journals), to 'reading all those books I've collected over the years, talking to everyone still alive on the telephone, watching old movies on TV, giving myself melanoma in the sun, gardening lackadaisically, and absolutely, positively, NO writing!'

That last promise had failed to develop beyond adjuration. By the turn of the millennium, the second volume of Weatherbury's *Reader* had been published, as well as Fleming's and St George's studies. A year later Cummings's monumentally influential *Nine Lives* came out. Suddenly everyone had to have work by surviving Purples. Von Slyke fell to with avidity. De Petrie had turned recluse and couldn't be bothered. Axenfeld fell somewhere between the two. He gave a few interviews. He sporadically reviewed books for major papers. He now and then allowed a piece of short fiction from work in progress to be published.

Through those years, as Axenfeld's social circle narrowed through the attrition of illness and death and those moving in search of lucrative employment, he'd managed to retain his privacy to such an extent it had been a stupefaction to many who'd thought better when Cummings's biography revealed that the author wasn't the 'girl about town bachelorette' he'd insisted upon for so many years, but instead settled into unobtrusive domesticity with a Chilean diplomat, a middle-level functionary at the United Nations, who spent a third of the year out of town on UNESCO business.

It was partly the retirement of this consort, with no alteration of the time he spent in South America, that seemed to allow Axenfeld to relax, sufficiently mollified to allow another novel to be evoked out of him, if with the least amount possible. *From the Icelandic* wasn't as snowily despondent as *At Imperial Point*, not as autumnally elegiac as the story collection. It was coolly burnished, vigorous yet deepened with maturity, by turns diverting and pensive. Its narrator's secret beloved, the 'irresistible Laurence Grace', was a character unlike any Axenfeld or indeed anyone had up till then delineated. A successful stock broker, a con artist, a renowned heart-breaker, and finally, when a good deed goes awry, a public disgrace, he was not merely a gay Gatsby, he was a portrait of an entirely credible gay man who lived large and high, who elevated then dragged down others alongside himself. Thousands of readers – gay and straight – fell for his considerable charms. Cummings reviewed the book in the London *Times*, declaring it 'masterly, a light-hearted yet deeply felt and complexly characterized glance into *fin-de-siècle* American life'. *From the Icelandic* had been my own introduction to Axenfeld's work, and after its gingerly handled multiplex brilliancies, *Second Star from the Right* seemed a post-adolescent not bad first try. I'd never said that to Axenfeld, but I had certainly implied it more than once. Gaining his regard.

I was torn from my reverie by the ringing of a phone indoors. I got up and looked in through the louvered porch toward the living room, but the phone was closer, on a side table out on the sunporch. I wondered if it was Axenfeld ringing from his neighbor's saying he'd be late. I'd stepped into the sunporch and headed toward it when an answering machine took over. The caller was someone I didn't know. I ignored the call, wondered whether I didn't want to refresh my lemonade now that I was already up.

It was then I realized where I was. The long narrow sunporch appeared to have been built onto this side of the house at some time after the original construction. From indoors, I'd not failed to notice the row of clerestory windows connecting it to the dining room and one side of the parlor, but I'd deemed it utterly accessory. Now that I was on the sunporch, I realized the contrary was true. For it was here, not anywhere else in the house, where Axenfeld's two-piece Canon SuperStar word processor had been placed, upon a small, stalwart-looking cherrywood table, placed in the deepest, bilaterally louvered corner of the sunporch, accompanied by a sturdy matching armchair. Upon the table were magazines, newspapers, and half under one end of the printer/keyboard, a folder which when I riffled it open proved to contain a typed manuscript of twenty pages.

This site, then, with its well-worn, homelike desk and chair, its serene yet complete view of the gulf, its breezes and sunlight, its right-at-hand telephone and answering machine, its commodious canvas-covered armchair and matching ottoman for reading, its low shelves of books and batches of manila envelopes full of what looked to be manuscripts, done or in progress, its various small tables and settees and lounge chairs beneath which many, many other boxes of manuscripts, paper bags full of manuscripts and newspaper-wrapped manuscripts had been shoved and packed, stacked like logs, this was the actual heart of the house, core of Axenfeld's life, center of his time spent here, the essence. As I realized it, I simultaneously came to grips with the fact that this narrow, airy, unprotected, exposed to the public sunporch must also be his Fibber McGee room.

Seconds later, I heard Axenfeld. I met him between the foyer and the carport. He was shaking what appeared to be cement off a trowel. He looked up at me, and his eyes from under the beaked painter's hat widened as though he'd seen a ghost. I recognized this as one of his social gambits – along with his long silences – for obtaining and retaining attention.

Axenfeld looked away and said in tones of such complete intricacy that I didn't know how to untangle them all, never mind interpret the results, 'He used to wear a navy blue Speedo too.'

'Len Spurgeon?' I asked, already knowing the answer. Then, 'You got a phone call. The machine took it.'

'He's invited us to dinner. My neighbor. Partly to thank me for putting up with him. Partly to slaver over you. He's not an old letch and he's awfully amusing on his topics. The food will be better than my cooking. Is that all right? Can you be ready by seven? Do you want to nap?'

I said yes three times. He smiled lopsidedly and said, 'There's an alarm clock at the bed-table.'

'What was Len Spurgeon doing here those months in 1981, staying with you and your father?' I asked outright.

It was no longer inappropriate to do so. Our dinner, at a local cafeteria-style restaurant – part of a still-extant traditional-meal homecooking Southern chain, where I was delighted to be able to get cholesterol-defying dishes like frothy succotash and thickly batter-fried chicken and coconut cream pie – had been easygoing fun. Rather than ogling me, throughout the meal the neighbor had defused the situation entirely by treating me as though I were a contemporary, with his own peculiar proclivities. At first I was apprehensive at his loud, easily overheard speech, especially when he'd say things like, 'Look at the biceps on that feller. Jeez, I'd like to see them ripplin' close by as he held me down and reamed my sorry ass.' Or, 'Lordy, that boy's hair is yellow as new-churned butter. Bet it ain't a sight darker where it warms his pecker.' Or, 'Look at the hose on that un' Christmas! He must have ter wrap it halfway round hisself when he draws on his jeans!' Either the folks who frequented the place already knew and were accustomed to him and therefore ignored him, or, more likely, they politely accepted his comments as praise. Axenfeld laughed quietly into his hands as comment.

'What was Len Spurgeon doing here?' Axenfeld asked me back. 'He was waiting for wood.'

'Excuse me.'

'Waiting for wood. That's the term that's used in the pornographic film business for getting and keeping an erection.'

'Len was making a porno film here?'

'Six. Eight. I'm not certain exactly how many. He had a good-sized contract. He'd been a Colt model in the late '70s, you know. So popular a Colt model with his lean, tanned athletic body and page-boy-length golden hair and tanned face and strawberry-blond facial hair that he'd been given his own magazine. Two issues. He went by the name of Chad Elkins. Then he'd done soft-core photos with another Colt model and that went over so big they convinced him to do a film cameo. Oddly enough it was about baseball, titled something like *Hard Sluggers* and in his portion, after a long late-night extra practice, he retires to two adoring male fans who catch him in the changing room and eat him front and back over ten minutes. After that, everyone wanted him. He signed up with the studio and they decided to shoot on a former alligator ranch near North Fort Myers. I can't recall how he got my phone number. Maybe from Mitch Leo. He phoned a day after he arrived, drove over, and had dinner with my father and me. They got along instantly; after all, Len was the son my dad wanted, that every red-blooded all-American father wanted. So when he complained about where he was staying, the noise and drinking and partying, my dad invited him here. What's the TV room was a guest bedroom at the time. Next day, Len moved in. He remained eight months. Earned I don't know how many thousands of dollars. He was as highly paid as

Casey Donovan, which for those days was high. Whenever anyone asked what he was doing hanging out on Sanibel Island, he'd always look them in the eye and say, "Waiting for wood, man. Best place in the world for waiting for wood".'

It turned out Axenfeld considered Len so far beyond his ambit he didn't at all mind him around the place while recharging his sexual batteries. Indeed, he told me he came to like the man, to relish his peculiar dry wit and point of view, as well as to appreciate how much he helped with Axenfeld Senior. The two would discuss sports, hunting, guns, weaponry—the allegedly manly pursuits. His father had been a difficult patient, having trouble recovering from his multi-coronal bypass and tamping down his natural activities and high spirits. With Len around, he began taking it easy and this relaxation, Axenfeld felt, may have added a year to his life. This extra time gave father and son more time to get to know each other as adults, as people. This aided Axenfeld when his father eventually did pass away. In addition, the new friendship considerably helped Len, who confided he'd gotten along miserably with his own father, the two at loggerheads since Len had been ten years old. 'He appreciates me!' Len had said more than once. 'I'm okay. I'm an all right guy. He says so all the time.'

A further benefit of the three residing together became apparent only after Len had reluctantly moved back to New York, when Axenfeld Senior's health seriously deteriorated. Aaron asked if he wanted Len back; he might be able to get him if he tried hard enough. His father said not to bother, then added, 'Having him around made me see what a good boy you are. What a good son you've been to take care of me as you've done. If you'd been more like him, which is the way I'd always wanted, I'd have been dead a helluva long time ago.'

'And your father had no idea where Len was going every day?' I asked. 'What he was doing?'

'Not a bit,' Axenfeld replied. 'I know you'll think me extraordinarily perverse for not telling him. I mean, he understood Len's character well enough after a while to presume he was up to something not completely salubrious. Whether he thought that was gunrunning for some covert, patriotic organization or fencing stolen goods or what, he never admitted. I hope you won't judge me

too harshly if I confess that I received the most titillation whenever
Len would come or go. After only a few weeks, they'd begun to kiss
each other's cheeks as though they were father and son. I never
ceased to speculate what exactly my father would say, what he
would think, had he fathomed that those lips that caressed his
cheek so fondly had an hour before been employed in, or were
about to be employed in, avidly rimming the anus of or conscien-
tiously fellating the penis of some marine lieutenant from Pensacola
named Hank.'

We laughed. 'But Len never told you anything about why he and
his father didn't get along?' I was trying to find out if the car story
was true.

'No. I could never bring myself to pry. You know whom he might
have told? You're going to him tomorrow, aren't you? Dominic!
I'm exhausted.' Axenfeld had been heating milk in a saucepan. He
poured it into a mug, added a spoonful of honey and sipped. 'I can
fall asleep. But I wake in a few hours. This will keep me out longer.
Has your fax arrived yet? Do you need to be up at a certain hour? Is
one blanket enough? Will the bed be comfortable?'

I responded no, no, yes, and yes.

That night I lay in the masterbed pondering what Len Spurgeon
was really doing here those months, twenty-five years ago.

Axenfeld was apparently awake long before I got up at nine. He
was out in the front garden, beaked painter's cap and industrial
gloves on, trowel in hand, repotting some otherworldly plant when
I wandered out into the dining room, found a place setting for
me, and poured myself coffee. He came in a few minutes later,
asked if I wanted breakfast, and put it together for me, despite my
protests.

'You're off to Truro then?' he said, sitting cattycorner to me and
sipping heavily sugared coffee. 'You shouldn't worry. If Dom invited
you, he likes you.'

'I'm still afraid,' I said. 'Were Len and he very close?'

'You'll have to ask him yourself . . . I have to confess something,
especially after yesterday . . . But first, you don't write yourself?
Stories? Poems? Novels?'

'No. A few essays, you know, for literary journals.'

'You don't aspire to write the Great American Novel of the twenty-first century?'

'I'll leave that to you, Mr Von Slyke, and Mr De Petrie.'

'The reason I ask is, I find I admire you where I thought I wouldn't,' Axenfeld said. 'It speaks of a humility, a true modesty that none of us can even pretend to possess. Not that the others do pretend, but . . . There is still one thing that I'm not entirely clear about. What is it that you want? I don't mean regarding the Purples. I mean in your life? For yourself?'

'That's just it. Now it's all tied up with the Purples.'

'I mean . . . I know you want to do this thesis on Len and the Purples. But you don't want to be Len, do you, by any chance.'

I must have looked flabbergasted, because he went on.

'The reason I ask is that you evince such an interest in him, I won't say an unhealthy interest, or even a morbid interest, but you have to admit an interest, maybe an obsession that it is to say, at the very least, a bit Hollywoodish.'

'I have been living in Hollywood. I don't get . . .'

'Hollywoodish in that *noir* sense. You know, the unnatural obsession to know absolutely everything about the deceased. What was that film? Films. Were there more than one?'

'I don't think so,' I answered. I knew the film he meant: *Laura*. 'As for what I want, as you asked it. I suppose I'd like to be . . . well, if it isn't too much to want to be, like Dr St George! You know, to teach young people literature – that's what I'm doing this summer and really enjoying it. And at the same time to write about writers. And who knows, maybe to get to know one well, as he has. To be connected in some way. As he's managed to do.' I let it drift. 'I know I could never be Len Spurgeon,' I began to defend myself. 'I know very well . . .'

'That's just my point,' Axenfeld interrupted. 'You could! You could be Len! Don't you understand? Oh, not the Len who lived from, when was it? 1948 to 1991? But an even better Len. Smarter. More personable. More Len than he was himself. Because now you've got the gifts of knowledge and of hindsight, you can do Len right! To do him better than he ever could, poor thing, not knowing what in the hell would make him stand forth, never mind what would happen to sidetrack him!'

My mouth must have hung open at this outburst. I didn't have a clue how to answer him. He was speaking about something that lay in the realm of the metaphysical, and was simply beyond me. At the same time, I wasn't anxious to let him know how far beyond me he'd gone, lest I seem even more of a naïf than he'd doubtless already judged me. How could I be Len, I wondered, since my times were so different? There was no young group of genius gay writers to influence as he had. His era had been unique and unprecedented, hadn't it? Not to be repeated? So how could I possibly . . . I kept wondering what it was I was missing in what he was saying. It had to be more. Yet what? I simply couldn't reach it. So, instead, I picked up my coffee and began to sip.

After a minute, Axenfeld must have recognized my inability to comprehend, to meet him as an equal. He said, 'Forget that. Forget everything I've said.'

More awkward silence ensued. I was terrifically embarrassed, even humiliated. At last I ventured, 'I'd better get going. Thank you for everything.' He mumbled something inaudible and went outside to his begonias.

Once I'd brushed my teeth and showered and changed and packed and was at the car, I had another thought. 'By the way, the fax I was expecting . . . It didn't by any chance . . .?'

'Yes. It came while you were still asleep.' Axenfeld turned to the toolshed and lifted out a manila envelope and handed me the sheets of single-spaced manuscript. I had to wonder if he'd planned to keep it back unless I'd specifically asked for it. 'As you thought, it is substantial.'

I looked at it and it was all I could do to hold myself back from immediately reading it, pouring the pages out of the envelope and reading them right there, leaning against the rented Tiburon. I resisted the impulse, not wanting the last thing I did in Axenfeld's presence to be anything that would detract from him. I slid it into the outside pocket of my laptop bag, shook his hands, waved good-bye, drove off.

An hour later, at the airport, settled and awaiting my plane, I at last was able to open the envelope and settle in to read.

It was Harve's idea to take the Cable Car up Mount San

Jacincto. Everyone agreed on that afterwards . . . After everything that happened.

They were driving along Interstate Highway #10 on their
way to Palm Springs, car windows open, their faces and hair
lightly buffeted by the summery breezes of an uncommonly
warm late February day. They had just passed the turnoff for
Beaumont and the until-then straight highway had concluded
a wide curve south when the chocolate-brown mountain hove
into view, rising out of an undistinguished ochre plain, a
drowsy giant commanding the entire prospect outside the
right windows of Theo's Volkswagen Beetle.

Harve commenced to whine. 'C'mon, Theo. We don't have
to be in Cathedral City any special time. It's only fifteen minutes up the mountain and fifteen down. We'll go up. Have a
drink and come right down. Dale and Tony said it's a terrific
ride. You promised we could go next time we were here.'

'We have a guest, Harve. What if Paul's claustrophobic?'
Theo asked, serenely self-assured behind the opalescent plastic steering wheel.

'Are you claustrophobic?' Harve turned around in his seat
to ask. 'Anyway, it's not that small a cable car. And it's surrounded by windows on all sides. Floor-to-ceiling windows at
times. Please say yes.'

'The question,' Paul clarified, 'is not whether I'm claustrophobic, but whether I'm acrophobic. How high does it go?'

'Five or six thousand feet,' Harve said. 'In several stages.
Only the last is said to be at all steep. It's supposed to be a
really spectacular view from up top!'

'Are you acrophobic?' Theo asked with mild amusement,
as though he wouldn't believe a positive answer.

'Not a bit,' Paul answered back.

They'd spent an unusually languorous and pleasant night
and morning in the Hollywood Hills, the three of them. First
in the large floor-sunk immersion tub, with that breath-taking
gridwork of yellow lights outlining darker squares visible
through wraparound 200 degrees of floor-to-ceiling windows.
Their mood enhanced by the view, grass, wine, music,
incense, each other's bodies and each other's presence, all

three had begun making love right in the tub and had only
gradually relocated to the bordering shag-covered bed, where
they'd consummated, Theo and Paul returning to pleasure
each other's bodies long after Harve had come and,
exhausted, fallen asleep. For Theo and Paul this engrossment
in each other had been a cultivated surprise. After all, they
hardly knew each other, and only through Harve. Paul from
up in San Francisco, where they'd dated years before. Theo as
Harve's lover these past two years in Los Angeles.

'Harve's acrophobic,' Theo said, the purposefully long
sides of ash-blond hair over his right ear riffling gently in the
breeze like the pelt of some elegant animal. 'Which he might
explain, along with his unnatural interest in going up.'

'Okay, as long as it's not too long. I've missed Palm Springs
each of my past three trips here because of one stupid reason
or another.'

The Aerial Tramway parking lot wasn't full. A car was just
docking, people exiting, others ready to board. The cable car
waited a minute, before its doors electronically hissed shut
and with an unanticipated lurch that caused a few women to
pitch and cry 'Oooh!' the car lifted off the ground.

The car rose above the arid landscape of rock and sand
interspersed with deep crevasses filled by parched-looking
piñon trees and creosote underbrush, the view opened considerably. Enough for him to observe as they approached the
metal girder 'station' upon a rocky ridge another cable car
coming ahead. It rode abreast, passed – people waving
through the windows at each other.

After a third girder station was passed, the parking lot
where they'd left the VW was a faraway slate lozenge amid
beige soil, the highway a snake cutting through prairie.

Theo and Harve were standing near a full-length window-
door, with their arms about each other. Paul saw a family:
parents in their thirties, three boys ranging in age from seven
to maybe ten. Most were couples. One elderly. Two in their
fifties. Four younger, including a man and wife Paul had seen
step out of a chauffeured limousine, as well as another duo
who'd tumbled out of a Hot Rod Deuce. Two barely

342 THE BOOK OF LIES

retirement-age men, so similar in appearance and dress they
must be brothers, at the front of the cable car, were talking
nonstop to a tanned, sable-haired youth in a gray uniform,
wielding the oversized cable car levers.

As the car rose the wind began to blow with more force.
Paul noticed the driver having to clutch at the levers.

After two more stations, it became apparent they had
crested the mountainside. The pinnacle rose ahead, a precipi-
tous granite wall. Paul could detect a pre-cast concrete and
steel portal jutting out from beneath the cliff face, into which
the cable car would berth, and above, upon the flattened-off
apex, an amazing redwood and glass edifice, two stories high,
circular to take advantage of the site, numerous glass panes
glittering as though with undeclared promise, reflecting like
the facets of some cyclopean sapphire the exact tint and
strength of the ante-meridian sunshine.

The other passengers spied their destination and began
pointing in a susurrus of anticipation. The cable car veered
perpendicular with a tremendous panorama unfolding below.
From their height, the mountain resembled a dusky wrinkled
tablecloth dropped and unevenly spread upon a lighter surface. The highway was a flimsy silver thread: autos and
tarmac and service roads condensed to a single shimmer. Paul
could ascertain the city of Palm Springs, a green tetragon containing brighter tints and hues, its little kaleidoscope apart
from the encircling buffed desert creams, olive drabs, and
sallow ochres.

Paul tapped Theo's shoulder to have him turn to look at
the wondrous sight of a city as Lilliputian as on a board game
when the winds picked up with such insistence, the cable car
shuddered.

'Whoa, Bessie!' one of the brothers up front joked. No one
laughed. Once begun, the wind seemed reluctant to let go of
the cable car. It buffeted them again and again, causing the
car to swing wildly. Their vulnerability, so far were they now
from either the rocky ground beneath or the concrete berth
above, was apparent. The wind continued to shake the car
and a woman called, 'Make it stop, Bob!' as two kids

laughed. Paul could see the car operator doing all he could to
not let the levers be wrested from his grip.

A stillness, then the car quivered more madly. Passengers
swayed insanely. Several, pried loose by centrifugal force, were
thrown into the seats where they slid about. The ritzy couple
were whirled into the Hot Rod kids. The women screeched.
The older lost her balance and was sent sprawling onto the
floor. The shaking went on, until Theo, not laughing, shouted
out, 'Enough already with the special effects!' Harve held him.
Paul could see terror filling Harve's eyes as his face went rigid.
The wind raged on until there was a fresh sound, an abrupt
'thuurranng'. The cable car went suddenly still.

Before anyone could express relief, it began rattling more
brutally than before. Women were sobbing, huddling into
their husbands' jackets. The Hot Rod girl had her poison-
green fingernails over her ears. Her pompadour-haired
boyfriend was looking around with fright distorting his
bland, handsome face. The elegant couple found a spot down
between seats. The oldest tourists had fallen to their knees,
wrapped their hands about a metal pole, lips dribbling in
prayer. Harve could no longer hide his terror and shoved
himself into Theo, who tried to comfort him.

Paul alone was unconcerned. Wait, the kids standing at the
car's back window, pointing down, also seemed unapprehen-
sive.

Paul slid over to where the boys were excitedly pointing
down.

The smallest looked up at him with the most cherubically
thrilled face. 'One of the cables snapped. We're hanging by a
single cable. Look!'

He pointed to where the shattered metal cable fluttered
like a black ribbon in the wind, tethered only at the girder
station they last passed.

'That was the loud noise before?' As the three boys let him
join them, he added, 'If that's true, we're in deep fucking doo-
doo.'

They laughed with the pure, heartless mirth of youth. Paul
felt himself connect with these unalarmed, heedless children.

'What do you think?' The elder quietly asked, 'of our chances?'

'Fifty-fifty!' Paul said.

'That high?' the boy seemed disappointed.

'They probably have some back-up system,' Paul said.

'None!' The older boy grinned with enormous delight.

'What if . . .' the middle boy, 'the other cable snaps?'

'Zero!' Paul said nonchalantly. 'We're all goners!'

'I told you, Zeb!' the youngest gloated.

'No survivors?' the middle one insisted.

'I figure,' Paul went on, cold-bloodedly, 'as the car plummets, most of us will black out. So we'll be unconscious when the car actually hits the rock and is smashed into pieces. But before that, the sudden fluctuations of air pressure inside and outside of an object this dense in a field of this gravity will probably suck in the windows. They'll shatter in and carve us into pieces.'

'A zillion pieces,' the youngest added gleefully.

'We'll be dog meat!' the older uttered.

'Chuck ground!' the youngest exulted.

'Out cold. Diced to ribbons. Flattened like pancakes,' the middle one persisted. 'Anything else?'

'The engine in back might burst into flames as we hit ground,' Paul hazarded. 'So whatever was left would be charred unrecognizably.'

'Cool!'

'I said we'd burn up before,' the youngest insisted. 'Remember?'

'You said we'd explode, dummy!'

'This is better.'

All three chuckled.

The boys' father was hovering at Paul's shoulder, his face was a mask of consternation restrained by vestiges of masculine dignity and parental concern.

'Don't you boys worry. This will only take a minute to fix. Hi!' he said to Paul. His mask wavered and Paul read upon it, Help! Don't let my boys die! 'You boys behave. Okay? When we get down I'll buy sundaes at Johnny Rocket. Okay?'

'Okay, Dad,' the oldest said in his let's-be-kind-to-this-jerk
tone of voice, which went unnoticed by his father.

The man stumbled to his wife, sitting with her head in her
knees.

'*Sundaes* at Johnny Rocket!' the middle boy sneered.

'He'll end up on the *menu* at Johnny Rocket,' the oldest
said.

Paul said, 'Ground clown!' All three boys snickered.

The operator was talking excitedly on a phone. When he'd
finished he faced the passengers. 'Uh, folks. We've had a sort
of mishap.'

'No shit! Roy-Gene!' the guy with the pompadour yelled
out.

'Let 'im speak!'

'I know you're upset,' the operator went on. 'But I'm in
contact with both stations, top and bottom. We're in no
immediate danger. They're going to do all they can to . . .'

The cable car was struck and everyone not holding on tight
was flung around. Including the operator.

'All they can,' he repeated, 'to get us up top. That's
closer.'

'How they going to move us,' the elegant man asked, 'with
only one cable?'

'Yeah! Stupid!' Paul heard one of the boys murmur.

'They're going to bring another cable. We'll hitch it to the
roof and they'll pull us up,' the operator explained. 'It'll be
slow, but sure.'

Everyone seemed to have a question. He good-naturedly
tried to answer them. The phone rang. Those passengers not
in despair began discussing whether it would work. He'd just
hung up the phone, when the pompadour asked, 'How they
going to get it here?'

'Helicopter! It's on its way.'

At that moment, the car began shuddering. The boys'
mother began to cry out, 'We're going to die!' before her husband got his hand over her mouth. The chic woman, the girl
in white leather and the old lady who'd managed to rise from
her knees closed around the pair.

'Mom lost it!' the middle boy declared with the objectivity of a newscaster.

'Shut up, Zeb!' the older one commanded, equally unemotional.

The youngest boy saw the helicopter come in from the westsouthwest. From one end dangled a chain.

The operator had begun unlatching a roof hatchway.

'He's not going outside, is he?' the old man of the couple asked.

The youth had lifted himself up. The two brothers held his ankles.

'Why can't we just move to the helicopter one by one?' Theo asked. 'These side doors open, don't they? Wouldn't that be faster?'

'Winds too strong!' one guardian-brother said.

Harve had been listening with apprehension. He hid his face in Theo's shoulder.

'They'll never make it,' the middle boy said, watching the helicopter approach. The cable hanging was lengthening, as it was played out, and swung in a great arc. The helicopter was fighting the wind.

The operator had to reach out and up for the end of cable being dangled and try to keep from being blown off his precarious roof perch. There was one especially close call when the hanging cable was slammed inches from the operator. The resounding noise as it struck the roof alarmed the women. Theo was doing all he could to keep Harve from falling. Was he having a fit?

A half-hour of heart-stopping trial and error before the cable was gotten hold of and attached to a grapple. The operator was brought in to a faint cheer.

'Now the real fun begins!' the perceptive middle boy said.

As the helicopter separated from the cable car, it played out the cable until it became a narrow black snake, appearing to furl and contort into some menacing form with every draft. The deafening noise as it hit the roof or once grazed the back window where Paul and the boys watched it with *sangfroid* terrified everyone else. Its antics, fascinating and beautiful to look at in an impersonal way, threatened to demolish them.

Once the helicopter had reached the wind-struck summit, another twenty minutes were required before the cable could be secured. The boys' mother had been tied up in clothing, her face hidden by a kerchief. Two other women were half holding, half comforting her on the floor. Harve had blacked out and Paul had to help Theo lay him across a seat. Theo knelt repeating, 'Why today? Harve? Why of all days, today?'

It was another half-hour before the wind-tossed cable tautened and another few minutes before they felt a terror-provoking vaulting forward.

Hours of slow movement. No one got used to the irregular pitching forward. It never pulled them more than a few feet. The wind picked up and the car was tossed like a salt shaker. Everyone feared one or both cables would break. Thereafter, the surges forward were slower and gained less ground.

It had been two in the afternoon when they ascended. By the time the car reached the concrete docking station on Mount San Jacincto it was after six. The winter sun had set, the external cold versus internal heat had glazed the windows with frost, through which the lighted yellow and green bauble of Palm Springs became tinier, increasingly fogged over and vague.

At the top, they stumbled, were half carried out of the car and led into the pinnacle's man-made structure. Two men kissed the ground. Harve had come to, but his eyes were blank and glittery as he allowed Paul and Theo to lift him upstairs. He was checked over by a registered nurse who'd been already stranded with fifty other people at the mountaintop restaurant. Harve and the boys' mother were put to bed. The mortified management made the newcomers comfortable and they were given free drinks and dinner. Paul brought the three young brothers to a window commanding the view of the cable-car route. As the boys chomped on their free burgers and sipped from the long pliant straws of their soft drinks, they spoke about the adventure.

'It was great all right!' Paul said. 'But now, how do we get down!'

Book Nine

RAVENS AT TRURO

...it is an address vanished, a name past divining, a costlier pain than you ever thought to possess. Aeons could not explain its sharp hold, its caress.

Dominic De Petrie, *Conversations in the Dark*

'Is THAT YOU? IT IS YOU! Hell and damnation! Stand up and give me a brotherly hug here in front of everyone or I'll be forced to break both of your ears off and bring 'em to the guys at the bar.'

Whom else but Bart Vanuzzi, my brother-in-law!

Naturally I stood up and gave him a hug, which he paid back by almost shattering my ribcage. As he did, and as I attempted to pull out of his resolutely Drakkar-flavored ambience, I became very aware that all 200 passengers in the lounge awaiting the hour-late jet to Boston were staring at us. Bart has that effect: he's so very public a person that even if there were no one else but two sight-impaired children who only spoke Urdu to witness it he'd turn our encounter into theater so unforgettable they'd not only recognize him but without fail gush about it to their very next interlocutor.

'What are you doing here?' I asked.

He looked at me as though from a long-angled lens. 'Don't give me that line! Your sister told you I was here!'

'In Fort Myers? I thought she said Fort Lauderdale,' I invented on the spot. 'I can *never* get these Forts right.'

The minuscule shift in his gunsight-narrowed eye showed he only half believed I was that stupid.

'What are you doing in the airport?' I'd assumed I'd be safe from him here.

'Some guys just came in from the coast to join practice. We were meeting them. And my teammate there, you know him, our Heisman Trophy fullback, Evan Davis, he turns around and whistles: "Look at the cute piece of ass in the tight chinos." Which, I forgetting that besides being our offensive co-captain, Evan is also our professional faggot, means he's checking out a guy. So I turn around to look and who is Evan leering at but my own little brother-in-law? By the way, that *is* a close-fitting pair of pants. You looking to join the Mile-High Club?' Before I could ask what he meant,

Bart went on, 'Your plane's late. Come to the bar and I'll buy you a beer and introduce you to the guys.'

His exceedingly muscled arm went round my shoulder and head, advancing me in the direction he wanted: this was more than a suggestion. A minute later, he'd maneuvered me across the airport's main corridor, down the hall, inside a dark, noisy, beery bar and grill. The half-dozen oversized men on stools yelling at soccer on the dropped-down Hi-Def TV screen were undoubtedly his Forty-Niner cohorts. Facing us as we advanced was, I recognized not only from previous TV viewings but also from his focussed concentration upon my person as we progressed through the Formica tables, Evan Beauregard-Davis. He probably seemed bullet-headed because the rest of him was so big. His face youthful: peaches and cream skin and periwinkle-blue eyes the size of Susan B. Anthony dollars. He would have looked a kid if not for his aquiline nose – a rudder that gave distinction – along with his trademark three-inches-high, bristle-straight, butterscotch-colored hair. His long, overmuscled arms gently but surely dislodged me from Bart's half-nelson, and drew me up to the bar between himself and an African-American watching TV who acknowledged me by a raised eyebrow as he scooped beer nuts off the bar.

'Hello, good-lookin',' Evan said in a husky molasses and mint-julep drawl I couldn't believe was natural. 'Bart said you were his bro, but I couldn't believe it. He's such an orang-utan.'

Evan took my hand in his huge one and released it slowly. He smelled of Joop, or Boss, not an aggressive scent. His green polo shirt seemed to be the exact hue of – and about the same breadth as – a snooker table. From close up, the baby blues were blondly, extravagantly lashed. A red comma left of his amused mouth and a tiny nick below one butterscotch eyebrow were all Evan possessed by way of scars. But upon his innocent countenance they looked deliberate. He kept his large warm hand against the small of my back, using it to turn me as though he were my puppeteer as Bart introduced me to one after another of their team members.

'You a detective?' backup quarterback Toby Hess asked.

Baffling me. 'I'm a scholar . . . a literary detective.'

'Oh yeah, that's right.' He lost interest.

'He a college professor, Bart?' another asked. Tapping my neighbor on his head. 'Hey, Tyrone! Here's your chance to get your degree.'

'I don' wan' no degree,' Tyrone growled.

Bart got the rest sufficiently confused about who I was, so when a particularly egregious foul was made on the TV, they all went back to the Galaxys.

Except for Evan, who guided me to face only him, and who said, 'How'm I going to turn you into my boy-toy love-slave if you fly to Boston right away?'

I was tickled by his attitude and intelligence. 'You're awfully confident, aren't you? You get everyone you go after?'

'Not always . . . right away!' He rectified it. 'Eventually!'

'Not everyone's gay, you have to admit.'

He shrugged. 'That don't mean coon-shit to me!'

As I looked at him, the good ole boy Evan suddenly resembled someone else, someone more substantial. I couldn't think who.

'Then I'll change what I said before. You're *over*confident.'

His lips puckered as though he were about to bawl. 'Now don't go making definitions. I jes want me a friend to play with. You about the cutest I seen all . . .'

'. . . afternoon!' I finished for him.

'All damn month I been in this hole of Fort Myers! If you want to know the truth. Good thing your brother-in-law's a completely evil son of a bitch, because I'd have you here on the bartop, if he weren't.'

'Whooaa!' I succeeded pulling away from him, uncertain what was going on. I thought we'd been flirting, fooling around. 'I'm glad he's here. And mean. And that I'm leaving soon.'

'Boy!' Evan leaned into my ear, voice huskier than ever, 'You don't half know what you're missin' turning me down! But I'm going to be a good sport. I'll give you another chance! I'm going to get your info and call you next time I'm in . . . where is it he said you live? – Los Angeles? I'll take you out to dinner in a tux an' all. Be a complete fuckin' gentleman. How about it?'

'Maybe,' I said, pulling away. 'Nice meeting you . . . all!' I said. I found my brother-in-law. 'I'd better get back to my lounge.'

To my surprise, Bart threw his arm around my shoulder and walked me back out. 'You give Evan wet dreams? He going to be on my case all week about you?'

'He could use some work on assertiveness.'

'Runs in the family. His daddy was Rutherford Davis. The guy who went to Siberia and opened those gold mines despite being shot twice by the Russian Mafia? Before him they are all dominators, going back to Jefferson Davis.'

'President of the Confederacy?' That's who Evan resembled.

'Johnny Reb himself!' Bart said. 'Now, I don't have to warn you, do I?'

'I can handle Evan.'

'I'm not just talking about Evan. At least he's open about what he wants. I'm talking about all these people you're going around seeing.'

'Thanks for your concern. I'm just, like, interviewing. Nothing else is going on!' And when he stopped dead and looked at me skeptically, I added, 'Okay! I bought a manuscript. That was it! It cost what you spend monthly on underwear.'

'The money is not the point,' Bart insisted. 'Not the amount. Not even that you paid it! I'm worried you're out of your depth. Truth is, I don't know what you're up to, and who all of these people are. Some may be great writers. Hell, the greatest in the world! That doesn't mean they're not going to fuck you over. Use you for their own ends. Who knows, just toy with you, for their own entertainment. These people are intellectuals, probably screwed up, and, well, they've all got a million more miles experience than you. Admit that!'

'I admit it. But . . .'

'I'll bail you out. No questions asked,' Bart said. 'Not just because of your sister.'

'That's really generous of you. But . . .'

'You don't know – you can't know – anyone's motives but your own. Just watch your step. That's all I'm asking. Okay?' He grabbed me in another half-nelson, half lifting me off the floor.

Someone on a public address system called my flight number. I heard it, and so evidently did Bart. He let go of me and poked me in the rib.

'Now get the hell out of here! Call your sister when you get home! You hear me! *Mi-nac-cio!*' he warned in a low snarl. 'If you don't . . . you're going to be my personal gift for Evan Cock-sucking Davis. You understand?'

*

The last photo I'd seen of Dominic De Petrie had been on the back inside cover of his last published book of memoirs dealing with the early 1980s: *Death and Art in Greenwich Village*. Despite its late publication date, according to Irian St George, the picture was taken a decade before. St George would know. In 1992, De Petrie had been barrel-chested, vigorous-looking, with still-curly, abundant salt and pepper hair and a distinguished squarish face, dominated by the sort of large, piercing eyes Romantic poets used to compare to those of eagles. I assumed after fourteen years as he'd moved into his middle sixties, he'd altered. I was prepared not to recognize the author at the little Provincetown Airport, where he'd insisted on picking me up, saying, 'Why rent a car? I can chauffeur you around, and if you want, you can drive one of my vehicles.' It might even be diverting to report back that we'd gotten into an identity mix-up.

But there he was, as I stepped down the stairway of the little commuter twelve-seater – I have to admit, feeling like an early RKO Picture. This was my first non-jet plane, jets being banned due to wetland environmental concerns. De Petrie was unmistakable in the small crowd waiting. He wore a white cotton vest over a yellow polo shirt, Roman centurion sandals, and baggy off-black shorts. His hair was almost white and he'd lost more, though what remained was curly. He looked healthy and vigorous, if thinner than in the glossy. When I got closer, I noticed his skin was loose under his chin and neck, though taut on his arms and legs. He was on the far side of the cyclone fence separating passengers in front of the single-story airport building as I stepped through the plane's hatch and peered around. By the time I'd reached the runway tarmac, he'd already figured out who I was. As I arrived at the gate's stationary luggage rack, De Petrie was there.

'They said it was uncanny!' he said. 'They weren't lying.'

'My resemblance to Len?'

'Though I didn't know him when he was your age, naturally. Is this all of your stuff?' De Petrie asked. 'Let me give you a hand.'

I wouldn't let him tote the heavier suitcase, but he almost tore my computer bag out of my hands and hefted it as though it weighed nothing. He guided us through the swarming little terminal and out into the peace of an immense back parking lot. 'It's not far,' De Petrie said. 'That pale green object ahead.'

'The Z-5?' I asked. The little Beemer roadster stood out from the heap of drab Mini vans, Sport Utes and sedans like a diamond in a coal chute.

'Dame calls it the De Petrie Fuckmobile,' he said. 'When Axey saw it he asked why I didn't get it in fire-engine red. But I couldn't forget the old adage, R-C-S-D! You've never heard it? Red-Car, Small-Dick!' De Petrie laughed: a distinctive laugh, a mix between a chortle, a cackle and a giggle, genial and masculine. The Beemer happily chirped and flashed its headlights at our approach. It started its engine and revved to a soft purr. I knew this was mechanical, in response to the proximity of De Petrie's keychain-sensor. To me it was like a happy puppy welcoming its owner, eagerly awaiting play-time.

My luggage was stowed and we were belted into the cockpit and he was shifting into reverse, awaiting a doddering woman in a 1970s Sedan De Ville to pull out, when I realized I'd still not made a formal salutation.

'I thought,' he said, 'that first, we'd drop into P-Town. It's more or less on our way. We'll pick up the papers and sweets there. You hungry? What am I saying, the young are always hungry! If you have special food needs let me know. After you're settled in and we've had coffee or tea and munchies, I thought you'd show me the manuscripts and other documentation you've collected supporting your thesis. We'll take it out to the beach. Given your tan, you look as though you enjoy sun. We've got a beach near me. Magnificent. Private. Besides, it'll give me a chance to check you out without seeming to be a dirty old man. After, we'll get dinner. Then you're free to pump me as much as you want. That sound like a possible schedule?' De Petrie asked. 'Let's *go*, lady,' he prompted in a low growl.

'It's fine. Great. Yeah.'

'Why do I sense there's something on your mind?'

'It's just that . . . I don't know how to say it . . . how incredibly honored I am to finally meet you.'

'Save that for the MLA, okay?'

'No, really, Mr De Petrie. I have to . . . Even if it sounds adoles-cent. *The Adventures of Marty* is my favorite book. I read it every year. It changed my life . . . in . . . a dozen ways. I wouldn't be here,

I wouldn't be . . . well, who and what I am if it weren't for that book – and your others too.'

'Okay, you said it. Feel better?'

'You don't believe me?' I said. 'Or you've heard it so many times before that you . . .'

'That what? I believe you. Now what? Am I responsible for changing your life? How am I supposed to deal with that? It's . . . this is why I've stopped going out, meeting people, why I've stopped interviews and all that publicity junk. I'm glad you liked it, but the sad truth is, I wrote *Marty* for my own selfish reasons. That book more than others. I had no intention of some sixteen-year-old changing his life. I'm not sure I like the idea you did. It's confusing. Too many issues. That's why I don't publish.'

'What reasons?' was, out the welter of questions, all I could think to ask.

'To buy this little fucker,' he slapped the steering wheel, 'for one thing! Foreign advances from the book went as downpayments. Continued royalties keep paying it off. Finally! She moves!' He threw the Z-5 into gear. We shot out of the parking lot, leaving curtains of sand on either side.

The two-laned road curved and twisted almost back on itself several times as it ascended into high sand dunes surrounding the airport. Perfect for De Petrie to open up the Beemer's powerful engine. He drove with confidence, a little flair, and fearlessness, accelerating into sharp bends, throwing the car into overdrive along a straightaway to pass a dilapidated pickup, maneuvering abruptly, effortlessly. In minutes, we'd approached an eight-laned islanded main road, which he leapt across, onto another rough two-laner headed into an area of one- and two- and infrequently three-story clapboard houses. We crossed two more good-sized boulevards and came out onto the main drag, Commercial Street, in front of the post office. I could partly see and even more strongly smell the waterfront, only a block away, and apparently at low tide.

Getting out, De Petrie said, 'I'm leaving the keys. Move it only if a cop asks.' Then he was gone.

Provincetown was a bustling tourist zone, but I got why De Petrie avoided it in summer. The half-dozen teens sprawled on the post office steps shadowed by its towering Doric columns were dressed in retro-grunge and post-punk outfits, their hair multiple shades of colors, the least expected parts of their anatomies embellished with rings and silver studs. Cars crawled along the street, as people hung out of back windows shouting. Pedestrians ambled slowly three and four abreast on the narrow sidewalks, spilling into the narrow main concourse, further slowing traffic. Shops selling every kind of merchandise went out of their way to attract passers-by. It was boisterous and obscurely happy, social and comfy. It was also blaring and vulgar and nerve-racking.

De Petrie threw a bundle of newspapers and a grease-spotted white paper bag into the netting behind his car seat as he hopped in.

We inched along a block of the stop-and-go main-street traffic before he veered left into what looked to be an alleyway. It never widened, but it did rise steeply, recrossed the avenues from before and ran parallel to the road we'd come into town on. At the highway, De Petrie swung a right, pushing two buttons on the car's console. One turned on the CD player. Kate Bush's second album began with lush orchestration and her characteristic wail. The other button had no apparent effect. I asked what it was. Despite our speed and the wind inches away outside the car windows, within was calm, so De Petrie didn't have to shout.

'That's an automatic variable governor. From here down to Hyannis, Route 6 changes top speeds every few miles without warning! The highway police hide just before the signs and nab anyone who doesn't immediately adjust. I've programmed all the changes into the Z-5's system, I know two cops in particular dying to cite me. They're frustrated as hell when I sail past doing sixty-four or forty-nine and a quarter miles per hour.' He laughed his distinctive laugh again.

The road narrowed to four lanes, suddenly closed in on either side by clay bluffs and heavy foliage. When that opened out, the scenery expanded to reveal, on the right, a seemingly endless row of tiny cabins, behind which I could make out the immense flat plane of the bay waters, and across it the tip of Provincetown glittering in the early afternoon sunlight. On our left, a salt-water lake appeared, a far more mysterious prismatic blue than either the sun-speckled bay or the matte sky. From the lake's most distant expanse appeared vast clouds of what at first I thought were insects but as we approached

realized were sea birds – terns, gulls, geese and mallards in the thousands – skimming low along the water surface, bending and curling
as though they were a single organism, metamorphosing in front of
us from a giant quivering sheet into a tight funnel before breaking
and scattering into their thousands, re-forming as a flattened bar
that as we watched became an arrow headed north. The Beemer
began a long ascent just as massive earthen cliffs on our left limited
the lake and, on the right, lofty trees began to conceal the bay
waters.

At the top of the ridge, the continuation of high bluffs on our left
was more exposed. The entire area, I noticed, was federally protected marshland. All at once, on the right, we were treated to a
Currier and Ives etching: a nineteenth-century New England town
with snow-white skyscraping church steeple, dormered houses and
outbuildings, all embraced by the fattest, roundest, fluffiest, green-
est tree tops.

'North Truro,' De Petrie said, as the highway narrowed to two
lanes and began to descend, at first sharply, then more gently. On
either side was forest, mixed in with what looked like abandoned
buildings that might have been farms or businesses. Just before
another rise, the road forked and the Z-5 took the leftmost tine, lev-
eling off and speeding through a completely residential area, houses
hidden from view by trees, hedges, and fencework, although those I
could make out were spread upon large plots, unnumbered, post
boxes collected at designated spots.

Five minutes of narrow, roughly paved road and we geed onto an
even less discernible path. We rose sideways to the view below,
allowing me to see more of it, from above. A flat circular drive
landed us in front of what might have been a carriage house or
early horseless garage, its top-windowed double doors latched shut.
Before it was parked a dun-colored Sport Utility. The house,
attached to the garage behind, extended along one side. It was
painted Crenshaw melon yellow, trimmed with ivory, a conventional
two-story salt-box of no great size, with a dinky filigree-columned
wooden side porch. Only a few fruit trees. But the front yard was
distinguished by robust, well-tended, red rose bushes, and a blue,
white and pink 'English garden' of daisies, hydrangeas, flags, nar-
cissi and hollyhocks.

De Petrie gave a quick tour of the house. Four rooms had been first erected in the second half of the eighteenth century, he said: the three ground-floor rooms and one above. When the property was purchased by a local ironworks manufacturer who'd made a fortune equipping whaling ships, the house acquired its formal entrance and foyer, the two parlors flanking it, a downstairs master bedroom and dressing room, and three more upstairs garret rooms for servants and children. At the turn of the twentieth century, the carriage house/garage had been added, and indoor plumbing installed. Fifty years later, a furnace had been put in the cellar and the kitchen thoroughly modernized. The circular driveway made its debut then. The house belonged to friends of De Petrie's, he told me, inherited by them and used as a summer place due to its neglect and deterioration. He'd come to rent it after the Pines season was over, from after Labor Day to Thanksgiving. When his friends decided to sell the house in 1984, he'd just made a 'financial killing' – a book contract with a sizable advance covering publication of *The Last Good Year for Cadillacs* and *Chrome Earrings*. De Petrie showed me how the entrance had changed position over the years, opening first from the kitchen, then at the long, formal drawing room, later at the foyer, then to the side porch, and back to the dining room again. When he'd moved in, he said, he was in such straitened financial circumstances, it was all he could do to keep the place in minimally required repairs. Eventually, income flowed in for further restoration.

'You'll be comfortable here.' De Petrie guided me through the dining room, into a little formal parlor, from there into the sunny square foyer, with stairs rising to the bright second floor, to a matching library and into a rectangular bedroom. 'You've got a bath and a short cut to the kitchen,' he pointed out. 'You should get around at night without breaking anything. I sleep upstairs.'

While I put my clothing away and changed into shorts, he prepared our noon snack in the long, formal yet also family-style dining room that seemed to be an axial point in the house. The phone rang as we'd only just seated ourselves and he'd poured coffee and laid out the pastries we'd picked up in town. De Petrie gestured for me to go ahead, and went to take the phone call in the library, several rooms away, so I couldn't hear what he was saying. For no reason I could put my finger on; I felt certain the caller to be Aaron Axenfeld, perhaps checking that I'd arrived safely, or checking De Petrie's opinion about my similarity to Len Spurgeon.

As I plunged into the apricot-filled Danish and fresh pineapple slices and heavy French coffee, I remarked through the quartet of tall back windows how ornithologically active the house and its surroundings were. A stolid, immovably rooted, abundantly leaved beech tree some twenty feet away supported several feeders, one of which attracted hummingbirds who hovered whirring as they sipped sugar water. I soon noticed other birds: a puffed-out, red-breasted robin plashing messily in the rust-stained, once-white cement bird bath as a quarrelsome cardinal family contentiously awaited their turn from the various branches of a mulberry bush; tiny brown tits, frosted white, braiding the lower branches of the bordering box-wood; tawny buff swallows buzzing each of the back garden's trees and shrubs, checking them out, before zooming out of sight; two pensive black-winged red birds daintily perched, snacking only inches away from where I sat, picking at seeds distributed in a drawer-like bird feeder installed athwart the windowsill; a preoccupied dusky-gray secretary bird barely placed on the feeder, busily preening itself until it presumed no one was looking, when it suddenly poked into the midst of the seed pile, came up with the biggest it could hold in its beak, and flew off to dine in private; myriad tiny gold and green finches bejeweling the leaf-umbrellaed air. Watching the birds I found myself relaxing for the first time all day. I must have spaced out a little watching their miniature antics, because I wasn't even aware De Petrie had finished his phone call and returned.

'Ready for the beach?' He took a final sip of coffee.

A short auto ride brought us to a small, nearly full parking lot approximately carved out of the adjacent thickets of beach plum. Beyond it a sand path led up and around a bluff. I could hear but not yet see the surf. A short trudge with our gear and there, abruptly, beyond the narrowing of two earthen walls, it was, spread out before and below us. I was amazed to find that we stood more or less atop a sixty-foot cliff. Those two diagonal, evidently man-kicked-out paths in the sand were the only means of access down to the wide, cream-colored sea strand. From this altitude I could catch sight of only a few people scattered upon the sands.

Once we'd reached bottom, the cliffs seemed to be even more daunting. Because of how empty the place was, we easily found a sunny yet private spot. One close to the water's edge, as the sun would cross behind the cliffs in a few hours, De Petrie said, blocking our light. At first I simply splayed out on the large beach sheets, absorbing heat, trying to nap. Unable to, I became restless and tried the surf. The water was cold and rough, but not excessively. I was laved and tumbled.

De Petrie remained sitting, a visored cap protecting him from sun glare, as he pored over all the material I'd managed to gather up and put into his hands: the four manuscript fragments – the kids in the car, the bar on Christmas Eve, the Flamingos, and last, but hardly least, the cable car mishap. Along with them were my reports of conversations with Bobbie Bonaventura, Thomas Dodge, Tanya Cull, Reuben Weatherbury, Camden Phoenix, Irian St George, Damon Von Slyke, and, just completed this morning while I was on the plane coming here, Aaron Axenfeld. In addition were the journal entries, letters, and other documents the heirs and executors had provided me with. A considerable body of evidence, I thought, and one I hoped De Petrie would add to. For the moment, I had to wait his verdict on what I'd so far amassed. So, after boring myself in the surf, I waved to him, gestured in a direction and began walking.

The cliffs closely approached the shoreline, constricting the beach at several points, and giant black rocks rose out of the sands. I realized I'd gone around a bend, out of sight of De Petrie. Once again, the cliffs withdrew and the beach widened, this time so much I could barely make out the couple half hiding behind beach umbrellas directly under the cliff's edge, although I was fairly certain they were nude. A few hundred yards, and I was surrounded by seagulls the size of turkeys. I was reminded of Damon Von Slyke at our historic first encounter saying to me with that poker face of his that he'd titled his new book *The Gulls*, and how everyone hated the title. At the time I'd thought it odd. I now wondered if it had been a complete and unblemished put-on. Like renaming the character in that short story Leonard. I mean, he'd not even been trying hard to fool me, had he? How stupid did he think I was? How naïve? Another narrowing of the strand ensued, this one so limiting the overarching cliff crumbled at the water's edge, eroded up to a height of fifty feet. Did the tide go that high during storms? Nor'easters? Another bend of shoreline, even larger rock outcroppings and a few more nudists, this time males of a certain age, alone and, I assumed – rightly? wrongly? – gay. One was dead asleep, his body as though dropped, but with a wideawake, friendly-looking, sand-covered Irish wolfhound that rose to its feet to carefully check me over, looking, sniffing the air, not barking or advancing toward me.

At last, wearied, I sat on a rock ledge, let the gulls come nearer, and scrutinized the ocean. I tried to sort out what was going on in my life. For the first time in months, I felt I had a future ahead. The thesis. The class. St George. The friendship of one, maybe two, maybe all of the remaining Purples. A calculatedly quiet ascent in the Languages Department at UCLA. A stately incremental upgrade in the academic world. Maybe Tanya Cull or St George or Weatherbury endorsing my thesis when it was published as a book by Stanford U Press. Not even Fusumi's tenured chair and that house in Little Holmby Hills seemed totally out of the picture. I'd get an office in Rolfe or Royce Hall, buy myself a Z-5, maybe in this same pale green with a tan convertible roof, and then, perhaps when I felt settled in, find someone to take Chris's place beside me.

I had purposely not thought about Chris for weeks. Chris had been the problem, the sticking point, the burr under my saddle for months. Chris; what Chris said that afternoon we'd broken up in that stupid park on Morningside Heights; how Chris had failed to react when I'd gotten this post at UCLA; what Chris hadn't said when our small group of friends had cheered me goodbye; what Chris thought and didn't think; what Chris would think and wouldn't think when I proved to Chris – and everyone! every goddamned arrogant, snooty, high-faluting son of a bitch student and teacher at the Columbia Grad program! – that I didn't need Chris, nor them, not any of them, to rise to the top.

Behind me I heard a dog bark. I turned to see the Irish wolfhound off its owner's towel, dancing about as its master stood up, just awakening, and stretched himself. He was tall, well built, maybe in his early thirties, totally naked, with thick curling black hair, a fuzzy-looking goatee, and a large erection that stood out in front of him and bounced whenever he moved. He looked like a more mature Ray Rice. I turned away the second he seemed to try to establish eye contact with me. After what I thought was a sufficiently apt amount of time to let him know I was ignoring him, I stood up and took off, lightly jogging down the beach. As I passed in front of his blanket, the dog briefly ran out to join me, caught up, and accompanied me on my run. He called it back – 'Bar-neeeee' sung out in a confident virile baritone, answered by a barrage of barking. I didn't stop racing until I felt a stitch in my side and thought I would scream in agony, drop onto the sand, and die.

' "Celebrations and suppressions," in the words of the master, "are equally painful to me," ' De Petrie said. 'Nevertheless, if you don't too much mind, as tonight is a sort of morose anniversary, let's raise a glass to it.'

We were in a sequestered candlelit booth in a Italianesque seafood restaurant in Wellfleet, not far from his house. Our waiter had just taken our order. The sommelier had just brought us a complex 1996 California Merlot.

'To the ravens at Truro,' De Petrie said, 'who never lie.'

We clinked glasses and sipped.

'By "the master", I assume you mean Henry James.'

'James the Younger, James the Great, and the Old Pretender, as Max Beerbohm called him. Do you ever read him?' Before I could answer, De Petrie went on, 'Does *anyone* still read him? James, I mean. I *know* no one reads Beerbohm anymore.'

I mumbled about re-reading *The Aspern Papers*.

He laughed. 'I don't for a second doubt it. You're sort of living out *The Aspern Papers*, aren't you?' Again before I could reply, he went on, 'I don't suppose you ever saw that frightful Hollywood movie based on the novella? What was it called? It starred Robert Cummings as the scheming editor and Susan Hayward as the allegedly frumpy grand-niece. Big stars in my day whom you've doubtless never heard of. In the film, every night she goes into a trance and transforms herself into her beautiful grandmother Juliana. Sporting jewelry with stones the size of your fist and a cleavage-deep velvet gown, she crosses over a mini Ponte Rialto to some chandelier-encrusted *atelier avec terrace* to play Chopin Nocturnes till dawn. One night Cummings follows and is seduced by her. I can't remember who played the old woman who'd been Jeffrey

Aspern's lover. She looked a million years old. It was beautifully
shot. Venice itself never looked so glamorously *louche*. Romantic
twaddle though it was, it was more faithful than more accurate ren-
ditions. It conveyed the flavor of the thing so well.'

'It was called *The Lost Moment*!' I said.

'You *clever* thing! You're right! What a *trashy* title.'

'I saw it on television when I was a kid. It was so over the top, it
blew me away. In fact when I read the James, I thought that was the
rip-off!' And immediately asked, 'What do you mean before by the
ravens at Truro?'

'You've noticed all the birds?' De Petrie asked.

'How could I miss them?'

'How could you, they've become so much a part of the place?
We've encouraged them – with feeders all year round – so that when
they're not there, and especially when they're both not visible *and*
silent, well, then it becomes *remarkably* noticeable.'

'Why would they become silent?' I asked.

'When ravens come they hunt and kill other birds. What we are
memorializing today is the first time I actually seized upon this
phenomenon. It *is* a phenomenon! Unmistakably so! It was this date
in 1991. I was downstairs in the dining room, waiting for Len, who
was upstairs getting dressed. We were to go into Provincetown for
his doctor's appointment. The CytoMegalo Virus had worsened the
floaters in one of his eyes. I refused to let him drive and said I'd take
him. He'd been dry-coughing for weeks, running heavy fevers for
nights. He'd grown uncommunicative. As I was scanning some
pages from *Marty* that I'd written earlier that day, there it suddenly
was: an amazing, unanticipated, absolute lack of birdsong.'

The waiter came with bread. When he was gone, De Petrie continued.

'I'm extremely hearing-sensitive. It's a curse at times. Like
Roderick Usher, I can hear rats in wainscoting six floors down. So,
it only took a few moments for me to notice the *total* cessation of
sound. I went out to the backyard. Didn't see any birds. I walked
deeper into the woods. Again, no birds. Not a peep, literally. Then,
in the distance, in the direction of the highway, I heard a caw-caw,
caw-caw. After a few minutes the ravens arrived. They were huge:
the size of eagles or buzzards. They especially go after younger birds,

you know, nestlings, eggs. I counted a dozen ravens lurking high in tree limbs. A hunting pack. I yelled to scare them off. They flew away. But not far. And a few minutes later I could hear them assault some hapless bird family. A few loud mixed squawks and then the caw-cawing again, terrifyingly triumphant. I went deeper into the woods, thinking I might still save a wounded bird. I found nothing. Not long afterward, I could hear them fall upon other birds up in the trees, near where the property adjoins the Fleischers'. I never *saw* anything of course, which almost was the most striking aspect of it all. When I got back to the house, Len was waiting. He'd been up the night before and he looked awfully ill.

'That afternoon the doctor confirmed not only that his CMV had spread, was still spreading, but also that he had pneumocystis. He wanted to hospitalize him. But Len said no. We drove over to Mechanic Street to the medical supplies place and got oxygen masks and tanks and IV racks and all the other equipment he would need. That afternoon when we arrived home, Len went straight upstairs to bed. He never came back down alive. It only took a few weeks. Of course they were frightening, ghastly weeks filled with alarms and crises. For me. Luckily for Len, he only remained conscious a fraction of the time. But that afternoon, as we drove back here with all the gear in the back and in the trunk, I saw the ravens again. They were on Joe and Armin's lawn, four of them, pecking at something. Incessantly pecking. If I had a gun I swear I would have killed them . . . Len never noticed.

'Since then, the ravens have come back three times. Each time, someone close to me dies. Ravens at Truro never lie.'

Our appetizers arrived.

'Not a moment too soon! Or we'd lose all appetite,' he quipped.

After we'd dispatched the food, I said, 'Naturally I've read about the AIDS epidemic in the '80s and early '90s. But I can't even begin to conjecture what it was like. You must have suffered awfully!'

'What is it James writes about Stransom in *The Altar of the Dead*?' De Petrie asked rhetorically. '"He had perhaps not had more losses than most men, but he had counted his losses more; he had not seen death more closely, but he had, in a manner, felt it more deeply." Except that I *have* seen it more closely. All *too* closely. All too often! But let's not talk about morbid things. Let's talk about you. About what I read today.'

Our entrées arrived, mine lobster on a bed of capellini, his stuffed calamari on linguine, compelling our immediate attention. I tried not to stare at De Petrie as we ate, but while I glanced at the waiters, the decor, my food, the other diners, I found myself pondering the reserves of courage he must have discovered within himself to have gone through so many illnesses, so many deaths, at such close range, so many years in a row.

When I – when virtually anyone I knew – thought of Dominic De Petrie, it was commonly as that unnatural prodigy, the successful author, one who'd managed to keep his career not only going but evolving, expanding over three decades. Of course it had helped that his talent was of the dazzling rather than the subtle kind. As a result he'd been fortuitous almost from the beginning. De Petrie's first three novels, predating the Purple Circle – and, really, gay literature – had nevertheless been decisive critical and commercial hits, each building on the other. The biggest hit, *Singles*, set in Manhattan's Upper East Side and told from the dual point of view of a young man and a young woman involved in an impossible relationship, was not only a best-seller, it was optioned for the movies by producers and film stars for years.

Not satisfied with high sales, not contented with a Hemingway and other book award nominations, De Petrie had the effrontery to forge into untried territory and publish a book of gay themed poetry. *A Choice of Faces* was scarcely noticed by his usual audience, barely reviewed except in the new gay media, but like Jeff Weber's volume of verse, it sold several small editions, and ended up influencing an entire generation of gay poets. Far more influential in varying, mostly unexpected, ways would be De Petrie's next book, the novel *Prowl*, an even greater departure for him, a psychological thriller set deep within the nucleus of New York's gay disco and club scene.

Prowl was the first, many since said the best, gay-themed thriller. It was hard-hitting, authentic in scene and customs, explosively violent, astonishingly candid about the sex and relationships gay men had with each other. This 'revelation of secrets', this 'washing of dirty laundry in public', led many prominent gay politicos to viciously attack De Petrie and his book, in print and in speeches. For

368 THE BOOK OF LIES

some months after the book's publication, his life was threatened so virulently, so often, he had to hire security guards and for a while even leave home. On the plus side, *Prowl* was the first gay-themed novel picked up by a major book club. That, and the reviews in the mainstream press, which veered from the highest praise to blistering criticism, rendered the novel's publication an event. Sales in hardcover, paper and in translation into a half-dozen languages ended up far surpassing his previous novels. For the following decade, gay youths coming out in San Diego, Indianapolis, Bangor, London, Berlin, Sydney, São Paulo and Tokyo would have *Prowl* as a guide, a promise – and a warning. It would be more than a decade before another of De Petrie's titles surpassed it in celebrity or sales, and that would be uniquely different, as controversial, even more beloved: *The Adventures of Marty*.

However spectacular for De Petrie's career, had he stopped writing or died after the publication of *Prowl*, his reputation would doubtless be far less than it turned out; above that of Cameron Powers and Rowland Etheridge, but below that of Axenfeld, Von Slyke and even Mark Dodge, somewhere in the general area of Jeff Weber or Mitch Leo. It was the second, quieter, phase of De Petrie's lifework that ended up attracting serious readers as well as scholars of Dr St George's stature. Because while it might have been sufficiently bold for an author to sacrifice an achieved name and recognition to go on to help create an entire genre – i.e. gay literature – and be responsible for some of its early masterworks, De Petrie went further. In the 1980s and 1990s, he assembled a succession of gay-themed books that crossed formal lines others never suspected were in place and then went on to fulfill the newly devised expectations to the utmost. In his study of the Purple Circle, Thaddeus Fleming admitted he didn't know which would ultimately prove the more important, De Petrie's middle-period fiction – the experimental short stories in *Gay Tragic Romances*, his idyllic *A Summer's Lease*, the satirical *Advice to a Jewish Prince* – or his nonfiction works – memoirs, essays, mixed genres – including, *The Last Good Year for Cadillacs, Chrome Earrings* and *Saturdays – and Rain!*

Even those paled, Erling Cummings, Reuben Weatherbury and Irian St George believed, to books De Petrie released after: the novel

The Adventures of Marty; the memoirs *Agent for the Deceased* and
Death and Art in Greenwich Village; the novella *Absolute Ebony*;
and his most recently published book, *Conversations in the Dark*,
about which critics were divided as to its genre if not quality.
Cummings voiced the not uncommon belief when he wrote 'that
final quintet represents a heady culmination of a consummate mas-
tery of form and style'. Fleming concentrated upon the work from
Marty on. 'Each book undertakes a giant vault into some unforsee-
able future of literature, which it predicts, then goes on to shape and
define.'

These were my own favorites among the Purple Circle's many
attainments. I felt I would have to re-read late De Petrie again and
again as I aged and grew more experienced to comprehend what I
sensed lay unrevealed beneath the more easily graspable surface
layers, as in those figures and scenes Old Masters underpainted that
only years of the most intimate knowledge and loving scrutiny dis-
close. I wasn't certain I'd possess the intelligence or vocabulary I
suspected was required to articulate it all, and I wondered how
much this weekend encounter would help or work against any ultimate wisdom.

Our few previous phone conversations, along with this encounter,
had confirmed for me Dominic De Petrie's urbane, accessible erudi-
tion and the facility with which he seemed able to manipulate his
intelligence and his listener's response, as though they formed a
single, brilliant, multicolored mantle that he, like a magician, waved
and spun in your face, to baffle, evoke thrills, chills and applause,
and ultimately enthrall.

Against that I had to place De Petrie's all too evident personality.
It was refreshing in one sense, as the no-longer-young *can* be brac-
ing, in that he evidently did not believe he had to accommodate
anyone by social inanities such as diplomacy, politeness, or unguard-
edness. On the other hand, he'd revealed aspects of himself I felt not
everyone would consider of the highest order: his puerile glee in
expensive, gaudy machines, in using them to outwit the police: his
adolescently fast – though so far unperilous – driving; his preening
attitude toward himself and all that was his; his air of presumption
about what he'd earned, what he possessed, what he'd accomplished, whom he'd known. I was doubtless meeting him too late to

suffer from what I suspected had once been a noteworthy personal vanity, but not, I sensed, by that many years. No surprise then, that the not-unperceptive De Petrie no longer allowed interviews, or indeed any but the rarest of public appearances. Since he had no apparent intention of bending to anyone's conception of whom he ought to be or seem to be or how he ought to act, but intended instead to follow his own whim of iron, why subject his reputation to further criticism? While I, adoring fan, and moreover an adoring fan who actually wanted something from him, well, I was hardly in a position to breathe the tiniest iota of criticism, was I? He was utterly safe with me.

Our dinner plates were being cleared off, and now we could converse again. I took the offensive.

'What do you think?' I got up the courage to ask. 'Do I make a case?'

'You mean of what I read today?' De Petrie asked, then uncharacteristically professed, 'I'm scarcely to be considered an authority. Irian St George would be more apropos. It's all intriguingly implicative. And a far richer vein than I would have presumed. I will say one thing: I learned a great deal more about Len than I'd known.'

'Unpleasant things, probably. I'm sorry if I . . .'

He waved that aside. 'New knowledge can only be an advantage. He's dead so long now, nothing will or indeed *can* alter my memory of him. But you may be amused to hear that I suspected worse of Len. He did have a reputation! Naturally that wouldn't stop me. It would only encourage me to take up with him, given the opportunity. Do you know how it was that he came to live here? How could you? We met at the Hookers' Ball. A drag competition show and dance held at one or another of the local *boîtes* in P-Town. It's an after-season affair. Generally around Columbus Day. Most of the tourists have left, so it's only year-round residents and the seasonal staff who've remained. A popular event. The final blow-out of the year. I attended the one in October 1985, as I had in the past. At one of the indoor bars sat an Australian celebrity *en travesti* who was to be the show's MC. He used to go around telling everyone he was straight, with a wife and kids. That might have been true, but that particular night he was trawling for boys. Men, rather. Because when I approached the bar to order a Heineken, he was trying to nab none other but Len Spurgeon. Who was by then over forty. Len remembered me. I remembered him. We amused the drag celeb with outrageous flirting and misleading promises to join him after the show for a three-way on his yacht parked out in the harbor. Then it was time for him to go on-stage. We two hung around for half the show, then found we were too horny. We went to Len's place and screwed each other's brains out.

'Now I'd met Len before. Maybe as early as 1978. I knew he'd been lovers with Mark Dodge, and that he'd had a relationship of some unspecified sort, probably romantic, with Jeff Weber. I possibly knew about him and Cammy Powers. I also recalled that after some initial attraction, Mitch Leo and Len hadn't gotten along, although I never heard or sought to discover why. I knew nothing about him and Rowland. Nor about him and Damon, nor about him and Frankie McKewen. And it wasn't until Len had moved in here that tight-lipped Axey told me about Len's residence in Sanibel Island, and then I suspect only because it had been a positive experience for all.

'The truth is, I'd never been all that attracted to Len before we met at the Hookers' Ball. At first, he'd been almost ostentatiously good-looking. Off-puttingly sexual. I've had my share of beautiful men in the '70s and '80s. Handsome as you are, you will be saddened, though not too surprised to hear, that the appeal of physical beauty is, after all, rather limited. Though Axey would, naturally, disagree. Even so, by the time we re-encountered, the initial gloss was off Len. Replaced by what I found to be a more impressive edge. Don't get me wrong. He wasn't a dog! Len had unquestionably aged well. That, and some other new, previously unexpected qualities I thought I saw in him at the time, vaguely interested me. Even so, when we did get together again over the first few months, it was casual. Len worked in P-Town at some photo and framing shop, had his own pals, his own apartment. He also had somewhere in his meanderings picked up a great amount of knowledge about and experience with horticulture, and he began coming out to Truro on weekends and days off to help with the gardens, about which I knew nearly zilch. I'd usually wait until he was done, rinsing off in the outdoor shower, before I'd accost him and drag him into the house for sex. It was utterly nonchalant and thoroughly harmless.

'When without much warning he had to move out of his flat in town, I realized I was alone in a big place here and we seemed to get along, so I offered Len the room you're sleeping in. Eventually Len totally redesigned the garden and in fact all the property's landscaping. He took over a portion of the garage and turned it into his workshop. He began getting me to restore the house. Which we did as much as possible together without outside help. Len settled in and here he remained. Which meant I also remained here longer periods of time. At last I gave up my apartment in Manhattan. Then, when Len began coming down with various symptoms and falling ill for longer and longer spans of time, he quit what little work he was still doing part-time in P-Town. He went on full disability and never went into town unless forced to, although we had several vehicles by then.

'We never defined our relationship to ourselves or to anyone else. It seemed pointless. We'd both had so many previous commitments that ended disastrously, it seemed best not to even hint at the possibility. We never made demands on each other. We never placed curbs on whom we might date or screw, or socialize with. We never argued. After several years, we simply became Dominic and Len, or Len and Dom. Holiday cards and postcards from traveling friends were addressed one way or the other, invitations to events and parties. Len remarked on it wryly once. In my hearing, he said to one of my friends, "My Mom would have shit her undies with joy if she ever guessed I'd end up living like a country gentleman with a rich and famous husband." I never knew if he was kidding or not. At any rate, Len came to cherish the house and grounds more than I did. So much so, he became part of it. Figuratively *and* literally. After he died and was cremated, I followed his wishes and scattered half his ashes in the garden and the rest out on Long Knoll beach, where we spent this afternoon.'

We ordered desserts. It was late. The place emptying out.

'This may sound foolish,' I said, 'but I can't help but wonder what it's like having known so many that are . . . gone!'

'I could dissemble, Ross, but the truth is you tend to become haunted! Don't get me wrong,' De Petrie was quick to clarify. 'It's not at all sensational and spine-tingling, as it's portrayed on television or in the movies. It's far more insidious. You remember a face

out of the past. It rises three-dimensionally, if for an instant, in front
of you. Or a fully inflected phrase comes to you, unbidden, complete
with its unmistakable, long gone, speaker. You hear other words
from others' voices, ones you know have been long-quieted. You
recall an incident not as a memory, but as though it is happening in
the instant, total and complete. You constantly feel a tenuous yet
unbroken connection to presences, to intelligences, you know can no
longer be in operation: yet which are, to you, alone. And with them,
you sense a subtle lessening of contacts to people your perceptions
tell you are actually present. It doesn't end there. Because it is continuous, unceasing: it goes on and on. After a while, you're surprised
to realize you're living segments of your life in the past, a good
share actually, and a specific not very large allotment in the present.
The future holds no significance to you. Planning for it seems . . .
insipid somehow. You're initially surprised that no one else notices
how you are living your life. Then you comprehend that's because
those who have been intimate enough or who cared enough to
notice anything at all about you are simply no longer present to do
so. To others you appear absent-minded, dotty, eccentric.

'It's all rather comforting when it has become so habitual,' De
Petrie confessed. 'I suppose because it is so quotidian and enduring.
I don't talk about it as a rule as it usually drives people to yawn
immensely. It was Henry James again who put it so wonderfully. In
that same novella. Stransom thinks about his many dead loved ones.
James writes, "They were there in their simplified, intensified
essence, their conscious absence and expressive patience, as personally there as if they had only been stricken dumb . . . They asked so
little that they got, poor things, even less, and died again, died every
day, of the hard usage of life." So, like Stransom I have my own little
altar, although mine is only a few photos on an upstairs credenza.
The real altar, I suppose, exists in my mind. In my books! Since the
mid-'80s, they're nothing but dirges and elegies and despondent tes-
timonials!'

'You don't mean *Adventures of Marty*?'

'Don't I? That book more than any other.'

'But . . . it's so funny! So exuberant! Not gloomy!'

'Well, then,' De Petrie smiled sourly, 'my little plot worked.'

'What little plot?'

'To rope in all you poor unsuspecting readers! To entice you and seduce you into loving the characters so much, to make you identify with them closely, that when I then killed them off, you would have to feel something, even if it were only a smidgen of the agony I myself had gone through with the originals.'

'Why do that? To divide, to lessen your own agony?'

'Clever you. Yes, I admit, it was all quite deliberately sadistic on my part. Only Axey ever fathomed what I'd set out to do, and how far I'd succeeded. He called *Marty* my "Surreptitious Days of Sodom".'

'Len isn't in that book?' I argued.

'*Isn't* he? Len is *everywhere* in the book. As he's also nowhere in particular! The way Len is, to this very day, everywhere yet nowhere in my house in Truro. The way devout Christians and Buddhists believe God is. Immanent, I believe, is the term theologians employ. Len's in everything – not to be discerned until you are actively pursuing him – I've completed since he died. You realize, of course, that I've written nothing *new* since Len died. I've merely rewritten and revamped, completed and then subsequently very slowly released all of what in those years I was so very assiduously at work on. Those terrible years I stood by helpless watching and attempting to help nurse Len. And before Len, Mark and Jeff and Cammy and Mitch. The only reason I wrote so much in those years, you understand, was to escape the unavoidable reality around myself. To elude and avoid what I could not accept, or do anything to slow down, never mind stop. Every volume was another brick I cemented into place in my useless bulwark against the undeniable.' De Petrie paused. 'St George doesn't believe a word of it He tells me I'm overdramatizing.'

'I believe you,' I said. I did.

'Good for the youth of America!' He saluted me mock-cheerfully. 'Because of your untarnished innocence and candor you deserve the prize! Which is . . . Ta-da!' he explained the flourish. 'Another manuscript fragment for your thesis. This one came out of nowhere, a year before he died.'

Our tab arrived and De Petrie paid over my protests. We finished our brandies, then sped home in the Z-5 through a moonless, star-studded, honeysuckle-drenched night. I changed into my sweat pants and T-shirt. De Petrie dropped the MS on my bed-table and went upstairs for the night.

'I don't really know where this came from,' the preface to the pages I held in my hand read. 'For a long time, I thought it was something I'd seen. You know, one of those full-length cartoons that used to be aired on television year after year around the Christmas holidays. I recall several such films set in Arctic locations, with beautiful magic white horses and dark long-bearded villains. I think they were made in Finland or Denmark. Not America or Japan. But whenever I mentioned this particular tale to my siblings, they said they didn't recognize it at all, although they did remember the others. So maybe I made it up myself. The way, I guess, writers make up stories and novels all the time: some image or idea sits in your mind for a long time, and then one day, there it is: a story. At any rate, this little tale seems to stand for something about my life. I've titled it, "A Fable".'

A FABLE

There once was a little boy who lived in a northern land. He was happy, and well loved. And in turn he loved everyone: his family and friends, the countryside and the farm animals and the wild birds and animals. But most of all he loved the wintry snows and ice. From the time he could toddle, even before he could talk, he loved to play in snow and ice. Nothing pleased him more when he'd grown a little older than to sled, or ski or, best of all, to skate the ice that formed over lakes and ponds and rivers and streams more than half the year. He would go out skating with his family and friends. But long after they were weary, the little boy would continue skating, gliding along the ice, skidding, sliding, racing, flying. He'd skate by himself, with nothing but the wind, with the snow, for companions.

One afternoon, long after all the others had grown weary and skated away to rest and warm themselves at an outdoor fire, the little boy continued to skate on and on. The snow began to fall again, not thickly but melting at the ice's surface. The little boy was so lonely and yet so fascinated with the patterns it made falling in the strong shaping wind, he

pretended he could see another person. He began to skate
with, dance with, this person. Together, they swung round
and round, pirouetted, allowed each other under and over,
swerved and spun, twisted into figure eights.

Without the little boy noticing, as he skated, the wind and
the snow grew stronger, until he found himself blinded from
seeing anything but snow. Faintly he heard his friends and
family calling him. He thought he heard them telling him to
hurry and come indoors with them. Cry babies, he thought.
Cowards, he scoffed. Why be afraid of the snow? The wind?
The ice? He wasn't afraid. As the snow came down around
him thicker and harder, he skated on, gliding along the ice,
skidding, sliding, racing, flying with the elements, enjoying
his solitude, his peace and quiet.

He was very surprised when, coming out of a revolution
he'd made with his eyes closed, he saw a stranger skating
nearby. An extraordinary, tall, beautiful stranger, clothed in a
gleaming silver jacket and shimmering trousers, both of them
adorned with innumerable diamonds. The little boy wasn't
certain whether the stranger was a man or woman. Its gloveless long hands and beautiful long hair were snow white. Its
face wasn't pink like the little boy's but instead of a pallor
like the finest ivory, and its eye the deepest, darkest blue the
little boy had ever seen, like that pool of water at the very
bottom of ice when farmers cut holes into it for winter-fish-
ing. In its shimmering beautiful voice, the stranger asked the
little boy if they could skate together.

Although none of his friends or family could ever skate as
well as the little boy and so he'd always danced alone on the
ice, he was afraid to be rude. So he said yes, and instantly felt
the gloveless ivory hands take his fingers. Even through his
own warm rabbit-fur-lined mittens he could feel the chill of
the stranger's hands. Still, the stranger's voice was silvery and
sweet, the stranger's face was lovely and calm, and the way
the two of them went on to skate together, to dance on the ice
as though gliding through mid-air, was wondrous, ecstatic,
beyond anything the little boy had ever experienced.

They skated, hand in hand, for hours. The way the little

boy had skated with the snow and the wind, that's how he skated with the stranger. Together, they swung round and round, pirouetted, allowed each other under and over, swerved and spun and twisted into figure eights. Hour after hour. Until at last the little boy began to tire. He'd never tired of skating before. But now he could see through the falling snow that the sun was setting, had set, it was midnight black around them.

'Enough!' the little boy cried at last. He tried to pull out of the frozen grip of the stranger, who begged him for one more dance, one more reel, one more spin, one more *pas de deux*. On and on they skated, dancing, until finally the little boy called out, 'Enough, or I fear I'll die!'

Reluctantly the stranger stopped dancing. Then the stranger bowed deep to the little boy. 'Never before,' it said in its voice of silver bells, 'have I met a skater who could keep up with me! Not a half, not a quarter of the time you have honored me with, little sir. Never before have I met your equal.'

No longer afraid, now he had been released and now that he felt warmth crawling back into his hands and arms and feet, the little boy politely said, 'Will you skate with me another day?'

'Alas, I cannot. I must go away,' the stranger said. 'But if you were pleased by our skating, grant me a boon – a single kiss.'

The little boy didn't even think but impulsively reached forward and placed a kiss upon the sterling lips. As he did, the little boy felt encompassed as though by frigid chains: tightly bound within the silver and diamond clothing and the freezing limbs of the stranger, with all warmth being drawn out of his body. He tried to pull away and succeeded enough to withdraw his lips and plead, 'Let me go, please!'

'Know then, impetuous child,' the stranger said frostily, 'with whom you have danced, with whom you have dared carouse all day! I am the Ice Queen, Sovereign of Winter, and after dancing with me, and knowing me, and being loved by me, a human may never know another! Death by freezing cold is your reward for consorting with me – and my heart's delight. But do not be afraid, it will be gentle, like sleep.'

'I beg you, great Queen, let me live, not freeze to death. My friends and family love me. They are good people and will take my passing hard. Let me go. I'll honor you hereafter. I'll skate with you, and you alone. I'll never care for any other the rest of my life.'

'Do you swear it?' the Ice Queen demanded. The little boy solemnly swore the vow. Then the Ice Queen put up an index finger and its silver nail grew into an icicle, sharp as a stiletto, and the Ice Queen said, 'I know the ways of men and how they lie and how they forget. With this bond we seal our vow.' The Ice Queen plunged it into the little boy's breast. To his surprise the boy felt no pain, no hurt.

'The ice now lodges deep in your heart. There shall it remain the rest of your life. You shall grow tall, fairest of all men in the land, adored by all. Princesses, the cream of the land, shall desire you for escort and companion. You may give them your body. You may give them your word. You may give them the sweetest dreams of hope. Never give them your heart. Should you ever warm to another but me, this arrow of ice shall melt away. Your heart shall break and bleed to shreds. You will instantly die!'

With those words, the Ice Queen drew off and spun itself into a silver tornado of sleet and rose to the sky and was gone. Shaken and stunned, not realizing all he had agreed to, nor exactly what he had vowed to make good his escape, the little boy skated away through the snow. When he reached home, his family and friends were barely awake, but amazed and joyful to see him. He'd been gone all night, believed lost in the blizzard, already mourned. They warmed him at their stove and cherished him.

From that day on the little boy went skating on the ice, but though he danced daily with the snow, and pirouetted with the wind, he never again re-encountered the Ice Queen. He grew strong and tall, fairer far than anyone else, just as he'd been promised. In time, his aloof beauty attracted friends from afar, some from great houses. At last he left his beloved

home and wintry lake and moved to the capital, and there by
his looks and cool grace, he gained favor with the royal
household and rose high at the King's court. As he'd been
promised, all desired him, high and low, rich and poor.
Nobles wanted him as chum and escort, Princesses demanded
him as consort. He wed one and became a great peer.

He lived long and prospered beyond his goals. But though
he was widely adored, he could never return a jot of their
love. One by one they turned from him, friend and courtier,
spouse and concubine, companion and child. Old and alone,
surrounded by nurses and hired help, he lay dying. And only
now did he come to see that his adult life had been a show, a
mime. For the price of more years had been direly high: a
frigid heart, a core of ice.

At last, he died, forgotten, unmourned. When they closed
his casket, the few who stood by, all remarked on the corpse's
great chill, on the snowy and overcast, ill-chosen morn, on
the hardness of the frozen earth. Also how fast, once the box
was shrouded in earthen dirt, frosty rime surrounded it,
encasing it in a silver shell – a carapace of rock-hard snow
and polar ice.

After I'd read Len's fable, I lay in bed a long time, thinking. I'd
never felt so close to him as then, lying in what, for some months,
had been his bed, sleeping in what for six years had been his house,
reading his story, his fable: a story – if I were willing to admit it – not
terribly different than my own.

I'm not certain when it was that I became aware of the cricket. I'd
almost fallen asleep when I was startled awake by its chirping. It
sounded so close, I turned to look. The window was open. I got up
and closed it and went back to bed. Closed my eyes. Ahhh! Sweet
sleep! I heard the cricket chirp again. This time louder. It must be
inside the house! Inside this room. Maybe if I ignored it? I was, after
all, very tired. That's what I tried to do, ignore it. It didn't work. As
though intuiting my intent, the cricket chirped on and on. Damn! I
got up and lit the table lamp and put a shirt over my bare torso and
went searching for it.

Not under the bed. Not under the furniture that I could see. I stopped and listened. There it was! Low down. My head down near the floorboards, I listened again, followed the sound. Yes, very close to the floorboards. Maybe it was *in* the floorboards. No. Couldn't be. I wouldn't hear it so clearly then. I needed more light. Put them all on! Was that it, scuttling along just under the poorly fitting lower molding and floor?

I followed the scuttling sound into the dressing room. It stopped. I kicked at the wall near where I thought the cricket might be. Then listened. The next time I heard the cricket chirp it had moved yet again. I kicked again, afraid I'd hurt myself or, worse, wake my host. Was his bedroom directly above this? I didn't recall. I'd not toured upstairs. Didn't know the layout of the rooms up there.

Wait, there it was! Headed toward the bathroom! I followed it again. Hoping that by kicking at the molding and annoying it, or better yet frightening it, I'd be able to move it out of my part of the house. This took effort. It went the wrong way for a few minutes once it had reached the floor and molding in the bathroom, and I thought that if anyone saw me, they'd conclude I was acting like a madman, kicking the floorboards, talking to someone or something no one, not even I, could see. Maybe I should just take a sleeping pill? They must have one in the cabinet here, no?

I rummaged through the bathroom shelves, all the while listening to the poor stupid, scared cricket chirping its brains out. At last I found a Sominex. Getting it out of its child-proof package was a chore. I realized how sleepy I was, decided to only take one. Took it with water. Then got angry and started kicking at the floorboards all around myself, immediately silencing the cricket. I stood listening. Nothing. Was it gone? At last. Or had it run back into the dressing area and from there would go back to where I'd first heard it, in the bedroom?

I was standing there, listening intently. Nothing! I opened the bathroom door into the dining room. Nothing. Wait! Was that it? A cricket. Maybe not mine but, yes, clearly a cricket. I went back to the dressing area and listened. No cricket. Went back into the bedroom. No cricket. Good! It worked! I knew that closing doors meant nothing to a cricket, which could sidle under them. Even so, I would go back and shut all the doors between me and the dining room, between me and the cricket chirping. I pulled the string chain of the overhead bathroom bulb to put out the light, with the dining-room door ajar, still listening to make sure the cricket was outside, not in. I didn't hear it. Fine. I shut the bathroom light.

What was that glow? From the other end of the first floor? Did it come from the kitchen? Hard to tell with the door between the dining room and the pantry ajar like that. Maybe it was my imagination? The Sominex? Sure!

I closed the dining-room door, the bathroom door, the dressing-area door and went back to bed. But although I could only hear the cricket at a distance now, I still couldn't sleep, thinking of that glow. Maybe De Petrie had left on the outside light, near the garage. I got up and went to the window on that side of the house. No, the porch light used for the driveway was out. But I saw the same glow. It seemed to come from inside that part of the house. Could it be a flashlight? A burglar?

I couldn't very well awaken De Petrie, could I? I grabbed one of the window sticks used to keep the heavy windows from falling closed and, wielding it before me as a weapon, I went out through the three doors, quietly padding into the dining room. From there I used the stick to nudge open the ajar door into the pantry. The pantry to kitchen door was also ajar, and the glow was beyond. I trod down the steps and once more braced myself for trouble and once more nudged open the ajar door. The kitchen was dark. Through one window I could see the glow was a light and the light was on inside the double-doored garage. I couldn't believe De Petrie kept it on intentionally all night. Had he forgotten it was on?

The door from the kitchen to the garage was locked and bolted. I undid the locks, trod cautiously, and carefully edged open the door. Before me were five steep little wooden steps down to the concrete floor of the garage. I couldn't see very deeply into the garage. But it was lighted. I slowly dropped down the stairs. No one was in the garage. On the left, just under the turned-on light-bulb, were the built-in cabinets, shelves, desk top, work bench, all of what De Petrie had called Len Spurgeon's workshop. It looked untouched. Tools put away. Nothing obviously out of place. Neither the Sport Utility nor the Beemer was kept indoors, except, I supposed, during winter months, so the garage was empty but for the workshop and, on the other side, three tall plastic garbage and leaf pails and a few slotted wooden boxes for deposit bottles and beercans. Remembering every B suspense movie, where the enemy is always hiding above ready to leap down, I looked up. Crossed slats – thinner than two by fours, maybe one by twos – barely holding up the weight of aluminum lawn chairs, paper lamp shades, a few light-looking boxes. It wouldn't support anything heavy as a man. I stepped forward. I felt funny. As though someone was here, present, with me. Where? I found a flashlight and switched it on. Its tight beam explored every shadowy corner of the place until I had ascertained I was alone. I put it back where I'd found it, noticing two other flashlights, and a lantern. I found the wall switch and turned it off. I walked up the few steps. As I turned and closed the door I said, 'Good night.'

To whom? I couldn't say. The presiding spirit of the house? The *lares* or *penates* that I felt lived exactly there? I didn't know. Maybe it was the Sominex working. Because by the time I'd gotten back to my bed through the darkened lower floor of the house, I was exhausted. My head hit the pillow and I was out!

Albinoni awakened me: two oboes intimately exchanging motifs in courtly larghetto, while violins sighed from the sidelines. After a few seconds, I realized the sound was, almost angelically, coming from above. I moved the curtains. Stark, strong sun. The clock read almost ten. That Sominex had really worked!

In the dining room, a place was laid out for breakfast next to the window bird feeder. A thermos of hot coffee, fresh croissants, confiture. I was starved. I ate for ten minutes before I wondered where my host was. After I'd cleared and washed my breakfast plates in the kitchen, I showered and changed. The Beemer and the Sports Ute were still in the driveway, the Z-5 parked slightly differently than he'd left it last night. I guessed he might be upstairs, and called from the bottom of the step in the entry foyer.

The Baroque concerto ceased. De Petrie called something in response and I took it to mean I ought to go up. I was greeted by a peaked-roof stairway landing the size of the downstairs parlor. Light slanted in from two dormered windows on one side, a small reading area made by placing an overstuffed armchair next to a Queen Anne tea table. Exactly opposite the stairway, flanked by an ancient highboy and antedeluvian painted pine chest, ajar doors disclosed windows in two small bedrooms. A modern-looking bathroom occupied the short side of the wide-planked landing, a corridor the long side. I glanced into a large, bright white and pale green bedroom I guessed to be his on my way to the end.

I knocked on the door, heard 'Come on in!' and opened to a narrow room with dormered windows on either end, the walls built out of plain lumber bookshelves. In the far corner another beat-up, cozy looking armchair and knee-high table. In the other, a modern computer desk with what looked to be a full array of the latest cybernetic office equipment.

De Petrie half twirled in his large mahogany deskchair. 'You're not interrupting anything in the least bit literary. I usually do correspondence and on-line finances in the morning. Did you have breakfast? Was it enough or are you still hungry? Did you sleep okay? Have you confirmed your flight? Do you need anything else? Have you read the piece? Do I sound exactly like Aaron Axenfeld?'

'Yes. Yes. No. Yes. Yes. No. Yes. And, precisely like him.'

'Have a seat. Give me a sec here, okay?' he said, and spun back around to finish what he was doing. I sat on the edge of the armchair, in view of the trees and birds and garden outside. Much as that was diverting, it couldn't compare to what was here. After a few minutes, I began to inspect the lines of books stacked almost carelessly and without organization upon the poorly sanded lath shelves. As I hoped, several were filled with De Petrie's own books, hardcovers, first editions, trade paperbacks, mass market versions, book club volumes, foreign translations, reprints, anthologies he'd been included in. On the shelves above were books in various versions and editions of the other Purple Circle members. Maybe another fifty or so volumes. A real treasure trove if they were autographed. When I drew one out to check, sure enough Mark Dodge had written on the flyleaf of a first edition hardcover of *Keep Frozen*, 'For Dom, on behalf of an intimate, long continuing intercourse with the Alfred A. Knopf Company', and it was appended, 'A representative thereof aims to please'. The *double entendre* brought me down from the literary empyrean as I realized what the dedication meant: they'd already had sex by then. Mark was telling De Petrie he wanted more.

Before I could slip it back into its place, De Petrie click-clicked the mouse, turned and said, 'Done! What do you have there?'

'I didn't mean to . . .' I handed over the book.

He looked at it barely a second. 'Well! My reputation is safe today,' he said and laughed his distinctive laugh. 'So? You read the fable?'

'I read it. I liked it. Someone should publish it.'

'By itself? It requires context.'

'Would Len have wanted it published?' I asked.

De Petrie shrugged.

'It's yours to do with as . . .? I began and stopped.

'As we both know, Ross, it's always more complicated than that.'

'I feel,' I began, 'there's still so much about him I don't yet know. His background. His childhood. His . . .'

'You mean is the car accident story true?' De Petrie interrupted. 'I don't know. I do know he was the second child of four. That the first boy died as a child. He never said under what circumstances. Is the story his? If so, is it, while fake, a dramatization of some less melodramatic incident, yet an objective correlative for the guilt the little boy felt? Who knows? Is the story about the Eagle's Nest on Christmas Eve true? I can't imagine young Len not getting whomever he wanted. Maybe it was about someone else. Len never told me anything about seeing a gazillion flamingos. Nor being on a cable car when a line snapped. But there was a great deal he didn't tell me.'

'What did he tell you?'

'He told me he was homosexual early on. That by eight or nine years old, he was having sex with boys. By the time he was fourteen, he'd had scores of local kids. When the other boys stopped fooling around and went after girls, he knew he was queer. He went after the horniest boys he could find then. The ones who were a little slow. The ones who couldn't hide their boners. The older guys who worked for his parents part-time on the farm. The jocks. He told me that when they moved to Bettendorf, he went into athletics because on the first day of Phys. Ed. he recognized that the track and field coach was also queer and had the hots for him. Between the two of them, they seduced most of the varsity teams. It helped Len was such a good athlete. When they needed a baseball star, Len came out and pitched and won. After every winning game, girls would throw themselves at him. He'd politely slip away and then pick himself another young athlete's cherry. He sucked and fucked his way through the minor leagues, and the majors. And he never hid it. Everyone knew he was queer. They'd joke about it, he told me. His teammates would actually help him bed guys. He'd come home and find someone waiting for him, he said. Anything to keep their star pitcher happy. This was the early '70s, when it was all very hush-hush. Then that football player came out. Dave Kopay! Len watched him do the talk-show circuits, the newspaper interviews, write that book – and be forced out of his profession! He figured the same would happen to him. Why bother? He'd stay where he was, and get what he wanted – most of the time, anyway.

'Then he met Mark Dodge and the unexpected happened. Len fell for him. Len had never felt anything but what Whitman called "the camaraderie of manly love". But Mark Dodge had that effect on many people.'

'Not on you!' I interrupted, remembering the inscription.

'Don't get me wrong! Mark Dodge was the absolute primo piece of male ass of the era. We did it a few times. But he didn't, you know, grip my imagination. His writing, now. *That* was something else! I *loved* his books. Of all my contemporaries, probably Mark and Axey are the ones I most enjoyed reading then, and now too. Possibly because they're so individual. Their imagined worlds are so very close to reality, yet totally their own. And utterly different from mine. Where was I? Right! Len fell for Mark. And for a while Mark fell for Len. And because they were both public figures, the affair went public very fast. Len didn't quite suffer from Kopay's problem, but he lost his privacy and a lot of the pixie dust that had surrounded him before. When Mark went on to even greater fame, and then moved on to an off-Broadway actor about to make it big, Len went into a depression and, worse, into a slump. A few years later, he was back in the minors. When his interest waned, he began working other angles. Coaching. Training. Modeling. Porn movies. Bartending. Whatever. The rest, you know.'

'Among the fragments I read, there's nothing about Mark,' I said. 'Nothing, you know . . . negative or bitter!'

'Oddly,' De Petrie said, 'I think the character Theo in the story about the cable car might be construed as a portrait of Mark Dodge. You know, a decade after, when Mark was living in LA and had another lover, a fellow I only met once. Maybe. Don't quote me on it,' De Petrie temporized. 'And since I'm suppositioning here, I think a case could be made for the bar story being told from Jeff Weber's P.O.V. Pretty as Jeff was, he struck out in bars and clubs all the time. Guys would pick up on all the edges and burrs and quirks in his personality really fast and that was it. So that piece might have a been a slap at Jeff. I have no idea at all if what Bobbie Bonaventura told you about that bank robbery was true or not. Mitch Leo's letter sounds totally true. So does Frankie McKewen's "Berlin Diaries".'

'And Cameron Powers?' I asked.

'Well, the C. A. T. is out of the bag. That's true. As for Dame . . . I don't understand it. I would have thought that of any of us . . . he would have been the one who took Len to the Caribbean. I guess we're all busy in our own way rewriting history at this stage of our lives. You packed and ready? I don't mean to rush you, but . . .'

De Petrie was out at the Z-5 rummaging through the car's back trunk for something when I brought out my luggage.

'You didn't happen to see a narrow flashlight back here?' he asked. 'It's supposed to be attached here, next to the internal CD changer. It's pale green.'

I said no, then remembered where I thought I might have seen it. 'Could it be in the garage? The workshop?'

Before he could ask how I could possibly know that, I headed toward the garage, and slipped in through a space in the slightly ajar double doors.

Not too long later, I was back out at the car with the flashlight in hand. As I handed it to De Petrie, the two of us found ourselves in a peculiar instant of *déjà vu*. He suddenly looked around. I did too. It had grown quiet, utterly without birdsong, all around us. But though we both listened for several minutes longer, looking at each other for signs, no ravens signaled their appearance with their characteristic caw-cawing. Another pause and the moment was over.

Book Ten

FROM THE PARADISE GARDEN

...I guess in the end it comes down to who has it and
who doesn't have it. All the rest is baloney.

Len Spurgeon, letter to a teammate

I'D NEVER BEEN THIS CONFUSED driving in LA before. I'd managed okay to get from Burbank Airport where I'd left the rented car for the weekend over to Route 170 going south. I knew that would connect to the Ventura Freeway, 101, and from there I could take any of three exits, Highland, Cahuenga or Vine, to Franklin Street and easily over to Casa Herrera y Lopez. But while I thought I was following the signs correctly, all of a sudden another Freeway, 134, going to Glendale and Pasadena, interfered. What was supposed to be a single break-off became two, one after the other. I took what I thought was the correct turn-off but once I emerged from the endlessly long cloverleaf, I found myself somehow wrong. The next exit should have read Moorpark Road. Instead it read Tujunga Avenue. What? I slipped into the slow lane and the next exit approaching was not as I'd hoped, Ventura Boulevard, but instead Laurel Canyon Boulevard. With another sign announcing Studio City. Meaning I was headed in the opposite direction. I flipped on my directionals too late for whomever was right behind me in a large black pickup, who proceeded to blow his horn long and loud to express indignation at my lack of thoughtfulness. Hey, I made a mistake! Sue me! Even so, I got off the freeway, thinking I'd immediately go around, get back on, and return the way I'd been originally headed. Only problem was, at night, in a strange part of town, I couldn't locate the on-ramp.

On the other hand, there directly in front of me was Laurel Canyon Boulevard and I knew where that went. At least, I knew in one direction. Not a week ago, driving home from Camden Phoenix's studio, I'd taken it and had a fun drive through the Santa Monica Mountains. Why not do it again? It had been a jam-packed airplane flight, a long, cramped ride back from Boston. And while productive – I'd spent half the trip writing up an explanatory introduction to my thesis which I planned to hand in to Dr St George tomorrow, along with all the documentation I'd shown Dominic

390 THE BOOK OF LIES

De Petrie – even so I'd still been irritated and felt a great deal put upon. My seat companions were an overweight, middle-aged married couple who liked to spread out, the family in front had a noisy, nosy eight-year-old boy and the folks behind were traveling with a cranky baby not even my earplugs could totally block. After close to six hours of all that, my nerves were more than a little jangled by the time we'd landed, thankfully after not circling overhead too long. No wonder concentration was difficult as I'd worked: words kept eluding me, well-known, often-utilized examples of sentence structure had proven evasive or, when accessible, had come out juvenile and cliché-ridden. Perhaps driving would make me feel more capable, more accomplished, lift my spirits a bit?

Within two traffic lights I recognized the road. The four lanes ascended smoothly, veered left, right and sharply left. It was past midnight and the traffic was moderate and, as before, fast. Around me I noticed a French-blue Z-5 with a ragtop, a Mercedes-Benz coupé, a Firebird, two Jeeps and was that the same black pickup truck I'd stiffed? Looked like it. We whirled up, around and past Mulholland Drive, then down, merging into a narrow two-lane road. I was once more surprised by how the road twisted in smaller and smaller Ss, rising, opening out into an abruptly appearing canyon, then closing down into a mere gulch.

As I completed a particularly sharp, angled left curve, and immediately countered that with a right curve, I realized the black pickup from the freeway had managed to get behind me. The road ran downhill, curling into tighter and tighter S-turns, and cars in the opposite lane seemed once more to fling themselves directly at me, their headlights in my eyes one after another. As before, all of us were moving so fast, it seemed we all but rode each other's tail bumpers.

Which didn't at all explain matters when the black pickup actually bumped the Celica from behind as the road spun and rose up to a stoplight flashing red. I felt it with a jolt and, in reaction, I pulled away with a burst of acceleration as I flew up and then down a shallow S that ended suddenly at another stoplight, also green, which I shot through like a bullet. Despite the fact that I'd picked up maybe five miles per hour of speed, I could see the black pickup also kept up and was only inches from my rear fender spoiler. Not because there were cars behind pushing it. There weren't. In front of me headlights flashed from around another unexpected bend, blinding me, swerving across my view, as I tried to pull away from the black pickup again. Was the driver harassing me because of a grudge? Because of that sudden slowdown I'd done on the freeway? It couldn't have bothered him that much? Could it?

The road curled up on itself, and I felt the pickup bump me again. And again. This was clear and intentional. I remembered now hearing students in my class talking about car assaults. How people in larger, stronger vehicles would purposely bump into, even crash into smaller cars, waiting until the driver in the front vehicle stopped and got out and then how they would assault, sometimes even shoot the driver. Was that happening? Was this such an onslaught? Or was I imagining this? My adrenalin was rushing. I was doing all I could to remain calm.

I raised the speed to sixty on the next straightaway but I had to brake suddenly for an upcoming tight curve and then for another. I'd always felt confident in this car, felt sure it could do anything I asked of it, but the black pickup was keeping up with me, and now I was becoming aware that my adrenalin was rising out of control, making me nervous, angry, open to mistakes as the road curved yet again, opening into two lanes per side as suddenly as it had closed down into one lane before and meanwhile kept swiveling to the right, going straight, curving, straight, corkscrewing down at an incredible angle. The pickup moved between the two lanes of space it had and continued bumping me again and again, blowing its horn.

I tried to see who in the hell it was as I accelerated faster, praying the Celica would retain its grip on the turns, and despite the darkness and how little I could keep him in my sights because of all the twisting and slewing, I could make out the figure at the wheel of the pickup was tall and thin and dark-haired. Ray Rice? He had a pickup, didn't he? I tried to remember as we swerved and I tried to get further out in front of him, praying there were no cars stopped directly ahead in case I had to suddenly brake. Ray Rice would be stupid enough for this kind of antic, wouldn't he?

Whoever the driver was, he kept bumping me, crashing his front fender into one back fender of the Celica then the other, rapidly swerving back and forth so I couldn't get a good look at him. Why?

Ray or whoever? For fun? To scare me? And wait, now we were headed into a straightaway and coming up ahead on the left soon, wouldn't that be my turn-off to Hollywood Boulevard? The one I'd missed before? Yes!

I swung into the left lane, determined to hold my place despite him even as he continued bashing my right back fender, now seeming to aim for my wheel wells, as though he was trying to knock the wheel off the axle. Meanwhile, we hurtled down the mountainside, going far too fast for the road, flew around two more tight bends. I saw cars approaching, but luckily they stopped at the streetlight, three of them, and I took that as my chance. Without warning or directionals, I abruptly swung left onto Hollywood, almost hitting a car approaching from its correct side, but in the loud horn-blaring mess managing my turn, even though the car did tip slightly and the tires squealed for mercy. I was clear. I'd lost the black pickup.

Sensing it would come looking for me, I slowed and made a left turn as immediately as I could, then a right, another left, and I pulled the Celica right into the driveway of a two-story Norman-style house on what I guessed to be upper Ogden. The automatic outside house lights went on. I shut off the car lights and sat, idling, my heart pounding. The house lights went off again.

Sure enough, a minute later, I could see in my back mirrors the black pickup slowly cruising by on Ogden, searching for me. From this angle, I got a profile, a tall one, and I could see it definitely wasn't Ray Rice driving the pickup, which didn't in the least pacify me.

Then who? Some lunatic? Wait! That profile, though brief, had not been totally unfamiliar? I thought I knew who it belonged to. Who?

I waited another four, five minutes, then with all of my car lights still turned off, I slowly pulled out of the driveway. With car lights off, I crawled along back streets parallel to Franklin and crept slowly up the road leading to Von Slyke's house. As I approached the gate, I could have sworn I just missed the black pickup by seconds as its lunatic driver trawled for me.

By this point, I was so freaked I parked on the side of the road by the Casa Herrera's main gate and slumped over to make the car look empty should he drive by again as I dialed my way in through the gate, all the while checking around for the pickup. I counted the long seconds it took for the gate to open completely. Then dashed the car in, again parked and again slumped over as I dialed the gate closed. Finally, the gate was shut, and damn it, there was the pickup cruising by. It even seemed to slow at the gate, as though the driver were peering in, looking for me. Then he was gone. I shot around the circular driveway and didn't stop until I was deep within the motor court, the Celica hidden by the foliage and house walls.

My heart was still racing. When I looked into the rear-view mirror to check that I was alone, I saw my face too, my face as I'd never seen it before: bloodless, haunted, gaunt with fear.

Although her car was parked outside, I didn't see Conchita in the house when I entered. I went straight to the kitchen bar and found an open bottle of bourbon in the cabinet and, standing in the almost dark room, I poured it neat into a glass and drank it. I was still shaking. I drank another shot. After a few minutes I felt a smidgen better. I went out and got my bags from the car and dropped them in my room. I was still shaking. I went back to the kitchen for another shot of bourbon.

This time Conchita was there, in a dressing gown, barefoot, not sleepy at all. She looked at me and did something with her upper lip. I looked at what I was doing and said, 'I had a terrible flight back. Driving back here from the airport someone tried to run me off the road.' I sipped again. 'He kept on crashing into me. I don't know why. I thought we were going to crash. Go up in flames. I'm lucky I'm alive. The car must be a mess!'

I was about to pour another drink, but her hand shot out and stopped me. 'I've got pills,' she said. 'They're better. They'll calm you down.' She took the bottle away from me and put it back on its cabinet shelf. She vanished into her room. A minute later she was back with two flat yellow pills in the palm of her hand. 'Go on!' she urged. 'Take them.'

I took the pills. Washed them down with water.

'You got a delivery. Urgent,' Conchita said. 'I left it in the library.'

'Who from?'

She shrugged.

I slogged up the stairs into the library and turned on the desk-lamp. A hand-delivered envelope. Same day. It was on Dr Irian St George's office letterhead and without greeting or preamble it read: 'Be in my office tomorrow morning at nine o'clock. Before your classes. This cannot wait!' No signature. What the hell?

Conchita was standing at the sill of the library door. 'Mr Von Slyke phoned. I said you were gone. He didn't sound too happy. He said he'd call again tomorrow.'

I tried to think what in the hell this was all about. Could the papers have not arrived at the Timrod Collection?

Whatever it was, on top of today, tonight, the last half-hour, it was more than I could handle. I shut off the library lamp and walked past Conchita back down the stairs and into my room. I don't think I even said good night to her. I did begin to brush my teeth. By then the liquor or the liquor and the pills or the liquor and the pills and the shock of the driving assault and all the adrenalin leaving my body conspired to totally enervate me. I dropped the brush in the sink. I did manage to get my clothing off and myself into bed. Barely.

That night I had strange dreams. In one of them, Conchita was straddling my body as I lay in bed. She was totally naked, sitting on my cock, her rouged, pointed breasts bouncing up and down, her head and hair swiveling back and forth, strange high whinnying sounds coming out her throat. I couldn't move, couldn't do a thing but lie there. I didn't feel any particular pleasure, or pain – anything, really. The dream seemed to go on a long time. It was replaced by others far more fantastic.

St George was on the phone when I entered his office. I took this as a good sign. He waved a finger in a roughly corkscrew direction, gesturing me to sit and wait. I did. He was listening to someone on the other end of the receiver. 'In-dis-put-ably!' he expostulated, then spun in his chair to face away from me toward the window overlooking the campus. He continued to listen. Said something I didn't catch.

That morning I'd awakened early and surprisingly refreshed, I supposed because of the pills Conchita had given me on top of the bourbon on top of the length and multitude of experiences of the previous day. I'd not seen Conchita and guessed she was out early on some domestic errand. But as soon as I'd had my coffee, I'd phoned the Timrod Collection, and spoken to the director's Connecticut-lockjaw assistant, who confirmed that the Von Slyke papers had arrived there intact, *in toto*, last Friday. He faxed me a copy of the receipt listing the number of boxes and confirming my own list of contents, and also faxed me a copy of the sizable check he'd cut for Von Slyke, which was to be sent directly to his bank account. Thus armed with nothing but good news, I'd tried phoning the author at the last number I had for him in Majorca. Received a high-pitched male British voice phone-answering machine. I'd left a message saying when I expected to be back at the Casa Herrera y Lopez, and I'd driven to UCLA early. I'd of course noticed the many new bumps and crunches and paint-scraping marks on the back and side fenders of the poor Celica, but it was far less damage than I'd feared. Now, a half-hour before my literature class was to begin, I felt a jot of contentment that whatever urgency St George wanted to see me about, it wasn't any bibliographic screw-up.

'In-dis-put-ably!' St George repeated again loudly, then spun around and flung a manila envelope on the desk. It was addressed to him at the English Department, and he gestured for me to open it. 'Then it's sett-led!' he said, and hung up the phone.

'This ar-rived this morning from Mr Rice Sen-ior!'

I opened the envelope and four eight by ten glossies slid out. All of them were taken from maybe fifteen feet away, all from the same angle, and all of them quite clearly showed a threequarters view over the lip of the Jacuzzi hot tub to within, picturing myself, half in half out of the water, receiving a blow job from Ray Rice Junior. I knew that when they'd been taken, I had been trying to push his head away from my genitals. Here, however, it looked exactly the opposite, as though I were pushing his head toward them. The snapshots looked as though they'd been taken from above the level of the terrace itself. From where, though? Maybe the open windows on the corridor of the house outside the dining room? Using what kind of equipment? I'd noticed no bright flashes. It must have been infrared film? The next question was who had done it? But since Ray had himself easily sneaked back into the house, it was apparent that someone else also might have come back specifically to take photos. It was a set-up from the beginning.

To say I was appalled by these photos doesn't begin to describe it.
That horror must have been clear on my face when I looked up at St
George, who was staring away from me, carefully, needlessly, check-
ing his perfectly manicured fingernails.

'Ad-mir-at-ion would be my na-tu-ral res-ponse!' St George said,
'if the sit-u-a-tion were not so fraught with ex-traneous im-pli-ca-
tions! Un-for-tu-nate-ly for us both, it is so fraught!' He moved his
gaze to his other hand. 'Al-so, un-fort-unate-ly, ex-plan-at-ions are
un-ac-cept-able in these very serious matters of teachers con-sor-
ting with students. You're aware of the rules. There can be no
ex-cep-tions. Someone else will take your class, of course! It's
already been assigned.'

Shock after shock.

'You mean someone will be taking it over today?'

'Nat-ur-al-ly! But all is not lost! I'm sure no charges will be filed
against you. And if so, I'll put them off somehow. The act certainly
ap-*pears* con-sen-su-al. Although they can argue otherwise. You're
not without re-sources. You have your the-sis to work on. The Von
Slyke papers too!'

'I finished them last week. I sent them off. They've been received
at the Timrod Collection.' I showed the faxed receipt. 'And paid for,'
I added.

He looked at the papers with a weary smile.

Encouraged, I went on, 'As for the thesis, I worked up a rough
first draft of it for you. After meeting with Axenfeld and De Petrie.
That went well. They were helpful, and very nice to me.'

'I'm very glad,' he said, not sounding it. 'You brought something
for me to look at?'

I handed him the envelope containing my intro and photocopies
of all the documentation. Len's five fragments, the letters and diaries
and statements of heirs and executors. My heart was thudding worse
than last night when the black pickup had been chasing me, but I
knew I had to soldier on, not fall victim to complete despair.

'These photos! They're not what they seem to be.' And when St
George looked at me as though to say please, don't bother, I added,
'I mean they are obviously what they seem to be. But it was all his
doing. He surprised me in the hot tub. I didn't make him do anything or even want him to or . . .' I trailed off. St George had said

before it made no difference what explanation I came up with. The truth sounded lame even to me. 'Ray told me before that he's gay and his father doesn't want him to be gay and he's very upset about it. Although I don't know why he'd set me up like this. Unless . . . Well, I don't know.'

St George was inspecting his cuticles again.

'At any rate, I'm sorry you have to be involved in all this. Really I am. Very sorry. Although to tell the truth, I don't know how I could have possibly avoided it happening. Except by not taking the class in the first place. Which is, I guess, what Ray Rice, Senior and Junior, wanted.'

Still no response. The phone rang and, given his usual languid manner, St George all but jumped for it.

A second later, he covered the mouthpiece of the phone and said to me, 'I'll have to take this call. Stop by the Bursar's office and sign for your final paycheck.' One of his perfectly manicured hands had fallen like a talon atop the envelope containing what I'd put together of my thesis. 'I'll look this over and get back to you.'

Despite that relatively high final note between us, by the time I managed to get out of the languages building without attracting anyone in particular's attention, I could feel my entire body sagging, my steps falter, my heart bruised inside me as though someone had been pounding upon my chest. I aimed toward the bursar's office via what I believe to be the longest and most circuitous path possible, partly to try to attempt to reintegrate myself from the blows I'd received as well as to avoid being seen in this condition and partly to keep off those campus short cuts students usually took. Despite this, I spotted Kathy Tranh – luckily before she saw me – on her way to Royce Hall, to my class, where in a few minutes she'd be treated to another teacher, astonished and, I hoped, grieved to discover I'd no longer be teaching. I wondered who actually had taken over the class, and how the person would react to my curriculum – follow it to the letter or amend it so much it totally warped the course.

My business at Administration was accomplished quickly and without questions asked or emotions expressed by the clerk or myself. Within a half-hour after arriving I was off the campus again, driving back to Hollywood. Not the most pleasant drive of my life, although for once traffic conditions had nothing to do with that, nor with my inner state. I couldn't stop thinking about those photos and how they'd been taken, how they'd been used, how naïve I had been to have been so easily framed. I still couldn't figure out why. I'd already made it clear that I liked Ray Rice and would pass him in class. Could this have been insurance? Or insurance that I'd not tell his father or anyone else what he'd done to me in that hot tub?

I also kept thinking about what my brother-in-law Bart Vanuzzi had said to me at the Fort Myers Airport, about how inexperienced I was, how open to being gulled. He'd warned me. He must have sensed something was going on. Everyone said that was one of Bart's major strengths as a quarterback, that he could intuit where the best receiver was and, even with three monster linebackers blocking his view, know exactly who to throw the ball to. I also couldn't help but wonder how this incident would end up being reflected on my record. Could St George just X the entire class and my part in it? Or note that the course had been divided in two and taken over by two instructors? He could. But would he? I also wondered what more the Rices planned. Criminal charges didn't seem likely, as Ray Junior was of age. There could be a civil action. It would be my word against his. That would be undoubtedly ugly.

Conchita wasn't home when I got there. I still felt terrible and wondered if I shouldn't go to bed. I'd just entered the house from in front and was passing through the library when the phone rang. I picked it up and got Von Slyke.

'The Timrod Collection received your papers and faxed me a receipt. They also faxed me a receipt for the check they deposited in your account.'

'Yes! I know,' he replied. 'That's what you said in your message.'

'I thought you'd be pleased,' I said.

'Yes. Very pleased. You'll be receiving a check for your services. Where should I have it sent?'

'Excuse me!'

'Well, it stands to reason that you can't possibly stay there any longer,' Von Slyke said.

'What? Why not?' Had he talked to St George? And anyway what difference would that make?

'Why not?' Von Slyke asked, sounded himself astounded. 'Because I can't very well be responsible for having you staying in the house at the same time Conchita is there. It's out of the question! I have obligations to her.'

'I gave up my apartment. Where will I go? Don't you also have obligations to me? I don't understand.'

'You don't understand?' Von Slyke scoffed. 'Well, let's begin with your initial lies and prevarications about yourself and your personal situation. Then move to your betrayal of my trust.'

'When? How did I betray you?'

'Ross, don't play innocent with me. Conchita mailed me your divorce papers. The papers sent to your address in Westwood and forwarded to my place which arrived as she was speaking on the phone to me here two days ago. She said they looked official and I asked her to open them. You do realize what I'm speaking about now, don't you? The papers finalizing your divorce from, what's her name? Here it is! Christina Ohrenstedt, née Crowell. Does that name ring a bell? Sound at all familiar?'

Chris. Again. I didn't know what to say.

'I take it the name is familiar, then,' Von Slyke said, triumphantly, 'and that your two-and-a-half-year marriage to her was not a figment of the imagination of the State Family Court of New York. I also take it that you are not going to attempt the extreme foolishness of trying, in this advanced day and age, to explain it away or deny it. Are you, Ross?'

'No.'

'Good! Now if you'll answer one more question. You're not gay either, are you? Not gay. Not even bisexual, are you?'

'You have to understand, Mr Von Slyke . . . I knew if I was going to write about the Purple Circle and be taken seriously by anyone, including yourselves, that I'd be totally suspect unless I fit in, unless I . . .'

'*Thank* you!' he interrupted. 'I've heard enough. I see now you aren't at all gay. Which is unfortunate, given how attractive you are. Not to mention how totally you fooled us all. However, it is also why you have to leave my house, today, Ross! Burton and I have advanced our air tickets. We're coming home early tomorrow.'

'You don't let straight people stay in your house?'

'It's not that, Ross. But it is partly the reason why I'm afraid I can't allow you to remain in the house with Conchita, not one more day. Or, rather, one more night. It's not entirely that I don't trust you, Ross, although why I should trust you after all of these lies I couldn't begin to say. No, even if you swore you'd be a perfect gentleman and never touch her, I just can't take the chance with Conchita also being aware of the fact that you're not gay. Not now. Not given the extremely tumultuous and mentally troubled life she's had. Her history of emotional problems, the various charges and allegations around sexual matters . . . I'm sorry, Ross, but I feel my debt to you is fulfilled. Or rather it will be fulfilled when you receive the check. As for Conchita, she's been with me for years. I promised her mother I'd take care of her. I cannot go back on my word, not to mention jeopardize years of work, all the progress we've accomplished.'

For the briefest of moments I thought I'd tell him all his work and progress *had* been for nothing, that Conchita had already gone and done what he was afraid of. It hadn't been a dream – she had indeed drugged and fucked me last night. Instead, I said, 'If I have to leave tonight, I'll have to stay in a hotel. I can't afford that on what . . .'

'I'll take care of a hotel for one week. Although it's the sheerest generosity on my part,' Von Slyke said. 'Your check will not be a small one, when it arrives. Whatever else, I really do appreciate all you've done there. The people at the Timrod Collection said it was superb. But I can't stake you to any fancy hotel. My hetero brother stays at the Holiday Inn in Hollywood. There are lots of "babes" around the pool, he said.'

I passed the slur and said, 'I'll leave the name of the place I find inside your desk. It'll probably be closer to school.'

Twenty-five minutes later I had my bags and papers packed and was headed out on my second trip to the battered Celica parked in front of the house. I stopped, noticing the extreme oddity of the Casa Herrera y Lopez being left wide open, and a second later the reason why. Stationary there was Conchita's Corolla and the same black pickup that had chased and crashed into me repeatedly the previous night. Conchita was talking to someone in the pickup. Not talking as though he were a stranger asking directions, but in a friendly, casual manner. I got the rest of my stuff into the trunk of the Celica. Using the cover of thick hibiscus bush that lined the circular driveway to the gate, I skulked my way to within ten feet of where they were. Given the quantity and location of paint scrapes on the truck's front bumper, I was certain it was the same one that attacked my Celica.

I was just in time to see Conchita take a single step up the tiny chrome running board of the black pickup and kiss the driver. This could only mean one thing. She'd told him when and probably also what flight I'd be on, coming into Burbank Airport, last night. She'd told him the car I'd be driving: the model, year and color. He'd followed me, not just after the freeway turn-off, where I'd noticed him, but all the while, possibly from the parking lot, maybe from the arrivals lounge. The attack had been planned in advance. I couldn't think why that might be, although I now did understand something else about the recent phone call with Von Slyke: Conchita had seen my divorce papers in with the mail, had guessed what they were, opened them and only then had she called Von Slyke. Now that I thought of it, she'd actually asked me that day for confirmation of where Von Slyke was before she'd called to tell him about the divorce papers and thus screw me. The question was, why had she done it?

As she withdrew from the open truck window, Conchita's hand lingered on the face of the man she'd just kissed. Thus I saw not only who the driver of the black pickup was, but I also understood in a flash all of what had happened and why. For the man driving the black pickup and whose profile I now realized was the same as the driver's profile I'd not quite been able to place last night was – Waterford Machado. My rival for Fusumi's chair at UCLA. Who had followed me from the airport. Who had doubtless been screwing Conchita for a while, or at least long enough to have seen his chance to do me in when I'd first moved into Von Slyke's house. He or maybe she or maybe the two together had taken advantage of Ray Rice jumping into the hot tub with me and had snapped those photos of us and sent them to Rice Senior. There had been no good reason why Ray would do it. But a very good reason why Machado would. Machado and Conchita had then made sure Von Slyke received my divorce papers. And who knew, but late last night had also been part of the plot too. They probably had photos, perhaps videos, of Conchita riding me in bed. Just to be certain, in case Von Slyke hadn't been totally offended by the news of my divorce and its implications, just in case he hadn't instantly kicked me out. They'd done it. The two of them together. And why was obvious: to get rid of me so Machado would be left in line for Fusumi's job

Upset as I was by all this, I still had to wonder how it had come about. Had Machado already known Conchita? Or had he approached her knowing she worked for Von Slyke? The maid had worked some years there, so she couldn't be a plant, could she? Well, hell, yes, anything was possible now. That Machado was putting out for Irian St George, for example. Much as we two got along, that had always been a problem; as I waited that moment when he'd put a hand on my knee or say something too clearly suggestive. But then if Machado and St George were more intimate, then did that mean St George was telling Machado what I was doing? Where I was going? Had this entire weekend trip East been part of that set-up? St George had, after all, paid for it. And what other things had occurred between him and my nemesis while I'd been blissfully unaware and out of their way?

I had to stop. I simply couldn't afford to become paranoiac. I had to keep my feet somewhere near the ground, despite the fact that it had so repeatedly opened up beneath my feet. I mustn't allow myself to go off on every tangent that lay so enticingly there, spelling out my doom. No. I had to think positively. I wasn't doomed. It wasn't by any means over yet! There was still my thesis! My brilliant thesis! That would stop them!

Machado drew away from the gate with a light horn beep of goodbye and a few minutes later Conchita stepped into her car and turned on the ignition. As she was entering the circular drive, I was already at the wheel and gunned the Celica. I zoomed past her so recklessly fast, so close, she had to sharply swerve to miss a head-on collision. The Corolla skidded onto the grass island and abraded the side of the fountain as she braked to a cacophonous halt. Every one of the scores of birds nearby rose into the air with a great screeching. I didn't see what damage was done to the fountain or the grass or her car, I was already hauling by too quickly. I was fairly sure she hadn't had time to recognize me. When I spun around and outside and past the wrought-iron gates of Casa Herrera y Lopez for the last time in my life, Conchita was slowly opening the Corolla's passenger side door, stumbling onto the grass. She looked as though she didn't know what had hit her. Got ya, bitch!

I made it to the Westwood Arms Hotel on Wilshire Boulevard a dozen blocks from UCLA as though gliding on air, without hitting a single red light.

I was in the nearly empty dark oak wood first-floor dining room of the hotel having breakfast and perusing the *Los Angeles Times* three mornings later, when one of the desk clerks I'd befriended found me and dropped an envelope from UCLA onto my table. I tipped him and opened it.

It was my thesis and documentation, as I'd assumed.

Also a covering letter from Irian St George, dated the night before:

> *What can one say? I'd hoped for so much, but this must be considered a complete and utter disaster. It's partly my fault. I've been so busy. And I'd feared that without close guidance you might go a bit awry. I never had a clue you'd end up so catastrophically in error.*
>
> *You've obviously not read all of the De Petrie journal entries as I have or surely you would have seen the attached and not fallen into such folly.*
>
> *Take a vacation. Rethink your commitment to the Purple Circle. To literature. To academia. Rethink everything! Then, and only perhaps then, contact me again.*
> *Sadly*
> *St George*

I signed my breakfast bill and walked out of the dining room and over to the elevator and took it up to my room without feeling my body, without feeling or thinking a single thing. Once I got upstairs into the little room. I sat at the desk chair looking out the window for the longest time. Naturally, I thought of jumping. It was twenty floors up. I'd end up a smear of corporeal paste on the street below before speeding autos further mangled the remains.

After a very long time, maybe hours later. I at last came to enough and then found the courage to read the attached entries from Dominic De Petrie's journals. What in the hell had St George meant by writing that I'd not read all the De Petrie journals. I certainly had read them. I'd read every journal entry that had been published, two volumes full of them. As well as reading everything that the Timrod Collection had put in its 'open' files over the past two years. Surely I would have noticed anything odd or relevant. Especially from these early dates when the Purple Circle was meeting regularly. There could only be one explanation for why I had not read them: these entries St George was not only citing but now throwing at me had to have been previously edited out of the finished books. Only De Petrie, their author, and, who knew, perhaps also Maureen at the Timrod Collection if she had bothered, knew that they had existed, and of course St George, the journals' editor, he also would know that they had already been edited out before publication.

This is what the deeply perfidious St George had attached:

April 17th, 1980

A rainy morning. I hate April rain. Have to go out and food shop today. Hate food shopping. I hate everything today.

Don't know why I'm in such a bad humor. Last night I was in a great mood. The Purple Circle met at Dame's place and we had a good reading session. First Axey read, a short story titled 'Plaid Flannel' a hysterically funny piece about urban disco queens trying to grow up and make it in the suburbs of Pennsylvania. Then it was Mark's turn and he read a section from the new novel he's been working on forever and seems afraid to finish, lest he actually have to publish it. After dessert, Dame himself read a proto-story/essay titled 'Instigations' which he thinks will be in his new novel. Three of us. Cammy, myself and Rowland, all thought it strong and unusual enough that he should open the new book with it. I read last, the opening chapter of *A Summer's Lease*, which everyone said was utterly new and different and which they all claimed to love. At least I was encouraged.

We all hung around a bit afterwards, having another go at finishing the peach and pear pies Axey had baked for the occasion. We got to talking about writing novels in which the protagonists are artists other than writers. We're all deter-mined not to fall into the writer-as-hero trap. Mitch Leo said

he thought I'd found an answer by making the hero of my
new novel a painter. He spoke of Henry James making
Roderick Hudson a sculptor, etc. Then Axey got a brilliant
idea. He suggested we not write about writers, but actually
create a fictional writer and write about him. All of us.

I leapt into the fray and said, sure, why not? After all,
what is fiction anyway, right, but what we say it is? Dame
and Rowland wanted to know how it could possibly work.
Axey and Frankie made some suggestions. Say Axey would
do a story and mention this fictional person along with other
real people. Cammy might do an essay also mentioning him.
I could do the chapter of one of his unfinished novels. Dame
could then mention the fake author in a review of some other
book he was reviewing. We'd begin mentioning the author to
others in letters. While to each other we could keep the fiction going by saying in letters to each other that we'd seen
him at so and so's party with such and such a number. Or
that Mitch and Frankie in Florence had bumped into him at
the opera or at the Farnese or Duomo. Dame could include
the fictional name in his new book, in his acknowledgment
page, along with real people, his editor, agent, favorite hustler, sister-in-law.

The conversation became more detailed and more rococo.
We went on for over an hour about it. Such fun.

The next entry was a month later.

May 22nd, 1980

I woke up late. Kicked out a very cute trick after sucking his
dick a half-hour till he finally – jaw ache – came. He wanted
to stay and 'play' all day. Mother told him she had work to
do. Have to try that stupid new chapter of *Summer's Lease*
before I forget what the hell I intended with it. I think
Rowland is wrong when he says sex doesn't feed but instead
derails the creative process. I always work better after hot 'n'
dirty sex.

Speaking of creative processes, last night the Purple Circle
met at Mitch and Frankie's and it was a so-so reading session,

but with another fun after-session. First Rowland read, a scene from his play *Mustang Sally*. An obvious rip-off of Sam Shephard, and awfully dreary. Hated it! Nor was I alone. But we were all relatively kind. All but Dame, who said, with his usual languorous delivery, 'I don't know. I still think the theater is dead.' Good thing Rowland didn't hear or Dame would have been dead.

Next was Frankie reading a chapter about a bar fight with broken bottles in some Midwestern saloon, a scene from this autobiographical novel about his childhood in Iowa that he's continually pulling out of mothballs a month or so at a time to polish, add to, and then put back into the drawer. (Ed. note: the scene would appear in the finished version of McKewen's posthumous *A Boy from Quad Cities*.)

After dessert and coffee – ice-cream cake from the local store, gloppy and messy, I adored it – Mitch read a really lovely piece about his grandmother from the new book. With *Refitting Tom Devere* such a (relative) hit, he's moving ahead with confidence and the writing shows it. Much applause. Then Cammy read a very Eudora Weltyish short piece that he believes will be part of *Via Appia*, if that book is ever completed in any of our lifetimes

Dame and Axey both brought up my novel opening from our last meeting. Partly because of Cammy's piece. Then I brought up our wonderful idea from last meeting about inventing a fictional character. And Jeff Weber said why invent one, when he already *had* a perfect character, one some of us already knew but not well enough to allow reality to intervene.

The person was his ex – a difficult break-up – of six months ago, whom it turns out also dated Mark a while back and whom all of us but, it seems, Rowland have met, mostly because of this guy's recent association with photographer Mapplethorpe and his sugar daddy Sam Wagstaff at their Robert Samuel Gallery, where Len for two months 'worked' (meaning where he got regularly sucked off by cock-crazy Robert). His name: Len Spurgeon. An attractive guy with all kinds of odd and haphazard background but also of sufficient mystery and that all-important element of being seductively attractive to each and every one of us, including Mark and Jeff, which is saying a lot since they've actually possessed the glorious Lenflesh. So he's got more than enough moxie to make him our Official Purple Circle Fictional Author/Person/Character. Rowland abstaining (out of sheer ignorance – the first time, in my presence or knowledge, he's ever admitted to ignorance of any subject) – we all voted Len S as our real-life model for the fictional person.

The question now is how much we've actually got to do to make him fictional. I mean, we're overworked as it is, doing what we're doing. Axey said that if we were smart, we'd take our time, not leap into it, and that way ensure the 'reality quotient', whatever that might be. But Dame agreed (for once! Whenever did they before this agree?) and said it could be a lifelong project. We were all thrilled by the prospect. But as I was walking to the subway with Rowland – both of us headed for the same subway line downtown – he said it would never happen. Why not? 'We're too lazy and too ego-tistical,' he said. Cammy joined up with us in the station and he agreed with Rowland. He wondered if we should tell Len of our plans for him. 'After all,' Cammy argued, 'we're making him sort of our mascot, aren't we?'

I love Cammy's choice of word. Mascot! *Vey es mir!*

Two months later was the third and final entry.

July 14th, 1980

A long and extremely boring phone call from my editor this morning. Boring despite the main topics being me and my books: normally intriguing subjects. What is this guy's prob-lem? At any rate after a great deal of digging and sleuthing I at last discovered that *Prowl* is doing well on all fronts. The fourth edition is out and shipped, the book club has mailed out over 20,000 copies! The British sale has gone through. A German sale is ready to be signed. The paperback will be out in October, a month earlier than anticipated, etc. etc.

I tried mentioning the new book to him, but couldn't get a

word in edgewise. Work on *A Summer's Lease* is going along
steadily. I know my jerk of an editor wants another book like
Prowl. But *that's it*, folks! No more like that am I ever going
to write. So they'll just have to settle for this.

Read another chapter from it last night to the Purples. We
met at Mark Dodge's super glamoro townhouse on West 24th
Street. It was a beautiful not too hot night, so he kept half of
the dozen or so French doors that lead onto that enormous
terrace open, and we stepped out there during our intermission and after the readings. God, it's gorgeous! Views of the
Hudson up to the George Washington Bridge and down to
the Verazzano Bridge. All of the West Village in view. Parts of
midtown etc. He'd had his 'houseboy' fix us canapés beforehand and make two kinds of mousse for dessert. If I didn't
adore Mark I swear I could easily murder him out of sheer
jealousy. But he's such a puppy about it all. Takes it as silly
fun. Never is snotty or anything.

At any rate, the readings. I did the early break-up scene
chapter from the novel and that was well received, though a
somber bit. Before me Rowland read something that looks
like it might be a novel. And since we were all thrilled it
wasn't that dumb play, we were enthusiastic. Jeff read an
essay about gay lit. he's trying to get into *Atlantic Monthly* –
very smart, mentioning us all, but good luck, Marie!! And
Axey read more of his new novel, which we adored, asking us
all for possible titles. When he explained to Dame how this
book was 'different in kind if not in type' from the last one, I
suggested that be the title. He pshawed this idea. (Ed. note:
Axenfeld did adopt the suggested title, *Different in Kind*, for
his second published novel.)

Afterwards, all sitting around on the terrace, we once more
discussed the fictional Len Spurgeon and his oeuvre. We all
agreed to write one piece each, which we would then put
together into a book at some unknown future date. 'A sort of
group novel,' Dame said, 'like – what was that lurid best-
seller a few years ago? *Naked Came the Stranger*.'

We've yet to figure out a plot, or character, but might do
the book à la the game Rumor. You know, one person begins

and another adds to it. So we drew lots and figured out
who'd do it first, then second, then etc. No title for it yet.
Though we all came up with several names, Cammy actually
with the best of the lot, *The Book of Lies*, since, as he said, 'It
will be one hundred percent lies!' We all liked that title, but it
wasn't officially ratified. Yet

Then the question of how we'd do it. Dame had chosen
first so he'll write the first piece. Then Mark. Next Axey,
Cammy, Mitch, Frankie, and finally myself. I'm glad I'm last,
but I frankly don't think it'll ever be written.

Meanwhile, as Dame brought up, what do we do about
Len if we ever do finish it? Give him the MS and have him
pretend to have authored it? Mark and Jeff and Dame all
think he'd really go for the idea, and actually enjoy being an
'author', so long as he doesn't have to do anything yucky like
actually write.

What about publicity? Photos? Interviews? Len could do
all that 'fun part', Mitch and Frankie argued. 'We'd train
him,' Dame said. He sounded as though he'd be personally
pleased to train Len, which got up Cammy's ire and they
began arguing and so we soon broke up for the night. As we
were getting into taxis etc. on the street, Dame told us, 'I'm
doing it. I know *exactly* how to begin!' Mark said he'd do his
part too. So maybe this group of disorganized, overextended
queens will actually complete it.

A note from the editor of the entries (St George himself) read,
'This topic never arises in the journals. There's no proof Von Slyke
began, Dodge seconded, or the others continued the project of the
completely bogus novel. So this *jeu d'esprit* was never written, nor
sections of it published anywhere under anyone's name.'

Except, of course, we both now knew differently. Von Slyke must
have at some time begun the novel, writing the fragment about the
boys in the car. Mark Dodge must have continued it, with that part
of a story about the youth Paul in Manhattan on Christmas Eve.
Aaron Axenfeld had to have written a third section, the strange,
imagistic piece about the flamingos. While the most amazing of all
sections, and the longest, the cable-car disaster, had been written by,

of all them, the Purple Circle member least associated with fiction, Frankie McKewen. The other Purple Circlers had failed to play the game, or had been unable to bring to the book any kind of publishable manuscript: there was no indication that Jeff Weber, Rowland Etheridge, or Mitch Leo had produced any part of it at all. But then they'd all four barely lived long enough to write their own work. While the prolific Dominic De Petrie had done what he said he would and had completed the pseudo-book with the fable about the little boy and the Ice Queen. Having known Len the longest and, I assumed, the best, he'd written what I supposed was probably the most personal, possibly the most appropriate, section.

I now had to wonder if in fact that fable wasn't at all about Len, but about De Petrie himself. Since, as I recalled it, he never actually told me that Len had written it.

In fact, the more I thought about it, the more I thought maybe I had it all wrong. Hadn't Axenfeld out and out said he hadn't written 'The Flamingos'? Was that true? Was I assuming those were the authors of the pieces merely because it was in their archives the fragments were found? Couldn't Axenfeld have *never* written it, but found the piece in his library under *Tales of the Offeekenofee*, as he'd said? Maybe Cameron Powers put it there? or De Petrie? Both had been on that sunporch? And hadn't Thom Dodge had *two* of the pieces? How did I know which, if *any* of them, Mark Dodge had written? What if there were the same five fragments somewhere in all eight of their collected papers? What if . . .? Whatever the truth was, I'd never discover it. They'd covered their tracks too well. That much was quite clear.

When I'd finished reading the entries, grasping how utterly I'd been had, fooled, screwed over, done in, mishandled by the Purple Circlers, both the living and dead, after I went over and over in my mind what had happened, or what I suspected had happened, and more importantly *why* it had happened, how it had been brought about via my complete and utter obsession with Len Spurgeon, what that obsession had done to me, led me to, where it had landed me, then and only then did I attempt to open the hotel window to throw myself out.

It was, like most legal hotel windows, of course, barred from opening beyond six inches. I did the next best thing. I took the elevator downstairs and jaywalked directly into the noonday traffic on Wilshire Boulevard, at that point six lanes thick, without a traffic light in a half-mile, moving at about sixty miles per hour. Others have died doing it. Among them, the 1960s activist Jerry Rubin.

I was struck three times. The first time glancingly, whirling me around on my feet and directly into the path of a second car, which veered to avoid me, but hit me anyway. I was rendered unconscious and slammed directly into the front left fender of another car. My body veered off and was hurled twenty-five feet against the trunk of a palm tree fifty feet in from the corner of Wilshire and Selby. I caused a fourteen-car pile-up and stopped traffic for several hours in both directions. It was on the five o'clock, six o'clock and eleven o'clock news. Also in the next morning's papers.

EPILOGUE

Needless to say, I didn't die. In fact, despite the photogenic spectacularity of the accident, I didn't suffer more than a dislocated right shoulder, three broken ribs, hairline fractured tibia, neckbone, wrist, cheekbone and nose. Oh, and I was in a coma for about three days. That was the bad part.

The good part was that the papers firing me weren't official until two weeks later, so I was medically covered by the school. Since I was so close I was taken to UCLA's own hospital , one of the best in the country, where – as a colleague – I received terrific care and healed with only the most minor of scars. Best of all, the news of my arrival in the Intensive Care Unit spread to my class within a few hours, and Pamela Agosian talked her way into my wardroom, lying about her relationship to me. She and the others from my class then took turns staying with me, and 'talking me' out of my coma. It was Pam's voice I heard, Pam's face I saw, when I came to. I asked her to stay, asked her to be my friend, little by little told her everything that had happened to me, to explain how I'd ended up there. I had to tell someone.

To my delight, she remained a friend, and more. After summer session, when I was well enough to hobble around on my own, I took up my sister and brother-in-law, Bart and Judy Vanuzzi's offer to stay with them in San Francisco until I'd fully recovered. Pam switched classes for her last term in January to Berkeley. By then I'd gotten my own place. She moved in with me.

We're still together and she's my biggest supporter. It was partly her doing that I got this job teaching at the College of the Canyons in Santa Clarita. Yes, we're back in southern California. She's teaching too, grade school, nearby in Castaic. I'm only an assistant professor, but with two incomes we've found an inexpensive place to rent. I teach four classes, really basic stuff, two freshman composition and two ordinary literature classes, in American lit. It's okay.

Because of Pam's continued support and belief in me, I've at last come back to work on the thesis about the Purple Circle. Redoing it, but not a great deal. It took a great deal of courage on my part, but when Pam and I at last told Judy and Bart what had happened, Vanuzzi said he thought it was the right thing to do. It was Bart who'd pointed out to me that not one of the three surviving Purple Circlers had said the fragments I called *The Book of Lies* was their work. It was bold, pushy Bart who suggested that I contact the three of them with the idea that I publish *The Book of Lies* with all of my documentation and my introduction as a book. That I send the MS to Von Slyke, De Petrie, Axenfeld and Reuben Weatherbury and ask them either to confirm their authorship of the pieces or to allow me to list Len Spurgeon as the author.

To my surprise, all four of them wrote back and said they would *not* accept responsibility for having written the pieces. So my supposition as to the book's authorship will have to remain as good as anyone else's.

The next step, however, was what really jump-started the controversy. One of my colleagues at the College of the Canyons was to deliver a paper at the next Modern Language Association Conference on some aspects of a contemporary African slang. Instead, he gave over his slot in the program to me and I delivered my own revamped introduction, calling the paper I delivered 'The Enigmatic Muse: An Unfinished Book by the Unknown Member of the Purple Circle'. The listing for my talk was not in the catalogue for the event. However, it very definitely was posted on those flyers handed out at the conference registration and orientation, showing 'amendments and errata' to the programs.

As a result, there were more than the expected number of people in the audience when I got up to speak than if it had been, as planned, Dr Anton Scherzer speaking on 'Non-glottal Agglutinative Origins of Contemporary Zimbabwean and South African Argot'. Among the listeners, Reuben Weatherbury, Tanya Cull, Irian St George – and, of course, his shiny new UCLA protégé, Waterford Machado. My paper caused a sensation. During the lengthy, stormy question and comment period, Machado and I ended up in a shouting match that almost turned into a fist fight.

While I was packing to leave my hotel room, two people from renegade MLA offshoot groups called my room asking to publish the paper. I gave it to them both and it appeared, with fullest editorial approbation, in their very next quarterly issues. Meanwhile, that final night of the MLA conference, Reuben Weatherbury had approached me in the hotel restaurant and we'd had late-night coffee, during which I'd revealed all of what had happened to me re: the Purples. 'I never thought you were gay,' he said. 'You never said or did anything to make me think so.' He also agreed to ask his editor, the one who'd put out the two volumes of the *Reader*, to look at my work, although he thought the project somewhat 'arcane' for them.

The next issue of the *MLA Journal*, coming out barely two months after the renegades' quarterlies, contained the expected response, a paper co-authored by St George and Machado decrying the 'wholesale, reckless aggrandizement and attempted heterosexualization of the works of the Purple Circle by scholars intelligent enough to realize how superior their work is to their own benighted people, but too greedy to leave gay work to gay academics'. Their attack was on several fronts, was well thought out, cogent, evidently a long-simmering offensive on St George's part, as it went after virtually every non-gay author who'd made the slightest foray into gay lit. in the past two decades. They knocked over a few big names, some of whom even I would admit needed a good bashing. Naturally, I was saved for the last, and the most virulent, assault.

Among the things they wrote was that I had gone into the affair with my eyes open, searching for, indeed hoping to find, 'some ignominious and belittling person or thing' to denigrate the group. Also that I had intended 'from the beginning to deceive, disparage, ridicule, and lower the Purple Circle members' literary standing'. I'd done so via 'calculated mendacity' in misrepresenting myself and my sexuality, going so far as to 'inveigle a defenseless and sexually unresolved undergraduate student into providing' me with 'totally specious credentials of hoaxed gender preference'. Furthermore, I had 'entranced, bewitched, cock-teased and even offered myself as bait' to whomever was naïve enough to be taken in by me. Capping it, I'd 'bought my way into possession of literary works'.

But worse, I'd done all this in an attempt to destroy not merely the work but, more importantly, the private lives of the Purple Circle members at their most vulnerable point: their affections. According to St George and Machado, from the onset, with my bigotry securely in place, I'd never for a second 'accepted, believed, thought possible or worthwhile the existence of, the strength of, or the efficacy of one man's sexual love for another'. It was this 'deep and unshakeable prejudice', they believed, which had 'driven me to fraudulence, lucre, and devastation'.

That's not true. No matter what anyone thinks or says, I know differently. I know unswervingly otherwise. Because while it's true that before I'd arrived at UCLA and moved into the Casa Herrera y Lopez, I'd had virtually no same-sex experience, I'd never been opposed to it. The truth is I'd been secretly fascinated by it, quietly wondering whether my absolute devotion to the works of the Purple Circle wasn't in fact extra-literary, even a result of unconscious latent homosexuality. My early good looks had pulled me in the other direction from the beginning. From almost before puberty, I'd been surrounded by, undressed by, caressed by, seduced by girls and women. I'd had a 'steady girl' since junior high. The minute one fell away, there had been six to take her place. I'd had all the sexual activity an American teenager would desire, with not a single conflicting complication – say, of unwanted pregnancy or sexually transmitted disease. I'd led a completely charmed heterosexual life, right up until the break-up and divorce from Chris Crowell while we were graduate students at Columbia.

It was at that time, headed toward UCLA, that I decided I would open myself up to men, give in to those unformed feelings and desires, and see what happened. Had he been less ambivalent himself – and less of a jerk – Ray Rice probably would have had me every way and any way he wanted. I'd kept hoping for one of the men I met on my quest to put the make on me, to demand sex from me in return for information or a manuscript, to crawl into my bed and ravage me as I slept. I couldn't believe not one of them would even touch me. But they didn't. Not one of the Purple Circle survivors, their heirs or executors! So much for fundamentalist propaganda!

No, it remained for someone else to do it. Someone who proved to me what no army of Machados or St Georges can ever otherwise persuade me may be altered, disputed, or doubted. The man whom

I slowly came to realize I'd fallen for, the man I was 'saving myself for', and whom I'd come to utterly desire. In fact, the only man who could possibly provide me with what I required. Because of him, and that experience with him, I now strongly believe in what Whitman called manly love. Indeed, despite the fact that I'll probably marry Pam Agosian next year and raise a family with her and live out the rest of my life as a conventional heterosexual, it was because of him that I've come to understand what had first and so much attracted me to what the Purple Circle was writing about, suggesting, aiming toward – a love stronger, more trenchant, more metaphysical than any other. I *do* understand that. I believe it. I accept it.

It happened that morning in July in Truro, Massachusetts, during the last minutes of my visit to Dominic De Petrie. Recall that I'd awakened late that morning, had breakfast, gone upstairs to his little office, talked with him, found out what more he knew about Len, experienced that sudden, odd sense of shared *déjà vu*, and when it was over, he'd asked if I was packed and ready in a voice that appeared to have undergone some kind of under-sea change. Minutes later, he was out at the Beemer rummaging through the car's trunk as I brought out my bags.

'You didn't happen to see a narrow flashlight back here?' he asked. 'It's supposed to be attached here, next to the internal CD changer.'

I said no, then recalled where I had seen it. 'Could it be in the garage?'

Before he could ask how I would possibly know that I headed toward the garage, and slipped in through the accessible double doors.

The place was as I recalled it the night before, though the light source now derived from a different direction: the three tall rubber pails, the boxes of beercans and soda bottles, the workshop bench, were all as I'd remembered. Beneath the workbench was where, the night before, I'd seen the pale green flashlight with its distinctive Beemer logo. I bent down to get it, stood up again with it in hand, instantaneously felt a return of that peculiar sense of *déjà vu* De Petrie and I had shared in his office not long before.

Of course I had been here before. Only hours before. Late at night. I registered that fact, but it was instantly swept away by another cognizance, that I was in the proximity of someone, something, perhaps the same 'house spirit' I'd intuited then. Whatever impression that was for me, it was short-lived, fleeting, transitory. This awareness began the same way but it quickly became more complex and far more concentrated. I had a sensation of total, sudden languor as though all vigor had been drawn from my limbs, rendering me powerless. At the same time, I remarked an indisputably new and until then unknown scent as it surrounded me, brushing my face, a cologne that only months later and after many trials and errors in department store men's cosmetics counters, I would discover was Guerlain's *du Coc* for men. Simultaneously I experienced . . . how can I put it that doesn't sound utterly deranged? I can't. So I'll come out and say I had the unassailable sensation that I was thoroughly enveloped by love. My body, my neck and shoulders, my hair, my ears, my face, all were wrapped in the most passionate unconditional affection I've ever experienced.

Its effect was so powerful as to dizzy me, to render me without capacity to resist as it continued to enfold me within wave after wave of the most unceasing ardor, until I vaguely thought I must surely be moaning aloud in pleasure, on the brink of losing consciousness, and drenching myself in the most intense, attenuated orgasm I've ever experienced. At the same time I felt supported, gently caught up, almost lifted.

I can't say how long this went on, only that it seemed a very long time and I wished it would never end. It did draw to an end, eventually, and I was left stunned and wholly drained. The very last actual manifestation I can recall was the sensation of a pair of lips longingly caressing the nape of my neck. When even that was gone, and when I'd felt the presence completely withdraw, I staggered, reeled, almost fell, held onto the worktable with my fingertips, and at last was able to turn back to the room.

There, rising up the five wooden steps into the house – those same wooden steps I'd used to come into this garage last night – was a pillar of what appeared at first to be ash-gray smoke that slowly spun and resolved itself into a six-foot column, and a shape. It was configured in place only a second, fifteen feet away, but there was no question at all of what was imaged. Wearing tight black Levi's and cowboy boots and a black T-shirt with sleeves rolled up on the biceps, who else could it be? He gazed at me fondly, lasciviously licked his tongue over his top lip, dissolved into whatever ectoplasmic state he diurnally existed in, swirled up the steps as squirming gray smoke, and was gone.

I remained where I'd been forsaken at the workbench, debilitated, wholly slaked, my thoughts a categorical muddle. Out of the corner of my eye I saw a figure to my left, and turned just enough to make out Dominic De Petrie standing in the space between the garage's double doors, stopped from entering. He was staring, almost gaping, not at me, but at those five wooden steps that led up and into the house. Staring for I can't say how long. At last, he made the effort and looked at me. As he did, the calm gaze of acceptance, the melancholic gaze he cast my way, filled as it was of so many different emotions – pride, proof, frustration released, yet also annoyance and, yes, even betrayal – all that forced my mind to finally conjoin my senses in grasping what had just occurred to me. De Petrie had seen it all! Seen and heard it all! He was a witness. He could corroborate!

My physical response to his unspoken confirmation of what had, impossibly, just occurred to me was utter consternation: the hair stood up on the back of my neck and my body temperature plunged. I began to shudder uncontrollably until I was sure I'd fall to the ground, where, who knew, I might begin frothing at the mouth. In a second, De Petrie was there, holding me, wrapping a sweater over my shoulders, murmuring unintelligible words at me, leading me out of the arctically chilled garage into the cinematically bogus-looking reality of a sun-warmed Cape Cod summer day. He continued to hold me even after I'd stopped shivering and had grown humanly warm again.

Warmed and suddenly embarrassed, I withdrew from him. He stood back, accepted his sweater, took the flashlight I held out to him with a hint of a laugh. Without a word, he tossed it into the car trunk. A few seconds later we were in the Z-5, speeding toward the airport.

We never spoke a word of it, Dominic De Petrie and me. Not in the car, not at the airport lounge waiting for my plane to land and taxi in, not when my flight was called and we shook hands. Not when I walked onto the tarmac and ascended into the commuter transport that would fly me to Logan Airport in Boston, and from there back to LA to face what would turn out to be my wholly unanticipated yet after all inevitable, and unmistakably individual destiny. Not then. Not later. Not ever. Yet every time we do speak – infrequent as that is – it's always present somehow, unverbalized, implicit, no matter what else we actually say.

There are rumors that De Petrie has made the final cut of those few Olympian authors being considered annually in Stockholm. And that Von Slyke is furious at the news, since he's the one who'd been doing all the international publicity. And that Axenfeld is, unsurprisingly, amused at the brouhaha. There are rumors that De Petrie has actually begun to write another book. It would be the first new one in years, decades, he'd himself admit. Of course, no one has any idea what its subject may be, although those in the know assume it will be autobiographical, another memoir. Naturally I've got my own ideas of certain material it might include. In fact, I once went so far in a phone conversation to allude to it. In the airiest of terms, of course, and to as amusingly as possibly bestow upon him the greatest possible freedom to work it up as he saw fit.

Don't consider this fawning, or even any sacrifice on my part. The controversy continued on and off in the pages of the literary journals and in certain 'academic rooms' on the Internet, then died down. After several years of trying, I've still not found an interested editor or foolish enough publisher for the manuscript and I'm beginning to think I never shall.

Still, there are days I still can't help feeling it would make a book. Even a not too inconsequential book, this *Book of Lies*. What do you think?

BIBLIOGRAPHY AND APPENDICES

AARON AXENFELD 1944–
Second Star from the Right (novel, 1978)
Different in Kind (novel, 1982)
Envoi to Obscurity (non-fiction, 1985)
At Imperial Point (novel, 1995)
Plaid Flannel (stories, 1999)
From the Icelandic (novel, 2001)

DOMINIC DE PETRIE 1944–
Who is Christopher Darling? (novel, 1975)
Singles (novel, 1976)
A Choice of Faces (poetry, 1977)
Prowl (novel, 1979)
Gay Tragic Romances (stories, 1980)
A Summer's Lease (novella, 1981)
Advice to a Jewish Prince (novel, 1983)
The Last Good Year for Cadillacs (memoirs, 1985)
Chrome Earrings (memoirs, 1989)
Saturdays – and Rain! (memoirs, 1995)
The Adventures of Marty (novel, 1997)
Agent for the Deceased (memoirs, 1999)
Death and Art in Greenwich Village (memoirs, 2000)
Absolute Ebony (novella, 2001)
Conversations in the Dark (memoirs, 2002)

MARK DODGE 1948–86
Buffalo Nickel (novel, 1975)
Keep Frozen (novel, 1977)

We All Drive Fords (novel, 1984)
Framed by Life a.k.a. Man in a Jar (autobiography, 1993; in Reuben
   Weatherbury (ed.), *The Purple Circle Reader*)

ROWLAND ETHERIDGE 1938–95
The Love Tribe (novel, 1968)
The Eleventh Commandment (novel, 1975)
The Thirteenth Trump is Death (novel, 1977)
Singular Sensation (play, 1979)
Desperately, Yours (novel, 1981)
Mustang Sally (play, 1984)
Beauregard in Brooklyn Heights (play, 1985)
On Buzzard's Bay (novel, 1992)

MITCHELL LEO 1941–88
Signals in the Sky, with Frankie McKewen (non-fiction, 1967)
The Younger (novella, 1977)
Refitting Tom Devere (novel, 1981)
After the Piano Recital (novel, 1983)
Serial Childhood (novel, 1985)

FRANKIE MCKEWEN 1943–88
Signals in the Sky, with Mitchell Leo (non-fiction, 1971)
I am You and You are Me (non-fiction, 1975)
In the Spirit of Chief Pontiac (non-fiction, 1976)
Switch Hitters (non-fiction, 1978)
Whitman's Sons and Sappho's Daughters (non-fiction, 1979)
A Boy from Quad Cities (novel, 1991)

CAMERON POWERS 1946–87
Along the Via Appia (travel, 1981)
'Miss Thing' and the '41 Bugatti (stories, 1999)

DAMON VON SLYKE 1941–
Representation in Indigo (play, 1966)
Systems for Approaching Emmeline (novel, 1974)
Instigations (novel, 1981)
Heliotrope Convertible (novel, 1983)

Pastiche Upon *Some Themes Alluded to by Gustave Flaubert* (novel, 1985)
Rejection: A Masquerade (non-fiction, 1986)
Verbatim (novel, 1987)
The Japonica Tree (stories, 1989)
Leaving Riverside Drive (novel, 1994)
DOS: Manuscript in Distress (novel, 1996)
Spun Sugar, including 'Fantasietta on a Sad Pierrot' (early stories, 1997)
Epistle to Albioni (novella, 1999)
Canticle to the Sun (novel, 2001)

JEFF WEBER 1945-89
Picking Up Men in Lower Manhattan (poetry, 1976)
Ode to a Porno Star (novel, 1978)
Sights and Offenses (stories, 1979)
The Odds in Ocean Park (non-fiction, 1985)
Cheyenne August (novel, 1988)
'In the Tree Museum' (story, 1993)

Books about the Purple Circle

Reuben Weatherbury (ed.), *The Purple Circle Reader*, Vol. 1, 1993; Vol. 2, 1999
Thaddeus Fleming, *Gauntlet to the Ground: The Purple Circle, 1978–1982*, 1997
Erling Cummings, *Nine Lives*, 2001
Irian St George, *On the Edge of the New: Dominic De Petrie and the Purple Circle*, 1999

Appendix 1: Len Spurgeon and the Purple Circle
   (*the works he influenced*)

1 1966–74 Sex etc. with Frankie McKewen – Iowa/Berlin – *A Boy from Quad Cities*
2 1976–7 Lover of Mark Dodge – SF & NYC – *Keep Frozen*

3 1978-9 Lover of Jeff Weber—NYC—story 'In the Tree Museum'
4 1980-81 Lives with A. Axenfeld—Fla—*From the Icelandic*
5 1981-2 Lives with Cameron Powers—NYC—*Along the Via Appia*
6 1982-3 Lives with Rowland Etheridge—NYC—*Beauregard in Brooklyn Heights*
7 1983-5 Tea with the Leo-McKewens—NYC—*After the Piano Recital*
8 1984 S/M sex with Damon Von Slyke—NYC—story 'Master and Man'
9 1985-91 Lives with Dominic De Petrie—Cape Cod, Mass.—'A Fable'

Appendix 2: Deaths

Mark Dodge—November 1986
Cameron Powers—June 1987
Frankie McKewen—March 1988
Mitchell Leo—June 1988
Jeff Weber—July 1989
Len Spurgeon—May 1991
Rowland Etheridge—September 1995

Appendix 3: Course Reading

The Yellow Room and Other Stories, Charlotte Perkins Gilman
The Great Gatsby, F. Scott Fitzgerald
My Antonia, Willa Cather
Black Elk Speaks: Being the Life Story of a Holy Man of the Ogalala Sioux, John Gneisenau Neihardt
Go Down, Moses, William Faulkner
In Cold Blood, Truman Capote
Five Plays, Tennessee Williams
Go Tell It on the Mountain, James Baldwin
Mr Sammler's Planet, Saul Bellow
Geography, Elizabeth Bishop
The Woman Warrior, Maxine Hong Kingston